Otherworldly

ALSO BY F.T. LUKENS

In Deeper Waters

So This Is Ever After

Spell Bound

F.T. LUKENS

Otherworldly

MARGARET K. MCELDERRY BOOKS

NEW YORK   LONDON   TORONTO   SYDNEY   NEW DELHI

MARGARET K. McELDERRY BOOKS

An imprint of Simon & Schuster Children's Publishing Division

1230 Avenue of the Americas, New York, New York 10020

MARGARET K. McELDERRY BOOKS is a trademark of Simon & Schuster, LLC.

Simon & Schuster: Celebrating 100 Years of Publishing in 2024

For information about special discounts for bulk purchases, please contact Simon & Schuster Special Sales at 1-866-506-1949 or business@simonandschuster.com.

The Simon & Schuster Speakers Bureau can bring authors to your live event. For more information or to book an event, contact the Simon & Schuster Speakers Bureau at 1-866-248-3049 or visit our website at www.simonspeakers.com.

Interior design by Rebecca Syracuse

The text for this book was set in PT Serif.

Manufactured in the United States of America

First Edition

10 9 8 7 6 5 4 3 2 1

Library of Congress Cataloging-in-Publication Data

Names: Lukens, F.T., author.

Title: Otherworldly / F.T. Lukens.

Description: First edition. | New York : Margaret K. McElderry Books, 2024. | Audience: Ages 14 up. | Audience: Grades 10–12. | Summary: In a land where the supernatural is believed to be real, nonbeliever Ellery and familiar Knox from the Other World form an unexpected alliance to strike a deal that could alter their lives forever.

Identifiers: LCCN 2023030201 (print) | LCCN 2023030202 (ebook) | ISBN 9781665916257 (hardcover) | ISBN 9781665916271 (ebook)

Subjects: CYAC: Supernatural—Fiction. | Demonology—Fiction. | Interpersonal relations—Fiction. | LGBTQ+ people—Fiction. | LCGFT: Paranormal fiction. | Novels.

Classification: LCC PZ7.1.L843 Ot 2024 (print) | LCC PZ7.1.L843 (ebook) | DDC [Fic]—dc23

LC record available at https://lccn.loc.gov/2023030201

LC ebook record available at https://lccn.loc.gov/2023030202

FOR THOSE READY TO HEAL AND THOSE STILL IN PAIN,
MAY YOU FIND COMFORT & LOVE

Otherworldly

Prologue

ARABELLE

In the middle of a collection of cornfields, in the middle of the country, in the middle of nowhere, a weathered wooden post marked the intersection of two roads.

The main road was a stretch of brown pea gravel rolled into a layer of asphalt that connected two nearby small towns. The other linked a row of family-owned farms. Few people besides the locals traveled them, as there was nothing for tourists to see except cornstalks in the summer and flat fields in the winter.

Atop the post sat two crooked, battered planks. The lettering that denoted the route numbers had faded with age, the paint blanched with time and rain and sun. Below them, a piece of plyboard nailed to the post held a single cautionary phrase, scrawled in dripping red:

BEWARE OF BARGAINS MADE HERE.

Arabelle scoffed at the warning as she eased her car over to the shoulder, threw it into park, and slid from the heated interior into the chill. She pulled the beanie she wore down to cover her ears, strands of her graying hair poking out beneath. She blew into her hands to warm her fingers as she stared at the sign. A towering oak with thick branches stood a few feet away, blocking the weak warmth of the afternoon sun. As she approached, her skin prickled at the potent, shimmering power that emanated from this crossroads. The average person who visited would be unable to feel it, but she was far from average, and she shivered in anticipation.

Arabelle had traveled from the city to this sacred place and spent the morning lost along snaking back roads until she'd finally found the correct location. Residents of the neighboring towns were reticent to share information, but she'd managed to piece together the clues all the same. The bloodied warning merely confirmed that she'd found the spot she'd been searching for, and she wouldn't be deterred from her purpose by an old strip of wood. Not after she'd made a promise to herself to seek knowledge and ability. Not after she'd been laughed at by members of her local circle, who were more interested in burning incense and selling essential oils than seeking *real* power. Arabelle would show them, when all was said and done. They'd bow in awe and respect when she returned with her boon.

Despite the sign, the intersection was well kept, and it appeared, by the recent offerings strewn across the base of the sign—a bouquet of witch hazel, a pyramid of figs, a wooden figurine in the shape of a dog, and votives with fire-blackened wicks—that some residents of the region still respected the chthonic goddess. She was connected to the harvest, after all, and it would be unwise to anger her lest it affect next year's crops.

Arabelle smiled to herself. Ah, the dichotomy of humans. Be wary but entreat anyway. Maintain a holy place but keep it secret. She understood why there wasn't an altar or a shelter there. A crossroads was not meant to be a final destination but a place between one point and the next. A liminal space where the barrier between worlds was thinnest. A perfect location from which to beseech the gods. A dangerous place, if the sign was to be believed.

No matter. She'd found it despite the vague hints on the internet and the unhelpful and wary attendant at the gas station a few miles back, who'd tried to caution her away. Flipping open a compact, she slid her sunglasses off, dropping them into the large canvas bag at her shoulder, and refreshed her makeup. She straightened her blouse beneath her wool coat, smoothing out the wrinkles and brushing off the snack crumbs from the long drive. She was glad she had worn leggings beneath her skirt, as the hem whipped around her ankles from a sudden bitter breeze that marked the impending winter.

She'd never quite done anything like this before. Of course she'd known of gods and goddesses all her life, of the three central deities—the god of the sky, the goddess of the seas, and the goddess of the dead. Per the myths, the realm of the earth was neutral ground between them—the space of humans—but the gods' children and their creations flitted in and out of the human world as they pleased. She'd prayed and made offerings before.

But this was her first time approaching a goddess with a request.

She cleared her throat and stepped to the center of the path, her boots leaving indentations in the stiff mud.

"Revered goddess," she called in a loud, clear voice. "I wish to make a bargain." From her bag she removed a jar of wine infused with honey, sprigs of fresh mint, and a pomegranate from the local supermarket that was overripe, the best she could do at the cusp of winter. She placed them at the other side of the intersection under the sign, then stepped back and waited.

Minutes ticked past. Another gust of wind ruffled her hair and clothes. Clouds laden with snow gathered overhead, obscuring the landscape in shadow for a moment before the sun peeked through again. She waited. And waited. Anxiety roiled in her gut. Another cloud rolled through, pitching the area in a darkness so deep that the shadows cast by the tree melted into it. Instead of drifting onward, the cloud miraculously stalled in place. Thunder sounded overhead, an anomaly for the time of year, and a frisson of fear and excitement ran through Arabelle. A slight drizzle began to fall, and the patter of sleet against the corn stover filled the air with a soft hum.

The color of the sky deepened further, as if it were suddenly dusk, and shadows grew and lengthened all around her. They slithered and writhed, distorted and feverish, then glided toward her offering. A swell of darkness rose and broke over the items like a wave washing over a sandcastle on the shore. When the clump of shade retreated, the gifts were gone.

Arabelle bit back a gasp as three wavering shapes broke away from the swirling mass, moved to the post opposite her, and slowly rose into vertical amorphous silhouettes. The churning shadows shuddered and coalesced into a semisolid form and, with a ripping noise, broke apart into three hooded bodies, faceless save for bright red eyes that glowed like embers. The wind didn't rustle their robes, and the sleet passed through them. They stared at her, unblinking and unmoving. The road lay between her and the frightening trio. If she wanted, she could've jumped back into her car and driven off, run away from the terrifying sight in front of her. She didn't want to.

"What are you?" Arabelle asked, taking a step forward so that she stood on the asphalt, breaking away from the safety of her vehicle. The fraction of timidity she possessed had fled, and she felt bold, empowered in the face of the true supernatural. "You're not the goddess."

"We are her servants," the middle one answered, their voice a rusty creak.

The one on the left continued. "We are shades from her realm."

"We represent the goddess," the one on the right finished.

Their voices slid from one syllable to the next as if they were one entity instead of three.

She swallowed, then clenched her jaw. "I want to speak with her and her alone."

"It is the day. She does not have dominion over the light."

"She is busy nonetheless."

"Preparing for the sleep of winter."

Arabelle crossed her arms. "Then I'll wait for moonrise."

"We will not. You will have to call again."

"With another offering."

"And we might not deign to appear."

They turned as if to sink back into the shadows and the earth.

No! She'd come all this way. She didn't have another offering. And now that she'd seen them, felt the presence of the otherworldly, she couldn't lose that. She wouldn't throw away her chance.

"Wait! No, wait, please."

They turned eerily as one. "You will speak with us now, human?"

"We have dealt with your kind before."

"We will strike a bargain on the goddess's behalf."

She stuck out her chin. "I'm not certain you are able. I'm not here for political prowess or fame and riches. I'm here for something greater."

They fluttered, shaking and hissing among themselves. "Speak what you want."

She released a long, slow breath. "I want power over death. I want immortality."

Their shaking increased as if they laughed, the ruffling of their robes sounding like the crunch of dead leaves underfoot.

"That is our queen's domain."

"We cannot grant that."

"She would not allow it."

"Why not?" Arabelle demanded.

"Immortality is for the gods alone."

"You are not a goddess."

"You are a human. You cannot escape death."

Arabelle chewed her bottom lip. She straightened her shoulders.

"Fine. I want knowledge. I want magical knowledge regarding the power of life. Life is not your queen's domain. And it wouldn't be escaping death, just putting it off for as long as I want. Until it's time for me to choose."

The shades stilled. The tallest one slowly tilted their head as if thinking. They exchanged a glance among themselves, bent their heads together, and whispered fiercely.

After a moment, they turned back to Arabelle. "We do not have the ability to grant you this power."

"We are shades. We have no knowledge of life."

The tallest raised a slender finger of wispy fog. "But we will give you someone who can assist."

"He is our queen's creation and is liminal in nature."

"Both of our world and of yours."

"He is powerful. Use his magic to create what you want."

Arabelle raised her eyebrow. "You're giving me a familiar?"

They nodded. The one on the end pinched their fingers and pulled out a rolled scroll and a quill from midair. With a flick of their wrist, the parchment unfurled. A contract. Words in a language she didn't know spilled down the page in black ink.

Arabelle paused and narrowed her eyes. This was too easy. She'd expected her gifts to open the gateway and allow her to make her request. She'd expected the goddess to respond with a task, something that would appear impossible, but that Arabelle would attempt anyway. She was not expecting dodgy shades. They had a plan, and she wasn't sure she wanted to be a conspirator. "A familiar in exchange for honey wine and mint and a deflated pomegranate?"

The shades laughed. The sound slipped down her spine, an eerie caress.

"A familiar and the knowledge of life," the tallest one said.

"In exchange for your soul."

"When the time comes."

She gulped. "Don't all souls come to your queen anyway?"

The shades shook in amusement. "All souls pass through our realm."

"Not all stay."

"But yours would stay with us *forever*."

Arabelle licked her lips. She took the hovering quill in her hand. The cold of it burned her skin. "What happens to the souls that pass through? Where do they go?"

"That is knowledge of death," the shades admonished in unison.

Arabelle squinted at the parchment. The words remained indiscernible, though she understood the basics. Her soul for a familiar who had the power to assist her in her quest for the knowledge of life. It wasn't quite what she'd expected or wanted. But a familiar would be a useful aid, especially one with magic. It was more than anyone else in the circle possessed. And an eternity in the realm of the goddess was a small price to pay, even if she'd never know what lay beyond. That was a problem for future Arabelle. Far in the future, if she accomplished what she wanted. She pushed the tip of the quill against the parchment and signed her name.

The scroll and quill disappeared in a puff a smoke.

The shades quivered. They moved as one, whispering to themselves as they slid across the landscape to the tree. The tallest reached out with a hazy hand and tapped against the wide, solid trunk. A light glowed from within, illuminating the edges of a door in the bark.

Arabelle's heart raced. Her familiar. Would it be a sarcastic cat? A wise owl? Hopefully not a goat, which would be hard to explain to her landlord. A raven, perhaps? That would be badass. She'd love to see the faces of the circle when she arrived at the next meeting with a large talking bird perched on her shoulder.

The door swung outward.

The shades laughed, a grating sound like corroded hinges that raised the hair on her arms.

A figure stumbled out. A figure in the shape of a boy. A teenage boy wearing jeans, thick-heeled boots, and flannel thrown over a T-shirt with an outdated saying. He looked like he'd stepped straight out of a magazine from the '90s, and Arabelle gaped as he brushed off the bark and bracken that clung to him. The door in the tree trunk slammed shut behind him, merging back into the wood.

He ran a hand through his shaggy raven-black hair and looked up at her, his eyes a flash of gold, the color of the sun beaming through autumn leaves. He raised his hand and waved, his smile wide and bright in his pale, narrow face.

"Hi," he called. "I'm Knox."

"What?" she said on a breath.

"I'm your familiar."

Arabelle's stomach dropped. "Well, shit."

"He is yours to command," the tallest shade said.

"He must listen to you."

"And cannot disobey."

She placed her hands on her hips and frowned at the shades, who slunk back to the signpost, blurring at the edges, as if moments away from retreating into the earth. "A teenage boy? Really?"

Knox held up a finger. "First, I'm thousands of years old," he said. "Kind of. It's complicated. But in human-realm time, I'm ancient. Second, I'm a familiar." He shrugged and rocked back on his heels. "And as you can see, a much more palatable creation to humans than those creepy creatures." He winked.

The shades made a growling noise in protest, a low, disconcerting rumble. Knox smiled sweetly at them, then wiggled his fingers in a mocking wave.

Anxiety knotted in Arabelle's chest along with the slightest hint of regret, though she couldn't do anything about it now. She'd struck the bargain. While future Arabelle would have to deal with the shades again later, current Arabelle had a familiar in the shape of a teenager on her hands.

"We'll take our leave." The shades had congealed back into one large formless mass. "Good luck, witch. We look forward to seeing you again when the terms are met."

Arabelle shuddered as the shades melted into the shadows. Once they disappeared, a shock of magic rippled over the crossroads; the clouds parted overhead, and the sinking afternoon sun bathed the area in watery light once more.

"What was that blast of magic?" She hugged herself to quell the goosebumps blooming beneath her clothes.

Knox stared at the crossroads. "I don't know. That was weird." He frowned, then shrugged, shaking off whatever concern had made him pause. He kicked a pebble as he sauntered toward Arabelle's car, all confidence and preternatural grace.

"So," he said, rubbing his hands together. "Last time I was up here was decades ago. What's happened since? I have so many questions. Because it's been a while, but also, I don't remember much. A few basic things seem to stick, but memories tend to fade in the Other World. Like, I don't remember my last boss *at all*. Wiped as soon as I crossed the threshold back over. So, like, if you ever feel embarrassed by something you do around me, don't be. I'll forget it the moment I go back."

"Other World?" Arabelle asked.

"Yeah." He shoved his hands into his deep pockets. "The realm of my queen."

Arabelle took a steadying breath. "Get in the car, Knox. We have a lot of work to do."

"No problem, Boss."

She slid into the driver's seat and massaged her temples. "And be quiet. I need to think."

Knox mimed zipping his lips.

"Shit," Arabelle said again as she started the car. "Okay. It's okay. This shouldn't take long. He'll be with me for a few months, tops. And then *poof*, back to the . . . *Other World*. It'll be okay." She cast a glance at Knox, who smiled as he clicked his seat belt on. She grimaced and gripped the steering wheel. "It'll be fine. I'll accomplish my goal and he'll go back. Everything will be okay."

1

ELLERY

ELLERY EVANS CURSED AS THEY HAULED ANOTHER PLASTIC tub of dirty dishes across the metal counter toward the deep kitchen sink.

Sweat gathered at their temples as they sank their hands in the steaming hot water, transferring the dishes into the basin to soak. The kitchen of the small diner was stifling. From the heat and sizzle of the stove, and the steam rising from the seams of Ellery's closest coworker, Hobart the industrial dishwasher, the room felt more like a tropical island than a restaurant. It was funny, in a way, that Ellery could grumble about the heat despite living in Solis City, a city renowned for the endless winter that had plagued them for the past five years, a weird weather phenomenon that no one could explain.

According to the calendar, it was supposed to be the middle of summer, but when Ellery biked to the diner that morning, wrapped up in their heaviest coat, gloves, hat, and scarf, it had been snowing. But that had been life for all of Ellery's teenage years. It was as if the seasons had just decided not to change one winter, and the warm wet of spring had never come. And without spring, there was no blazing heat of summer, and certainly no harvest in autumn. That was the way it had been for the last half-decade. And while there were scientists who had researched and tried to explain the situation—everything from climate change to the movements of the poles to changes in the ocean currents—no one quite understood what had happened, or why it had happened to this one particular region. Which also meant no one had any viable solutions.

Ellery was twelve when the seasons had stopped and now, at seventeen, didn't rightly care *why* their patch of the world had freezing temperatures year-round and snow every month. Ellery only cared about the consequences.

They used the spray nozzle to rinse an obscene amount of ranch dressing from a salad plate. A glob shot out and landed squarely on their apron, which, *gross*. Ellery made a face as they shoved the plate in the rack that they would run through the dishwasher once full. They grabbed a handful of utensils from the bus pan and dropped them into the suds. Elbows deep in the water, sponge in hand, Ellery scrubbed, absently humming along to the radio that played a random pop tune in the background, ignoring the cooks yelling at each other again. The sound of pressurized water beating against the inside of the metal box that was Hobart mostly drowned out the cursing.

The door to the kitchen swung open, and Ellery looked up briefly to catch their cousin's head popping through a slim crack. Her red hair was piled high, a pencil threaded through it; her freckled cheeks were flushed. The white apron around her waist had a blobby stain that might have been spaghetti sauce.

"Hey, El," she said, holding up her cell. "Phone. Your mom."

Ellery sighed. Of course she'd call in the middle of a shift. And she called Charley's phone because she knew Charley would answer. Ellery's phone was tucked away in the pocket of their jacket, Ellery having learned quickly that a sink full of soapy water wasn't conducive to healthy electronics. A day in a bag of rice later, and Ellery's phone was still spotty at best. "Can you tell her I'm busy?"

"Like the last three times? I don't think so. I'm not taking that heat."

"But it'll all be—"

"Supernatural bullshit. Yes, I know. You've said. Many times." She thrust the phone toward them. "Take a break. Diego won't care. Lunch rush is over anyway."

"There was a rush?" Ellery muttered.

Charley frowned and pointed aggressively.

Groaning, Ellery straightened from their hunch over the sink and stripped off their long rubber gloves. They pushed their short brown hair out of their eyes, snatched the cell from Charley's hand, and escaped through the back door of the restaurant out into the alley. They wedged an old pipe, which Frank had left on the stoop after being locked out one too many times, between the door and the jamb to keep it slightly propped. Overhead, Ellery spied a rusted horseshoe nailed over the entrance and rolled their eyes.

"Hey," Ellery said into the phone, standing on the concrete steps outside. The blast of chilly air when they exited had felt nice for a few seconds, until the absolute bone-piercing cold started sinking into their skin. Their T-shirt wasn't an adequate defense against the temperature. At least it wasn't snowing, though the sky was heavy and gray, ready to open at any minute. It wasn't even close to dusk, but the alley was dark with shadows cast by the dim glow of the streetlamp a few yards away.

"Ellery," their mom said. "How good of you to take my call."

Ellery tipped their head back and took a fortifying breath. They slipped one hand in the pocket of their worn jeans, fingers brushing the acorn wrapped with iron wire that resided there. "Hi, Mom. How are things?"

"Good," their mom said. She didn't elaborate further, which meant she was lying. After all, nothing had been "good" for the last five years.

Ellery swallowed around the sudden lump in their throat. "How's the farm?"

"Oh, it's going along okay. One of the greenhouses failed because we had some problems with the electricity. But other than that, the farm has been fine."

"It failed?" Ellery asked, rubbing the toe of their sneaker into the slush piled on the steps. "What does that mean? Did you lose the crops?"

A beat of silence. "Not all of them. And it's okay. The other greenhouses are working, and we'll have quite a yield from them."

Another lie. Ever since the winter set in, the family farm had struggled to produce anything. It couldn't. Not until Ellery's dad and uncles were able to construct a few greenhouses. Even then, the crops weren't as abundant, because the greenhouses were small and there wasn't as much space in which to plant. Also, greenhouses used heat, and between that, the farmhouse, and the barn, the electric bill had grown exponentially, too much for the extended family to afford. In fact, everything was too much for the family to afford, so Ellery had moved in with their older cousin for the summer to work in the city and send money back home.

"Well, I was just checking in to see how you were doing. How is Charley? Is she treating you well? Are you eating enough?"

Ellery winced. "Yes. Things are good. Charley is great. My job is good. Everything is fine."

"Oh, that's good. When I don't hear from you, it makes me think something bad has happened."

Guilt twisted beneath Ellery's ribs. "Sorry. I've been busy working."

"Not too much, I hope. We didn't let you move to the city to live with your cousin just for you to spend all your time working. I hope you're getting out and doing things. Having some fun? Experiencing new things?"

"Sure." It was Ellery's turn to lie.

"Do you still have the iron acorn I gave you?"

Ellery's lips twisted into a wry smile. Their mother believed the acorn's iron-wire cage could combat the magic of the supernatural, providing Ellery protection from any creature with ill intent.

Once upon a time, Ellery, too, believed in the myths of the faeries who lived under the hills in vast, glittering kingdoms, and the fae king who ruled over them. They believed in the garden gnomes who made the plants grow if they left them gifts, and the nymphs who coaxed the rivers to run and the wells to fill and who required offerings during the droughts, and the mischievious pixies who would lead travelers astray for fun, unless the individual had a pretty rock or sunflower seed to give to them. Most importantly, they believed in a gracious and loving goddess who ensured a bountiful harvest each autumn to those who brought offerings and burned incense and prayed like good little sycophants. That she would bestow her favor on and protect those who worshipped and revered her and showered her with trinkets like they'd been taught to by their elders.

Ellery believed in all the stories—that magic was real, that people were inherently good, and that if they believed in something desperately enough, it wouldn't fail them. Until they learned it was all a lie.

"Yes." Despite not believing anymore, it was the last thing their mother had given them before they left, and sentimentality was difficult to let go of. "Did you get the money I sent?"

"We did. You don't have to do that."

They had this same conversation every time. "But it helped, right?"

She sighed over the line. "Yes. Of course it did. We used part of it to buy an offering for the goddess. I have a good feeling this time. I'm certain she'll hear us."

Ellery's stomach sank. "Mom," they said, their tone almost admonishing. "Why did you do that? You could've used it for something else, something important."

"Ellery. It is important."

Ellery ducked their head and squeezed their eyes shut. This was another line of conversation they had each call, one that Ellery would've liked to avoid. "How can you still believe in her? It's a waste of money and time."

Their mom huffed. And Ellery knew they had crossed a line. But they couldn't understand how their mom still held fast to her beliefs. Ellery had watched for years as their parents and the rest of the neighboring farm folk begged and pleaded to an empty shrine in the corn, only for nothing to change. Ellery's faith shriveled and died, like the plants in the field, and the fruit on the vine, and the livestock without feed. All of it had only served to drive Ellery away, to solidify their skepticism when it came to anything beyond what they could see or touch. Especially as they made the difficult decision to pack their bags and leave, to be one less mouth to feed, one less burden.

"I know you don't understand," their mom said, and Ellery bristled at the condescension. "But I wish we didn't have to have this discussion every time, Ellery."

"I wish for that too," they mumbled. "Look, Mom—"

The back door swung open. "El!" Charley yelled from the other side of the threshold. "The hot weird guy is back."

"Mom, I have to go. The hot weird guy is back, and I cannot miss this."

"The *what*?"

Charley snatched the phone from Ellery's hand. "I wouldn't interrupt if it wasn't important, Aunt Nance. But El really needs to go. We'll call later. Promise."

Charley ended the call, then grabbed a handful of Ellery's T-shirt and yanked. Ellery stumbled into the diner, and one of the cooks yelled at them for letting in the winter air as the door slammed shut. The shock of heat from the kitchen after standing outside made Ellery dizzy, but it did not deter them and Charley as they jostled against each other for space to peek through the small circular window into the diner's seating area.

Sure enough, the hot weird guy stood at the counter, long, pale fingers drumming on the linoleum countertop as he talked to Marisol, one of the other waitresses, to pick up his order. His black hair was cut close at the sides and long on top, brushed forward with what Charley had dubbed "emo bangs." He wore large sunglasses that he didn't take off despite being indoors, and when he smiled, it was wide and cheerful and showed off perfect straight teeth that would have made an orthodontist weep.

"He's so hot," Charley said, pressing her nose against the glass.

"You have a girlfriend," Ellery reminded her.

"Not even just hot, but dreamy. Like he stepped right out of a movie or a runway. I mean, those cheekbones alone would land him on a magazine cover, but do you see those lips?"

"We literally live with said girlfriend. Her name is Zada, if you remember."

Charley swatted Ellery's shoulder. "I'm aware, but I can appreciate beauty in the form of a person. I mean, *look* at him."

Ellery looked, definitely appreciating his sharp jawline, smooth skin, and pink bow mouth. And while Ellery could also *appreciate* the visage, they weren't one to say it out loud. Or do anything about it. Admiring from afar was good enough for them, thank you. Because anything else would require social interaction, of which Ellery was not usually a fan. And, well, hot weird guy was 1000 percent out of Ellery's league in every reality. They couldn't deny that the "hot" part of the nickname was apt.

"I bet he's a vampire." Charley nudged Ellery's arm with her pointy elbow. "He gives off that vibe."

"There are no such thing as vampires."

"Fine—a sprite, then. Or a nymph. Something supernatural."

"Still all myths and still all not real."

Charley clucked her tongue. "You're no fun. Besides, who says they're not real? Zada's sister's best friend knows a club where a water nymph sings, and I've totally seen a dryad in the produce section of the grocery store."

Before Ellery could retort, a clattering of pots and pans sounded behind them, followed by shuffling footsteps. Diego leaned in, his large frame looming over the two of them.

"He has a bad aura," Diego said.

Ellery sighed. "Also, no such things as auras, unless accompanied by a migraine or seizure."

Diego sniffed, insulted. "You should stay away from him. He's trouble."

"Agreed," Charley said with a sharp nod. "He's weird."

The thing was, hot weird guy wasn't really that weird. He came in every so often and picked up an order under the name of "Arabelle," paid in cash, made some stilted small talk, then left. The thing that set him apart from every other customer, aside from his otherworldly attractiveness and the ever-present sunglasses, was the fact that he was never dressed for the cold. Never wore a thick coat, or a scarf, or even a pair of gloves. He appeared impervious to the weather, the same weather that had Ellery shivering within seconds.

And when he stopped in to pick up the food order, he looked at everything with an expression that was slightly wistful and a little sad. Ellery could relate.

Today wasn't any different. He glanced around the diner while he waited, wearing a long-sleeved shirt and jeans and an expression that was too open for the city.

Ellery couldn't ride their bike without at least four layers of clothing, a hat, gloves, scarf, and doubled socks. Maybe hot weird guy had a car he parked around the corner that none of them had seen. That seemed like a more probable explanation than superpowers.

Hot weird guy grinned when Marisol handed over the paper bag with his order, and Ellery wondered how she didn't swoon. His fingers wrapped around the handle, and he gave her a friendly nod. He turned his head to where Charley and Ellery's breaths fogged the kitchen window and raised his hand in a wave.

Ellery ducked down, cheeks aflame. Charley squeaked and giggled, burying her face in Ellery's shoulder as she laughed.

"Oh my gods and goddesses," she said, hands clapped against her burning face. "He saw us."

Ellery's insides tumbled in embarrassment, and they wrapped their arms around their torso. "Shit."

"Serves you both right for spying instead of working," Diego said, wagging his spatula at them. "Now break time is over. You can ogle on your own time."

Charley straightened, smoothed down her waitress uniform, and retied her apron. "Yes. Let me go serve all three of our customers."

Ellery raised an eyebrow. "We have three customers? I thought you said the lunch rush was over?"

Diego grumbled about sarcastic teenagers and went back to the basket of onion rings he'd dropped in the frying oil a few minutes ago that were now probably crispier than they should've been. Ellery extracted themself from Charley's arms and headed back to the waiting dishwater.

Ellery worked for the next few hours sliding loaded racks of dishes into Hobart for their steamy, pressurized wash, then pulling them out and stacking them once dry. Eventually they ran out of dishes and ventured on the other side of the kitchen doors into the diner proper. Sitting on a stool, Ellery wiped down menus and rolled utensils into napkins while listening to the chatter from Charley and

Marisol, and the continued bickering between Diego and Frank in the back.

Customers were few and far between. Even the dinner crowd was only a handful of patrons.

"I used to be the busiest diner on this side of the city," Diego lamented when he emerged from the kitchen a few minutes before closing, hand towel draped over one shoulder, frown lines in his brow. "Now I'm lucky to afford the power it takes to run the grill." He shook his head. "The city is dying, and soon the entire region will be left to the shadows."

"Maybe someone will figure out what's wrong and fix it?" Ellery asked softly. It was a weak sentiment. They had given up hope a while ago but had found that voicing their cynicism wasn't great for conversations.

Diego huffed. "Maybe. But it's been five years. It is no longer news. Even our local media has accepted this new reality and moved on to other things. We've been forgotten, Ellery. The rest of the world turns, and we'll remain stuck fast in winter forever."

A shiver worked its way down Ellery's spine, and it wasn't because of the cold. "What will you do?"

"Stay open as long as I can, and then . . ." He sighed wearily. "My brother lives in Olympia. They're experiencing a boom from everyone leaving here. Maybe I will go there and open a new restaurant. A bigger one with more seats and a larger menu." Diego patted Ellery's shoulder. "You have a good aura. I'll save you a job if it comes to that."

Ellery bit back the instinctive retort regarding auras but settled on a subdued "Thanks." But what Diego had said was unsettling. Ellery couldn't move again, not even farther away from their family farm. They knew their parents and extended family would stubbornly cling to what was left, try to hold on to a legacy. They'd die beseeching an imaginary goddess for a reprieve.

"Closing time," Diego said, with a nod to the door. Night had fallen, and the remaining residents of the city didn't often venture out once the sun went down. "Don't forget to take out the garbage when you're done."

"I won't," Ellery said as Charley turned the sign on the door to CLOSED and locked it. "I'll see you in the morning."

The others left as Charley and Ellery began closing procedures. They wiped down the counters and tables and stacked chairs, and Ellery ran Hobart one last time to catch the last remaining dishes. They both bundled up into their jackets and scarves. Ellery tugged a knit hat low over their ears.

Charley checked her phone. "Zada is here in the back. Do you want a ride, or are you biking home?"

"Oh, so you do remember her name."

Charley glared. "Fine. You can walk."

"No! Sorry." Ellery laughed. "Sorry. I won't tell her about the guy we ogle."

"Oh, she already knows. She wants to witness him in person one day. So, ride or bike?"

"Ride, definitely."

Charley winked. "Good choice."

Ellery grabbed the two bags of trash and trundled into the alley. After tossing the garbage into the large metal bins, Ellery unlocked their bike from the nearby post and followed Charley to where Zada's car idled. Ellery threw their bike into Zada's trunk, then slid into the back seat, sighing at the blast of heat from the vents.

"Good day at work?" Zada asked, smiling as she leaned over and pecked Charley on the lips.

Charley launched into the story of the return of hot weird guy and the utter embarrassment that had followed as Ellery settled into the cushion and tried not to dwell on their conversation with Diego.

But they couldn't help it as they watched the bleak landscape slide by outside the car window and noted all the closed stores and restaurants, as well as the drifts of dirty snow on the sidewalks, which hardly anyone walked on anymore. Diego wasn't wrong; the whole area was dying—not just the farms, but the city as well. People were leaving in droves, and soon all that would remain would be the shadows and the snow and vacant buildings.

Ellery hunched down into their coat. What would they do then? Would they be forced to move? What would happen to the farm? To their family? To the city? Ellery tucked their chin to their chest and pulled their hood up over their head to block out the view. Ellery didn't have any answers, but one thing was clear. Life as it was with an endless winter was not sustainable. Something would have to change. But Ellery had no clue as to what.

2

KNOX

KNOX LEANED FORWARD IN HIS SEAT ON THE COUCH, ELBOWS propped on his knobby knees as he watched the drama unfolding on the screen. His eyes widened as the actress playing the teen protagonist held up a gleaming knife, ready to plunge it into her best friend's heart.

"I'm sorry," she said, eyes brimming, voice choked, as she hovered over the boy writhing on the ground. A curse burned through him, turning him into *something* frightful. The TV show didn't boast the clearest details on their lore regarding the supernatural, but that didn't change the fact that Knox was still fascinated.

He shoved a handful of fish-shaped cheese crackers into his mouth as the two characters wrestled. Tears streamed down the actress's face as she gained the upper hand and raised the knife higher.

"Wait!" another character yelled as they ran into frame, holding a small bottle.

Ah. Knox knew that would happen. The best friend was a series main, and they wouldn't kill him off just yet—not midseason, anyway. But Knox stayed glued to the television because, in all honesty, it wasn't the climax of the episode that he loved the most. It was the end moments, the soft scenes, the displays of affection. He stared wistfully at the brief seconds before the credits rolled as the group hugged and laughed and held on to one another, grateful their found family had survived another hour-long adventure.

That was his favorite part.

But it was over too soon, and Knox would have to wait a week until the new episode. Which, in the age of binge-watching, seemed unfair.

He flicked through a few other TV shows on the streaming service menu but, finding nothing interesting, dropped the remote on the end table. With a sigh, he fell back onto the couch cushions.

He was restless. Arabelle had been acting frenzied for the past few weeks, and she'd given him little to do beyond going to the diner to pick up food. As a familiar, he couldn't leave the apartment without Arabelle's permission and specific direction. He wasn't sure if he'd been cooped up like this before, but he was certain he'd never felt so unsettled. At least he *thought* this feeling was new. That was the thing with being liminal, with existing between two worlds. Each trip back to the Other World meant a loss of knowledge from the human realm. Memories would fade into nothing, specifics lost as soon as Knox crossed the barrier, and over time, whole lifetimes would be forgotten. Important things remained—like his name and general knowledge of human life—but details would soften and disappear.

One thing he knew for sure was that no matter how lonely or bored he'd been, he'd never had trouble connecting with his goddess. Until now. She'd been quiet. His messages had been blocked, and she hadn't reached out to him at all. A sense of unease had settled heavily in the pit of his stomach over the past few years.

He craned his neck and peeked out the window of the apartment at the city, which was being blanketed in yet another layer of white. Knox imagined going outside to the small yard in the back of the complex and kicking up the snow or building a snowman. He daydreamed about visiting the nice folks at the diner and interacting with them, or maybe even finding the other supernatural creatures he knew were out there. Well, he imagined were out there. He hadn't encountered any on his limited trips in this life, though he had a strong feeling he'd met a few in his previous one.

But it didn't matter—he couldn't do any of those things. His bond with Arabelle wouldn't allow it, and if he tried to disobey, the insistent tugging behind his navel would become unbearable. And while Knox loved skirting the rules, he wasn't one for pain. Which meant he wasn't allowed much freedom.

He could ask Arabelle for permission to go out. She wasn't so bad as a boss. Knox didn't have to eat, but she bought him his favorite snacks anyway. And there were the nights they sat on the couch together, watching reality TV shows and commenting on the ridiculousness of humans, where they felt more like friends than boss and familiar. But with the way Arabelle had been lately, it was better for him just to stare moodily out of the window and wait for a task.

Arabelle knocked around in the kitchen, muttering to herself as she tinkered with a potion. Just like the potions she'd tried before, this one would most likely end in failure. Arabelle would curse and yell, and the process would start all over again. That had been the routine since Knox had stumbled out of the oak tree. Except she'd been a little more harried these days.

"Knox," Arabelle barked from the dining room.

Knox startled and flailed, his bag of crackers flying out of his hands. It launched upward, golden fish exploding into a shower of crispy crumbs. One of Arabelle's first edicts when she brought him home had been *Clean up after yourself, no messes*. And, well, this qualified. Knox unleashed a blast of magic that suspended the inevitable disaster in midair. With a snap, the crackers reversed their trajectory and refilled the bag. The bag then gently landed on the coffee table.

With a satisfied smile, Knox dusted off his hands.

"Knox!"

He jumped again and pressed a palm to his chest to feel his racing heart, because, wow, Arabelle's tone hadn't been that harsh since the first year he'd been here. He slid off the arm of the couch and landed lightly on his bare feet with a flourish, to cover up the fact that he had been so absorbed in his thoughts that she'd scared the nightlights out of him.

He cleared his throat. "Yes?"

"Come here. I need you."

"Of course," he said with a forced smile.

He crossed the living room and entered the dining area. Arabelle beckoned him closer. She licked her cracked lips. Taking in the scene, he couldn't help but notice how uncharacteristically chaotic her work area was. Clutter wasn't usually her style. She always put her scrolls and books away when she was finished, worried they'd become ruined in some way, but now they were scattered everywhere. Come to think of it, she'd barely stopped to eat in the last few days. She always said that a well-nourished body meant a well-nourished mind. Whatever that meant. Knox didn't need to eat or drink; he just liked to, because, well, it was great.

She grabbed his arm, her fingers a bruising grip, and yanked him closer. On a hot plate sat a bubbling cauldron. Upon closer inspection, Arabelle's cheeks were flushed pink with excitement and her hair was a wild mess. She ladled a portion of a green liquid from the cauldron into an ornate vial, slamming the stopper shut and holding it with both hands.

"I think I've done it," she breathed.

"Done what?" Knox craned his neck to look at the brew. Arabelle had made a ton of potions over the years. Everything from cough medicine to good-luck juice (which, for the record, didn't work).

"The elixir of life," she said.

Oh. Was that all? That happened at least once a year, sometimes twice in years Arabelle was industrious. "Right."

She wrinkled her nose. "No, this is it. I'm certain."

Knox shrugged. "Okay."

"I mean it. This is the one. I've figured it out. I just need you."

"My magic?"

She shook her head. "Your blood."

Knox froze. "What?"

"I thought all this time it was your magic that would complete the potion, but I should've known the shades wouldn't have specifically mentioned why you would be needed. You're the last ingredient. Your liminality. Your ability to exist in both worlds. That's what I need to complete the elixir."

Uh-oh. That sounded like it might actually work.

"Um . . . Arabelle, I don't—"

"Don't try to talk around it, Knox. You're here for a reason. And this is it. This is your reason. So get to it. I command you to add your blood."

Knox squeezed his eyes shut. The power of her voice rippled through his body, and try as he might to resist, he could not. This would definitely not make his queen happy. She ruled the Other World, the place where all human souls passed through. This would allow Arabelle to stay in the earthly realm indefinitely, extending her life and the lives of anyone else she chose, for as long as she wanted.

"Arabelle," Knox said through clenched teeth. "Think this through."

"This is your purpose. To help me. So help me."

Knox's shoulders slumped as he gave in and held out his hand. She grabbed it and pricked his finger. A bead of red blood welled at the tip. She uncorked the vial with her teeth, then tipped the drop into the glass. It splashed against the side and slid slowly into the mixture. Knox jerked his hand away and stepped back, awaiting the inevitable chemical reaction.

As soon as his blood hit the concoction, it glowed. Arabelle popped the cork back in place quickly as the substance sloshed in the enclosed space like a maelstrom in a bottle, frothing and swirling, deepening into a dark blue. The stopper creaked but held firm as the potion inside it thrashed. After a few moments, the storm calmed and left behind a shimmering blue and purple liquid, one that held the power of immortality.

She held the vial to the light and stared as the setting sun highlighted the color and the magic that swirled within. "I did it," she breathed. "I can't believe it. It took years and a lot of mistakes and a series of obscene grocery bills," she said, tossing Knox a wry look, "but finally. *Finally.*"

Arabelle laughed, her hands clasped around her ultimate goal.

Knox shivered as the lights flickered in the apartment and clouds rolled in front of the sun, casting the room in darkness.

"Arabelle," Knox said softly.

He trembled as the shadows lengthened. He gulped and took another slow step out of the dining room as the darkness around them writhed, spreading from the shadowed corners of the apartment along the walls and onto the floor, until there were many more shadows than what bright overhead lights should allow. Knox's hands shook as the darkness coalesced into bodily shapes, and the shades, servants of the queen, broke off from the shadows around them, emerging from the depths of the Other World.

Arabelle, so caught up in her own adulation and enamored with the elixir, didn't notice them right away.

"Witch," the air hissed, as one of the rippling pits of darkness spoke.

Arabelle spun on her heel, and her face drained of all color as the shades gathered closely around the cluttered dining-room table.

"What are you doing here?" she said, clutching the vial close.

"You've done it, then," one of the shades said in a low tone.

"You've harnessed the knowledge of life."

"You've completed your quest."

Arabelle wrapped her fingers around the potion in a death grip. "I have."

Their bright red eyes, fixed on the vial, glittered like rubies. "The terms of the deal have come to an end."

Knox shuddered as he felt the tether between him and Arabelle cut and release. The relief was instantaneous. Knox sagged against the arm of the couch, breath releasing in one long sigh. No more pressure, no more tension. His magic dimmed as well, no longer powered by the bargain but still present for now.

Arabelle cast a pitying glance at Knox over her shoulder. "I'm sorry, Knox. I didn't realize they'd come for you so quickly. But I hope you at least enjoyed your time here."

Knox grimaced. "I don't think they're only here for me, Arabelle."

"What?"

The shades quivered. "Payment is due when terms are met," the tallest one said, their voice a brittle breeze rustling dead leaves.

"But . . . that was not the deal we had!"

The second shade lifted a hand, pinched the air, and unzipped the boundaries of the realm, opening a rift through which the signed scroll fell out.

"Payment upon completion of the task."

Arabelle grabbed the back of her dining-room chair to steady herself.

"I want another bargain, then. Let me gather the offerings, and I'll meet you at the crossroads in a few hours and—"

"No! It is time. You have the knowledge of life." The shades leveled their gaze at Knox. "And now you must pay your end of the deal."

"I'll just drink it, then!" She grabbed the stopper at the top of the vial.

The shades moved quickly—like sharks scenting blood in the water, as Knox had seen once on a nature documentary. In one moment they were on the other side of the room, and in the next they crowded around Arabelle's shuddering body.

She cried out in shock as the third shade thrust out its shadowed arm, fingers reaching through her chest. Her mouth fell open in a silent scream, eyes wide with fear. Tears streamed from their corners and froze on her cheeks. The potion fell from her lax hand, the landing cushioned by the bright area rug beneath the table. It rolled, as if having a mind of its own, to the hardwood and traveled across the polished floor, stopping at the lip of the carpet where Knox watched from the living area.

Knox stared at it. Better to focus on the swirling liquid than the gruesome scene in front of him where Arabelle was losing her soul. Knox considered the elixir. The power of life. He had no need for it. He was immortal. But that immortality came with caveats.

The Other World was cold and dark and lonely. Who knew how long it would be until someone else needed a familiar? It could be ages before he'd be back in the earthly realm. And he'd gotten to experience so little outside of Arabelle's apartment. Not to mention the silence from the queen herself. What would he even find if he was pulled back to the Other World right now?

He lifted his head in time to see the shade finish extracting Arabelle's soul and watched as her lifeless body fell to the ground with a thump.

"Take this," the shade said, handing the glowing orb to the other.

"Where is the potion?" the tallest demanded, searching the carpet around Arabelle's body. "Where is it?"

That was odd. Why did they care about it? They had her soul. And they would have Knox again shortly. But their interest was disconcerting, and Knox used his toes to push the vial behind the leg of the couch.

"Why do you need it? You're immortal."

The shades stilled as if remembering he was there. "Knox," the one holding Arabelle's soul said, voice scraping out almost in surprise.

"We cannot allow it in the hands of the humans."

"We must protect our queen."

"The potion endangers her reign."

That did make sense. Kind of. But why would they even allow Arabelle to try to create it if the result would be so dangerous? One soul wasn't worth putting the queen at risk.

"Why hasn't the queen answered my messages?"

They rustled in clear agitation, and Knox's earlier apprehension welled into his throat.

"Come see for yourself." The tallest shade extended a hand.

Knox shuddered at the ominous invitation. His instincts screamed at him that something was off.

"Knox," they hissed, when he didn't move. "It is time to go home."

Knox wondered if he'd ever hesitated before returning home, because he was certainly hesitating now. He hated the idea of not knowing what awaited him, especially when the shades were acting so, well, shady. At least here, there was potential. He could play in the snow. Visit the cute person in the window at the diner.

Maybe he'd watched too many movies with rebellious teens, but his trepidation twisted into resolve. He didn't want to go back to the Other World just yet. There was so much to explore, and now that the bargain was complete, he was free for the first time in years. It was impulsive, reckless, and probably a very bad idea. But once the thought was there, he couldn't ignore it.

He snatched up the vial, shoved it in his pocket, and ran for the apartment's front door. His bare feet slapped across the hardwood of the hallway. The shades screeched behind him, demanding that he stop, but he didn't listen.

Instead, he slammed out of the apartment into the corridor of the complex, running faster and faster with each joyous step, the elixir of life burning in his pocket as he slung open the door to the stairs. He had no idea what he was doing or where he planned to go as he fled the servants of his queen, who were no doubt furious at his decision to defy them. But he didn't care.

Knox burst onto the street, feet sinking into the drift of snow on the sidewalk. He ran.

And he didn't look back.

3

ELLERY

"Come on," Charley said, tugging on Ellery's hand. She dragged them out from the kitchen to the front of the diner. The door had already been locked and the sign turned, and Diego and Marisol had left for the night.

Zada leaned on the front counter, her dark brown skin gleaming with a blue sheen from the neon lights of the storefront across the street. Her long black hair wound over her shoulder in a cluster of braids, with vibrant strands of different colors woven through. Between her huge brown eyes; long, curled lashes; perfect makeup; and leather jacket, she was entirely too beautiful and stylish to be at the counter of a diner on an early Saturday night.

"Have you asked them yet?" Zada said, tapping her fingernails on the laminate.

Charley shook her head. "Not yet."

"Whatever it is," Ellery said, removing Charley's grip from their wrist, "the answer is no."

"Don't be like that, El," Charley whined. "It's not a big request. Zada and I want to go to this club."

"There's a nymph," Zada clarified.

"No such thing."

Zada rolled her eyes. "Okay, fine. There's a singer that we both

33

really want to hear, but the line forms, like, now. We'd have to leave in a few minutes to have any hope of making it in."

Ellery blinked. "Oh, you're asking for Charley to leave work early?"

"Yes. Look, I know it's a pain in the ass completing the closing procedures on your own, but—"

"Go," Ellery said quickly. "Please leave. Like, I'm not even kidding, it will make my life so much easier. I might even get out of here quicker."

Charley frowned. "What?"

"Not to be insulting, but I would love to be alone for the next hour rather than hearing you sing off-key to the music in your head. Also, sometimes you make an even bigger mess that we then have to also clean up before we get to leave."

"How is that not insulting?" Charley demanded, hands on her hips. "I can't believe this. Back talk from my younger cousin. I feed you. I clothe you. I take care of you. I raised you."

"You literally did none of those things."

Zada hid a laugh behind her hand.

"What?" Charley pointed at Zada. "You're with them?"

"Babe," Zada said, a smile teasing around her mouth. "You know I think you're beautiful and perfect, but Ellery has a point. Do you not remember cleaning the kitchen last week with a towel that was covered in glitter? Or when you did our laundry and forgot the pen in your pocket? Or when you mixed bleach with another cleaner in the tub, and we had to evacuate the apartment for a day while the noxious gas was aired out?"

Charley gasped. "Slander. Absolute slander."

"Do you want to go or not?"

"Oh, I want to go," Charley said, snatching her purse and looping the strap over her shoulder. "But I don't know if I want to go with *you* any longer."

Zada laughed. "Babe. Oh my gods and goddesses. Babe!" She hopped off her stool and skirted around the counter after Charley as Charley stomped toward the kitchen.

Zada huffed as she paused at the kitchen doors. She looked to Ellery. "You'll be okay getting home?"

"Of course," Ellery said with a nod. "You'll be okay in the doghouse?"

Zada smirked. "I won't be for long. I have my ways." She patted Ellery on the shoulder. "Use my bus pass if you need to, and don't stay here too late. The city gets strange at night."

Ellery opened their mouth, but Zada cut them off. "I know, I know. You don't believe in strange. But text me when you get home."

Ellery gritted their teeth but acquiesced. "Yes, ma'am."

Zada made a face at the "ma'am" but scampered off after Charley. Their bickering faded as the back door slammed, leaving Ellery by themself in the diner.

They sighed and grabbed the cleaning supplies, getting to work. As predicted, it took an hour to wipe down all the counters and tables, turn the chairs over, and sweep and mop the floor. They cleaned the windows, then pulled down the blinds and twirled them closed. Then they turned off all the lights in the front. Moving to the back, Ellery ensured all the supplies were put away and the dishes were stacked neatly.

Since the sun had already set, the temperature had dropped from bone-chilling to certain death, so Ellery bundled up as best they could. Hoodie, overcoat, gloves, hat, and scarf. Grabbing their keys from the hook on the wall by the door, Ellery slid them into their pocket. They took their backpack and slipped it over their shoulders.

They grabbed the two tied bags of trash and opened the back door. It slammed shut behind them. Stepping out on the small stoop, Ellery accidentally kicked the pipe. It skittered off the raised steps and fell into the alley. Ellery wilted. They'd have to find it later when it was light out. Right now the city was dark, save for a few blinking neon signs and the moon.

Diego had once told Ellery that before the unnatural winter, the city had never slept and the lights had drowned out the stars. But now that half the populace had fled, and the rest were too superstitious to traverse the city in the cold and the dark, the stars were clear to see. Almost as bright as they had been when Ellery lived on the farm. The only sound was far-off music on the breeze, muted by distance and the blanket of snow.

Ellery tossed the bags in the dumpster, then walked to the post where they'd tied their bike. The alley had a steep incline that connected the main street down to the back door of the diner. With the snow and ice, Ellery knew better than to try and bike up the thin strip of pavement. They unlocked their bike and considered Zada's advice to take the bus home as they walked to the top of the hill. But it hadn't snowed much that day. The plows had come by to clear much of the road, and, well, the bus was money that Ellery didn't want to spend. They straddled their bike, shoving one foot into the stirrup on the pedal as they fiddled with their gears.

Once they were ready, Ellery lifted their head in time to catch a glimpse of dark hair and gold eyes before they were absolutely flattened.

A body collided with theirs, snapping their head to the side, knocking the breath out of them in a surprised and pained gasp. They toppled over, feet tangling in the pedals, and slammed into the cold asphalt.

Their assailant fell with them, and the two of them became a knot of limbs and metal as they slid down the incline. They didn't tumble over each other per se—the fact that Ellery's foot was stuck in the bike prevented that—but between the force of the hit and the icy slush, the slide was uncontrolled. The person's elbow dug into Ellery's stomach, robbing them of any breath they had left. The ice and gravel scratched against the slivers of exposed skin not covered by Ellery's thick clothes. The world spun in flashing colors: yellow from the streetlights, white from the glow of the moon, the ash gray of the dirty snow and the black of the asphalt, until they finally skidded to a painful stop, smacking into the wall at the back of the alley.

Ellery wheezed, their face inches from a frozen puddle. One arm was tucked underneath their body while the other was wrapped awkwardly around their middle as they blinked away tears.

There was a scramble next to them as the other person gained their feet, cursing as they slipped.

Despite the rolling waves of pain and nausea, Ellery pushed to their elbows and craned their neck to glance at the person who'd knocked them over. The guy blinked, meeting Ellery's gaze, gold eyes glittering in the speckling of moonlight, black hair disheveled, cheeks pinked, chest heaving.

His mouth dropped open as they looked at Ellery, eyes widening. "The dishwasher."

"Hot weird guy?"

"What?"

"What"—Ellery's voice was a breathy sound, with barely enough force for a whisper—"the fuck?"

Hot weird guy spun around, eyes searching the alley, before his whole body stiffened. "Oh no." He bent over Ellery, pawing at their body, wrapping his hand around their arm and yanking. "We have to run."

"What is wrong with you?" Ellery had gained enough breath to talk. They shrugged out of his grasp. "Why did you tackle me? Who are you? And why are you running around barefoot in the snow?"

Hot weird guy let go and stumbled back, feet sinking into the slush up to his ankles. "Now's not the time. I have to run. *We* have to run."

Ellery pushed to a sitting position, pulling their leg from underneath the bike. Their shoulders and spine ached and protested every small movement. Their right arm twinged. Blood dripped down their chin from when hot weird guy's jaw had collided with their nose.

Ellery hobbled to their feet, leaning heavily on the wall, unable to straighten fully due to the absolute searing pain in their back. Their backpack thankfully remained on their shoulders, and their bike seemed okay, as far as they could tell. Somehow they only had one glove on their hand. At least they didn't think any bones were broken, which was a small consolation.

Hot weird guy spread his hands. "My name is Knox. I'm a . . ." He trailed off, brow furrowed as if he wasn't sure what word to use, which was strange. "I'm a person. And I'm running from something very scary, and you should be running too."

Ellery raised an eyebrow. "I'm not afraid," they said.

Knox laughed, a strange, raspy sound. "You should be." He held out his hand. "We have to move. Come on."

"No."

He frowned, features twisting, then dropped the offered hand to his side. "I'd forgotten people were so stubborn. But fine. Stay here at your own risk."

The wind whistled through the alley, rustling through the scattering of debris on the ground. A strange sound accompanied it, a susurration of a name that sent pinpricks of unease along the back of Ellery's neck.

"Knox," the cold breeze called.

Knox spun around as a group of figures appeared from the shadows at the mouth of the alley. They descended toward them, steps not making a sound, more like fog than footfalls. The three of them wore all black, and they moved oddly in tandem. Every hair on Ellery's arms stood on end at their approach, and their heart thumped as they real-ized their back was against the end of the alley. The group of black-clad figures blocked the only route out to the main road. Somehow Ellery had unwittingly become part of whatever was happening.

"Knox," they called again. "You have nowhere to run." It was said in a singsong voice, a parody of a lullaby.

Knox trembled but narrowed his eyes defiantly. He stuck out his chin. "I have not yet begun to run, thank you."

"Give up, Knox." The sound was an echo of everything horrible. "There is no escaping."

"No."

Ellery gulped. "What did you do?" they whispered to Knox.

He didn't break eye contact with the figures. "Nothing."

Okay. That did not help them get a read on the situation. Ellery licked their lips and tasted copper. "Then why are they after you?"

"They're trying to abduct me."

Ellery stilled. Oh.

"Stay out of this," one of them hissed in Ellery's direction. They shivered, and it wasn't because of the cold.

"Knox. It is time to go home. Come, or we will be forced to drag you," another said.

Knox's throat bobbed. "You can just let me go."

"We cannot."

"Please?" he said, plaintive, his voice breaking. "You don't have to do this."

"We do."

"But I want a choice."

Knox's plea struck a chord, and, despite Ellery's better judgment, they let go of their death grip on the wall to stumble to his side.

"He doesn't want to go. Back off."

Ellery wasn't sure if it was the fall or how dark the alleyway had become, but it was difficult to make out the features of these . . . well, Ellery wasn't quite sure who they were. Muggers? Criminals? Family members? Whatever they were, they were in Ellery's way, and they were not doing anything to hot weird guy, even if he had brought Ellery to the ground. Not if Ellery had any say.

Knox sucked in an audible breath. "What are you doing?"

"I don't know."

Ellery didn't have a weapon. They reached into their pocket and found the useless iron-wrapped acorn still there. They clutched it in their fist, and hysterical laughter bubbled up their gullet. Right. Protection. Not a lot an acorn was going to do against three attackers. But in their other pocket was the diner key, and the back door was *right there*, only a few feet away. Ellery took a step to the side. Their heel struck something solid, and they glanced down. Well, that could buy some time.

"You're making a mistake," one of the trio said, their voice low.

Ellery sighed deeply. "Wouldn't be the first time."

The closest attacker lunged. Ellery stepped in front of Knox, pushing him behind their body. The figure recoiled and hesitated for a moment, and it was long enough for Ellery to duck and grab the pipe by their foot. They swung upward. It connected with one of the attackers, whose head snapped to the side, the force of the hit jarring the weapon in Ellery's hands. The iron was so cold, it stung Ellery's unprotected palm. The assailant staggered and fell with a strange sizzling sound, like cold water hitting a hot grill. Ellery tried not to think too much of it and jabbed the pipe into another's stomach as they reached for Knox. They bent double, wheezing and coughing, the smell of rotting eggs wafting from their dark robes. Ellery gagged, hoping the stench was from the nearby dumpster, then swiftly brought the end of the pipe upward, catching the second assailant under their chin. They hissed, staggering away.

The third didn't approach but stalked along an imaginary line, waiting for Knox and Ellery to try and escape. Ellery couldn't see their features in the shadows, but the threat of malice and retribution dripped off them and was apparent in the way they moved as their comrades writhed on the ground.

"What about that one?" Ellery asked, pipe clenched in their fist. "Are we making a run for it? Are we standing our ground or are we—"

Knox grabbed Ellery's wrist, his touch burning against the bare skin of their gloveless hand, holding the pipe at arm's length. "You're going to run while I distract them and—"

The last of the assailants charged. Distracted, Ellery didn't have a chance to swing the pipe or even really see the attack. It was as if one moment the attacker was at the end of the alley, then suddenly right in front of them. They grabbed Knox's arm, a blur of movement in the dark, the fabric of their outfit obscuring any identifying features. Knox cried out and wrenched his arm away with such force that his elbow knocked hard into Ellery's chin. Surprised by the blow and suddenly off-balance, Ellery fumbled backward and slipped on a patch of ice, feet flying out from underneath them. The pipe clattered to the ground as they fell, their back smacking into a gross mound of ashen slush. The breath was knocked right out of them, and they stared at the stars above, gasping for air.

The sound of a scuffle registered, and they rolled to their side, pushing themself up to their knees with one gloved hand. Knox. They had to help Knox, or they were about to be witness to an abduction. And Ellery really didn't want that on their conscience.

The pipe. Where was the pipe? The alley was so dark and shadowed that the moonlight didn't reach all the way to the ground in some places, obscured by the high walls on either side and the shadow cast by the dumpster. Ellery reached out with their frozen fingers, searching along the ground for the cold cast iron.

"Would you stop? I don't want to go back with you!" Knox yelled through gritted teeth.

"You must. But first, where is it?"

"I said—" Knox said, biting off each word, "*no!*"

The air crackled with energy. A hot flash of bright white light followed, and for an instant, the whole area was blindingly illuminated, as if there had been a sudden strike of lightning. And just as with a thunderstorm, a roar of sound rent the air. Ellery curled into a ball and pressed their palms against their ears as the blast echoed off the asphalt and concrete. They scrunched their eyes closed against the brilliance and pressed their forehead to their knees, shielding their face from the explosion. As soon as it happened it was over, and the alley was drenched in darkness again.

Ellery blinked open their eyes, head aching, every sound muffled as if through water, after the earthshaking detonation of whatever that was. They uncurled and looked, blinking away the stars in their vision.

"What?"

Knox had one hand pressed to the nearby dumpster, bent over and gasping. There was no sign of the others. Had they left? Run away after whatever the hell that was? A freak lightning strike? That seemed weird. But as Zada had warned, the city was strange at night. And Ellery had been living in a never-ending winter for the past five years. A random lightning strike didn't seem out of the realm of possibility. But if that was what had happened, why wasn't Ellery fried? Why wasn't Knox?

"What happened?" Ellery asked. They felt like they were shouting, like they had driven up a mountain and needed to pop their ears to hear clearly again.

Knox shook his head, gathering himself.

Ellery stood unsteadily, knocking their foot into the pipe,

which had been right next to them, the scrape of it along the pavement sounding a million miles away. Yawning, Ellery tried to regain equilibrium.

"Hey," Ellery said, about as steady as a newborn lamb on the farm. They had a thousand questions. *What the hell happened* being the most immediate. *Who the hell were those people* being the follow-up. But neither of those came out. "Are you okay?"

Knox lifted his head. His eyes shone amber in the moonlight. "What?"

"Are you okay?"

His brow furrowed, like he was confused. And maybe Ellery was reading into his expression based on their own issues, but it was almost like no one had asked him that question before.

"Yeah," he said at last, straightening. "Yeah. I'm fine."

"Okay. Good."

"Are you?" Knox asked. He gestured to his own face.

Ellery prodded their split lip and winced. Their skin stung from the cold. Their body hurt from their multiple falls. And they still couldn't see very well after that flash. But they were alive and not kidnapped, so they counted that as a plus.

"I've been better, but I'm okay for now."

A small smile curled at the edge of Knox's mouth. "That's good."

"Great. We've established that neither one of us is dead or dying. And the danger seems to have passed, because otherwise we'd be running, correct?"

"Correct."

"Then *who the hell were those people?*"

Knox's smile slipped away into a frown. "People?"

"Yeah." Ellery threw out their arm, gesturing with their gloveless hand to their overturned bike and the disturbed snow and slush showing signs of a scuffle. And to where Ellery's weapon of choice lay innocuously on the ground, now that it wasn't being used to bash hooded figures in the head. "The ones who were trying to abduct you? The ones who chased you? The ones I hit with a pipe? *Those* people."

Knox's gaze dropped to the pipe. He sniffed. "Cast-iron. Lucky."

"Yeah. Lucky. It was heavy and solid and available."

Pushing off from the dumpster, Knox took a few steps toward the mouth of the alley. He flexed his fingers as he stared off in the distance. "They won't come back for a while. They won't risk the light again, and they will need to recover from their injuries."

"I know the feeling," Ellery mumbled, rubbing their chin. They weren't sure what Knox meant by "risking the light," but Ellery assumed it had something to do with the attackers' identities being exposed. They were hooded, after all, and Ellery would not have been able to pick them out of a crowd. "What was that flash? And why are you not wearing shoes? And why did you try to run down a dead-end alley?"

Knox blinked. "I have no answers that will make sense."

Ellery nodded, still dazed and suddenly exhausted down to their very bones. And despite how odd that sounded, it was a good enough answer. "That's fair. Look, are you going to be okay getting back to where you belong?"

"I'll be fine. Will you?"

Ellery thought about biking to the apartment and immediately grimaced. They would have to try and take the bus now, if they could catch one at this hour. They could aways call Zada . . . oh shit! Zada!

Ellery dug their hand into their pocket and pulled out their phone. They cringed upon seeing the alerts from both Zada and Charley demanding Ellery give an update on where they were and if they had made it home. Ellery fired off a text that they were almost there, which was a lie, but Charley and Zada didn't have to know.

They shoved their phone into their pocket. "Yeah, I'm good. I'm going to be sore tomorrow, but I don't think anything is broken."

Knox studied Ellery with narrowed eyes, head tilted to the side, as if waiting for Ellery to do something or say something, or for Ellery to melt down there in the street.

Ellery cleared their throat. "What?"

"You're not freaked out."

Ellery laughed, on the edge of hysterical, definitely too loud in the stillness of the night. "Oh, I am. I very much am. But on the inside. Internally. I mean, I literally stopped an abduction and hit people, and I fell down a hill. And I'm totally going to break down when I get home. But I can hold it off until then, if you're worried you might have to deal with tears."

Sighing, Knox ran a hand over his face. "No. That's not what I was thinking." He smiled tightly. "Never mind. Thanks for the help. I owe you a debt." He patted down his clothes. "I don't have anything to give you right now, but—"

Ellery sputtered and waved him off. "Owe me? No. Don't worry about it."

Knox paused. "You don't want anything?"

"No. Of course not. Just get home safe."

Knox stared; his mouth parted in slight surprise. Then he smiled. "Okay. I will. Thank you again." He lightly touched Ellery's shoulder with the tip of his fingers, the faintest of pressures. "Goodbye."

"Ellery," Ellery said.

Knox dropped his hand and raised an eyebrow.

"'Goodbye, *Ellery*,'" Ellery clarified. They grabbed the straps of their backpack that had miraculously stayed on their shoulders. "You called me 'the dishwasher.' Which I am, but I have a name."

Knox's lips tilted up at the edges. "You shouldn't give your name to strangers."

"Well, you gave me yours. And I did save you, so we're not really strangers anymore."

"Oh. Yes. That is true."

"Okay then. Well, um, I'll see you around, Knox."

He touched Ellery's arm again, wrapped his long fingers around Ellery's forearm and squeezed. "I'll see you around, Ellery."

Then he turned and strode off into the night, his bare feet crunching through the freezing slush and snow. Ellery shivered in sympathy. They righted their bike, grabbed the handles, and walked up the hill to the street. They looked both ways, but Knox was already gone, disappearing as quickly as he had appeared.

Ellery shook their head, then groaned. Their body did not appreciate the excitement of the last hour, and they needed a hot shower and painkillers and a long sleep. They threw their leg over the bike frame, jammed their foot in the pedal strap, and took off down the empty street toward home.

4

KNOX

KNOX WENT BACK TO THE APARTMENT. KNOWING THE SHADES could not return, at least for a little while, it would be his safest and probably only chance to gather a few things, along with his thoughts.

He rubbed a spot on his chest. His magic trembled beneath his skin, gasping and feeble, dimmer now than it had ever felt. He'd used too much with that blast of light, but it had been his only option to avoid being dragged to the Other World against his will. Without the strength of a bargain tethering him to the human realm, his magic would only grow weaker.

Taking out a key from the hanging potted plant on the exterior of the apartment, Knox let himself in, closing the door softly behind him. The space was dark, and he crept silently from the cramped entryway into the living room and adjoining dining area.

Arabelle's body lay where she fell, her hair splayed in a graying brown curtain around her. She looked like she was asleep, but Knox knew she wasn't, and a sharp pang pierced through his middle. The hot sting of tears gathered behind his eyes.

Despite the businesslike nature of their relationship, he would miss her. Her short twitter of a laugh. Her horrible cooking skills. Her thirst for power. Her unrelenting need to always be correct. Her gentle praise when he helped her with her goals. But she was gone now, her soul taken by the shades, and when he saw her again, he wouldn't recognize her.

Knox gasped. Emotion clogged his throat, and it was suddenly difficult to breathe. The tears bubbled over and spilled down his cheeks in rivulets. This was new and weird and *uncomfortable*.

Was this overwhelming feeling *grief*? Was this what the sorrow and loss he'd watched on TV countless times felt like?

He'd never been given a chance to grieve before. He'd never had to witness the aftermath of the deals made at the crossroads. That was the benefit of existing in liminality. When his bargains were over, he'd go back to the Other World, and his memories would disappear as soon as he crossed the barrier. Sometimes feelings and flashes would linger, but by the time he was called again—years, decades, centuries later—they would be gone completely. This time, though, he had to soak in the sting. And as unpleasant as it was, he realized that there was the chance to feel the opposite as well. That there could be moments out there that felt as good as this pained him. And that was something to stay for.

He turned away from her body and took a steadying breath. He couldn't linger. He knew the shades couldn't return quite yet, but that didn't mean they weren't planning on showing up as soon as they could. He didn't want to be there when they did. He was lucky enough that he'd run into the dishwasher, Ellery, who'd not only had some kind of protection charm in their pocket, but also had cast iron handy. And with his limited magical reserves, he was unlikely to get that lucky again.

In Arabelle's bedroom, Knox grabbed a duffel bag. He crossed into his own space, a spare room Arabelle had furnished with a bed because he enjoyed the occasional catnap, even if he didn't physically require sleep. He shoved some clothes and the last bag of fish-shaped crackers into the bag. Ellery had pointed out his lack of shoes earlier, so he pulled on socks and a pair of boots. He needed to blend in better, because if he was going to avoid the shades, he had to be indistinguishable from humans.

In his haste, he bumped into the small nightstand next to the bed. A stack of papers fluttered to the floor, and Knox paused. It was his collection of letters written to his queen, on torn notebook paper, pages from Arabelle's journal, and even a few Post-it notes. They'd all been undeliverable. He'd started writing the week he'd emerged from the tree and had sent each note using his magic. With his liminal power, they'd cross through the barrier at his crossroads and make their way to his queen. But for some reason, they had returned crinkled and torn and stained. And she had never reached out herself. It wasn't all of them—some must have made it through, or had become lost on their way back to him. But either way she had been *silent*, and that unnerved him. With a sigh, he left them on the floor and exited the room.

He smoothed out the lumps where his clothes bunched beneath his hoodie and his puffy jacket. His hand brushed against something solid in his pocket: the hard knot of the vial he'd grabbed on his way out. In all the excitement he'd forgotten about it. He pulled the vial out and held it up to the dull light coming in through the window. It sparkled, swirling midnight blue and sparkling purple.

The cost of Arabelle's soul. The secret to human life. The shades had been weirdly interested in it, almost more so than in Arabelle's soul. They said it was dangerous, and it probably was, but their concern made it valuable. He might be able to use it to buy himself more time in the human realm . . . or to buy his queen's forgiveness for delaying his return home. Also, Arabelle had died for it, and that made it . . . special. He slipped it back into his pocket.

He cast a glance to the dining room and spied the cauldron on the hot plate. He crept toward it, giving Arabelle's body a wide berth, and peered into the pot. He was certain there had been half a cauldron of unfinished potion remaining when she'd poured a sample into the vial. But the cauldron was empty. Maybe what had been left had boiled out? With a wrinkle of his nose, he unplugged the plate. No use risking a fire, especially for the other residents of the building.

Knox paused and glanced at the leather-bound journal splayed open next to Arabelle's workstation. Her handwriting sprawled across the page, detailing every step of the recipe for the potion she'd died creating. That is, every step except the one involving Knox's blood.

Despite the missing ingredient, Knox decided it was too risky to leave it on the table. He grabbed it and shoved it into the top of his duffel bag.

Okay. Now that he was all packed up and his immediate concerns were addressed for the moment, Knox took stock of his situation.

He had limited time before the shades would find him. If he wanted to stick around in the human realm, he needed to make a bargain of his own, something to tether himself and his magic for a little while longer. He just needed someone willing.

Knox bit his lip.

He *had* lamented the fact that he'd wanted to talk to the cute dishwasher more. And now he knew the dishwasher's name and where they were likely to be in the morning. It was a long shot, but it was the only shot he had. Ellery had intervened. Ellery had asked if he was okay and displayed genuine worry. Ellery hadn't asked for anything in return for their help. Ellery had stared at him through the window in the diner the last several times he'd been there. Based on all the TV shows Knox had watched over the last few years, those seemed like encouraging signs. Knox couldn't offer much, but based on their actions that night, Ellery might not mind.

Regardless, Ellery was Knox's only chance at staying in the human realm. And he was not going to let it pass him by.

5

ELLERY

ELLERY TOOK ONE LOOK AT THEMSELF IN THE MIRROR AND realized there was no way they were going to be able to hide the fact they had been injured from both Charley and Zada. They had a split lip, bruises along the curve of their jaw and the bridge of their nose, and a few scrapes across their cheek. They could feel more bruises under their clothes, but at least those would be easily hidden. The purple on their face was a different matter.

Ellery didn't necessarily have to tell them the whole story about the fight and the almost abduction. They could lie and say it was a bike accident. But even then Zada would insist on driving them every day, and that would make Ellery feel even guiltier than they already did. Zada and Charley had given them a free place to sleep; Charley had found them a job, and they only asked for a bare minimum to cover groceries. Zada didn't need to waste gas and time on driving Ellery to work when they had a perfectly acceptable mode of transportation.

Ellery dabbed concealer along their jaw and then under their eyes to at least lessen the dark circles. They hadn't slept well, the adrenaline still very much rocketing through their body until well into the early morning. The little sleep they had gotten was filled with the weirdest dreams about rows of corn and snow and sentient shadows and a crossroads.

The makeup helped a little. But still, Ellery was going to put off the inevitable awkward confrontation for as long as possible. Luckily, Zada and Charley had stumbled in long after Ellery, so they were still passed out in their bed. Which meant Ellery could slip out and make it to work, no problem.

Ellery hissed in pain as they dressed in their normal hoodie, jeans, and double layer of socks, along with sneakers, a scarf, and an overcoat. In the pocket of their coat, the wire-wrapped acorn remained. Ellery pressed the acorn against their palm for a moment, the metal biting into their skin, before releasing it back to settle in the seam. They snorted. Their mom should've given them a can of mace to ward off *real* attackers. That might have actually prevented them from being injured and coming home sore and missing a glove. Without it, they had to borrow a pair of Charley's. They slipped out quietly after shoving a snack cake in their mouth for breakfast and chugging water from the tap.

The bike ride to the diner wasn't too bad. Using the key, Ellery let themself in the kitchen and found Diego and Marisol already there, preparing the grill and the ingredients for the small Sunday breakfast crowd. Ellery hung their outerwear and their backpack on the hooks by the door and rolled up their sleeves to prepare for the day, keeping their head down and their sweatshirt hood up. They vaguely wondered about Knox. Had he had made it to where he needed to be the night before? Was he as sore as Ellery this morning? Would Ellery ever know who they had assaulted to save a random person in a dark alley? Ellery maybe should've asked for Knox's number in case there were consequences from the night before. The thought made Ellery flush, knowing how that could have been interpreted, and they were grateful they hadn't humiliated themself by accidentally asking Knox out on a date.

Ellery's thoughts then slipped to dating and the fact that Knox was unfairly attractive, and how they maybe harbored a little crush just based on the few times they'd spied him through the window of the diner. They shoved those thoughts and the subsequent butterflies away about as hard as Knox's tackle from the night before.

They made it a few hours working quietly and more slowly than normal before Charley barged in for her shift, phone in hand.

"Yes, Aunt Nance. Ellery is right here. They slipped out early for work this morning, and they took my favorite pair of gloves." Charley paused. "Oh no, Aunt Nance, it's fine. I'm sure it was an honest mistake. No need to give them a stern talking-to or anything. Ah, here they are."

Charley nudged Ellery's shoulder and handed them the phone. "Your mom."

Ellery took it and made the mistake of rolling their neck to ease the tension gathering there. Their hood fell backward.

Charley gasped. "What happened to your *face*?"

Ellery lifted their finger to their lips in the universal *shush* gesture, touching the split in their lip and wincing, before adamantly pointing at the phone.

"Hi, Mom," Ellery said, shooting a glare at Charley as they pressed it to their ear.

"What did Charley say? What about your face?"

"Nothing," Ellery said, rolling their eyes. "It was not my face. She was talking to another coworker."

Charley mouthed something emphatically, and Ellery flipped her off. They headed outside via the back door and sighed when the pipe was not where it should be to prop open the door. Of course not. It was across the alley by the dumpster where Ellery had dropped it the night before. They shivered at both the cold and the memory.

"Is everything okay?" Ellery asked, wedging their foot between the door and the frame to keep it propped open.

"Everything is fine, dear. We're just taking precautions."

Ellery furrowed their brow. "What does that mean?" They hoped their parents hadn't spent money on another offering to an imaginary goddess.

"The Johnsons down the way had two cows that recently became sick. The vet couldn't make it out there to them, and eventually the cows withered and died."

Ellery's throat went tight. "And?"

"Well, they were fairly certain that there was a parasite of some kind. Maybe something from the feed. So they changed their vendor and the food, but the heifers died anyway."

"I'm sorry to hear that. But what does that have to do with precautions?"

"Oh—well, the Johnsons seemed to think it was a creature of some sort that was feeding on the stock. So they made sure to burn the cows' hearts and livers, then buried the ashes along the fence line to keep it from coming back. The rest of their livestock is doing okay, so they think they're in the clear."

"They . . . what?"

"We've decided to salt all the entrances to the barn and hope that keeps whatever it was away from the goats and the horses."

Ellery rubbed their forehead. "Mom—"

"Ellery!" Charley knocked hard into the door. It slammed into Ellery's hip.

"Ow!" Ellery yelled into the phone. "Oh my gods and goddesses, Charley! That hurt!"

"Sorry," Charley said, hand over her mouth. "I didn't know you were *right there*. I thought you'd used the pipe!"

"What's going on?" Ellery's mom demanded.

"It's fine! I'm fine. Charley just nailed me with the door."

"Hot weird guy is here," Charley said.

Ellery's mouth fell open, and they flailed in surprise. Charley snagged the front of their apron to keep them from toppling off the steps.

"He's asking for you. By *name*." Charley's eyes were wide, her cheeks pink. "And you are going to tell me every single detail of how he knows your name. And if it has anything to do with . . ." She trailed off, glancing at the phone. "Your liberal application of foundation this morning."

Ellery inwardly groaned.

"Ellery!" Their mom's tinny voice echoed from the phone from where Ellery had dropped it in their shock.

Ellery shoved the phone at Charley and pushed past her back into the kitchen. They crossed to the small window and glanced out. Sure enough, Knox sat at a booth, hands folded, sunglasses back in place as he stared out of the window. He looked no different than he had any of the previous times he'd visited the diner, except he was actually dressed for the weather, with a sweater and a large coat that he'd draped across the back of the booth behind him. He also appeared unfairly unblemished, as if the previous night had not happened at all.

"It's fine, Aunt Nance. Ellery is an absolute joy to have at our apartment. Zada loves them, and they're doing great. But right now, hot weird guy is here, and I must watch the disaster of Ellery interacting with him because this is going to be the best moment of my day."

Ellery frowned but really couldn't begrudge Charley, because she was right. This was probably going to be a disaster.

Charley stood by Ellery's side and slipped the phone back in her apron pocket.

"Well?" she asked. "Are you going to talk to him?"

Ellery gulped. "I don't know."

"Why not?" She peeked through the window. "He's waiting for *you*. What's keeping you in here when he's out there?"

Ellery looked at Knox's painfully beautiful face, then down at their graying hoodie that had been black at some point, their unintentionally tattered jeans, and their red, chapped hands. "Everything."

"Right." Charley placed her hand flat between Ellery's shoulder blades and pushed.

Ellery stumbled forward through the swinging kitchen doors to the space behind the counter, clattering into the stand with the rolled silverware.

Knox looked up at the commotion, and a small, amused smile curled over his lips.

Ellery waved awkwardly.

Knox gestured to the seat across from him in the booth with an elegant wave of his pale hand.

Taking a deep breath, Ellery crossed the diner and eased into the booth, their jeans squeaking against the fake leather of the seat with an embarrassing sound. The blush on their cheeks deepened.

"Hello again," Knox said.

"Hi," Ellery breathed.

Knox pushed his sunglasses to the top of his head and waved his fingers toward his own face. "I'm sorry. Do they hurt?"

"Oh." Ellery tentatively touched the cut on their mouth. "Yeah, but it's okay. I'll live."

Knox paused, staring at Ellery as if trying to see through them. Ellery stared back, caught in Knox's gaze, because looking at him in the light of day was very different from looking at him through the dirty kitchen window or in a dark alley. He was strikingly pretty this close. Ellery was finally able to see the gold of his eyes and how they were framed by dark lashes and perfectly arched eyebrows. And how smooth and unblemished his skin was, like he'd never had a pimple in his life. And how his dark hair looked soft and glossy, even caught in the frame of his sunglasses.

Ellery cleared their throat. "Are you hurt?"

Knox shook his head. "I'm fine."

"Are you . . . are you safe?"

Knox worried his lower lip. His fingers tapped a rhythm on the table. "For now. I . . . um . . . wanted to speak to you about that."

Ellery fiddled with the hem of their apron. "Yeah?"

"Why did you help me?"

Ellery shrugged. "Uh . . . it seemed like you needed it."

"That's all?" Knox asked.

Ellery stiffened. "Look, I'm not a jerk. I don't need a reward or anything. You don't owe me."

Knox raised his hands. "No. I'm just trying to understand."

"Oh. Well, I wasn't going to watch while you were getting kidnapped, if I could help it. You said you didn't want to go, and they didn't really give off friendly vibes."

"You weren't scared?"

Ellery scratched the back of their neck. "I was terrified."

Knox narrowed his eyes as if studying Ellery, his head tilted slightly to the side. "But you helped me anyway," he prodded.

Shrugging, Ellery scraped their fingernail on the tabletop. "I could be cool and say it was nothing, or that I don't like bullies, or something cliché like that. But I don't know. I just acted. I've probably just watched too many movies, which has instilled a false confidence in me about how to handle things in unreal situations."

"You like movies?" Knox asked, all pretense of caution tossed away, his smile wide.

"Yeah. Doesn't everyone?"

"No. I do, though. I love them."

Ellery huffed in amusement. "Me too. But like I said, probably not the best guidelines to follow."

"Oh," Knox said, sagging back against the booth. "Well, I'm grateful for your assistance. So thank you."

"You're welcome."

Silence descended between them while Knox studied the curtains. Ellery studied the sharpness of his jaw.

"Here you go!" Charley shouted, walking up to the table and dropping steaming plates of food in front of them. "Pancakes and waffles and eggs and bacon and sausage."

"Charley," Ellery said, leaning back to allow room for the warm plates. "What is this?"

"I didn't order anything," Knox said, brow furrowed in confusion.

"On the house, of course! It was a mistake for another table. I wrote down their egg order wrong. Silly me. And the other items needed to be cooked before we switched to the lunch menu for the afternoon."

Ellery narrowed their eyes as Knox peered around the diner, which was empty save for the lone man at the end of the counter sipping coffee, his used plates stacked in front of him.

"Right," Ellery said.

"Don't argue with me, dear cousin," Charley said with a manic smile, green eyes gleaming. "Just giving you something to do other than *stare*."

Ellery dropped their gaze to the fluffy waffles, mortified. "Oh."

"Yes. Oh." She smiled at Knox and batted her eyelashes. "Eat up and enjoy. Would either of you like coffee or water or orange juice or a milkshake?"

Knox blinked. "Um . . ."

"Milkshake it is," Charley said sweetly. "Hope you like chocolate. Be right back!"

She flounced away, and Knox looked a little stunned. "What?"

"That's my cousin, Charley," Ellery said, unrolling silverware. The snack cake hadn't done much to fill them up, and that had been hours ago. Ellery wasn't about to turn down free food, even if it was just a guise for Charley to eavesdrop. "I've learned to just go with it, so feel free to eat."

"Okay." Knox ran his fingers over the handle of the fork before picking it up.

"So," Ellery said around a bite of scrambled eggs, "was there anything else you wanted to talk to me about?"

"Yes. I—well, this is a little difficult to say. And it might be even harder to believe."

Ellery wanted to reassure Knox that they would listen to and believe him, but Ellery had learned that belief was a complicated thing tied inherently to trust, and Ellery had difficulty with both. And Knox was strange, and last night had been weird and frightening, and Ellery wasn't quite sure they wanted to be caught up in whatever Knox had going on. But they were intrigued, and that was a rare thing for them.

"I am not from the city," Knox began.

Oh. Was that all? "I'm not either," Ellery said. "I'm from a small farm about two hours away."

"Ah. Well, I'm not from a farm." He squinted as if thinking. "Or a town. Or a suburb."

"What else is there?" Ellery asked, squeezing syrup onto a waffle. Was Knox from a commune? Or an island in the middle of the sea? Had he been raised on a boat?

"I'm from another place. Another realm, to be exact."

Ellery snapped their head up in surprise, their stomach sinking. Syrup pooled in the hollows of their waffle.

"What?" they asked carefully.

"I'm not human. Well, I'm sort of human. I'm liminal. A . . . 'familiar' is probably the most accurate term. Anyway, my boss, who I lived with, is dead. Her soul was taken to the Other World by the shades because she made a bargain at my crossroads. I was supposed to help her, and I did, until the terms of the deal were met. When it was all said and done, instead of going home like I was supposed to, I ran away."

Ellery stared, stunned. Their mind spun, thoughts pinging around like a pinball machine. The conversation hadn't been quite normal to begin with, but it had definitely taken a turn for the worse.

Knox shoved a piece of bacon in his mouth. "Um . . . your syrup."

"What?"

"It's spilling."

"Oh!" Ellery righted the bottle. They grabbed their napkin and blotted the sticky runoff that had leaked onto the table. "Um . . . I'm sorry. But what?"

Knox leaned forward, forearms on the table, gold eyes glinting. His voice dropped to a conspiratorial tone, as if imparting a huge, urgent secret only the two of them could know. "Those things you saved me from last night were shades from the Other World. They're servants of the queen, kind of, and they do her bidding. They can't remain in the human realm long and they loathe light, but they're very good at harvesting souls. And they were trying to drag me back with them."

Ellery tilted their head to the side. "To the Other World?"

"Yes."

"Because you're not human," Ellery said slowly.

"Correct. I can exist in the human realm and in the Other World, but there are rules. Lots of rules. And I'm currently breaking a few of them. And they're *not* happy with me."

Ellery set down their fork, their forgotten waffle slowly disintegrating in the deluge of syrup. "Because your boss is dead? Arabelle?" Ellery asked, hazarding a guess based on the name used on all the orders Knox had picked up in the past.

"Yes," he said, softly. "She . . . died last night, before I met you in the alley."

Stomach churning, Ellery lost any semblance of their appetite. "Because the shades . . . took her soul?"

"Yes," Knox said softly. He sniffed and wiped his sleeve across his eyes. Then he snapped his fingers. "I knew you'd understand."

Ellery did not understand. In fact, they felt a little sick. The butterflies from earlier had died and become a heavy weight in the pit of their stomach. "I have a question."

Knox nodded eagerly. He bit into a sausage link. "I figured. It's a lot to process. I'll do my best to answer, but fair warning that my memory is foggy when it comes to certain things."

Ellery wrung their napkin in their hands. "Who put you up to this?" they asked. "Because it's not funny. At all. And I understand that you might not know why it's not as hilarious as they told you it would be. But it's actually pretty mean."

Knox's face fell. "I'm sorry. What?"

"Milkshakes!" Charley yelled, running up to the table and slamming the tall glasses between them. "One chocolate and one strawberry. You can fight over them. Or you could share. Here!" She dropped clean metal straws on the table.

"Was it her?" Ellery asked, jabbing a finger at Charley.

To Knox's credit, he did appear genuinely confused. It only served to make Ellery angrier.

Charley tugged on her apron. "Was it me, what?"

"Who decided to pull a gross prank on me?" Ellery stood. Tears threatened from behind their eyes.

"A prank?" Charley asked, gaze darting between the two of them. "Who is pulling a prank?"

"You don't believe me?" Knox asked softly. He stood as well, fingers knotted in front of him. "What about last night?"

Charley's eyes almost popped out of her face. "What about last night? What happened last night? Is that why El looks like they were hit by a truck?"

"What about it?" Embarrassment welled in Ellery's gut like a hot, sour shame. "I was happy to help you, but now . . . now . . . Maybe I shouldn't have intervened in a dangerous situation if I was just going to be made fun of and *humiliated.*"

Knox balked. "You regret helping me?"

Ellery ran a hand through their hair, tugging on the strands. "No. Yes. I don't know." They took a breath. "You didn't even tell me who those people were, and now you expect me to believe they were supernatural beings?" Ellery tossed up their hands. "How was I able to *hit* them with that pipe if they weren't real?"

"They were real," Knox said vehemently. He shoved his hands in his pockets. "The pipe was iron. They're susceptible to iron."

"Is *that* where the pipe went?" Charley asked.

Ellery ignored her. "Fine. Then what was the flash of light?"

"It was a blast of magic. I told you, they don't like light. It was the only way to protect myself."

"To protect yourself? Not me?"

"You had a protection charm in your pocket. That's why they couldn't touch you."

Ellery froze. They had the acorn in their pocket. And thinking back, the attackers had never touched them. Knox had knocked them over first. And Ellery had stepped between the *shades* and Knox . . . but no. No, Ellery was *not* believing this at all.

"You're unreal," Ellery said around a lump in their throat.

"Again, I'm very real, just different. And look, if I am going to stay in this world, in *your* world, I need help. I need to make a deal to tether me to this plane, and you were the first person I thought of."

Ellery stared at Knox incredulously. "Why me?"

"I saw you staring at me through the window yesterday."

Ellery's face lit on fire.

"And you helped me last night when most humans would've felt the unnaturalness of the shades and *run*. But you didn't. You're . . . you're special."

"Fuck off."

"Ellery!" Charley, who had all but melted at Knox's words, snapped to attention and threw an admonishing frown in Ellery's direction. She planted her hands on her hips. "That was rude. I'm so sorry," she said turning to Knox. "Please sit and finish eating while I have a talk with my cousin."

Ellery crossed their arms, protecting themself from further pain. "No. I'm done talking. I don't have time to waste on fairy tales and myths. And I'm certainly not striking any kind of deal with a person who lies about something as serious as why they were almost kidnapped. I have work to do."

Charley grabbed Ellery's ear and twisted, pulling them away from the table. "We'll be right back. Try the milkshake!" she called as she dragged Ellery behind the counter and through the silver swinging doors into the kitchen.

"Ow, ow, ow," Ellery said in a mantra under their breath. Charley released them once they were in the safety of the kitchen. She stood in front of Ellery, her body tense, wearing the angriest expression Ellery had ever seen on her.

Ellery rubbed the tip of their ear. It stung. "What the hell, Charley?"

"First, I'm not pranking you because I'm not heartless, which, wow. It hurts that you think I'd do that. And second, I'm the older cousin, and with that comes certain privileges, like telling the younger cousin off for being a jerk. Why are you being an asshole to hot weird guy?"

Ellery gripped the lip of the sink, hands curling around the metal. The warmth of it grounded them. So it wasn't a prank. Charley was the only person in the city who was both silly enough to pull a practical joke and who knew Ellery well enough to push those particular buttons. Which meant Knox was delusional. "His name is Knox," Ellery said begrudgingly.

Charley frowned. "I want the whole story."

Ellery's shoulders rose and fell in a sigh. "Last night—"

"Wait. Hold that thought." Charley tugged her phone from her pocket and hit a button without looking. It rang once before Zada's voice came over the speaker.

"Babe," Zada said, surprised and happy. "I thought Diego banned phones during work? Is everything okay?"

"You're on speaker, pumpkin," Charley responded with a bright tone and a frankly scary smile. "Ellery is about to tell us all about their very interesting night last night."

"Oh, this sounds juicy. I'm all ears."

"You're both horrible, and I weep for your future children."

Zada laughed. Charley poked Ellery in the cheek. "Spill or I'm calling your mother."

Ellery wilted. Knox had all but given them away, so they might as well tell the truth. They took a breath, bowed their head, and told the story to the soapy water in the sink rather than watch Charley's reactions. They recounted everything: how they had locked the diner and were about to bike home when Knox had come running out of the dark, how three robed people had tried to grab Knox to kidnap him until Ellery had hit them with the door pipe, how a freak lightning strike had come out of nowhere that forced the black-clad attackers to flee, and how they'd biked home and crawled into bed and then gotten up early so Charley and Zada wouldn't see the bruises.

"Let me get this straight," Zada said. "You stepped into a fight because hot weird guy was in trouble?" She hummed. "Sounds completely normal. I believe it."

"Very much agree that it's in character for our darling Ellery. And the evidence of this wild story is all over Ellery's face. It's quite frankly a mess."

"Now who's being rude?" Ellery muttered.

"Oh, me," Charley said, raising her hand. "Definitely me. But not as awful as you were to Knox. This kid cannot be much older than you and is obviously in trouble, supernatural or not. He needs our help."

"Seriously?" Ellery asked, raising their head. "Did you hear what he said? What he believes?"

"Of course. I've been eavesdropping. It's like you don't even know me," Charley said with a huff and a roll of her eyes. "Anyway, may I remind you that Zada and I offered to help *you* because you were basically in the same situation?"

Ellery scoffed. "How in any world is this the same situation?"

"You're both running from, and I quote, 'supernatural bullshit.'"

"Oh, good one, babe," Zada said with a laugh. "Using Ellery's own words against them."

Ellery groaned and rubbed their temples. "You're a menace."

"I'm your favorite cousin who has taken you in and loves you despite your general dislike for anything fun and interesting." Charley pursed her lips. "I'm not saying we make him our new roommate or anything like that. But let's hear him out and see what we can do."

"As the girlfriend to the cousin," Zada said, "I agree with this plan. If we can help, we should. Who knows? Maybe he is what he says he is, and then we'll finally have an authentic supernatural encounter."

"I love the way you think, my darling dearest. Your brain is as sexy as your body."

"Babe," Zada said, drawing out the vowel, "not in front of the kid."

Ellery frowned. "I'm seventeen."

"You're right. Their poor innocent ears cannot handle the depth of our love and longing for each other."

"I'm literally only four years younger than Zada."

"Four significant years, El. Anyway, I have to go, but I'm working from home today, so keep me updated."

"Will do. Ellery will be apologizing momentarily."

Ellery opened their mouth but snapped it shut at the look on

Charley's face. Charley ended the call, then rested a hand lightly on Ellery's shoulder. Ellery did their best to control their flinch when Charley accidentally knocked into one of the sore spots.

"I know that uncritical belief has hurt you, and the choices your parents have made the last few years have jaded you to anything that seems remotely supernatural. But that doesn't give you the right to be cruel."

Ellery closed their eyes. "He said he was from another *realm*."

"He did. Maybe it's a metaphor for something else, or maybe it's his way of dealing with grief. You heard him say that someone close to him died recently."

Ellery swallowed down the retort on the tip of their tongue. Charley was right. Knox seemed lost and unsure, and if the quick swipe of his sleeves over his eyes to dash away his tears was any indication, full of grief. Grief was something Ellery understood, something they'd felt on a molecular level since they'd moved to the city months ago. They could sympathize, but they couldn't fully set aside their deep resentment over finally being interested in someone, only to find out that he embodied everything Ellery had run from.

Still, even though Ellery was living through a world event that no one could explain . . . yet . . . that didn't mean there wasn't a reason grounded in reality that would eventually be revealed.

Charley squeezed Ellery's shoulder. "Come on. Your future boyfriend awaits."

Ellery opened their eyes and glared. "Shut up."

"I see many kisses in your future," she continued.

"Stop. You're horrible."

"You love me."

Ellery frowned and didn't respond as Charley led the way back into the dining room.

Knox looked up at their approach, his expression open and

hopeful. He had a little smear of chocolate right under his bottom lip that Ellery definitely did not stare at.

"I'm sorry," Ellery said. Charley shoved her pointy elbow into Ellery's side. "For telling you to fuck off. That was rude."

"It's okay." He rubbed his hand across his face, wiping off the ice cream. "Does that mean you'll make a deal?"

Ellery shook their head. "No."

Knox deflated. "Oh." He stared at the table. "Okay. Well. Thank you. And sorry for taking up your time."

Knox grabbed the duffel bag from beneath the booth and stood to leave.

"Wait," Charley said. "I talked with my girlfriend, and we can at least offer you a couch to crash on for a few nights if you need it. It doesn't sound like you can go back to where you had been?"

Shaking his head, Knox shouldered the bag. "Thank you, but I can't ask that of you, especially with the threat of the shades."

Ellery pinched the bridge of their nose. The action brought tears to their eyes. "We're only open until four o'clock on Sundays," they said. "At least stay here in the warmth until then, and we can help you find a place if you don't want to stay with us."

Knox checked the clock on the wall. It was almost noon. "Okay."

Sliding back into the booth, he hid the duffel under the table and sank into a sprawl, looking dejected, a far cry from the openly friendly Knox who had bounded into the diner a few days ago. It plucked one of Ellery's limited heartstrings.

"Great! I'll call Zada. You wait here until we close, and we'll all go home together."

Charley bounced back to the kitchen. Ellery shuffled their feet by the table. "I have to go back to work."

"Okay."

Ellery ran a hand through their hair. Without their hat, it fell in greasy strands around their chin. "Um . . . I'll just—"

"Ellery," Knox interrupted.

Ellery lifted their head and met his gaze. "Yeah?"

"Thank you."

Ellery's cheeks warmed at Knox's sincerity. "Don't thank me, thank Charley."

"But I am thanking you. So thank you."

"You're welcome." They took a step back and jabbed their thumb toward the kitchen. "I have to work."

Knox's smile grew. "So you said."

"Right. Bye."

Ellery spun on their heel and all but ran away, face flushed. They were still confused and distrustful and a little angry, but they had to admit that their silly superficial crush still existed in full force.

6

KNOX

Zada picked them all up at the end of Charley and Ellery's shift. Knox sat next to Ellery in the back seat. Ellery kept their hood up and face tilted down, more subdued than they'd been in the diner, especially after Zada had clucked her tongue at Ellery's bruised face.

Zada drove them to the apartment building and pulled into the parking deck of the complex. Knox grabbed his duffel bag from the trunk and followed behind the others. Once inside, they descended a staircase to a lower level.

"It's not much," Charley said, unlocking the door. "But it's homey and warm. Mostly."

Knox stepped over the threshold cautiously, peering around. The floor plan was open, with a counter that separated the living room from the kitchen. A tiny round table surrounded by four chairs in varying states of disrepair served as the dining room. There was one door that led to what Knox thought must be a bedroom, another to the bathroom, and a third that was a coat closet.

The basement location meant the street-level windows provided a view of piles of gray snow, which was nothing like the beautiful view of the city he'd had from Arabelle's balcony.

In the cramped foyer, Ellery toed off their shoes and stripped out of their outerwear, revealing a slight form, messy dark hair that hung below their chin, and skin pale from the lack of summers. They brushed past Knox and headed to a daybed in the corner of the living area, where they dropped their backpack before flinging themself into the blankets.

Knox realized that they didn't have their own room, merely a corner with the small bed and a dresser crammed between the bed frame and the radiator.

"Don't mind them," Zada said with a smile and a pat to Knox's shoulder. She crossed the room and sat on the edge of the small bed. She leaned down and whispered to Ellery, who sat up and followed Zada behind a closed door.

The apartment could barely fit the three of them, and yet they had invited him to stay. A bloom of something warm unfurled in his chest at their kindness.

"You can have the couch, Knox," Charley said as she ran the tap water in the kitchen into a glass. "It's a little lumpy, but it has served us well."

"It's nice," he said. "Thank you for letting me stay."

She beamed. "You're welcome."

He gently placed his duffel bag by the couch and tentatively sat on the cushion. It was a comfortable enough place for Knox to lay and pretend to sleep during the night.

Charley rummaged through the cabinets. "How about an early dinner? I don't know about you, but I'm exhausted. While you and Ellery were having a good old-fashioned brawl in the alley last night, my girlfriend and I were unsuccessfully trying to get into a club. Word in the city is that there's a nymph who performs there."

Knox straightened from his slump on the couch. "A nymph?"

Charley nodded. "Apparently her voice is amazing, and she charms everyone who hears her. I'd love to see her live."

A feeling of déjà vu settled over Knox, as if he might have known a nymph who resided in the area near his crossroads. "Huh."

"What?"

Knox shook his head. "She just sounds familiar."

Charley's eyes sparkled, and she clasped her hands in front of her. "Really? Do you think you could get us in? Zada would die."

Knox visibly flinched.

"No!" Charley held up her hands. "Not literally. She'd just be really excited. Sorry. Poor choice of words." She tugged on a strand of red hair.

Knox smiled slightly. He wasn't sure if he even knew the nymph, but it was one of his goals to find others like himself who might be out there. And Charley and Zada had been so kind to him already. It wouldn't hurt to try to repay them.

"Maybe," he offered. "We could try."

"Yes! Let's go tomorrow night. We can kill two birds with one stone."

Charley placed her hand over her open mouth.

"Sorry again. But what I meant was that if she is your friend, then we could take you to her and she could help you. Right? And then we get to see an amazing singer."

Knox's smile grew into one more genuine. "Yes. That sounds like a good plan."

Zada appeared in the bedroom doorway. "Yeah. That sounds good."

"How's El?" Charley asked.

Zada's lips pinched. "Really bruised. They're going to nap for a while. Honestly, I don't know how they worked a whole day."

Guilt bubbled in Knox's stomach. He hadn't meant to involve them the previous night. And now Charley and Zada had gotten pulled in too. The shades would still be after him, but he doubted they'd try to come for him here, in the presence of ordinary humans. And if they did, he'd just run again, lead them away. It would all be fine.

"Oh. Well, you know how they are about work," Charley said with a wince. "They won't miss it unless they're dead, and even then they'd try to make it in." Her tone was sad, but she forced a smile. "Anyway, how does spaghetti sound?"

Zada and Charley moved around each other in the kitchen with the ease and familiarity of those accustomed to another person in a shared space. They prepared a quick dinner and gathered at the table. Perhaps understanding that Knox wasn't much in the mood to talk, Charley commanded the conversation with anecdotes about working at the diner. If the pair had any reservations about having a supernatural being in their presence, they hid them well.

After dinner, Charley made up the couch with sheets, a heavy blanket, and a soft pillow while Zada cleaned the kitchen.

"The heating sometimes gets overwhelmed at night, especially down here in the basement apartment. I recommend sleeping in socks if you have them," Charley said, smoothing out the blanket. "Tomorrow Ellery and I both have to work, and Zada has class. Do you have something you can do during the day?"

Knox didn't. But he nodded. "Yes."

Charley smiled. "Great. And sorry about Ellery. They're having a rough time." She glanced at the empty daybed. "Anyway, feel free to stay up and watch some TV. Bathroom is right through there if you want to freshen up and change. Zada and I are going to bed. Night!"

Charley flipped off the light and disappeared into the hallway, arm linked with Zada.

Knox lay on the couch, his socked feet propped on the arm. He drummed his fingers on his sternum, staring at the popcorned ceiling and the fan lazily spinning above him on its lowest setting.

A series of soft footsteps down the hallway alerted him to someone moving about. The pipes shuddered when the shower started.

Knox sighed. Despite the circumstances, he was grateful for the trio's help, even if Ellery had been avoiding him since their tense discussion in the diner. Knox understood the information was a lot to process. He wasn't even sure if Charley and Zada believed him or were just willing to help for something interesting to do. But Ellery had completely closed off, and Knox didn't know them well enough to discern whether that was their default setting or if it was due to what Knox had revealed.

He had expected Ellery to be shocked and maybe even frightened after revealing that their attackers had been denizens of the Other World. But he hadn't expected disgust. The sting of it was surprisingly painful.

They all intrigued him, though. He hadn't encountered kindness for the sake of kindness before—not that he remembered, anyway. He didn't quite understand it. All his relationships were transactional, based on contracts or bargains. Even the one with his queen, who had created him. He worshipped her, carried out her bidding with the shades to gather souls for her, and in return she bestowed on him her benevolence and attention. Which was why her lack of communication was so worrying and hurtful.

The bathroom door opened, and Knox peeked over the back of the couch. Ellery emerged into the hallway wearing a large shirt and sweatpants, hair damp, skin pinked. The bruises on their face were stark, even in the low light filtering in through the windows, and the knot in Knox's chest tightened at the sight. They dropped a pile of clothes onto the floor and kicked them under the low daybed. Then they turned and startled violently, one hand clasping in their loose shirt, the other hand grabbing the frame of the bed to keep from tumbling backward.

Knox waved shyly. "Hi."

Ellery scowled. "You scared me."

"Sorry."

They shook their head. "Somehow I'm not so sure you are."

Ouch. "I didn't mean to startle you. I promise."

Ellery pursed their lips. "Fine. Whatever. I'm going to bed now. If I can get my heart rate to slow down."

Knox rested his chin on the cushion. "I make your heart race?"

Ellery paused in the straightening of their sheets and blankets, and their blush deepened. "No."

"Pity."

"*Good night*, Knox."

He grinned. "Night, Ellery."

Ellery crawled into their bed, and within a few minutes, their light snores filled the room, a comforting sound and rhythm.

Knox didn't need to sleep, but he tucked himself into the sofa all the same. This was not how he'd thought his day would end, but here he was, comfortable and potentially on the path to bargaining his way into an extended stay in the human realm. He just had to continue avoiding the shades and somehow convince these humans to believe him. And hopefully meeting a real nymph the following day would help.

7

KNOX

THE SUN SLOWLY SANK TOWARD THE HORIZON, AND KNOX nervously tapped his foot while they waited in line in front of the Siren Club. Which was a fairly unoriginal name, but who was he to judge?

He had spent the day wandering around the city, familiarizing himself with the area around the diner and the apartment, sticking to places that were well lit. The shades hadn't returned. But he knew better than to think they wouldn't. And the wait only made him more anxious, unsure if he would be able to escape them a second time. He needed a bargain. And he needed one quickly.

The music coming from inside drowned out the street sounds. Knox didn't like that he wouldn't be able to hear anyone approach. Not that the shades made noise when they moved.

It also made it difficult to make any kind of conversation, except if he wanted to whisper in Ellery's ear, but he thought that might get him shoved. They hadn't interacted since the night before, and he had a feeling that if it were up to Ellery, he would've been out on the street by now. As it was, he would have to prove to Ellery that he was telling the truth to have a chance at a bargain, and a more solid plan for staying in the human realm. It might be easier to pick someone else, *anyone* else, to try to persuade into a deal. Charley could be a possibility, or maybe Zada. They'd at least seemed open to the supernatural. But there was something about Ellery—a person who had bravely stood between him and the shades and faced them down, for no reason except to help. Any other human would've run, but they hadn't. Also, Zada and Charley appeared deeply in love and satisfied with their lives. They didn't seem to want for anything Knox could offer.

"You okay?" Ellery asked, huddled down in their coat, hat, and scarf, bouncing in place on the balls of their feet in an attempt to keep warm.

"Huh?"

"You seem a little"—Ellery scrunched their bruised nose—"far away."

"I'm fine," Knox said, watching as the sun set, bathing the street in orange. "Thinking."

"I hope you're thinking about how you're going to get us into this club, because I am not standing on this street freezing for much longer, and I think you'll break Zada's and Charley's hearts if they don't get in tonight."

The corner of Knox's mouth lifted. "You won't be heartbroken?"

Ellery snorted. Knox couldn't help but find it cute. "No. Clubs aren't really my scene."

"What is your scene?"

They shuffled forward as the bouncer allowed a few people in front of them in. "Working at the diner."

Knox raised an eyebrow. "That's it?"

Ellery shrugged. "I moved to the city to work. That's all I have time for."

"Doesn't sound like much fun."

"Life isn't fun."

"That's a bleak outlook," Knox replied.

"Well, I wouldn't expect a supernatural being to understand."

Ouch.

The line inched forward again. The sun disappeared behind the curve of the horizon, casting the city in twilight. Knox's breath hitched at the incoming night. His time was running short. The shades would have surely recovered by now.

"Name?" the bouncer asked.

Knox startled. "What?"

The bouncer was a tall woman in chunky boots and a long red buttoned coat. She held a clipboard in her hand and wore a headset.

"Name?" she asked, rather bored. "Are you on the list for tonight?"

Knox rocked back on his heels. "My name is Knox. I'm a friend of the performer."

"Last name?"

"Don't have one."

The bouncer raised a skeptical eyebrow and scanned down the clipboard. "You're not on the list. I can't let you in until everyone on the list is in first—then we'll allow overflow. But only if we have room."

Charley groaned from behind them. "This is what happened last time."

Knox pushed his sunglasses up to rest on his head and batted his eyelashes. "Could you please let the singer know I'm here? She's not expecting me, but we are old friends." He hoped. It had been decades since he'd last been in the human realm. She might not remember him. He only had a vague *feeling* that he might have known her. But what if they weren't friends? Shit. What if they were enemies instead? That wouldn't be unheard of. And what if it wasn't even the same nymph he might have sort of known? There were only a few left; most had returned to their waters years ago, forsaking human society and sticking to their own immortal kind.

The bouncer pushed a button on her headset by her microphone. "Someone named Knox is here." She waited, pursed her lips, then nodded when a response crackled in her ear.

"How many in your party?"

"Four," he said.

"She'll see you. You," she said, pointing at Knox, "go around to the side of the building by the stage door and knock. The rest of your party, come into the club."

She unhooked the red velvet rope. Charley squealed and jumped up and down, clapping her hands. Zada followed at a more sedate pace as they walked past the rope and under the awning.

Knox grabbed Ellery's gloved hand. "Come with me," he said with a tug. "Please."

Ellery looked to where Zada and Charley stood hugging each other and rubbing their cold noses together, and made a noise in their throat.

"Yeah. Okay."

Zada waved. "We'll see you inside!"

"Be careful!" Charley yelled and was immediately shushed by those around her as they disappeared into the entrance.

Knox led Ellery down the sidewalk, ducking through the crowd, grip tight on Ellery's hand. He coughed.

"You don't like their relationship?"

Ellery frowned. "I do. Of course I do."

"They look happy together," Knox said.

"Because they *are* happy. It's just that the effusive compliments and the sweetness can be a little much sometimes."

"It's difficult to see others happy?" Knox asked, his head tilted. "Because you're not?"

Ellery slowed their steps as they turned the corner to the side of the building. "What? No. I'm happy," they said, pulling their hand from Knox's grip now that they were through the crowd. "I happen to be very happy. Where did you get the impression that I'm not happy?"

"At the diner. When you yelled at me. And just now, when you said life wasn't fun."

Ellery paused. "I didn't yell. And that doesn't mean that I'm not happy. I *am* happy."

"Oh." Knox blinked. "If you say so."

"I *do* say so."

Knox held his hands up in surrender. "Okay."

Ellery shoved their hands back in their pockets. Their irritated breaths came out in little puffs, framing their face with a cloud as they pouted. They were adorable, standing there all annoyed, face half hidden behind the fabric of their scarf. Dark strands of hair poked out over their ear from where their knit hat was pulled down. And if Knox were a teenager in one of the television dramas he'd watched over the years while lounging on Arabelle's couch, he'd make a romantic overture, like tucking that piece of hair behind their ear or poking their pink cheek or wrapping his arm around their shoulder and pulling them in for a side hug.

But Knox didn't, because they weren't in an entertaining teen drama. Though Zada had reapplied Ellery's makeup expertly, the blue of several bruises was still faintly visible, bruises that Knox had caused. And Ellery had made their lack of interest in him and his situation clear. He'd have a hard enough time convincing them to enter a deal. It would be best to abandon any thoughts beyond that. So he let it go.

"Come on," he said, turning away. "There's the door."

The side of the club was beige cinder block, not at all as impressive as the front with the neon lights and colorful canopies and red velvet rope corralling a crowd of people jostling to be allowed inside. The alley was darkened now that the sun had gone down, lit only by the glow of the streetlamp and one naked bulb that hung above the door. The door was gray with the word STAGE in black painted lettering across it.

Knox rapped on the door with his knuckles. There was no response. He leaned on the doorframe with one shoulder. Ellery huffed in annoyance.

"I know you don't believe me," Knox said.

Ellery sighed heavily. "No, I don't."

"How can I prove it to you?" he asked.

Ellery adjusted their layers of fabric, covering as much of their skin as possible. "I don't think you can," they said.

"I'd offer to show you some magic, but I have so little left . . ."

A stiff breeze whistled down the narrow alley, and every hair on Knox's body stood on end. The shadows shifted, and the light above them flickered out with a pop and a spark. Ellery yawned beside him, leaning their head back on the building, none the wiser. Knox slipped his arm through the crook of their elbow and moved closer as the air shifted, the atmosphere becoming heavy.

"Ellery," Knox said, gulping.

The gloom stirred and moved, ripples spreading across the ground like a rock had been dropped in a dark pond. The small swells became waves that undulated and gathered until they coalesced into forms.

Ellery's body stiffened next to Knox, and they unconsciously moved closer to his side.

"What?" they breathed.

"They're here."

Ellery didn't ask who; Knox had a feeling that deep down they knew, even if they didn't want to admit it. Magic and power rolled in like a low mist, whisking wayward debris along the sidewalk.

"Knox . . ." The susurration of his name scraped along his spine.

And suddenly the three shades rose from the ground in front

of them, draped in wispy shadows, standing in a half circle that did not leave any avenues for escape. Not only did they seem to be fully recovered from the altercation in the alley, but their presence was also somehow bolstered. They were more substantial than they'd been last time, and Knox had no idea how that was possible. The air was dense with their anger, and it pricked along every nerve in Knox's body.

They approached, floating a few inches above the asphalt.

"Believe me now?" Knox whispered.

Ellery paled. "What *are* they?"

"The shades. You don't happen to have that pipe on you, do you?" Knox asked, licking his dry lips.

Ellery shook their head. "No."

"Didn't think so. Do you have your protection charm?"

"It's in my pocket."

"Good. They can't harm you while you have it."

"What about you?"

Knox shivered, his gaze fixed on the shades. They closed in until they were merely an arm's length away. "I'll think of something."

He couldn't think of anything.

The shades stopped. They had more definition than before: solidly shaped with sharper details, like the gleam of buttons on their cloaks in the moonlight and folds of the heavy fabric that fluttered in the breeze. But their faces were the same, pitch-dark ovals unformed beneath their hoods, with blazing red pinpricks for eyes. Instead of the shifting shadows Knox was used to, they were almost corporeal. Knox's unease increased with each passing moment they all stood in silence.

"Time to come, Knox," the leader said.

"You've been truant long enough."

"Your fun is over."

Ellery turned and grabbed the doorknob, making a frustrated

noise when they found it locked. A sharp metallic clicking followed as they tried to jostle it open. "Help!" they called, pounding their fists on the heavy door. "Help!"

"Quiet, human!"

The shade on the far left moved quick as a blink, slipping behind Ellery and sliding their arms around Ellery's body like writhing snakes.

"Get off!" Ellery yelled.

Panicked, Ellery clawed at the strands of darkness, unable to pry them away. They struggled and fought, only to become helplessly entangled. The shadowy ropes pinned their arms to their sides and oozed up the column of their throat, sliding beneath the scarf to caress Ellery's skin.

"Hey!" Knox yelled. "Hands off!" Knox lunged, but his arms were caught fast in the hold of the other two shades. They held him frozen as tendrils of smoke and shadow enveloped him in their cold embrace. "Knock it off! Let's talk about this!"

"Knox!" Ellery shouted, voice high-pitched and panicked.

Knox spun, meeting the shade eye to eye, close enough for their stale breath to wash over his face. "Don't touch them," he pleaded. "They didn't know."

"Let go." Ellery's voice was breathless and small, terrified, as smaller wisps crawled over their jaw to their mouth, pressing their lips shut.

"You can't hurt them!"

"We cannot," the shade agreed.

"We will not."

"We will release them once you agree to come with us."

Knox struggled. "I'm not! If this is about the—"

"It is about your disobedience!"

The shade clapped a hand over Knox's mouth, yanking his head backward and lifting him in a cloud of dark fog so that only his toes scraped the ground. He trembled in the hold, twisting as best he could, but he was stuck fast. He reached for his magic. He only had a weak, fledgling amount remaining, but it might be enough to conjure another blast of light. He took a constricted breath, intent on unleashing what he could in a flash. The magic quivered beneath his skin, glowing brighter.

A spike of shadow plunged into his chest, and he screamed in pain behind the gag. Shadow encased the ball of light, smothering it and snuffing it out. It was a feeling unlike anything Knox had ever experienced: utter physical pain and the stark, brutal absence of magic. The coldness of the world around him seeped in, and every inch of his body shuddered with *hurt*.

He gasped through his nose, and tears streamed from the corners of his eyes. It appeared his rebellion would be short-lived, and he would be returning to the Other World against his will much sooner than he wanted.

One of the other shades pushed aside Knox's clothes, their hand wandering through his pockets until they found the hard lump of Arabelle's vial.

"He has it," they said, tone almost gleeful.

"Good. Let us go."

Knox glanced to Ellery's wide eyes, fear reflecting in their brown depths. He had no idea how the shades were able to hold on to Ellery, when they hadn't been able to touch them the other night. The protection charm should've prevented it. They'd somehow tethered themselves to the human world more securely than ever before.

Knox looked down and saw Ellery's fingers wiggling into their pocket. They extracted a small brown object, an acorn encased in iron wire, and with surprising dexterity held it between two fingers. Twisting their wrist, they pressed the object against a cluster of shadow.

The shade hissed in pain, the darkness parting around the place Ellery had touched it with the charm. Well, then—the acorn *did* still work.

"What are you doing?" the shade said, shaking from the sting.

Ellery couldn't respond, not with their jaw locked, but with each scant inch of wiggle room, Ellery poked the charm deeper into the shadows. The shade howled once Ellery was able to bend and contort and place the charm against their mouth. The darkness holding their lips broke and dissipated.

Ellery screamed.

Knox doubted anyone could hear it over the music in the club. But it did shock the shade into receding slightly, allowing Ellery more room to press the charm against them.

"Desist, human!"

"Then let me go!"

The shade acquiesced and withdrew, releasing Ellery. They dropped to the ground with a grunt, sprawled on their stomach. They staggered to their knees, their breaths coming out in shallow, frightened pants.

Knox fought against his own bonds, wanting to reach out and ensure Ellery was okay, but he was hopelessly stuck.

"The human matters not," the shade clinging to Knox said. "We have Knox. Let us leave."

"The queen will not be pleased."

"It does not matter now that we have what we need."

Knox didn't know what that meant. They had spoken with the queen? When? And why would she not be pleased? Because he'd run away? He wanted to tell them that she had not responded to his messages, that he'd been afraid of returning because he didn't know what had happened. If only they would release his mouth, allow him to speak and explain.

Ellery snapped their head up and scrambled toward the door. They tried the handle again, to no avail. They resumed pounding their fists, a steady drumbeat beneath the music washing out through the seams.

The shades paid Ellery no heed, dragging Knox toward a clump of shadows. He managed to slide down in their grasp and dig in his heels, his boots scraping across the asphalt with a grating sound. It didn't stop them, and he knew once they were in a place that was dark enough, they'd use their powers and drag him across the barrier into the Other World. He'd disappear from Ellery's eyes, and he'd never see them again.

Oh well. It was good while it had lasted. It wasn't like he would remember Ellery once he crossed the barrier, anyway. And in time, Ellery would forget him too. He was only the hot weird guy who had made Ellery's life unpleasant for a few nights in a row. Easily forgotten.

A familiar tingle worked its way down Knox's spine into his fingers and toes. The veil was close. The power of the shades rippled over Knox and the human realm wavered in front of him, distorting like frosted glass. He expected to feel the tug behind his navel, the feeling of the Other World calling him back, the welcoming embrace of his first home, but he didn't. He didn't feel anything other than the presence and magic of the shades, and that scared him more than facing his queen.

Something was wrong.

"Knox!" Ellery yelled, abandoning the door and stumbling into the alley. "Knox!" they yelled, brandishing the acorn like a weapon. They tripped, landing on their knees, weak from being wrapped in the hold of a shade. "Knox!"

Goodbye, Ellery, Knox thought.

Suddenly the back door banged open, and a beautiful woman stepped out. Her long hair flowed over her shoulders and down her back in a silver waterfall. Her bright blue eyes shone like jewels in the darkness as she scanned the scene. She narrowed her eyes at the corner of the building where the shades had Knox in their hold, able to perceive what Ellery could not.

Knox did his best to show he was being taken against his will, writhing in the shadows, making as much noise as possible against the gloom over his mouth.

She glanced at Ellery's bowed figure.

"Cover your ears, kid."

Ellery didn't argue, slapping their gloved hands against the sides of their head.

She took a breath and released a blast of sound. The song was loud and beautiful and sharp, potent enough to pierce through the shadows. The shades cried out, lit up from inside by the magic of a minor goddess. They loosened their hold on Knox, and he dropped to the ground. He scrambled on hands and knees toward Ellery.

He reached them and covered them with his body, pressing his own hands over Ellery's ears just in case.

The shades writhed, their cloaks blown backward by the force, their hoods falling back. Soaked in the siren's magic, their true selves were revealed. Creatures of the Other World made of shadows and bone and roots of ancient trees. The flames of their eyes burned in withered gray faces made of little flesh.

They screeched and ran, dispersing into flickering shadows.

"That'll keep them away for a while," she said with a firm nod, brushing her hands off like she'd completed a job well done. She spun and addressed the two of them huddled on the ground. "Long time no see, Knox."

Knox stood from his crouch, pulling a pale-faced and unsteady Ellery up with him. "You remember me?"

She brushed her silver hair over her shoulder. "Yes. Of course. The question is, do you remember me?"

"Yes. I mean, no. Maybe?"

She shook her head. "Figures. Come inside. Bring your friend. They look like they've seen a ghost."

With a dramatic flourish, she sashayed to the door. Knox had no choice but to follow. He checked the ground, found the acorn undamaged, and slipped it into Ellery's jeans pocket before guiding a shaken Ellery inside.

8

ELLERY

ELLERY'S HANDS TREMBLED AS THEY HELD THE CUP OF HOT tea that was handed to them in the dressing room at the back of the club. They'd been peeled out of their coat, which was wet and dirty thanks to the time they'd spent rolling around on the frosty ground. Then Knox had steered Ellery to the couch into which they gratefully sank, moving on autopilot, because those things . . . those *things* . . . were *real*. Well, Ellery had known they were real from their first encounter, but that was when Ellery had been convincing themself that they were a group of criminals dressed in weird robes. But they weren't. They were what Knox had said. They were not human. They were supernatural.

Ellery pressed their fingers to their throat and shivered at the lingering cold from where the shadows had touched their skin.

Despite the space heater the nymph had aimed at their feet and the blanket Knox had tucked around them, Ellery could not stop their teeth from chattering. It was as if the combination of a near-strangling by sentient shadows, the exposure to the bitter cold of the night, and the absolute shattering of a carefully crafted worldview had left Ellery shaken to their core, their body unable to warm itself, their mind unable to process anything. Even the body heat from Knox's shoulder pressing into theirs didn't help.

"Drink," the beautiful woman—no, *nymph*—said, touching Ellery's hand that was holding the saucer. Her touch sparked against their fingers, and the sensation brought Ellery back to the present, at least physically. Mentally, they were still having a difficult time catching up. In the light of the room, Ellery was better able to appreciate the ethereal effect of the nymph's long silver hair, bright blue eyes, and golden-brown skin. "It'll help. I promise."

Her words were soft, holding no trace of the power from a few minutes prior. Ellery shuddered at the memory of the sight of the shades drenched in the magic of her voice. They squeezed their eyes closed, trying to shut out the horror of what they'd looked like under their robes. And the fact that Knox had been telling the truth. The supernatural was real. It was all real. And fuck, it was real.

"Will they be okay?" the nymph asked Knox.

"I hope so," Knox said. "It might take some time."

She hummed a tune, effortless and lovely. "Did they not know?"

"I told them, but they didn't believe me."

"Ah," she said. "Must be a shock."

No shit. Ellery wanted to tell them to stop talking about them as if they weren't sitting right there. They sipped the drink instead, not trusting their voice. The tea was warm, and the heat of it traveled down to their stomach, thawing the cold places.

Knox let out a helpless laugh bordering on hysterical. "Yes. Must be."

"As long as they'll be okay. It wouldn't look good for a human to die in my dressing room."

"Good to know your priorities," Knox said wryly.

Ellery blinked and took another gulp of the tea.

"I'm being pragmatic," the nymph said. She sat in the chair by a vanity across from them and crossed her legs. She wore a flowing, gauzy blue dress with a slit up the side and strappy silver high heels that highlighted her painted toes. "I'd have to relocate, and well, there aren't many places I could go that would be close enough to my river and aren't basically abandoned." She laced her fingers. "Let's cut to the chase, Knox. What brings you to my door?"

It was an abrupt segue. But the extreme events of the night had probably suspended the need for social graces.

Knox sat forward, elbows on his knees. He bit his bottom lip, a habit Ellery had noticed that he did often when he was thinking. "So you do remember me?"

The question plucked another one of Ellery's heartstrings—the content of the words themselves, but also the soft pleading quality of Knox's voice, a tinge of hope cracking on the end.

"Yes. I thought that was obvious. I wouldn't have allowed a stranger to enter through the stage door, and I certainly wouldn't have used my magic against shades for someone I didn't know."

He sagged in apparent relief. "That's ... that's good."

"What do you remember of me?"

He ran a hand through his hair. It stood on end. "Not much. A feeling, really. A vague sense that we might have known each other. I don't even remember your name, to be honest."

She smirked. "I'm going by Lorelei right now. It's ... an inside joke."

"Okay, Lorelei. Are we friends?"

Another heartbreaking question.

Snorting, she gripped the armrests on her chair. "Old friends. This is the fifth time we've met, Knox. You've known me in four of your previous lives."

Knox blinked; his mouth formed a small *O* of surprise. "I'm sorry. I don't remember."

She waved away the apology. "Happens each time. I've accepted that the barrier between worlds really screws with your memory."

Ellery raised an eyebrow. "What does she mean?" they said, their voice a shaky rasp.

"Oh, they speak," Lorelei said with a smirk.

Knox sighed, shoulders taut. "When I cross the barrier between realms, I forget things," he said, wiggling his fingers at his head. "Not everything. Memories of people, *humans*, don't stay in here." He tapped his temple. "But sometimes other things do. It's one of the costs of being liminal."

Frowning, Ellery took another swig of their drink. "Sounds lonely." They froze, mortified. They hadn't meant to say that aloud, but they had. They ducked their head and downed the remaining tea. At least their teeth had ceased chattering.

Knox shrugged.

"So what are you doing?" Lorelei asked. "Why were those shades after you?"

"Oh." Knox perked up. "I ran away."

Lorelei's eyes widened. "You ran away? How were you able to pull that off? I thought you were limited by the terms of your bargain."

He rubbed his hands together. "Well, when my last boss died, I just . . . I ran."

"Any particular reason?"

He bit his lip again. At that rate, it would be raw and bleeding before the conversation was over. "Have you heard anything from my queen?"

At this, Lorelei uncrossed her legs and spun in her chair to peer in the mirror. She picked up a sponge of makeup and dabbed at a spot on her forehead. "No. I have not. But if I had, I'd give her a piece of my mind."

"Why?" Knox asked, brow furrowing.

Lorelei's expression darkened. "What do you mean, why? I don't know how long you've been here for this life, but it's fairly dismal, if you haven't noticed."

"I don't understand," Knox said, his voice low, almost more to himself than anyone else.

Lorelei heard him. "My river froze. Why do you think I'm in this club and singing each night for humans who can't comprehend the true power and beauty of my voice?" She looked at Knox in the mirror's reflection. "My river fucking froze, Knox. *Five years* ago. I couldn't stay in it or near it in any of my forms after that first winter, and all my powers as a minor goddess couldn't break whatever *your* queen has done. I tried everything, even contacted my father." She glanced at Ellery. "River god, son of the goddess of the seas," she said by way of explanation. "And *nothing*. Still frozen."

Ellery dropped the cup. It bounced on the plush rug with a quiet thump. "What?" they breathed. Their thoughts whirled. Not only was the supernatural real, but . . . but . . .

Knox shook his head. "I don't understand. My letters can't get through, and she's not reached out to me. It's not like her. Something must be wrong."

Lorelei tossed her hair and huffed. "Knox, I know you're only involved in the magic side of your queen's duties, so this may have passed your notice. But this city and its suburbs and the surrounding area are trapped, waiting for a spring that hasn't arrived."

He blinked, then frowned. "Only more reason to think something has happened."

Lorelei shook her head. "The rest of the world has moved on. It's *only* here. Which means she's abandoned the humans and all the creatures of this area. Including *you*."

Knox sucked in a sharp breath. "But I'm her creation. She wouldn't . . ." He trailed off.

Ellery resisted the urge to touch Knox's arm, to offer comfort, though they weren't sure if it would be accepted. And they weren't quite sure what the conversation meant. It was so confusing. And they were so tired. And they were still processing the fact that gods and goddesses were actually real.

Lorelei's expression softened. "No one knows why. It could be that she's forgotten, or it could be a punishment. You know how gods are. How fickle they can be. How time is irrelevant."

Knox bowed his head, his jaw clenched. "I know."

"Whatever the reason, she's upset the balance of this realm more than she knows. She's made a mess."

Knox stiffened. "What do you mean?"

Lorelei tossed down the makeup and stood. "Human belief is waning. The offerings have all but stopped, not only to your queen but to us minor regional deities as well. The pixies are pissed off and have abandoned their meadows. The garden gnomes have fled for greener pastures." She crossed her arms. "I would've left as well, but I'm bound to my river."

Knox fidgeted in his seat. "I've been . . . stuck. My last boss was a recluse and a workaholic. I've only been able to leave the apartment at her command." His throat bobbed. "I didn't realize what was happening."

"Well, now you know. Your queen has doomed me to sing to humans for the rest of my days. Well, the humans that remain. Most of them have left, opening space for others to move in. Others who are not as nice and kind as river nymphs."

Ellery's stomach twisted into a knot as they remembered the conversation they'd had with their mother earlier in the day about the Johnsons' cows. Could that have been . . . one of these other not-so-nice creatures Lorelei alluded to? Ellery couldn't believe they were considering that their mother's unhinged story might be true. But they'd been proven wrong on many fronts that evening, so it didn't seem as farfetched.

Lorelei gestured to the cup on the floor. "Hey, human, are you okay?"

Ellery nodded quickly. "Yeah. I'm good."

"Good. Look, I do have to go out there and sing for a bit. You can wait in here. The doors are locked, and I'm fairly certain those shades will need to regroup before they can wreak any further havoc."

"My cousin and her girlfriend are out there."

"Really? I'll give them a good show. What are their names, and what do they look like?"

Ellery answered the question, still feeling dazed and like they were living on a different planet. Their heart thrummed rapidly, matching the rhythm of their thoughts of *it's real, it's real, I can't believe it's real. All of it is real.*

Lorelei gripped Knox's shoulder. "I'll have the cousin and girlfriend escorted back here after my set for a meet and greet. Hopefully your human will be back to normal by then."

"Not his human," Ellery managed.

Knox flinched.

Lorelei laughed. "Sure. Okay. Whatever. Don't make a mess."

She left, talking to the staff as she did, letting them know the two teenagers in her dressing room were okay to stay. The music from the club filtered in through the open door and muffled again once it shut behind her. In the distance, the tune changed, presumably when Lorelei took the stage. The applause was muted but fierce.

Knox picked up Ellery's cup and placed it on a table of headshots and autographs.

"Are you okay, really?"

Ellery wanted to say they were fine, but it was far from the truth. The phantom touch of the shade lingered on their skin. The image of their true forms was branded in Ellery's brain and burned behind their eyelids. Everything Ellery had believed as a child and then given up on, abandoned in the face of unheard prayers and ignored offerings and the long-lasting cold, was true. And the truth of that settled in their middle like a stone.

"No," Ellery whispered.

"What can I do to help?"

"Unless you can rewind the last few days, I don't think you can do anything."

Ellery met Knox's gaze, stared at his face for the first time since the altercation outside the club. Ellery sucked in a harsh breath. Knox had a bruise blossoming on his cheek, and his eyes, which previously glowed, had dimmed and now sported dark bags beneath them. And while he still appeared unfairly good-looking, he no longer looked untouchable or otherworldly. He looked . . . human, shockingly so.

He swiped his thumb along his lip. "Do I have something on my face?"

"You look different."

"Oh. Good different or bad different?"

"Just . . . different."

"Okay."

Ellery rubbed their forehead. They had so many questions. And they were scared that the answer to each one would only bring more questions. And their mind was too hazy, too overloaded, to parse out the meaning of the answers anyway. They settled on something simple, immediate.

"Why didn't you use your magic?" Ellery couldn't believe they were asking such a question. "You created that lightning with it, right? It drove them away, and earlier you said you'd had some left."

Knox pressed his fist over his chest, his expression troubled. "They snuffed it out."

"What?"

"One of the shades was able to . . . smother what little I had left. It was . . . They've never been able to do that before, or if they have, they've never seen a need to. And now I'm empty." He frowned. "And exhausted."

"It's been an exhausting three nights." Which was the understatement of the year.

"Yeah, but I don't get tired. I don't need to sleep. I don't need to eat." On cue, Knox's stomach rumbled. He frowned and rubbed his arms. "And I'm freezing."

And that's when Ellery knew that something had to be wrong. Knox had always seemed impervious to the weather; it was one of the reasons he'd stood out on his trips to the diner. It was what had branded him as *weird* along with the *hot*.

"Hold on," they said, squirming from beneath the blanket. They scooted closer to Knox's side and draped the fabric over them both. "There."

Knox wrapped his long fingers over the edge and wriggled down until he was covered from neck to feet. His pointy elbow dug into Ellery's arm.

"Thanks," he said. Then he yawned.

Ellery's remaining questions fizzed on the tip of their tongue, but they swallowed them down as Knox's eyelids fluttered closed and he leaned heavily into Ellery's side.

Ellery knew they should stay awake, should press Knox for answers, should find Charley and Zada and run away and leave this mess behind. But those were the probable actions of future Ellery.

Right then Ellery was tired, and finally warm, and relatively safe.

They allowed their eyes to slide shut and followed Knox into sleep.

9

KNOX

"How adorable!"

Knox rocketed out of sleep at the sound of Charley's excited squeal. He blinked awake to find Lorelei, Charley, and Zada standing around them with varying expressions on their faces. Open delight on Charley's, tempered amusement on Zada's, and outright confusion on Lorelei's.

Ellery grumbled next to him, shifted in their sleep, and tucked their face into Knox's neck. Knox held utterly still, Ellery's wild hair tickling his jaw, their breath brushing along the skin of his throat. Knox's heart double-thumped at the casual contact. He didn't know the last time someone had *touched* him willingly, not in the service of a magical goal or in the throes of absolute panic, and he didn't realize how touch-starved he'd been until that moment, until the sensation of Ellery's weight against his body sent sparks traveling down to his fingers. Okay, this was a situation he had no idea how to navigate gracefully, and he stared helplessly at the top of Ellery's head, wondering if he should shove them off or let them rest.

"Ellery!" Zada said sharply, pushing two fingers hard into Ellery's shoulder, nullifying Knox's internal dilemma.

Ellery snapped to sitting, but their eyes were still closed.

"What?" they said, voice thick with sleep.

"Wake up. You were about to give Knox a heart attack."

Ellery froze as they opened their eyes and took in their surroundings—the couch in Lorelei's dressing room, the shared blanket, the position they had just been in—and a blush bloomed across their cheeks.

"Knox," Lorelei said. "Since when do you sleep?"

"Since now." He tilted forward, elbows on his knees. Despite the catnap, he was still so tired. He could go right back to sleep if given the opportunity. "I'm exhausted. The shades suffocated my magic, and without a contract and a tether . . ." He trailed off.

"Interesting." Lorelei pressed the back of her fingers to his forehead. "Your skin is clammy." She shook out her hand. "Anyway, I talked with Charley and Zada and told them everything I know. You'll be safe with them for a while. I gave them tips on how to fortify their apartment against any supernatural intruders."

Oh. Knox furrowed his brow in thought. He hadn't really considered that. Per Lorelei, who knew what lurked in the city now. The shades were annoyingly difficult to hinder, but any bit of protection could help. Though it'd just be easier for him to stay with Lorelei. As a minor goddess, she could overpower the shades any day. And it would be safer for him, and for the humans, now that the shades could somehow maneuver around protection charms and had showed they had no compunction about hurting them. "Can't I stay with you?"

"No." She shook her head. "I'm sorry, Knox. But I can't be seen aligning with you. Everyone knows where you belong, and your queen isn't the most well liked at the moment."

Knox pressed his lips together. Of course. He couldn't blame her. They'd been friends for four of his human lifetimes, and when he inevitably returned to the Other World, he'd forget again. And she'd be left to explain herself.

"What does that mean?" Ellery asked.

"It means she doesn't want to risk her relationships with other supernatural beings for me."

Lorelei smiled sweetly. "Sorry."

"I understand."

"It's fine," Charley said, arms crossed. "You can stay with us for a little while."

"Are you sure?"

"Yes." Zada smiled. "Until you figure things out."

"Good," Lorelei said. Then she clapped her hands. "Now it's time for you all to go. I have another set to prepare for, and as cute as you are, you're cramping my style."

Ellery disentangled themself from the blankets and stood. They were not as unsteady as before or as dazed, but they were quiet again.

The four of them left through the club, Knox being unwilling to go through the stage door, and exited back on the street. He immediately shivered and huddled down in his coat, the cold annoyingly sharp on the walk to Zada's car. Was this what it was like to be human? Did Ellery feel this all the time? No wonder they were always cranky and bundled-up.

The ride back to the apartment was punctuated by Charley's animated discussion of Lorelei's singing and her set list. Zada drove and responded to Charley with short statements and the occasional hum. The radio was a low murmur in the background. Ellery silently stared out the car window, deep in thought.

Zada pulled into the parking deck of their complex. At the door to the apartment, Knox hesitated, unsure if he should enter. Maybe it would be best if he found another place or went back to Arabelle's apartment. That last encounter had shown that his presence could be dangerous to the humans, and he didn't want anyone getting hurt because of him. But he'd never been this vulnerable before, and who knew if he'd be able to find another safe place in this condition? Plus, it felt so good to be cared for, to be welcomed in.

Unbidden, his stomach growled loudly. He winced.

Charley raised an eyebrow. "Would you like a snack?"

He gently set his bag down on the floor and leaned it against the wall. "I'd love a snack."

Ellery shed their hoodie, then brushed past Knox and headed to the kitchen table, plopping bonelessly into a chair and taking the glass of water Charley handed them.

Charley offered Knox a package of frosted strawberry toaster pastry. He opened the foil wrapping and unceremoniously shoved most of one into his mouth. There wasn't much space in the apartment, so he perched on the arm of the couch, drawing his legs beneath him to stay out of the way.

Zada danced around Charley, narrowly avoiding an elbow, and grabbed a shaker of salt from a spice rack. She crossed the room back toward the doorway. After flipping several locks into place, she knelt on the floor.

"Um . . . ," Knox said. "That's not actually going to work. The shades can appear anywhere there are shadows, so blocking an entryway isn't going to help."

Zada uncapped the shaker. "It's not necessarily for them. Lorelei said there were other beings, right?"

Knox nodded. There were others. Lots of them, historically scattered across the world, and based on what Lorelei had said, many had moved nearby thanks to the recent thinning of the human population. He shuddered. He didn't want to think about the possibilities.

"And will a salt line stop them?"

"Most of them."

"It won't hurt you, will it?"

Knox was touched at Zada's concern. "No. I don't have ill intentions."

"Good." She poured the line. Satisfied, she turned and faced him. "What else?"

"Do you have any iron?"

"Oh!" Charley said. She hunted in a cabinet and pulled out a pan. "This was our grandmother's." She hefted a large cast-iron skillet. "Will this work?"

"Undoubtedly."

"Excellent." She set it on the counter within easy reach. "Anything else?"

Knox hummed. "If you have a lucky charm, you should keep it on you at all times."

"Oh! I think I have a rabbit's foot somewhere." Charley yanked open a drawer and started rummaging.

Ellery watched the proceedings with narrowed eyes. "What are you two doing?"

"Getting ready for bed," Charley said with a smile. She made a high exclamation of delight when she located her rabbit's foot, which was inexplicably dyed blue. "Lorelei told us everything. About the shades, and who Knox is, and how she's a nymph from a nearby river, and how there are other supernatural creatures around here who aren't so nice. So we thought we'd set up a few fail-safes and then get some sleep."

Ellery stood. "There are . . ." Their throat worked. "*Things* after him. They're dangerous. They"—Ellery touched the reddened skin of their neck—"are real and frightening. And you're both just—what? Taking him in? Trusting that a fake rabbit's foot and a bit of salt are going to protect us? It's dangerous. *He's* dangerous."

Zada cocked her head to the side. "You say this like you weren't just cuddling him on a couch in a nymph's dressing room."

Ellery sputtered. "We weren't cuddling! And I was . . . I was not thinking clearly. I had just been attacked by those . . . by those things."

"Shades," Knox said helpfully.

"And I had just learned that everything I don't believe in is real."

"I *know*," Charley said. "Mind-blowing, right?" She mimed an explosion with her hands. "Like, we met a *river nymph* tonight. And that time in the grocery store—I'm certain now that it was a dryad that I bumped into in the produce aisle. Like, what else do we not know about?" She shook her head. "So trippy."

Ellery ran a hand through their hair and tugged. "How are you both not freaking out right now?"

Zada sat the saltshaker next to the skillet. She reached over and patted Ellery on the shoulder. "Look, I know this is difficult for you. But think of it this way—a minor goddess from a river confirmed that there are multiple realms and that gods, goddesses, and everything in between could potentially be real. And that's legit terrifying. I'm going to sleep with the closet light on tonight. So I get you. But, on the bright side, we do have our own expert."

Zada gestured to Knox, who still balanced on the arm of the couch.

"I would not call myself an expert. But I do know some things."

"See!" Charley said. "He knows some things! It'll be fine."

Ellery bristled. "He's not telling us everything."

Knox stilled. "What do you mean?"

"Your queen . . . ," Ellery said slowly, arms crossed over their torso as if holding themself together. "What is she the queen of?"

"The Other World," Knox replied around the last bite of his pastry. "Which is basically where all human souls go at first."

Zada paused. "At first?"

"Yeah. At first. Don't ask me where they go next. I don't know. I do know that some stick around with us, though. That is the queen's decision. It is her domain, after all."

Ellery cleared their throat. "So she's a goddess? Of the dead?"

"Sure."

"What else is she the goddess of?"

Knox chewed thoughtfully. "Lots of things. Goddess of magic, for one. Which is why I exist and why my last boss, Arabelle, summoned the shades. Goddess of physical boundaries, like crossroads and city borders and the boundary between the living and the dead."

"Anything else?" Ellery asked carefully.

"As Lorelei said, she's the goddess of the seasons and the harvest."

Ellery's whole posture went rigid. Their face turned a deep red.

"El," Charley asked, "why all the questions?"

"Don't you get it?" Ellery said, words clipped with anger. "His queen and our goddess are one and the same. The harvest. The seasons. She's one of the big three—the chthonic goddess. Her brother is the god of the sky, and her sister is the goddess of the seas. She's the goddess my family prays to, which means his queen is the reason that we're stuck in eternal winter!"

Knox's heart sank. He had hoped that Ellery hadn't been paying close attention to his and Lorelei's conversation. But they had pieced it together.

"Ah," he said softly. "You were listening."

"I was."

"And you understood?"

Ellery scoffed. "We don't use words like 'Other World' and 'shades.' But yeah, I figured it out."

"Oh. What do you say, then?"

"Generally, we say 'afterlife,'" Zada said gently.

"Oh. Well, it's not really an afterlife; it's a different life."

Ellery slammed their hand on the table. "Not the point. The point is that the goddess you call your queen is the reason my family is ruined. She's why I had to move to the city! Why the farmland is failing." Ellery looked to Charley and Zada and thrust their finger in his direction. "Don't you get it? His queen is responsible!"

The last bite of his snack lodged in his throat. "I thought you didn't believe in this stuff."

"I don't!" Ellery crossed their arms. "I mean, I didn't. I don't know." They sputtered in anger. "But Lorelei blames your queen."

Exhaustion tugged behind Knox's eyes. The pastry had done little to ease his hunger. The combination of sugar and fatigue made him irritable, and he matched Ellery's angry stare. "Oh, and you believe her?"

"Maybe," Ellery said, stepping into Knox's space. "You asked how you could prove yourself to me. I know how. Contact the goddess. Ask her why she has forsaken us."

"Ellery," Zada said, stepping between them calmly, a mediator. "It's late. Maybe we should save this argument for the morning."

"No! We've been waiting for answers for five years. And like you said, he's an expert." Ellery stomped forward and shoved Knox in the chest. "Contact your queen. Call her, or send a pigeon, or whatever it is you need to do."

Knox lost his balance on his precarious perch and fell backward into the cushions. He scrambled upright, knocking the decorative throw pillows to the floor, and jumped to his feet.

"I can't."

"Don't lie."

"I'm not lying. I can't."

"Why not?"

"Because it takes magic to send a message. And I don't have it."

Ellery frowned and crossed their arms. "Bullshit. You used magic against the shades. I saw you."

"Yeah, and then they snuffed it out, or did you not hear that part of my conversation with Lorelei?" he snapped back.

"Okay. Fine. Find another way, then. I'm sure you can. There are plenty of shrines to visit, and there won't be a wait to go in."

Knox clenched his fists. "I can't. I'm sorry, but I can't."

"Ellery," Charley said, warning in her tone. "Back off."

"No! There's something he's not telling us. Something he's hiding. And magical liminal being from the afterlife or not, I'm not going to stop asking questions until we get answers. Why can't—?"

"Because you weren't the only ones forgotten!"

The words burst from his mouth, loud and bitter. And they hurt. They *hurt*, as if Ellery had reached in Knox's lungs and ripped them out themself, roots and all, leaving a gaping, bloody wound behind. Knox pressed his palm to his chest, breaths coming in rapid pants, sorrow of a different kind pricking tears behind his eyes. He bowed his head, didn't risk seeing the confusion or, worse, the pity of the others.

"Like I told Lorelei, I've tried to contact her. I've tried and I've tried, and she hasn't answered me in *years*." He swallowed down the hot sting of grief. "And I don't know why. I don't know why she's forsaken your family and the people of this region. I don't know why she has abandoned any of us. I only know that even if I did have my magic at full strength, it would make no difference. And even if I wanted to go back to the Other World and tell her about all your problems, to try and help that way, I would forget the moment I crossed the barrier. And all memory of you and what's happened here would be gone." Knox took a ragged breath. "So no. I don't have the answers you're looking for, Ellery. I'm sorry."

He took a moment to compose himself, hastily wiped at his eyes, then raised his head.

Ellery's face was still red, but their hunched posture and refusal to meet Knox's gaze suggested it was now the result of shame rather than anger.

"Well," Zada said softly. "That's certainly an answer."

Zada and Charley exchanged a look. Ellery didn't move, staring fixedly at the carpet.

"It's been a long day," Charley said, breaking the tense silence. "Emotions are high. We can revisit this later."

Zada touched Charley's hand. "Right. Let's get some rest."

In a blur of movement, Charley fixed the cushions and the pillows on the couch. She straightened the sheet, jamming in the loose corners.

Charley gently touched his arm, and Knox's body sagged in relief beneath her warm palm.

"Things will look better in the morning," she said kindly. "Right now you're tired. We're all tired. We'll talk again after a good rest."

Knox nodded.

"Thank you."

Charley smiled.

They all took turns in the bathroom, and Knox changed into a pair of pajama pants, a shirt with long sleeves, and a pair of fluffy socks. He snuggled down into the blanket, hands tucked close under his chin.

Ellery padded into his line of sight, wearing a large T-shirt and pajama bottoms, and switched off the light. Then they dove under their covers.

Knox tried not to think about Ellery, tried not to think about Arabelle, tried not to think about the shades or his queen or anything else.

He was unsuccessful.

And despite his exhaustion, he stayed awake long after the others had gone to bed.

10

ELLERY

Ellery tossed and turned. They rolled around, trying to get comfortable, but their pillow was too soft, and their mattress was too hard, and their blankets were both too scratchy and not warm enough. Not that the blankets and the pillow and the mattress were any different from the nights in which Ellery slept soundly. But it was easier to deflect than admit the truth.

Which was, Ellery just felt kind of awful. Every time they closed their eyes, the image of the shades' true forms floated across their mind's eye. And every time they tried to curl into the warmth of their blankets, they felt the leeching cold that had slipped around them. And every time they tried to shut off their brain, all they heard was the echo of Knox's devastating confession. And every time they tried to push down the shame at being such a prick, it came roaring back and clogged their throat.

Ellery rolled over again and sighed loudly.

"Are you awake?" Knox whispered from his place on the couch. He lifted his head and peered over the arm, his golden eyes wide, reflecting the dim light from the moon that filtered in through the window.

"Ugh," Ellery answered, voice low. "I can't fall asleep."

"Why not?" He squirmed until he was draped over the back, long arms dangling, chin on the top of the cushion. His dark hair stood on end, and again Ellery was struck at how human Knox appeared, even in the low light filtering in from the windows above. He had dark circles under his eyes and a crease on his cheek from the pillow, and the mystical air that had exuded from him so brilliantly had faded.

It made Ellery feel a little worse, but also a little closer to Knox than before, as if they were at least on the same plane of existence now.

"Just . . ." Ellery scrunched their nose, trailing off. How could they put into words that their entire belief system—the whole reason they had left home—had shattered, and it had messed with their head? But also that they felt awful for how they had treated Knox since their altercation in the diner? That the cognitive dissonance pinging around their brain was making them nauseated and tired and so, so confused? "I feel bad."

"Oh, are you sick? Do you need me to get Charley?"

"No, not 'bad' like 'sick.'" Ellery buried their head in their blanket, half hiding their face. "I feel awful for the way I talked to you. For pushing you. I didn't . . . I just . . . The last few years have been hard. But that's no excuse for how I acted. So I'm sorry."

"Apology accepted," Knox said, small smile tugging at the corner of his mouth. "Does that mean you can fall asleep now?"

Ellery huffed in amusement. "No. But it helps a little."

"Good."

"Are you okay?" Ellery asked.

Knox tilted his head to the side in thought. "I'm exhausted." He looked away. "And I'm . . . sad."

"I'm sorry." Ellery swallowed. "I know what it's like to have a strained relationship with your parents. It sucks."

Knox snorted. "It's not a great feeling."

Ellery winced. "Well, be prepared for Charley and Zada to smother you with affection now. Taking people in is kind of their thing."

"That doesn't sound bad." He shifted and met Ellery's gaze. "Can I ask you a question?"

"Sure."

"You said your life has been hard. What happened?"

Ellery blew out a breath and tugged their blankets tighter. Huddled in the dark, they found it easier to reveal their truth, to confess their secrets in whispered words, not loud enough for anyone else to hear other than Knox, an almost stranger. "I told you I lived on a farm."

"Yes."

"Well, farms don't work when it's been winter for five years. And my family couldn't afford for me to live there anymore. So I moved here to live with Charley and work. And despite how much we fought, I miss my family. I miss my parents. I miss my home."

Knox blinked. He crossed his arms and rested his cheek on top of them. "Oh," he breathed softly. "I didn't realize."

"It's okay. It's not something I talk about."

"Why?"

"Because it sounds selfish. I mean, I'm upset because instead of having a typical teenage experience and going to parties and finishing high school and preparing for college, I've had to work and worry and be an adult way faster than I wanted. And it's sucked, but there are tons of people who are in the same position and people who have it worse than me. At least I have a roof over my head, and my own place to sleep, and food. And I have Charley and Zada looking out for me. I'm lucky."

Knox hummed. "I'm not human," he said. "Well, I may be more human now than normal because of the missing magic." He waved his hand lazily. "But in my limited experience, I think you can feel unhappy about your situation and still acknowledge the challenges others have. It's not one or the other."

Knox wasn't wrong, but it did little to untie the knot of complex emotions that resided within Ellery.

"For what it's worth," Knox continued, "I'm sorry."

"Why? You didn't have anything to do with it."

"I know," he said with a yawn. "But I'm commiserating. I know it's not easy being human. It's not easy being a familiar, either."

Ellery sat up and pulled their blanket over their shoulders, tucking it around them. They didn't want to fall asleep now. "What does it mean? To be a familiar?"

"Well, I'm a creation of the goddess. I exist to serve in either the Other World or this one. I'm bound to someone who needs magic and has made a bargain. I do the human's bidding until the terms of the contract are met. And then I'm supposed to go back through the barrier and serve my queen until I'm called again."

"Sounds restrictive."

"One of the reasons I ran away."

"And the shades?" Ellery asked, shuddering at the memory of their forms beneath their robes. "Can they be summoned at any crossroads?"

Knox hummed. "No. There are a specific few. Mine is the one for this region. Unfortunately I'm tied to it as well, which makes me as stuck as Lorelei."

Ellery furrowed their brow. "That adds another level of difficulty to hiding."

Knox huffed in amusement. "I know. It's only a matter of time before the shades find me again."

"I can't believe people would willingly make a deal with them." Ellery shivered at the thought and huddled farther into their blanket.

"I know, right?" Knox said with a low chuckle. "Who in their right mind would strike a bargain with those terrifying creatures? But some people do."

"They must be desperate," Ellery said softly, their stomach churning as they considered the potential circumstances that would drive someone to do so.

"Arabelle wasn't desperate, but she did want to prove herself."

"I'm sorry you lost your friend."

Knox rubbed his face on his sleeve. "I wouldn't call us friends. She was my boss."

"Still. She was all you knew in your life here."

Knox bit his bottom lip in thought. "Normally, when it's over, I go back to the Other World right away, and I lose my memories as soon as I cross the barrier. There's no time or need for sorrow. But I'm glad I feel it this time. Makes me more human."

"So it's true that you forget?"

"Basic information about the human world seems to stick. Things I need to know to function here. General knowledge of other supernatural creatures and minor gods and goddesses remains as well. It's the specifics of my assignments that fade." He tilted his head. "Sometimes I get echoes of feelings and emotions I've had about things that may have happened. Things that left a strong impression."

"Like how you thought you may have known Lorelei?"

Knox nodded, his chin digging into the fabric of the couch. "Yeah. Like that."

Ellery picked at a string on their blanket. The process seemed so sad and unfair. "Why do you forget everything else?"

"It's the nature of the Other World. It makes it easier to leave this world behind, not just for me, but for the souls who pass through as well. But there are always souls who are restless or souls who recognize each other in the afterlife, as you call it. I've always thought it wonderful, the souls who find each other, remember each other. It means they had a strong connection in life. They must've loved each other very much." Knox smiled softly.

"When people make a request . . . do they always get a familiar?"

"No. Sometimes the shades can grant what the person wants. Some requests are easy, like the ability to sing or wanting to be famous. The people who need magic are the only ones that I help."

"And if you're already with someone . . ."

Knox shrugged. "The shades figure it out. They don't turn down a bargain they can use in their favor. Especially if it means more souls for our queen. That's basically their job."

"Are you the only one?"

Knox's lips twitched into a smile. "Why? Want to summon your own familiar?"

Ellery's cheeks heated. "No. I'm just curious." They ran a hand through their unruly hair. "And wondering if that's one of the reasons the shades want you back so badly. Because they need you for another assignment."

Knox's smile dropped. "No. I'm not the only liminal being my queen created." He frowned. "After Arabelle's contract was complete, I ran. I was scared," he admitted. "The shades followed, and they'll keep at it until I can find a way to tether myself here. Just for a little while. Just to experience a bit of the human realm. Have some fun before I have to go back and face my queen." Knox said it blandly, but his expression went tight, his jaw clenching in obvious worry.

A chill ran down Ellery's spine. They pulled their blankets tighter. They hadn't really considered the situation from Knox's point of view. Would he be in trouble for running away? Even in light of the goddesses' abandonment of the city and its surrounding areas?

They rubbed their chin, an idea forming in their mind, remembering how Zada had called Knox their expert. Knox had knowledge and access to a world that Ellery couldn't ever fully grasp. They only had the basics of religion that they'd learned from their parents and the farming community, which appeared to be very much lacking beyond worship of the chthonic goddess. Knox could potentially help them figure out how to bring the relentless winter to an end.

But it could be dangerous. What if Knox wasn't telling the truth? What if Ellery lost their soul? But . . . wouldn't it be worth it if it saved their family? If it saved the city? Was Ellery desperate enough to risk it? Ellery pushed a hand against their chest, felt the rapid beat of their heart beneath their palm.

"Have you fallen asleep?" Knox whispered.

Ellery smothered an unhinged laugh. "No. I'm thinking."

"About?"

"You need a tether."

"I do."

"A bargain."

"Yes."

"To keep the shades from dragging you back."

"That would be ideal, yes."

"And I need information. I need this winter to end."

Knox sat up straight. "What are you suggesting?"

Ellery licked their dry lips. "I suggest we make a deal. I'll be your tether, and you help me contact your queen, my goddess, and ask her to end this winter."

"I told you; she's not answering me."

"I know. But there must be another way. We could find an alternative line of communication. Right?"

"Maybe? But I can't make a guarantee. And if I can't hold up my end, then we'll be trapped."

Ellery shrugged. "Fine. You just help me find information about why your queen is not answering any of our prayers. Does that work?"

"Yes," Knox said, hesitant.

"Great. And I'll . . . protect you from the shades."

Knox winced.

"What?" Ellery asked, defensive. "That's not good enough?"

"It's dangerous." Knox frowned. "And I don't know if it's possible now that protection charms don't appear to work against them."

"Point taken. Fine. I'll tether you to the human realm."

Knox blew out a loud breath.

"What now?"

"It's . . . vague."

"Then what should it say?"

"I don't know! I didn't draft the contract language. That was the shades' job."

"Fine. Is there something you want?"

Knox tilted his head. An expression passed over his features that Ellery couldn't interpret. After a few long moments, Knox grinned slightly. "I want to experience human life."

Ellery's eyebrows shot up. "And that's not vague?"

"I can make it not vague."

Ellery gestured. "Then by all means."

"I'll make a list of experiences." Ellery opened their mouth, but Knox cut them off. "It won't be a long list. A feasible one."

"What kind of experiences?"

Knox's eyes glowed. "Like eating at the diner."

"We did that the other day."

He snapped his fingers. "Exactly! We've accomplished one already."

Ellery rubbed their eyes. "Okay. Yeah. That sounds good."

"Are you certain?"

Ellery was not certain at all, but they had to try. "No souls involved," they added quickly.

Knox's eyebrow quirked, but he agreed. "No souls involved."

"Then yes."

"Okay."

Ellery extricated themself from their blankets with renewed energy. Striking a deal with a magical being was reckless, but so was intervening in a fight in an alley, and so was leaving home for the city. "How does this work?"

"Usually the shades draft an agreement, and the petitioner signs with a magic quill."

"Okay. I have a paper and a pen. Does that work?"

"I don't see why not."

Ellery scrambled from the mattress and crossed into the kitchen. They found Charley's work apron hanging off the handle of the oven and took out her notepad and pen. They tore out an order slip and slapped it on the counter.

Bargain between Knox and Ellery, they wrote at the top. In careful handwriting, Ellery laid out the agreement in plain language so that there was no question as to the terms. Ellery would assist Knox with experiencing human life, and Knox would help Ellery find information about the perpetual winter. It was foolproof.

Knox left his place on the couch and padded to the kitchen, leaning over Ellery's shoulder. He was taller than Ellery, lean and pale, and he smelled like the perfume that had permeated Lorelei's dressing room. Ellery could feel the heat of him against their back.

"This okay?" Ellery asked once finished, setting the pen down.

"Looks fine to me."

Ellery took a deep breath. "Okay."

"I'll sign first," Knox said, slim fingers twirling the pen. "In case you want to back out." He smirked, like it was a taunt. But a pause did give Ellery a chance to think things over before signing the document. A document that would bind them with a supernatural being, one that they hadn't believed in just a scant twelve hours ago. And that only solidified Ellery's decision.

Knox signed with a flourish, his signature full of twirls and curlicues, beautiful and elaborate. He held out the pen.

With a shaking hand, Ellery took the ballpoint. They signed their name, scratchy and small.

Nothing happened. Or at least Ellery didn't feel any different.

Knox's brow furrowed.

"Huh," he said. "That didn't seem to have worked."

"Why not?"

Knox hummed. "Magic. We need magic."

"And yours isn't working at the moment."

He shook his head. "No, it's not."

"Where do we get magic?"

"I have an idea. Where do you keep your knives?"

Ellery paled and pointed to a drawer. Knox yanked it open, the cutlery clacking against one another from the force. "Oh, this is even better." He pulled out a cake tester from when Charley had gone through a baking phase after watching a challenge show. Her new hobby had lasted a week.

"What are you doing?"

Knox's tongue peeked from the side of his mouth as he concentrated. He pricked the end of his finger, a small bead of blood welling on the end. He squeezed the tip, skin turning red. "Arabelle used my blood as the last ingredient in a potion she made, and it worked. It was the missing piece." He dipped the tip of Charley's pen in the blood and tapped it at the end of his name, leaving a red dot.

He offered the pen to Ellery, eyebrows raised. "Your turn."

Well, Ellery had already signed. This was just another weird step. In for a penny, might as well go for a pound. Carefully Ellery touched the pen to Knox's finger and, with a gulp, added a dot to the end of their name.

The result was instantaneous. The contract sparkled and fluttered, then hovered in the air in front of them. The thin paper transformed before Ellery's eyes: the white-and-blue-lined order slip shimmered gold and became something different, something magical.

Knox gasped and doubled over, pressed a hand to his chest. "Oh," he said, grinning widely. "It's back."

"Your magic?"

"Yes. The bargain worked." He breathed and tilted his head back. "Thank the goddess. Feeling the cold was awful. As was the hunger and exhaustion."

Ellery snorted. "So you're saying you aren't a fan of those parts of the human experience."

"Zero out of ten. Do not recommend."

"Good to know." Ellery smiled wryly.

They picked up the paper from where it had fluttered back to the counter after being magically possessed and studied it. With a shrug, Ellery folded the note in half, only for it to bounce back flat and for the crease to disappear.

"What?"

"There's a reason everything is a scroll in myths and fairy tales." He took the paper from Ellery's hand. He pinched the side with both hands and tried to tear it. The paper simply twisted and flexed as needed, then popped back straight. Knox opened his palm to a small flame and held the contract over the fire. The flame danced and flared around the golden paper, but it would not catch. "Indestructible," he said, closing his palm, causing wreaths of smoke from the snuffed flame to curl from between his fingers, "until our deal is complete."

Ellery's throat tightened. "Nice," they said, but it came out wobbly.

Knox didn't notice or didn't care. He rolled the paper into a tiny scroll and passed it to Ellery. "I'll let you hold on to it."

Ellery took it, their hands brushing over Knox's. Knox's smile was once again bright and wide, and his eyes sparkled gold. The human Knox was gone, replaced by the being that Ellery had come to know through the diner window.

Ellery's insides tumbled in a mixture of fear, dread, and attraction. Their mouth went dry as they wrapped their fingers around the scroll.

"Hey!"

Ellery and Knox jumped apart. Charley stood in the doorway between the kitchen and the hallway. She had on pajamas. Her red hair was everywhere. Her tank top strap slipped off one shoulder, and she yawned wide. She had her rabbit's foot clutched in her hand as if she was going to defend herself with a fluffy key chain.

"What are you two doing up so late? And making noise? Why the noise?"

"Midnight snack," Ellery said quickly, unsure if Knox would tell Charley that they were signing a contract in blood. She didn't need to know that right then. And Ellery had no idea how she would take it. "We were hungry."

Charley smacked her lips. "It's way past midnight, but whatever. Just go to sleep and don't make a mess."

"We won't."

"Good night."

Charley turned and smacked her shoulder into the doorframe. She grumbled a curse and stumbled back to her bedroom.

Ellery quickly slid the notepad back into Charley's apron. They considered the pen and realized they didn't want Charley to accidentally seal an order in Knox's blood, so they washed off the end in the kitchen sink with a little soap and warm water. Hopefully they hadn't ruined the pen, but whatever.

"You should try to get some sleep," Knox said with a gentle nudge.

"What about you?"

Knox blinked, brow furrowed in contemplation, then slowly smiled after his self-assessment. "I'm not tired."

"What did you do when Arabelle slept?"

"I watched a lot of television shows."

Ellery squinted. "Okay. Well, try to keep it down."

Crossing the room, Ellery dropped on their mattress. They slid the scroll into the pocket of their hoodie, which was crumpled on the floor, and plopped down on their pillow. They couldn't believe what they'd just done. They couldn't believe it had worked. They couldn't believe they were now bound to a supernatural being, a familiar with magic and a sly smile and a bubbly personality and . . . Ellery was so screwed.

They pulled the blanket up to their chin and turned away from where Knox sat on the couch and watched the television turned down low, the light from the screen highlighting the line of his jaw.

Yep. Ellery was so very screwed.

They tucked their hands under their pillow, and despite the unease and turmoil and hope coiling in their gut, they fell into a deep sleep.

11

KNOX

The tugging sensation behind Knox's navel had returned along with his magic, the telltale sign that he was tethered to the terms of an agreement. But this time he'd made the pact on his own, with his own interests in mind—no one else's. There was power in that aspect of the decision he hadn't really considered before, but now that it had happened, he was ecstatic.

With that, his magic was his own to use and wasn't tied to any command or rule that Ellery might give him. It pulsed warm and bright and unfettered in his chest. With Arabelle, Knox could only use magic if she allowed it, because magic was part of the deal she'd made with the shades, and he could only access it within the rules she'd set. And when that bargain was completed, his magic had withered. Now it *flourished*.

Ellery had asked him to be quiet while the others indulged in their beauty rest, and he would out of common courtesy, but he also knew that if he wanted to make cymbals crash with his magic, he *could* despite the request. He wasn't as powerful as a god or goddess or even one of their children, but he could match another being like himself— like the shades—if it was ever needed. He hoped it wasn't.

Speaking of which, Knox dipped his hand into his pocket and

pulled out the vial. It glistened in the moonlight. The shades had searched for it when they had assaulted him and Ellery. It was clear they wanted it, and that made the vial valuable. He might even be able to use it as a bargaining chip if they somehow got the better of him. He looked around the room, and his gaze lighted upon a small curio cabinet crammed in the corner. It was full of knickknacks like porcelain thimbles and tiny spoons and bells with various city names on them. It was a great place to hide the vial, which would look natural among the assorted objects.

With a zap of magic, he popped the lock and slid the vial in between a shot glass and a deck of playing cards. It fit right in. Once in place, he closed the door with a soft click.

That done, Knox turned his attention to another detail.

With the information he'd gleaned from both Lorelei and Ellery, it was obvious that his queen had forgotten him. He didn't know if it was neglect or if it was a punishment, but it was clear it was targeted to this area, which included him—her own creation. And it *hurt*, sliced him down to the marrow. He had told Ellery he was sad, but the word was inadequate to convey the depth of his feelings. He felt *betrayed*. And now he understood why Ellery had turned their back on their own beliefs. But it also solidified his course of action. He didn't owe the queen his allegiance, and for once, he would put his wants first.

While the others slept, he made a list of all the things he wanted to do. He left off a few things he knew wouldn't be probable, with the world the way it was. And he didn't want to bind Ellery to him for a decade, so he pared it down. He read the items over with a quiet sense of satisfaction and to the comforting rhythm of Ellery's deep and even breaths, pleased with his ideas. Much of it was inspired by the teen dramas he'd watched at Arabelle's apartment. He carefully folded it, because as thrilling as it was to express his wants and desires, he didn't want to share until he had to.

The kitchen light flicked on behind him, and he turned as Zada emerged from the hallway, robe cinched tight, silk scarf wrapped around her braids. With a yawn, she shuffled over to the coffee machine and pressed a button. Charley followed, slipped behind Zada, and wrapped her arms around her, resting her chin on Zada's shoulder. Zada sagged in Charley's embrace, and Charley placed a light kiss to the side of her neck.

"Morning, sunshine," Charley said, voice gravelly from sleep.

Zada hummed in reply, then said something in a low, husky voice Knox couldn't hear.

Knox looked away, guilty that he had inadvertently spied on a tender moment between the two. But it did spark an idea. He reopened his scrap of paper and added two words to the bottom before tightly refolding it and slipping it into the pocket of his pants.

"Oh hey, Knox," Zada said, sitting in the armchair next to him. She crossed her legs, pink bunny slippers on her feet, cup of coffee in her hand. "Did we wake you?"

"No," he said, blushing. "I've been up for a while."

Zada quirked an eyebrow. She took a sip of her coffee and gave him a once-over. "You look better than you did last night."

Knox ran a hand through his hair. "I feel better."

Charley clanged around in the kitchen. "Not to say you looked bad," she shouted. "Just—you looked different! Tired. A little peaked. Not yourself."

"I think he knows what I meant, babe."

The sound of the refrigerator door opening and closing rang through the apartment, followed by the sound of a pan hitting the coils of the stove. "I was tempering the sentiment, honeybun."

"Oh my gods and goddesses," Ellery grumbled from their blanket burrito on the bed in the corner. "Please be quiet."

"Nope!" Charley cracked an egg. "Rise and shine, cupcake! It's time for a new day. A new outlook. A fresh start."

"I hate you with every particle of my being."

"You *love* me. Anyway, time to get up. Things to do! People to see! Problems to solve!"

"It's my day off," Ellery said, rolling over and pulling their pillow over their head. One foot popped out of the bottom of their blanket roll, and a low string of muttered curses followed. The foot disappeared quickly as Ellery curled into a tight ball.

"You're being a poor host, El," Charley chided. "Besides, I thought you wanted to solve all the ills of the world today, and you can't do that with your head buried in a pillow."

"It's fine!" Knox said quickly. "It's perfectly fine. We talked last night and figured things out. So we're good."

Charley shoved bread into the toaster. "Nope. It's not. Ellery is being rude with a capital *J* as in 'jerk.'"

Ellery disentangled enough to raise their hand and flick Charley off. Which only made Charley giggle.

Knox's eyes widened, and he stood. "It's really okay."

Zada took another sip of her coffee. She reached out and tugged on Knox's sleeve. "Ignore them. They have a teasing relationship that even I don't understand sometimes. But it's all in fun."

"Ellery is notoriously difficult to wake in the morning. It's routine for us to bicker."

"Charley is notoriously chipper in the morning. It's routine for her to be annoying." Ellery sat up slowly, hair sticking in every direction, face puffy from sleep. The sun streamed weakly through the high windows, bathing them in buttery light. They wiped the sleep from their eyes and yawned so wide, their jaw cracked.

It was entirely too cute, and Knox's heart stuttered at the sight, something warm and fond growing in his chest right next to his magic. Especially when they ended up just rolling to another spot on the mattress and falling over.

Knox muffled a laugh.

Zada cast him a knowing look but didn't comment.

"Come, tell us how you worked things out," Charley said, grabbing the toast that had popped up and dropping it on a plate. She buttered both sides, then scooped fluffy eggs on top, adding a slice of cheese and a sausage patty before mashing the other piece of toast on top. She cut the sandwich in half and set it on the table. "Egg sandwich à la Charley, hot on the table. Come get yours before they're gone."

Zada gestured to Knox. "After you."

Zada and Knox gathered around the table as Charley made more sandwiches and Ellery's soft snores emanated from the mattress.

"How did you resolve your conflict?" Zada asked, unfurling a napkin. "Did Ellery admit to being completely wrong about the situation?"

"Yes. No. Not entirely." Knox tented his fingers. "We made a compromise."

"Really?" Charley said, joining the table after plating the last sandwich. The fourth sat steaming on a plate, awaiting Ellery. "El compromised? Wow. That's not like them at all. Intriguing. Do elaborate."

"I am going to help them find out information about my queen and what is happening with the climate, and they are going to help me experience human things."

Charley choked on her sandwich and grabbed her glass of water. She took a long gulp. "What?" she said after a few seconds, her voice tight.

"Mind out of the gutter," Ellery said, finally emerging. They plopped down in the empty seat and propped their cheek on their fist. They still appeared half awake. "Like Zada said, he's a expert on the supernatural. And he wants to have human experiences, like having fun."

Zada smirked, then winked at Charley. Charley giggled.

"I made a list," Knox interrupted to cut off whatever inside joke he was missing. "Of places to go and things to try."

"Oh!" Charley squealed. "Like sightseeing? El, you should totally take Knox around today. Show him the sights."

Ellery sighed. "What sights?"

"The sights!" Charley said, throwing her hands up. "The cool things of the city. Thinking about it, I don't think you've even seen it all. You showed up one day and started working the next." Charley suddenly stood. "I'll make a list!"

"You all have fun," Zada said. "I have class and work."

"I have work too," Charley said, scribbling onto her order pad. "Just a few hours in the late afternoon, so I'll bring home dinner from the diner. But you two have so much fun. Use the bus pass, and don't get in trouble." Charley returned to the table and held out the paper. She then pinched Ellery's cheek. Ellery didn't even flinch, just muttered something under their breath and took a large bite of their sandwich.

After breakfast, the morning was a flurry of showers and getting ready for the day. Knox waited his turn by looking through his duffel bag. He removed a set of clothes for the sightseeing trip, and in his search for them, his hand knocked into the solid leather-bound book of Arabelle's. He pulled it out and sat heavily on the couch. He ran his hand over the cover, then opened to the last entry. Her words were still there, missing the last ingredient. Not that he was expecting them to change.

He took out his folded list.

"What's that?" Ellery asked. They had emerged from the bathroom in a cloud of steam, skin flushed from the warm water. They wore a long-sleeved shirt and a pair of jeans with hems that brushed the tops of their feet. They toweled the damp strands of their chin-length hair and peered over Knox's shoulder.

"Arabelle's journal," Knox said, shoving his list in the crease and snapping the book closed. "Ready to go?"

"Yeah. I have Charley's 'agenda of fun,' as she's calling it. We can leave whenever you're ready."

For the first time in this life, Knox felt a genuine thrill at the prospect of going out into the city. He had Ellery with him, and he was under no obligation to complete a task other than having fun. Excitement coursed through him.

Knox ran to the bathroom and washed and dressed, and when he emerged, Ellery was wrapped up in their winter outerwear.

"I know you don't feel the cold anymore, but if you want to blend in, you should at least wear a coat. You know, for appearances' sake. Just a suggestion."

"Noted," Knox said, slipping on boots and sliding his arms into his heavy winter coat.

Ellery tugged on their gloves. "I want it stated that if this isn't fun, it's Charley's fault. Not mine."

Knox nodded. "Okay."

Ellery pulled their hat down over their ears and wound their scarf around their neck. They looked more like they were about to hike in the wilderness than venture downtown, but they were cute with only their brown eyes visible and the tips of their hair sticking out from the bottom of their hat. "Ready?" they asked, eyeing Knox's ensemble, which consisted of a simple pair of jeans, a sweater, and Arabelle's long black coat.

Knox fished around in his pocket and found his sunglasses. He perched them on his nose, then pushed them up with one finger in a flourish. Ellery rolled their eyes, but their lips tugged into a smile. "Ready," he said. "Let's go."

Ellery stepped over the salt line, and together they left the apartment.

They rode the bus to a museum of modern art that was free to the public and wandered around the displays. Knox didn't understand several of the pieces but was glad to learn that Ellery didn't either. They walked to a sculpture garden that had been at one time surrounded by beautiful flowers, according to the postcards that were in the adjacent gift shop. As it was, a temporary tent had been erected around the statues to at least keep the snow from piling up on the stone. Ellery blushed at some of the more evocative pieces and rushed past them, a high flush on their cheeks. Though it could've been the cold.

Next they rode a glass elevator to the top of the tallest building in the city. The open-air view was brisk and dizzying, and while Knox expected Ellery to stay back from the edges, they surprised him by walking right up to the railing and peering out at the city below.

"Wow," they said, eyes wide.

"You can see for miles," Knox said, standing next to Ellery's shoulder. "It's beautiful."

"I wouldn't go that far. It's a patchwork of urban sprawl, and there's questionable slush everywhere from the pollution. And if the clouds weren't hanging so low, you could see farther and—"

"Just . . . ," Knox said, licking his lips. "Enjoy it. Please."

Ellery shoved their hands in their pockets. "Yeah. Okay."

They stood together in silence, looking out over the city. The noises from the street didn't reach them that far up, and they were the only two walking around save for the elevator attendant, who was barely paying attention.

"When I first moved here," Ellery said, voice soft and low, a confession, "I couldn't sleep at all. The noises from the streets were too loud, and the lights were always on. Not at all like home, where the loudest thing was the occasional owl, and the brightest light came from the stars. It took me a few weeks to be able to block it all out." Ellery laughed. "I was so grumpy from lack of sleep. Charley almost sent me back home."

"Grumpier than you are now?" Knox asked.

"Hey!" Ellery protested, though they were laughing. "I take offense. And yes, I was very irritable. I've mellowed in my months here."

"I can't imagine," Knox said.

"Oh, shut up. Is the"—they swallowed, still having trouble with the words—"Other World like this?"

"No," Knox answered. "The noise is different. Especially by the main docks, where the new souls are brought in. They are often loud. But the older souls, the ones that have been there a while, are silent." He didn't tell Ellery that the loudest sounds came from the new souls lamenting their deaths. They probably could imagine why.

"What about buildings?"

"The queen has a grand palace. And a magnificent throne. But that's it, other than the boat houses by the docks and a few scattered structures here and there. There's no need for more than that. It's nothing like this." He spread his arm out to encompass the city below.

"Do you have a room at the palace?"

"Yes." Knox had a room, just a small place to exist by himself.

"If you don't sleep, what do you use it for?"

"What do you do when you're not sleeping?" Knox asked with a smirk. "I have duties for the queen around the palace. I have hobbies. Did you know I can play several stringed instruments? The fiddle, guitar, harp, and so on and so forth."

"That must be so weird," Ellery said, their breath a smoky puff wreathing around their face. "To have all the time in the world."

"It's all I've known, except for those brief hours yesterday that I was human. But you have to understand, time works differently in the Other World. When you're immortal, five years is . . . nothing."

"So, our five years of winter here . . ." They trailed off.

Knox suddenly wished he hadn't brought it up. "It's insignificant to a god."

"Wow." Ellery echoed their earlier sentiment.

"Yeah," Knox said. "It stings to think about."

Ellery frowned. They tentatively reached out and touched Knox's arm, and he knew the frown wasn't because of him, but *for* him, an acknowledgment of their shared pain. And Knox was relieved at the progress, glad that the understanding that had passed between them in the small hours of the morning remained in the light of day.

Ellery released Knox's shoulder with a squeeze, then turned. "We should go. Charley's list is long."

Their next stop was on the very edge of the city. As soon as Knox stepped off the bus, he knew this place was not like the others.

"It's basically an ode to corn," Ellery said, picking up the glossy pamphlet about the attraction and flipping through it. "I don't understand how a series of stone obelisks shaped like corn makes any kind of sense, but it is what it is." Ellery snorted as they read through the history of the statues. "Charley *would* pick something like this. I really do love her, but she is so weird. I mean, my parents' farm grows—" They coughed. "*Grew* corn but also other things, like soybeans and oats. We had a vegetable garden and . . ."

Knox only half listened to Ellery's rambling while they walked around the attraction. It was indeed weird. There was a rectangular fence around the corn obelisks, presumably to keep them from being damaged or toppled over by visitors. Around the outside of the fence was a brick-paved walkway that allowed visitors to see the statues from any angle. Benches dotted the path. Luckily, it had been swept of snow, so there was minimal slipping hazard. But despite the amenities for tourists—even a souvenir stand—there weren't many people out and about.

They stopped at a large informational plaque that had the history and significance of corn through the ages laid out along a timeline.

"I'm so sorry. This is probably not what you meant when you

wanted to sightsee. In retaliation, I'm going to buy Charley a phallic corn key chain."

Knox snorted. Ellery was wrong, though. The area was interesting. As soon as he stepped off the bus, he'd felt a familiar tingle of power trace its way down his spine.

He leaned over and looked at Ellery's pamphlet. "This is a sacred place."

Ellery paused. "For real?" They dropped their voice. "To your queen?"

"No," Knox said. "To someone else."

And that's when Knox spotted him. The man was dressed all in black, standing at a corner of the fence, near a bench. He stared out into the field. Knox tracked his line of sight and spied the remains of a wooden windmill. It obviously wasn't part of the current attraction. It sat on a small, wooded area, locked behind the fence, and it was mostly in disrepair. The sails had rotted and hung limply off the cracked veins; the tower listed, and there was no telling if the millstone was still inside. But it had been something once, and Knox wagered that the stranger knew what.

"Do you still have your acorn?" Knox asked, voice dipped low.

"Yes?"

"Good. Stay here."

Knox strode away from Ellery's sputtered questions, but Ellery didn't follow. Or at least didn't follow right away.

"Hello," Knox called and waved, slightly jogging over.

The man turned slowly and peered at Knox through a pair of designer sunglasses. His face remained placid except for a slight tick of his jaw. He exuded power, much like Lorelei. He was definitely a minor god, but of what?

"Hello," he replied, voice deep and rough. "Do I know you?"

Knox smiled. "Maybe? I don't have a great memory."

At that, the man's lips twitched. "What do you want?"

"Why are you assuming I want something? I could just be friendly."

He scoffed. "Why else would you approach?" He tugged on the cuff of his long jacket with gloved fingers, and a single black feather slid out and floated on a sudden cold breeze.

Knox's eyes widened. "Raven?"

He pursed his lips. "Bram, currently. I have been known by Raven as well as other varied monikers over the centuries, but it feels a bit pedestrian. Now, who are you?"

"Knox," he said, holding out his hand. "From the Other World."

Bram eyed the offered handshake with disdain. "I know where you're from."

Knox blushed and dropped his hand when Bram didn't take it. While he and Lorelei had been friends over several lifetimes, he was still only a creation of the queen. He wasn't a god. Not like Lorelei, and not like Bram. And while Lorelei didn't care about hierarchy, Bram apparently did.

"Right."

"What do you want, familiar?" Bram asked, his tone weary. "I prefer to enjoy the time at my shrine in peace."

Knox licked his lips. "I was wondering if you had heard anything from my queen."

Bram raised a single finely shaped eyebrow. "No."

"You're a messenger god. I've not been able to send a message to her for several years. Would you be able to—?"

Bram raised a hand, and Knox bit down on his next words, cutting himself off with a strangled, quiet noise.

"No. I'm a messenger for my king *only*. You know, the god of the sky. I have no interest in the Other World. I barely have interest in this realm," he said, peering at the field with an arrogant sniff. "And whatever trouble your queen has created with her negligence of this region is not my concern."

"But the winter—"

"Hasn't ended in several human years. Yes. I'm aware." He tugged on the collar of his coat. "It's so blasted cold here. And if my shrine wasn't right there," he said, with a gesture to the windmill, "then I'd be off flying around somewhere else. Which I usually am," he added, puffing out his chest. "I merely made a stop for old times' sake. I certainly didn't expect to be accosted by a magical pet."

Oh. That stung. Knox hunched his shoulders and stared at the ground. A slow trickle of snowmelt wound down from where Bram stood and inched its way across the brick.

"Hey, Knox!"

Ellery bounded up, shouldered their way between Knox and Bram, and held up a key chain that was a weirdly shaped ear of corn with googly eyes. "Bought it for Charley. Isn't it ugly? She'll love it!" Ellery cackled.

Knox's tension eased slightly, and he smiled.

"Excuse me," Bram said. "We were talking."

"Oh," Ellery said, turning. "I thought you were finished. I heard that last insult, and it really seemed to put the nail in the coffin of that conversation. My bad, though. Did you want to continue being a jerk, or . . . ?" Ellery trailed off.

"A rude human. How quaint. Do you know who I am?"

Ellery tapped their chin. "I'm not sure. I have built many a scarecrow in my lifetime, but I don't think I've ever had the pleasure of making your acquaintance."

Bram bristled. More raven-colored feathers slipped from his sleeves and from the hem of his long coat, blowing in a circular pattern around them.

"Watch yourself, human."

Ellery snapped their fingers. "Oh. I know who you are. You're a minor god who is a messenger for a bigger, more powerful god. Right?"

"Such insolence."

"Me?" Ellery asked, pointing a finger to their chest and affecting a completely innocent expression. Knox found it unfairly attractive. Ellery batted their eyelashes. "Is he referring to me?" Ellery asked Knox, feigning confusion.

Bram sneered. "You're either very brave or very foolish to mock a god to their face." Bram pulled down his sunglasses and peered at Ellery with his black eyes. "Based on the fact that you're cavorting around with a familiar, I would wager that you land on the side of the latter."

Ellery pulled themself to their full height, which wasn't much compared to both Knox and Bram. They lifted their chin. "Hey, I've faced down shades from the Other World twice," Ellery said, pointing at their bruised face. "And I've witnessed a nymph use her powerful song, and I haven't run away yet. So if you think I'm going to allow a generic minor god of the wind, who doesn't even have enough of a following to have a properly maintained shrine, to disrespect my very magical and amazing friend, then you are mistaken, sir. Furthermore," Ellery said, pushing a finger into Bram's chest, "maybe if you actually did your job and carried messages between the gods, then you'd have more of a fan base. As it is, I've certainly never heard of you, and like I said, I grew up steeped in farm culture. You'd think I'd know of a god who is basically a bird."

Bram removed one glove and revealed his long, thin fingers that curved like talons. He rested his hand gently on the top slat of the fence, and his claws instinctively curled around it, long, pointed nails scraping along the wood. "I am a god of the wind. I'm not simply a messenger. And my powers can easily overcome the adorable little protection charm in your pocket."

Knox fisted his hand in the fabric of Ellery's coat and yanked them backward. "I apologize for our mistake, breeze-friend. We didn't mean to cause offense."

"Maybe *you* didn't, but—" Ellery began.

Knox clamped a hand firmly over Ellery's mouth. He tamped down the small flutter of *something* that happened with the feeling of Ellery's lips moving against his skin, even if it was in a muffled rant.

"We'll be going." Knox dragged Ellery away.

Knox released Ellery once they were out of earshot but looped his arm through theirs and marched Ellery back to the bus stop.

"What was that?" Knox said, bewildered. "Why were you picking a fight with a *god*?"

Ellery crossed their arms. "Minor god."

"Fine. Minor god. But one with enough power to have you sucked into a tornado. Why?"

Pouting, Ellery kicked a stray pebble. "I heard it all," they said. "He was a jerk to you. You asked for help from a fellow"—Ellery made a few large hand gestures—"supernatural being, and he chose to be a dick instead."

Oh. Oh. Ellery was being protective. Knox's smile bloomed across his face, and his eyes crinkled in delight. "You defended me? And to think that last night you wanted to throttle me."

"I didn't want to throttle you."

"You most certainly did! And a few mornings before that, you were going to throw a milkshake in my face after I told you the truth."

"I was not going to throw a milkshake!" Ellery protested with a laugh.

"Fine. But you were not happy with me. And then not happy with me again. But you've also defended me from the shades and then sought help from Lorelei—"

Ellery raised a finger. "Lorelei coming out of the stage door at that precise moment was total luck. I had nothing to do with that."

"You banged on the door, *loudly*, if I remember correctly. And now you're defending me from a god like I'm some kind of damsel in distress and not a magical being myself."

"So I don't like bullies." Ellery pulled their hat lower, hiding the red tips of their ears. "And just because you are magical doesn't mean you don't need help."

"Very true."

"What was his problem, anyway?"

Knox sighed. "There's a hierarchy. The top tier consists of the three main siblings—my queen, her brother of the sky, and her sister of the seas. They are the rulers of their realms. And next in power are their children and their children's children. And at the bottom are their creations." Knox gestured to himself. "Like me." He shrugged. "It can get complicated." Which he hoped conveyed that he didn't really want to get into all the politics and relationships of the gods and their ilk. "But it's fine."

"If you say so. That doesn't excuse his behavior, but whatever." Ellery searched their pockets and found Charley's list. "Have you had your fill of weird stone corn statues? Because it's lunchtime and I'm starving, and Charley wrote 'Bob's Barbecue Food Truck' on here, and that sounds excellent."

"I'm not hungry," Knox said with a smug grin. "But I could try anything."

"Great, let's go."

Ellery shoved the list back in their pocket and resolutely started marching down the street back toward the city. Knox hummed in delight when the familiar tug of a command failed to yank behind his navel. There was only a hum of magic in his chest and a slight twinge across the bond between them, like the vibration of a plucked harp string. He smiled, happily following Ellery of his own free will. But before he did, he cast a glance over his shoulder. Bram was gone. All that remained was a small fluttering of black feathers and the muted sound of a caw in the distance.

Despite the bad interaction, it had given Knox an idea. One that might meet both ends of their bargain.

12

ELLERY

"RISE AND SHINE, CUPCAKE!" CHARLEY YELLED IN ELLERY'S FACE. Ellery jerked awake and groaned. "No," they said, rolling over and shoving their head under their pillow. "Go away."

The four of them had stayed up late the night before, playing a card game at the kitchen table after dinner. The game involved passing and stealing cards and slapping the table when needed. Ellery lost each hand, but it was fun watching Zada become stubbornly competitive and Charley laugh uncontrollably each time she messed up and Knox grin wildly as he learned the game. He ended up winning the last few rounds, and Ellery wasn't entirely convinced he hadn't been using his magic to cheat. But whatever, it had been fun.

When they finally decided to go to bed, Zada checked the line of salt and Charley set the cast-iron pan on the end of the counter, just in case. Ellery dropped off into sleep almost immediately.

That had only felt like five minutes ago.

"Come on, Ellery! The sun is up; so must you be."

"I will strangle you."

"In order to do that, you have to actually get out of bed."

"Ah, the daily morning struggle," Zada said from the kitchen.

"Didn't you live on a farm? Weren't you awake before the roosters crowed every morning?"

"That was different."

Zada huffed like she didn't believe Ellery in the slightest. "Well, you'd better get up so you can grab breakfast before work if you plan on going. Or are you playing hooky with Knox today?"

As much as Ellery needed the money, they were tired and wouldn't mind having another day of running around with Knox if it meant they were allowed to sleep in longer. The cognitive dissonance of the past few days had been exhausting as well. But as much as their parents protested Ellery sending money home, they knew that their family needed it, or else their parents wouldn't have allowed Ellery to leave in the first place.

Ellery sat up slowly and pressed a hand to their forehead, pushing their hair out of their face. It fell right back down. "I have to work," they said.

"Then what is Knox going to do all day?" Charley asked. She was already dressed, makeup and hair perfect, beautiful as always. "I have a shift too. We can't just leave him here to watch TV. That's not fun at all."

"It's okay!" Knox said, sounding cheerful and energetic. "I'll just go to work with Ellery. I have an idea!"

Ellery squinted. "An idea? Why don't I like the sound of that?"

"Because you are inherently mistrustful and you are allergic to fun," Charley said without missing a beat. She smiled sweetly to soften the sting. Ellery merely rolled their eyes.

Knox chuckled. Ellery hated the way it made their insides squirm.

"We met a minor god yesterday," Knox said, knees on the couch, arms draped over the back, chin resting on the cushions, while watching Charley and Zada prepare breakfast in the kitchen. He too was already dressed for the day, and his face glowed in the dim light, his eyes sparkling their normal golden hue. How had Ellery thought him anything other than supernatural in the first place? "At the corn shrine."

Charley held up her keys. "Thanks for the key chain, by the way. I *love* it."

Ellery mouthed *told you* to Knox.

"Wait." Zada paused, Knox's words catching up in her brain. "You met a minor god yesterday? And you didn't mention it at dinner? What the hell?"

"Yeah, a wind god. Bram. He's a messenger for the god of the sky."

"He was a jerk," Ellery said. They untangled themself from their blankets and stood.

"Aw," Charley said, placing her hands over her heart. "Did you make a friend, Ellery?"

"Fuck off."

"Anyway," Knox said, undeterred, "it gave me an idea. Lorelei sings at a club. And Bram was visiting his windmill shrine. Lorelei said that many of the gods and goddesses and other creatures that remain have moved into the city."

Ellery arched an eyebrow. "Wherever we go, we could potentially run into them."

Knox snapped his fingers. "Exactly. I knew you'd get it. You understand me so well."

Ellery's face warmed. They turned away, cheeks flushed, and busied themself with making coffee and toast.

"Okay," Zada said. She moved to the kitchen table, bowl overflowing with chocolate puff cereal and almond milk. "So, at any given time, we could potentially meet a supernatural being and not know it. That is totally fine and not at all concerning."

"You should be protected as long as you keep your charms on you."

Charley held up her keys again, and the rabbit's foot dangled next to the googly-eyed corn. Zada reached into her shirt and removed a pendant of a four-leaf clover that had been encased in resin.

"Great. You should be fine, then. Mostly. I mean, you at least won't be easy targets."

"Right."

"Comforting."

"Knox's point," Ellery said, steering them back on track, "is that they're out there. We met one."

"Yes! Which means each time we do a fun thing on my list, we can also look for information. One of them is bound to know more than we do or at least give us direction on how to contact my queen. We can, as Charley says, maim two fowl with one rock."

"Close enough," Charley said with a nod. "But do you honestly think you'll meet a god or goddess at our diner? Would they need to eat or drink? Why would they be drawn there?"

"Lots of reasons," Knox said with a wave of his hands. "Feasts were common celebratory gatherings, for one. For two, you have beautiful young people who work there, and the supernatural are always drawn to beauty and youth to either admire, steal, or trick."

"You flirt," Charley said with a blush. "But yes, I agree." She twirled her hair around her finger. "There is such an abundance of beauty at the diner. But I don't agree with the stealing and tricking part. That's wrong."

"I imagine the tricking stems from the misconception that youth equals naivety," Zada said calmly, eating her cereal and scrolling through her phone. "We should be offended the gods think of us that way."

Knox ticked off another finger. "And three, it's the only operating diner in that part of the city right now."

"Which means the chances of someone supernatural wandering in are higher." Ellery frowned. "Except—wouldn't we have noticed? We noticed you. How come you were the only one who stood out?"

As soon as Ellery said it, they wanted to shove the words back in their mouth. Charley cackled. Zada snorted into her cereal. Knox stared, eyes wide, a blush blossoming over his perfect cheekbones. Ellery was never going to hear the end of it.

"That's not what I meant!" they protested quickly, face burning.

"Oh, really?" Charley said with a sly smile. "Maybe you should tell us exactly what you meant, then? Because the way that came out, it sounded like you noticed how striking Knox was when he visited."

Ellery wished a hole would open in the floor and swallow them. They realized they probably shouldn't wish for dramatic things while being under contract with a supernatural being. Better escape before they made it worse.

"I'm going to go get ready for work."

Ellery abandoned their buttered toast and moved into the hallway. They pressed their back flush along the wall and thunked the back of their head against it. They steadied their breathing as they listened to Knox's soft, timid answer explaining how others probably hid their supernaturality better than him, since he was still relatively young in comparison and hadn't been in the human realm very long.

Ellery placed their hands on their face and felt the heat of their cheeks against their palms. They'd basically just admitted their physical attraction to Knox. And while that had been fairly obvious from the beginning based on their actions, any shred of plausible deniability had fled out the window. Crap. Crap. Crap.

Ellery shook their head. Whatever. It was fine. Knox was only going to be in the human realm a while longer, and Ellery took solace in the fact that when Knox did return to the Other World, he'd promptly forget this ever happened. Yes. Excellent. That was good.

With that thought, Ellery readied for work. They showered and brushed their teeth. They dressed in their regular jeans-and-T-shirt combination, then stared despairingly at themself in the steamed mirror. The bruises on their face had faded to a sickly green. They picked through the pile of cosmetics in the basket on the sink. A knock, followed by Zada's voice, cut through the noise of Ellery's rummaging.

"Ellery," she singsonged. "Let me in."

The bathroom was so cramped, Ellery only had to turn slightly and take half a step to reach the doorknob. They turned it, and Zada wasted no time joining Ellery at the sink. She peered into the basket and chose the correct concealer.

"Do you want my help?"

Ellery deflated. "Are you going to make fun of me?"

"Absolutely not," she said, tapping the makeup on a sponge. "He's cute. I'd have a crush too if I had any interest in men."

Zada touched Ellery's chin and lifted their face, pushing back the damp hair that had clung to their cheek, then dabbed the sponge across the bruises.

"That's not what I meant."

"It's totally what you meant. And it's okay. It's perfectly human to have crushes on people because of how they look."

"I haven't really had crushes before," Ellery admitted, voice low.

"I know."

"I don't know what to do about it."

"You don't have to do anything," Zada said with an encouraging smile. "Just enjoy the feelings that come with it. It's kind of fun, right?"

"It's terrible."

Zada laughed. "Really? That bad, huh?"

Ellery groaned. "No. Yes. I don't know."

"And that's okay too," Zada said, patting Ellery's shoulder in sympathy. "You know I love your cousin, right?"

"Yeah."

"But before I loved her, I thought she was really hot. And I was a mess about it. And then I got to know her and was like, 'Wow, she's really hot and really fucking weird.'"

Ellery couldn't hold back their laugh, and it turned into a strangled snort-slash-bark, which sent Zada into a fit of giggles.

"Right?" she said. "But that initial attraction grew into love, and yeah, now I can't imagine life without her. Even though we're still pretty young, she's it for me." Zada finished with the sponge, then grabbed a tube of tinted lip balm and swiped it across Ellery's mouth. "There. Bruises hidden, and now your lips look soft and pink."

Ellery looked in the mirror. "Thank you."

"Now do something with your hair. Since all three of you are going, I'll drive so you don't have to hide under scarves and hats."

"I don't hide. I'm just always cold."

"Spare me," Zada said. "Everyone is cold. That doesn't mean you have to look like you're about to battle a snow beast."

Ellery opened their mouth to protest, but Zada bodily threw them out. "Nope. No complaining. And it's my turn."

Thirty minutes later, they were all ready to go. Zada led them like ducklings out of the apartment and up the stairs to the first level. They piled into the car she'd parked on the street. Ellery shivered the whole time without their usual added protection of a hat and scarf. But they had zipped their coat all the way up, and that at least kept the back of their neck warm. As they waited for the car to heat up, Ellery decided they didn't care that they looked like they were battling a snow beast when they bundled up; they would not let hormones dictate what they wore in the name of comfort and warmth again.

The three of them spilled out of the car at the top of the hill that led down to the alley. Knox stiffened slightly at the scene, and Ellery couldn't blame him. The last time he was there, they'd only escaped from the shades by the luck of a cast-iron pipe and an acorn.

Charley and Zada shared a lingering kiss that Ellery normally didn't mind, but with their conversation with Zada still ringing in their head, it made them squirm. Knox didn't seem to notice, his hands in his pocket, his sunglasses on his nose, the fog of his breaths wreathing around his face in the weak morning light.

"I'm freezing," Ellery finally said.

Charley broke away from Zada with a pout. "Sorry, lollipop. I have to go to work. We'll see you after."

"Have a good shift, babe. Later, kids."

"I'm an immortal being," Knox said, deadpan, at the same time that Ellery let out a "Hey!"

Zada threw her head back and laughed as she slid into the driver's seat and started the car.

Charley watched wistfully as Zada drove away and blew a kiss into the wind.

"You're ridiculous."

"It's called love, Ellery. And I'm in it. You'll understand one day."

Ellery pushed past her and made their way carefully down the hill into the alley, gripping the side of the building when encountering an icy patch.

At the back of the diner, Knox paused and stared up at the horse-shoe nailed over the door. He sniffed, then grimaced.

"I'll go around to the front," he said.

Ellery frowned. "Wait, the horseshoe works?"

"Yes," Knox said with a sigh. "That one is made of mostly iron. Iron repels all; intention doesn't matter. It's one of the reasons I couldn't pick up the pipe in the alley that night." Knox gestured to where the pipe had been restored to its usual resting place on the stairs by the door.

Ellery's eyes widened. They hadn't realized that. "Oh."

"I'll just—" He pointed to the road and turned, making his way back down the alley to walk around to the front of the building.

"It's better this way," Charley said, using her key. "I didn't want to explain to Diego why we were bringing hot weird guy through the kitchen, anyway."

Ellery huffed a laugh. Together they entered the diner, where Frank and Diego were already arguing in the back over the grill.

"I'm telling you, if they let Vanderhook have any ice time, they would win more than once in a blue moon. You can't have your best player on the bench for most of the game and expect results."

"And I'm telling you that he shouldn't even be on the ice. He is the worst player on the team."

"You're so hysterically wrong."

"Look at his stats!"

"That's because his stats are based on his limited playing time."

"Ovetsky is better."

A clang of a spatula on a grill followed. "That is the saddest thing I've ever heard."

"Oh yay," Ellery said, hanging their items on the hooks by the back door. "Sports. A perfectly calm topic for the two of you to discuss."

Diego's head popped up from where he was observing Frank gently flipping an egg. "You," Diego said, pointing his finger and wagging it between Ellery and Charley. "You two! I hope you have worked out whatever fight that was the last time you both were here."

"Yeah," Charley said. "About that. We have a friend who is going to be with us today at the diner. He'll stay out of the way, we promise."

Diego's eyes narrowed. "Is it that boy?"

"Which boy?" Charley asked sweetly, tying her apron around her waist.

"The one you call 'hot weird guy.'"

"Funny story."

"No."

"He needed our help."

Diego narrowed his eyes. "He has a bad aura."

"Maybe it's changed?" Ellery offered. "Since the last time you saw him."

Diego's eyes narrowed even further. "Now you believe in auras? What has happened?"

"More than I can even explain," Ellery said with a forced smile. "But just trust us, Diego. You know we wouldn't do anything stupid."

He pointed at Charley. "Her, maybe. But you—" He switched to Ellery. "You, probably not."

Ellery didn't know if making a deal with a familiar counted as stupid, but Diego didn't need to know that part.

"Thank you for the reticent vote of confidence. I'll take it."

"Okay. Fine. He stays out of the way, though. I do not want another scene in my diner."

"Understood."

Charley hurried out of the kitchen. Ellery spied through the small window in the swinging kitchen doors as she let Knox in. He shed his coat and hung it up on the coatrack that no one used. Charley guided him to a booth in the corner, out of the way of the counter, which Ellery admitted could become quite busy at times. Charley handed Knox her phone and her earbuds and showed him how to play games and watch TV if he wanted.

Knox spotted Ellery through the window, reminding them of one of the first times they'd met, and he waved. This time Ellery didn't duck and run away but waved back. Knox smiled brightly, and Ellery's heart stuttered as the tingling of infatuation returned. Ellery did as Zada had said and enjoyed the feeling instead of fighting it. It was weird but not bad.

Diego cleared his throat behind them.

Ellery jumped and ran to the dishwasher. There was a smattering of dishes from the early birds of the day, and Ellery took a breath and got to work.

A few hours later, during their small lunch rush, Ellery was elbow deep in suds when the door peeked open, and Knox tentatively stepped inside. He was definitely not allowed back there, but that didn't stop him from making a beeline toward Ellery, who was curved over the sink. He hopped up on the counter, where the tubs of dirty dishes would be dropped for Ellery to run through Hobart.

"You can't sit there."

"I won't be in here long. I'm bored, though. And I wanted to see you."

Ellery flushed. "Well, it's work. It's not supposed to be fun." They scrubbed at dried egg yolk. "But thanks for the visit."

Knox smiled. "It was fun coming here when I lived with Arabelle. It was one of the things she allowed me to do. And I liked talking to the waitresses."

Ellery used their forearm to wipe the sweat from their brow. They were sure the steam had undone all the effort they'd put into their hair and makeup that morning.

"Was there anything else that you wanted to do when you were here?"

Knox pulled up his leg and rested his chin on his bent knee. His shoe being on the counter was a total health hazard, but Ellery didn't have the heart to tell him to put it down. They'd just wipe it with cleaner once he left.

Knox hummed in thought. "I wanted to sit in a booth, order whatever I wanted, and eat."

Ellery looked up from a sticky plate of syrup. "That's all?"

Knox grinned and nudged his elbow into Ellery's arm. "I also wanted to talk to you."

Ellery blushed wildly. Hopefully Knox would chalk it up to the steam from Hobart. "Really?"

"Yeah." He shrugged. "I wanted to be around people, talk, have fun, eat. I aimed small because it felt attainable."

"More attainable than running away?"

Knox laughed. "Yeah. More attainable. And for the record, out of all the humans that I encountered in my trips to and from the diner, you were the one I noticed the most." He smiled softly.

Ellery dropped a plate in the sink. It fell with a plop and a splash. A clump of suds hit their cheek, right below their eye, and slowly slid down to their chin.

Knox chuckled. "May I?"

"What?"

"Here." Knox slid his fingers along Ellery's jaw, skin smooth, touch gentle. Ellery's breath caught, and every atom of their body froze, as Knox swiped the suds away with his thumb. The soft brush of it sent a shiver down Ellery's spine. Knox gazed at them intently and tucked a strand of Ellery's hair behind their ear, fingers light and quick on the shell, before trailing down Ellery's neck, goosebumps blooming in his wake.

Knox's lips parted. Then he pulled away and wiped the excess suds on the hem of Ellery's apron. "There," he said, voice thick.

Every nerve where Knox had touched was alight, sending sparks right to Ellery's brain, and their whole body went hot. "Thanks," they said, whispery and breathless.

"You're welcome." He looked away, hands gripping the shelf beneath him. "You know," he continued, soft smile playing at the corners of his mouth, "when I ran that night, I didn't plan to run to the diner. It just happened." He swung his leg. "I'm glad it was you I ran into."

Hope flickered in Ellery's chest. "Really?"

"Yes. If I was going to be able to stay here, I needed a human to make a deal with. So it was lucky I ran into you. Someone who had already noticed me." Knox smiled, then winked.

And oh. The frisson between them suddenly disappeared, popped like one of the soap bubbles in the sink. Ellery's heart sank like a stone and settled in their gut. Knox needed a human. *Any* human. But he had happened into one with a crush, one who could be manipulated with a flirty wink. How lucky for him indeed.

Ellery pressed their lips into a thin line and went back to the dishes, scrubbing vigorously at a spatula, shoulders hunched. The atmosphere had soured.

Knox noticed the change in mood immediately. He dropped his leg. "What? Did I say something wrong?"

Luckily, Charley barged into the kitchen. "Knox!" she said, and Ellery winced, certain she was about to berate him for the way he was sitting. She hurried over. "There is a girl here who is short, and she ordered a salad with everything in it. And no dressing. I think she's someone like you."

Ellery's body sagged. "Charley, just because a girl is short and probably vegan doesn't mean—"

"She has a hat pulled over her ears. And she's unfairly pretty. Like, really pretty. Like Knox–level of pretty. Oh, and her eyes are a deep green."

"Your eyes are green."

"I don't eat salad without dressing. Hello."

Knox blinked. "I'll go see." He placed a hand on Ellery's shoulder and squeezed.

He jumped down and followed Charley through the kitchen doors into the dining room. Once they were out of the way, Ellery ran over and peered through the window.

And oh. Charley was right. The girl was beautiful. She sat at the counter, and when Knox approached, she grinned brightly and offered the seat next to her. He settled in and they talked. Ellery couldn't hear what they were saying, but there was no awkwardness in their body language. She lightly touched Knox's forearm, her fingers curling over the skin of his bony wrist, purple sparkly fingernails flashing in the sunlight. He smiled at her in return and patted her hand. She ducked her head, grinning, cheeks round and dusty pink like ripe apples. Ellery's gut churned.

"You're right," Diego said from over Ellery's shoulder.

Ellery jumped. "Would you stop sneaking up on me?"

"Sorry. But it's true. His aura has changed."

"It has?"

"Before, it was shadowed. I interpreted it as him having bad motives. But I think he was sad or lonely. Now his aura is bright. Not as bright as Charley's, but brighter than before."

Ellery licked their dry lips. "What about mine?"

"Right now, yours is very green." Diego chuckled.

Ellery scowled. "That's not funny."

Charley appeared in the pass-through and grabbed the big bowl of salad Frank had prepared. She gave Ellery a thumbs-up, and Ellery's heart sank. Charley placed the bowl in front of the girl, who said thanks with a high, sweet voice, the words shaped by her lush cherry lips. Even Charley gave heart eyes in return.

Ellery pushed away and shuffled back over to the sink, shoving down the flare of jealousy that threatened to overwhelm them. And oh, Zada was wrong. Having a crush wasn't fun at all. Not when it was probably one-sided and not when it was being used against them for a bargain.

The door swung open again, and Charley breezed through and quickly crossed to the sink.

"Her name is Aubri. She's a pixie," she whispered. "Kind of. Her mother is a pixie, and her dad is a human. And they fell in love, but she was raised mostly human, so she has no information on Knox's queen, even though she's kind of from the same family because of her connection to the earth and forest, which is kind of part of the harvest."

"Okay."

"But she's really nice. She's like you too, because she had to leave the little garden home her family had on the outskirts of the city because of the winter."

"Great."

"And she—"

"I don't really care. She doesn't have information on the goddess, so whatever."

Charley blinked. "Oh." She furrowed her brow. "Ohhhhh."

"What?"

"You really like him, don't you?"

"I already talked with Zada, so I'm sure you know everything."

"Contrary to your belief, Zada doesn't spill all her secrets. She's certainly not told me what you two talked about in the bathroom this morning. But I can guess."

Ellery sighed and kept their gaze glued on the suds lazily floating in the water. "I like him," they whispered.

"I gathered," Charley said. Ellery was grateful there wasn't any judgment or pity in her tone. "And based on what I walked in on earlier, I think he may like you too."

"He doesn't." Saying it out loud stung, made it more real, made the loneliness Ellery felt twist a little sharper. They blinked back tears. "I didn't tell Zada everything."

"You didn't?"

Ellery shook their head. "No."

"Ellery, you can tell me. I'm not just your cousin, I'm your friend. And there's nothing that will shock me. I promise."

Ellery stripped off their rubber gloves and dropped them next to the sink. They crossed the room and fished around in the pocket of their hoodie hanging by the door and found the small, rolled-up scroll. They clutched it in their hand.

"Remember when we woke you up that night?"

"Somewhat. I was basically asleep. But I saw how close you two were, and you were whispering like you were doing something you probably shouldn't. It was cute."

"Yeah, well, you're not totally wrong." Ellery passed Charley the scroll.

Head tilted to the side, she unrolled the receipt. "Why is this golden? And humming? And is that blood?"

"He needed a human. And I needed information."

Charley snapped her head up, eyes wide. "I take back what I said. I'm shocked. What the goddess have you done?"

"I made a deal."

"*This* is the compromise? You didn't give up your soul, did you?" Charley asked harshly, gaze quickly scanning over the words. She made a face at the two drops of blood. "Please tell me you didn't use the pen from my apron for this."

"We washed it off," Ellery muttered.

Charley gagged.

"Anyway. No. I didn't sell my soul, but . . . I know he's acting like he likes me. But he doesn't. He needs me. That's all. He wants to stay here and play at being human for a little while because his queen ignored him and hurt him. So he needed a human to make a deal with. And that's who I am. That's what I've done."

Charley's jaw clenched. Her face went red. Her nose flared. "Why?" She bit out the word.

Ellery swallowed. "We need information on how to stop the winter. He could give that to us. We could save the city. We could save my family's farm."

Charley pinched the bridge of her nose. "You have to stop taking on other people's problems, El."

Ellery flinched. That was not what they were expecting. They knew Charley would be upset, which she was—but about doing something foolish, about entering a contract with a supernatural being they barely knew. Not trying to . . . save the world. "What?"

"This is classic Ellery. You take on your parents' problems and come to the city to make money to send home. You defended Knox in the alleyway when you should've run."

"Leaving home was as much for me as it was for them."

"Bullshit. If it had been for you, you wouldn't be in this diner working right now, and you wouldn't be sending half your paycheck back to the farm. You'd be traipsing through a city holding hands with a cute boy or girl. Maybe even the boy who is currently chatting with a pixie." She squinted at the scroll. "And now you're trying to end a supernatural winter? Why do you always have to be the self-sacrificing hero?"

"I don't."

"You literally do! Ever since you were a kid. I don't get it."

Ellery crossed their arms. "So? Someone had to do something. If not me, then who? This is a singular opportunity. I had to take it."

Charley closed her eyes. "In this instance, you're right. I just wish you would lean on people a little more. On your parents. On me. On Zada."

"I do."

Charley opened her eyes and frowned. "You ride your bike in the snow instead of using the bus pass because you know Zada pays for each trip. And you don't like it when she drives because it uses gas. You won't even consider letting us find a bigger apartment so you can have your own room at the risk that it would cost more. And the part of your paycheck you don't send home, you hand to me for a bed in the living room, when I've told you over and over you don't have to." She placed her hands on her hips. "It's okay to need a little help sometimes, El. You don't have to do everything alone."

Ellery crossed their arms over their chest. "Fine. What do I do about the bargain?"

Charley stared at the contract. She grunted as she tried to tear it, but then gave up on the third try when it wouldn't budge. "I guess it won't get destroyed if I put it in the oven or drop it in the sink?"

Ellery shook their head. "No."

"Well, I don't know what to do. This is not in the cousin handbook." She twisted the paper one more time, and it immediately bounced back to pristine condition. She glared at it. "I guess you'll have to see it through and do what you can."

"And what about . . . Knox?"

"What did Zada say?"

"To enjoy it?"

"She's so smart. One of the many reasons I love her. Normally I'd agree with her, but Ellery, this story"—she held up the scroll—"has 'star-crossed lovers' written all over it. It's going to hurt. So I guess it's up to you whether you enjoy the ride or if you jump off before it can get going." She handed the contract over. "I don't envy you, kid."

Ellery took back the paper and shoved it in their pocket. "I don't envy me either."

The kitchen doors swung inward. Knox barreled through, and his expression lit up at spying Ellery and Charley.

"Aubri had to go home, but she said she'd ask her mother if she's heard anything from the queen. She gave me her number to contact her and follow up."

"I'm sure she did," Charley said with a put-upon sigh. "Come on, Knox. Let's use some of that charm to earn some tips."

"Oh, okay."

Charley put her arm around Knox's shoulders and turned him back out of the kitchen. Ellery was grateful for Charley's intervention. They had a lot to mull over and didn't think they could concentrate in the face of Knox's . . . everything.

Charley was right, though. They had a choice to make. Either hurt now or hurt later, and honestly, Ellery wasn't keen on either option.

They slid their work gloves back on and faced the mounting pile of dirty dishes. At least this was something they knew how to fix. With a sigh, they went back to work.

13

KNOX

KNOX HAD NEVER BEEN HAPPIER.

With the three humans having to either work or study, his list of fun human experiences was placed on hold for a few days, but that didn't bother him at all. He went with Charley and Ellery to the diner and helped Charley make tips. After work, Zada had tried to teach him how to cook, and when he'd burned the food, their group had tromped to an all-night noodle restaurant and laughed at how red their faces turned when they ate the spicy ones. At night, they played games, and Knox delighted in Ellery's blush when their hands touched as they swapped cards, or when they squished together on the couch, Ellery's body a comforting heat along his side as they watched TV.

He grocery-shopped with Charley, met a nice dryad in the produce aisle, and endured Charley's squeals when she found out she'd been right. The dryad had no information about Knox's queen, but they were proof that Knox's hypothesis had been correct—that they might encounter other supernatural beings as they traveled around the city.

But his favorite time was when Charley and Zada went to bed, and it was only him and Ellery and their whispered conversations. Sometimes it was nothing more than a raspy "good night" or "see you in the morning." But other nights, it was long meandering chats recounting their day: how Charley had laughed until soda shot out of her nose, or how Zada had used all the salt on the line by the door and didn't have any for her recipe, or how the neighbors' cat had gotten out and allowed Knox to pet her. He loved how Ellery's drowsy voice was quiet, words softly slurring as they drifted toward slumber, until they fell asleep between one sentence and the next.

Knox imagined this was what it would be like to have a family, to be a part of a unit, and he reveled in it. He loved lying on the lumpy couch at night, listening to the comforting rhythm of Ellery's deep, even breaths and the occasional cute snort. He loved being part of the bustle of the morning. And he loved helping when he could, using his magic to tidy up or warm the living room on the nights the heater sputtered.

And though it wasn't some grand adventure, it was domestic, and intimate, and lovely. With the bargain sealed in blood, he didn't worry quite so much about the shades. And it was the first time in a long time that he could just exist on his own terms: his magic a quiet hum for him to use at his own discretion, his return to the Other World a distant future, while he fell deeper in love with humanity, especially the three humans that were closest to him.

Before he knew it, a week had passed since he'd met Ellery in the dark alleyway.

At the end of another day at the diner, which had included another visit with Aubri while she ate lunch, Knox lounged on a stool by the counter, propping his elbows behind him while he gently spun on the seat.

"Closing time," Charley announced as the last customer of the evening left the restaurant. She quickly locked the door and turned over the sign. "Time to clean up."

Diego, Frank, and Marisol had all left about thirty minutes prior, when the last order had been filled. So it was just the three of them in the diner, and as Charley pulled the shades and switched off the outside light, Ellery emerged from the back.

They appeared tired. Their apron was covered with stains and suds. Their eyes were red, and Knox couldn't tell if it was due to exhaustion, or if they had been crying. He didn't like the thought of either.

"Here, let me help," he said as Charley hauled out a tub of cleaning supplies. "Wipe down the counters first, right?"

"We'll do it," Ellery said, shuffling toward the cleaners, stifling a yawn as they waved away the offer. "It won't take long."

Knox paused. "I'd like to help."

"You've helped enough," Ellery grumbled.

"What does that mean?"

"It means," Charley said, cutting off Ellery's response, "you can take out the trash!" She beamed. "Gather up all the bags from the cans and bring them to the dumpsters in the alley."

Knox gathered the garbage as Charley and Ellery wiped down the tables to the soundtrack of Charley's bad singing. Once he had all the bags, he exited the back door, the tingle of the horseshoe overhead reminding him that once he exited, he'd have to walk to the front to enter the diner again.

Ellery confused him. There were times when he felt they had an understanding, and others when he felt he had no clue about them at all. He thought they'd shared a moment in the kitchen a few days ago, a moment where he'd touched Ellery's skin and thought about the last line he'd written on his list of human experiences. He'd thought they'd grown closer since their whispered conversation in the middle of the night, since their deal signed in blood, since their fun day of sightseeing. But maybe he was wrong. Humans were puzzling. And Knox wasn't used to dealing with so many emotions.

Lost in thought, Knox tossed the bags in the dumpster. A few leaves of wilted lettuce were dislodged and fell. They were caught by a sudden cool breeze that swept through the back street and stirred into a small whirlwind before settling on a pile of slush. At the same moment, the moon hid behind a cloud, and the streetlamp at the mouth of the alley winked out.

Knox dusted his hands, happy with his job well done. He turned to head back toward the diner entrance and found himself face-to-face with the shades. A whisper of cold slid down Knox's spine, and he cursed himself for not recognizing the signs of their presence. He'd been too wrapped up in his thoughts. But at least he had the protection of the bargain he'd struck.

"Knox," the leader said.

Knox raised his hands. "You can't take me. I've made a deal."

"We know," another said, drawing out the vowel. "You've been busy."

Knox blinked. "So have you. What do you want?"

They surrounded him, blocking his exit. While they couldn't forcibly take him now, thanks to the scroll signed in blood currently in Ellery's pocket, he'd learned through their last encounter that they had tricks up their sleeves. But so did he. He lifted his palms, and light like firecracker sparks popped from his fingers.

"You should also know that with my new deal, I regained my magic."

"We're not here for you."

They floated a few inches off the ground. Their cloaks absorbed the scant light, tattered hems scraping along the asphalt. Their red eyes were bright glowing coals in the blank, dark ovals of their faces.

"Why are you here, then?" he said, lowering his hands and snuffing out the light. His magic pulsed in his chest along with his heartbeat, a rhythm of warmth in the face of their cold.

They exchanged a glance. "To bring you the information you seek."

Knox raised a wary eyebrow. He didn't trust them. But they'd cut off his escape routes, and he wasn't sure what they would do to him if he angered them.

"What information?"

"The human wants to know why the queen has forsaken this land, why she has not answered the calls to end the suffering of the humans, why the winter has not changed to the spring, as it should have years ago."

Knox shivered, unnerved with their knowledge, but he dared not to show it. He lifted his chin and nonchalantly examined his perfect nails. "How do you know that is what the human wants?"

They chuckled, an eerie rasping sound, like dead leaves scraping across stone.

"We know the terms of all the bargains made in the name of the queen."

"My bargain wasn't made in her name, but in mine." Knox tapped his chest. "It was *my* bargain. No one else's."

Another laugh sent a shiver through Knox, and his skin crawled. He twitched. Every cell in his body screamed to run, to get away, but he stayed frozen and faced them, curiosity and necessity overriding his fear.

"It was signed in your blood. You are her creation, as are we. We feel all and know all that pertains to the crossroads."

"Great." He crossed his arms. "So what is the cost of this information?"

The leader stepped forward, wrapped a fogged hand around the lapel of Knox's coat. "Where is the vial?"

Knox's heart stuttered, his suspicions confirmed. "The vial?"

"The elixir," they said with a sibilant hiss. They shook Knox in their grip and lifted him, his toes barely in contact with the ground.

"I don't have it."

"It was in your possession that night with the nymph."

Knox's lips pulled into a smirk. "Well, you have me there. But don't worry. It's safe. And I'll present it to the queen when I deem it's time for me to return to the Other World. She can determine what to do with it, because, as you said, it shouldn't be in human hands."

"*We* want the potion, you fool." The second shade closed in on him. They grabbed Knox, wrapping smoky fingers around his bare arm. His skin stung with their frozen touch, and Knox shuddered. He was impervious to the weather of the human realm, but not to the effects of the supernatural, and the chill soaked into his skin.

"Why do you want it? It's a potion of . . ." He trailed off. It was a potion of life. The shades were not alive. They were not like Knox, able to flit between worlds and live as a human. They were denizens of the Other World and could cross the barrier, but they could not remain as he could. They were not alive as he was. Knox furrowed his brow. "Wait. You . . ." He licked his lips. "You, what? Want to be human? You're immortal. Why the hell would you want to be human?"

"We have watched for centuries as you have lived several lives, enjoying the human realm and our home in equal measure. You and your siblings are the unique creations of our queen, her favorites, her children who exist in both worlds."

Knox scoffed. He was obviously not her favorite. She had *abandoned* him. "And you want that?"

"We want *life*."

Knox blinked. "You tricked Arabelle."

"We did not deceive the witch," the third said, voice harsh and grating. "She did not read the fine print."

"But that's what you did. You gave Arabelle what she wanted because it was going to benefit you. Not her. And when you came to take the payment, you were hoping the elixir would work for the three of you."

"She was a means to an end."

"And for what?" he demanded. "What is your plan? The queen is a goddess. You'll still be under her command."

"We will be human. The human realm is neutral territory."

Oh. They were right. The human realm was not ruled by the major three, in the eyes of the gods. She ruled the Other World. The sky god ruled the Clouds. The water goddess ruled the Oceans. But *earth* was ruled by humans. The powers and presence of the gods and minor deities could impact the human realm, but they were not meant to rule.

Knox let out a laugh that sounded slightly unhinged, even to him. "And your endgame is to live as humans? It's not all peaches in this realm, you know. Life is hard. There are all these laws and social norms, and you'll need money and—"

They snickered in return. "Do you think we haven't been planning this for centuries? We do not intend to live as normal humans, like those you have cavorted with."

Okay, that sounded ominous. "So, what? You're going to *rule*? That's against the natural order of everything."

"Enough! We do not need to reveal our plans to you. Where is it?"

"Like I said. It's not here." Knox thought about the vial tucked safely away. "Wait, you went back to Arabelle's apartment after I ran, didn't you? You drank the dregs that were in the cauldron." He snapped his fingers. "That's why you were different last time. Why you could do the things you could. When you couldn't recover the vial at first, you drank the unfinished mixture."

The shade slammed Knox against the side of the dumpster. "It was not enough. We are suffering, Knox. Crossing the barrier causes us pain. Being in the human realm causes us pain. We need the vial with the full potion, or we will be trapped in a half-life."

"That does sound like a problem," Knox said, reaching up to rub the back of his head where it had connected with the side. "But it's not mine."

The shade pressed in, the void where its face should be close to Knox's; their breath was so cold, it burned against Knox's cheek.

"It's your fault," they said.

The others chuckled.

Knox's throat went tight. "What do you mean?"

"When we gifted you to the witch, we closed the crossroads. We sealed this region from the queen's sight to keep the details of our plan from her."

"What? How?" Knox demanded.

"Our tricks are our own, familiar. But we have always controlled the crossroads."

"We knew we would be safe for several years."

"Time matters not to a goddess."

Knox squirmed in their grasp. "You knew Arabelle would be able to figure it out before the queen noticed."

"She was smart and powerful."

"More so than the others who came before her."

Knox's stomach dropped. His world spun with the new information. He took a shuddering breath. "If I had returned . . ."

"Everything would have been restored to normal for the humans, and the area would be free of this winter. The queen would see again, but only after we'd drunk the potion and freed ourselves."

There was a pause, then the other spoke. "But you ran."

"And the winter continues."

Knox's knees went weak. "I didn't know."

"Did you not think it more than a coincidence that this winter has lasted five years, and you have been here for that same amount of time?"

Knox's thoughts whirred. That couldn't be true. Could it? Was it his fault? "The queen hasn't called for me," he whispered.

"Because she cannot."

Knox sucked in a harsh breath. She hadn't abandoned him? She just couldn't reach him?

"That will not change until you give us the potion and you return home."

"Until then, this winter will continue."

"And your human friends will suffer."

"I . . . I can't," Knox stuttered. His throat was tight, his tongue clumsy around the words. "I made a deal."

"And now you can fulfill your end of the bargain. Tell the human the reason for this winter and how to end it. And the terms will be met."

"When I return . . ."

"We will take the elixir."

"And you will forget."

The shade released him. His legs gave out, and he fell forward onto his knees, catching his body with his palms. He heaved, his back arching, bile burning his mouth.

"We suggest you do not wait much longer."

"We are not patient."

"There are other ways to break a contract."

Knox snapped his head up. "You wouldn't."

"Do not test us further."

They floated away from him and melted into the darkness. The clouds covering the moon receded. The streetlight flickered back to life. The unyielding cold seeped from Knox's body.

But the guilt remained. He was the reason for this winter. He was the reason Ellery had been forced to leave their home. The reason their life had been difficult the past few years, the reason they'd lost their childhood. And oh, Knox's heart *hurt*. Like those few hours he'd been human, when his magic had been snuffed out by a being that was half life and half death, and he could feel the hurt and the hunger and the exhaustion of the human body. His heart felt like that now; each beat of it sent a shock wave through his frame. His stomach knotted, his arms trembled, and it took every ounce of willpower for him to push upright, to stumble on shaky knees to standing and lean against the alley wall.

He was the reason.

He tilted his head back, swallowed down the tears and the remorse. He'd initially run because he had been afraid of what the queen's absence had meant. But he'd also been selfish. Then he'd thought he'd been forgotten. But that wasn't true either. The queen might not even know something was wrong. She might not even realize that he had not returned. Or what if she had? A different fear settled in his stomach at the thought. What if he returned and she thought him truant?

He could go now, though. Take the elixir, return through the tree at the crossroads, and run to her with the vial. But as soon as he crossed the barrier, his memories of the humans here would be lost, and the shades would be waiting. And what were their plans for the human realm?

They could not be trusted.

There were too many variables.

And he could not tell Ellery. He would not tell Ellery. If they knew *he* was the reason for the winter, they'd hate him. He'd lose the only friends he had. And besides, he didn't want to ensnare them in this mess more than he already had.

No. This was a burden he'd have to shoulder alone. For now. Until he could figure out a way to thwart the shades and remember everything once he crossed the barrier. He wanted to *remember*. Until he had a plan, he'd have to continue playing human. And, well, that piece wouldn't be such a hardship since it meant more time with Ellery, Charley, and Zada.

"Knox!"

Knox shook his head and pushed away from the wall. He pulled down his sleeves, hiding the deep red-and-blue mark where the shade had gripped his skin. He took a steadying breath and centered himself, fought to control the shaking in his limbs. Once he was composed, he walked to the mouth of the alley.

Ellery and Charley waited for him, all bundled in their heavy jackets and scarves.

"What happened? We thought you disappeared," Charley said, looping her arm through the crook of his elbow.

He did his best to hide his wince. Ellery studied him with a frown, and he hoped that they couldn't see how shaken he was.

"Funny story. I slipped."

"Oh, are you okay?"

"I'm fine."

"Good. Ellery thought you might have run off with Aubri."

"I did not!" Ellery protested quickly. "That is not true. I was worried that something bad had happened again, like the *shades*. You know, scary shrouded figures with no faces and cinders for eyes and devastatingly frigid hands?"

Knox waved the concern away. "The shades? They can't do anything to me."

"Because of your deal?" Charley asked sweetly. "That you signed in blood? With *my* pen?"

"I told her," Ellery muttered.

"Oh," Knox said. "Well. Yes. Anyway, everything's all locked up? We're good to leave?"

Ellery narrowed their eyes. "Yes. Zada is on her way. Are you sure you're okay?"

"Why wouldn't I be?" Knox asked with a wink. "I just took out the trash. You do that all the time, right?"

Ellery didn't look convinced. "Okay."

Knox gave them his brightest smile. He hoped it worked. He rubbed his hands together. "Now, let's talk about my next fun idea."

Charley bounced in place. Ellery groaned playfully.

"I'm thinking," he said with his brightest tone of voice, attempting to mask the aftereffects of his encounter, "that I'd like to experience the raucous enthusiasm of a sports match."

Ellery's next groan was sincere.

Later that night, once everyone was asleep, Knox took the vial from where he'd hidden it in the curio cabinet and held it in his palm. Its contents swirled like a tempest. It was now the singular most important object that Knox possessed. The key to *everything*.

The potion could not fall into mortal hands. But he couldn't allow the shades to have it either. He should destroy it. Somehow. Or give it to Lorelei to sink it into the depths of her river. Or ask Bram to fly it to safety in the Clouds.

But . . . it was Knox's only proof of what the shades had done. It was his fail-safe. His only leverage against the shades. The only evidence he'd have to show his queen. When he did return to the Other World, he'd need it to explain his truancy. Would she understand how hurt he'd been by her absence? Would she understand his fear of potentially returning to a home in shambles? Would she understand his need for a connection to others? He hoped she would. He hoped he would be able to explain.

Until then he'd have to keep the elixir close, tucked against his chest, safe from the shades, as he mulled over his options. And if that meant a few more days or weeks of human experiences, of time spent with Ellery, then all the better.

14

ELLERY

FROM KNOX'S ACCOUNTS OF HIS LIFE WITH ARABELLE, HE had spent most of his time on her couch watching teen television dramas. As such, his list of experiences seemed to be heavily influenced by the tropes he found onscreen. Apparently a lot of the shows had at least one episodic arc centered on a homecoming football game or lacrosse match or whatever it was called when people played soccer or baseball, which Ellery found unforgivably repetitive. But due to this penchant for TV show writers to include a sporting event, Ellery would now be forced to endure one.

"It's too cold for most sports, unfortunately," Zada had explained to Knox. "But we do have an amateur ice hockey team, and the games are pretty fun."

Ellery normally really liked Zada, but this was an egregious betrayal, because it led to the four of them walking into a freezing arena to watch the Solis City Yetis slap a hockey puck around with long wooden sticks.

"This is so exciting," Knox said, lowering himself into the hard plastic stadium chair. "We're so close to the ice!"

Zada had indeed outdone herself with the seats. They were only a few rows away from the glass. Which meant they were surrounded by hardcore fans decked out in jerseys and memorabilia. The four of them stuck out in their regular clothes and absolute lack of team spirit.

"Thank one of my professors," she said from the other side of Charley. "He had tickets that he couldn't use."

"How fortunate," Ellery said, squirming in their seat.

"Hey!" Charley leaned over Knox and poked Ellery in the cheek with her finger. "At least pretend to enjoy it. Besides, when was the last time *you* came to a game?"

"Never," Ellery said. "Absolutely never."

To fit as many people as possible into the arena, the seats were squished close. So when Knox turned his head, his golden eyes fixed on Ellery, his knee a warm press against the outside of Ellery's leg, it was a little overwhelming. Ellery did their best to remind themself that Knox only saw them as a means to an end. But in the face of Knox's beauty and his intense attention, it was difficult to remember anything. Except him. Ellery's traitorous heart knocked hard against their ribs.

"You don't like it?" he asked, hands folded in his lap.

Knox's dimmed expression made Ellery feel like an ant at a picnic ruining the fun. "I just don't get it," they said with a shrug. "I'm not a 'rah-rah-yay-team' kind of person."

"Oh." Knox's brow furrowed. He took in Ellery, gaze catching on their scarf and hat and large jacket. "It's cold in here. We can go."

Ellery shot up from their slouch. "Oh. No. No. It's fine. Part of the deal. This is for you."

Knox frowned. "I don't want you to be uncomfortable because of me."

"It's fine!" Ellery said, holding up their gloved hands. "Besides, we could meet another supernatural being here and get information we need, right? This could benefit me as much as it does you."

Knox looked away. "Right. Yes."

Ellery winced. Even though Knox had made it clear that their relationship was transactional, every time Ellery mentioned the contract, Knox's mood changed, and not in a good way.

Well, Ellery could at least try and cheer him up. With a complete lack of grace, they knocked their knee into Knox's playfully and smiled. It was a little bold, a little flirty, very out of Ellery's comfort zone, but why not? "So who could we meet here?"

Knox stared at the contact, a small grin playing around the corners of his mouth. He slid his foot along the sticky concrete and pressed it along Ellery's. "Anyone, really. But I was thinking about gods or goddesses who are related to fortune and luck. Or those who feed off the energy of a crowd."

"Let's hope they're friendly."

The sudden alarm signaling the beginning of the game was almost as jarring as the change in Knox's demeanor. He startled, his attention swinging to the teams who appeared, skating around on the ice. He leaned forward in his seat, eager, as the crowd started cheering.

He didn't move his foot.

"What is *that*?" Knox asked, yelling over the crowd. He pointed to the team's mascot, a tall fuzzy blue-and-white monster with googly eyes.

"That's Zetty the Yeti!" Charley yelled. "She's the chaotic mascot."

"Huh."

"What? Is the mascot a . . ." Charley leaned in. "Is the person in the costume someone like you?"

Knox laughed, boyish and loud. "No," he said, giggling. "Oh my goddess, no, not at all."

Ellery's stomach flipped as Knox leaned hard into Ellery's side and chuckled into their shoulder. "Can you imagine?" he asked. "A god hiding inside that outfit?"

Ellery did try to imagine Bram or Lorelei inside, and that made it all the funnier. They hid their chuckles behind their hand. "Maybe mistakes were made?"

Knox laughed harder. "Maybe," he agreed, straightening.

Once the game began with the face-off at center ice, Ellery found themself watching Knox more than the action between the two teams. Knox's eyes went wide, and he perched enthralled on the edge of his seat, asking Charley questions when the referee blew their whistle and when certain things happened on the ice. During the first fight, where gloves went flying and punches were thrown, Knox was on his feet yelling with the rest of the crowd.

Ellery didn't join, but that didn't mean their heart wasn't pumping fast or that their hands weren't sweaty or that adrenaline wasn't running through their veins. Because Knox was beautiful and enthusiastic, and he glowed as he had fun. He wasn't human, and he was horrible at blending in with the general crowd, but the clear delight on his face and the easy laughter he shared with Charley and Zada were all evidence that he belonged with their little family.

At the end of the first period, Knox dropped in his seat, chest heaving. "This is fun!" he said, turning to Ellery. "Are you having fun?"

"Yeah," Ellery said, and they couldn't help how it came out soft and fond. Because despite the environment and the crowd and the sport that they couldn't care less about, they *were* having fun. Because watching Knox and Charley and Zada have fun was better than any lonely night staying in.

During the break, Zada returned from a trip to the concession stand and passed out nachos, popcorn, and drinks.

And while Ellery itched to ask if Knox had felt or seen anyone who was maybe a god or goddess or being like him, they didn't. They didn't want to spoil Knox's good time and didn't want to see the displeasure or disappointment that passed over Knox's features whenever

Ellery mentioned the bargain. So they sat in the uncomfortable arena chair and watched the ice and the crowd and ate popcorn and watched Knox make faces at the questionable cheese on the nachos.

During the second period, the other team scored.

The guy in front of them in the red jersey jumped to his feet and waved his banner, while the crowd around him, all wearing the white-and-blue of the home team, eyed him with disdain.

"That's what you get for keeping Vanderhook on the bench!" he taunted the crowd around him. "Your coach doesn't know what he's doing, and neither do the players!"

Popcorn rained around him as the crowd threw handfuls. At the chorus of boos, the guy danced and yelled, miming crying by rubbing his eyes. "Boo-hoo! The Yetis suck. But what did you expect from a dying city?"

Knox, who had been watching the exchange with wary amusement, sank back into his chair, a grimace on his face.

Ellery wasn't quite sure what happened next, as their gaze was glued to Knox, but the good-natured jeering became a little more pointed, a little meaner. Suddenly there were more people on their feet, and the yelling was louder, and the proximity of the standoff was much too dangerous The strained atmosphere only grew as the opposing team scored again.

Charley leaned over. "I think we should all go take a break outside and come back once this cools off."

Ellery nodded in agreement and stood. The four of them linked hands, Knox reaching out and taking Ellery's, gloveless and slippery with melted butter from the popcorn they'd been eating. Ellery led the way out of the aisle.

They didn't make it far before the first punch was thrown. The brawl had started on the ice, but now bled into the stands, the tension exploding, and from there chaos descended. People dressed in both red jerseys and blue-and-white joined in throughout the stadium, yelling obscenities, throwing fists and elbows. But most of the crowd had the same idea as Charley, and the aisles flooded with those trying to leave.

"Excuse me," Ellery said as they were jostled as they tried to exit. "Excuse me!"

They were stuck, being pushed down by angry fans who barreled toward the brawl and being pushed up by fans trying to flee. Ellery came face-to-face with a woman who shouted at them with beer-soaked breath before pushing them backward so she could squeeze between the gap in the metal railings and descend.

Knox's grip tightened as Ellery was jarred harshly, feet slipping on the concrete stairs, back knocking hard into Knox's chest. Ellery's body went tight, their breathing thin with panic, as they were squeezed on all sides by the raucous crowd while standing in a precarious position. Thankfully Knox was solid and tall. His breath was hot on the back of Ellery's neck, and when he spoke, his voice was right in Ellery's ear.

"Hold on," he whispered.

Ellery tightened their grip on his hand. He wrapped an arm around Ellery's waist and lifted his upturned palm to where Ellery could see. Then a tingle spread down their spine, and Knox snapped with his fingers.

The crowd, which had been heaving dangerously on the stairs, froze. The commotion stopped on a dime. Where once their path had been blocked and the stairs dangerously packed, the way up was clear.

"Go," he said, his whisper harsh in Ellery's ear, his shoulder nudging Ellery forward.

Ellery didn't need to be told twice. Within a few seconds, the group of them had maneuvered to the safety of the landing. Once they were on flat concrete and out of the way, Knox snapped again.

The commotion and crowd resumed, and the only difference was that the four of them were no longer in the midst of it.

Ellery didn't look back and burst out the door into the concourse area, dragging the train of their friends along. It was significantly less crowded, and once Ellery felt like they were in a spot where they could breathe again, they dropped Knox's hand and whirled around. "What did you do?"

Knox smiled evenly. "I just paused everyone for a moment." He shrugged. "No big deal. They won't even notice."

"That was so cool," Charley said, hands clasped, eyes wide. "Our hero."

Zada eyed the crowd around them. "I think we need to go."

"Why?" Charley asked, leaning into Zada's side, throwing her arm over Zada's shoulders. "You don't think it's going to calm down?"

"Actually, I think it's going to—"

She didn't finish her sentence. A rowdy group emerged from the arena escorted by security, all shouting, all covered in beer and popcorn. Ellery recognized the woman who had shoved them.

The noise of the goal alarm blasted from the door. And another fight erupted between two of the men. The woman then pushed a security guard and broke free of the group, making a break for the exit, passing by right where Ellery stood with Knox. The security guard caught up with her and grabbed her by the shoulders. As she spun, cocking her fist back to punch him, her elbow slammed into the bridge of Knox's nose. Knox made a high-pitched noise and clamped his hand over his face. Blood oozed between his fingers, dripped down the front of his shirt in a concerning gush.

"Oh my goddess!" Charley screeched. She grabbed the arm of the woman and spun her around and jabbed her finger at a stunned Knox's face. "Look what you've done!"

"Let go, princess!" the woman yelled. She shoved Charley hard. Charley staggered; her foot slipped on a hot dog wrapper, and she fell backward into Ellery's arms. Surprised, Ellery couldn't keep their balance, and they fell in a tangle of limbs. Ellery landed hard on the concrete right on their hip, and it was so reminiscent of the night they'd first spoken to Knox, they couldn't help but laugh at the irony.

"Charley!" Zada yelled. She helped Charley to her feet, then they both grabbed Ellery, hauling them upright. "We need to get out of here."

"I agree."

Ellery grabbed Knox's free hand and tugged him through the gathering crowd, following on Charley's heels as Zada pushed her way through to the outside of the arena. Once away from the exit, they paused under one of the streetlamps.

"Knox," Zada said softly. "Are you okay?"

He hadn't made a sound since he'd been clocked. His pupils were uneven, his eyes unfocused. Blood spattered his white T-shirt and stained his hand.

"Let me see," Ellery said. They lightly touched Knox's hand and pried his fingers away from the damage. Blood slid from both nostrils, and it poured down his mouth to his chin. His nose was rapidly swelling, and a darkening bruise had already spread across the bridge, seeping under both eyes. "Shit."

"I'm fine," Knox finally said, voice thick and nasally.

"You're not."

Knox blinked slowly. "What?"

"Okay, you're obviously concussed."

"We need to get him home," Charley said.

"I'm okay," he said again. "It'll be fine. I'll just fix it with my magic, and I'll be fine. Fine. Just fine. Fine." He grinned, blood in his teeth. Ellery shuddered.

Knox's bloody hand sparked.

"No!" they all yelled.

Knox flinched.

"I mean," Ellery said, holding out their hands. "Wait a minute, okay? Why don't we wait until we get to the apartment and make sure you can't accidentally magic something you don't mean to. Or, you know, we could try ice and painkillers. That could work too." Ellery gestured to their own face. "And hey, we'll match."

Knox tilted his head slowly. He raised his hand and booped the tip of Ellery's nose with his finger and giggled. Then he winced. "Okay." He nodded, then winced again.

The walk to find the car in the parking lot was stressful, not just due to a wobbly Knox, whom Ellery kept one hand on at all times, but also the stream of cars and people leaving the game. They finally found the car, and Ellery managed to guide Knox into the back seat. They slid in next to him and stayed close.

Knox blinked slowly, wincing when the bright beams of oncoming headlights shone on the car. At least the blood had slowed to a trickle. Charley found a packet of tissues in the glove compartment and handed them over the seat. Ellery opened them and pressed one in Knox's hand, then guided Knox's hand to his nose to mop up the blood.

"How are you doing?" Ellery asked.

"I'm fine. That was fun."

"Your definition of fun is suspect."

Knox chuckled. "Yeah? What is your definition?"

Ellery shook their head. "Not this."

They remained quiet for the rest of the ride, and once they got back to the apartment, Ellery helped Knox remove his shoes and jacket and tugged him to the couch. Charley and Zada disappeared while Ellery helped make Knox comfortable. The pair returned moments later with a wet washcloth, painkillers, a glass of water, and an ice pack.

"I don't know if these will work on you," Charley said, handing Knox the two small pills. "But it can't hurt."

Knox eyed the pills, then tossed them in his mouth and swallowed them with a gulp of water.

Zada eased Knox back to lay his head on the arm of the couch, pillow propped behind his neck and head tilted slightly back. She carded her hands through his hair, moving the sticky ends of a few strands away from his face. "There. Just relax."

Knox's eyes fluttered shut, his dark eyelashes a sweep across his cheekbones. Ellery sat on the edge of the cushion next to Knox's torso. They took the washcloth and gently, gently cleaned the blood from his face, being careful not to knock into his nose or scrub his skin too hard. It was intimate in a way, even with Charley and Zada right there, and Ellery's face went hot when Knox's breath skirted over Ellery's skin as Ellery dabbed away the evidence of the injury. Once most of the blood was gone from his face, Ellery cleaned the mess on his hands, scrubbing the soft skin between his fingers.

Knox hissed when Zada touched the wrapped ice pack to his face. His jaw went tight, and his fingers clasped around Ellery's, grip tight.

"Sorry!" Zada said. "Sorry. Sorry."

"It's okay," he said, muffled, using his other hand to balance the cold pack on his face. "Thank you."

"Twenty minutes on," Zada said. "Then take it off. I'll set a timer."

"Let us know if you need anything." Charley wrung her hands, her face pale. "Sorry, Knox. We should've known that something would happen. Tensions have been high in the city, and well, it felt like the crowd just needed a release. Sorry it was on your face."

Knox grunted. "It's not your fault. You couldn't have known."

"Are you okay, El?" Zada asked.

Ellery set the washcloth on the coffee table. Their hands trembled with fading adrenaline, and their hip ached from where they'd fallen. "I'm fine."

Zada arched an eyebrow but didn't refute them. "Okay. We're going to bed. But wake us if either of you need anything."

They left the room. Once Knox was settled on the couch, and his grip on Ellery's hand had eased, Ellery went back to the hallway and stripped out of their coat and kicked off their shoes. They reached into the pocket, where they kept the acorn, and found it had cracked in half. They held it in their palm. The acorn had been crushed when Ellery fell, and the wire had snapped. It was ruined.

"Ellery," Knox whispered from the couch.

Ellery shoved the remains of the charm back into their pocket. They'd deal with it later. Knox needed their attention right now. They rubbed their palms on their jeans, brushing off the acorn crumbs, then ran back over to the couch.

"Yeah?"

"You never answered."

"Answered what?"

"Your definition of fun."

Ellery sank onto the cushion near Knox's stretched legs. His eyes were shut. His voice was slightly slurred. "I don't know."

"You don't know?"

Ellery stared at Knox's face—the pained wrinkles in his forehead, a small smear of blood near his chin—and took a slow breath. "When I was a kid . . . before . . . I liked to ride my bike along the farm road. And I liked fishing in the stream behind our house. I liked taking care of the barn cat. I also liked going to movies and playing video games."

"What kind of movies?"

"Horror, if you can believe it."

Knox laughed, a raspy exhausted sound. "I do. Kind of."

"Well, you should. Horror movies are fun. And they're safe in a weird way. Like, you can be scared but also know that it's just a movie and that usually someone prevails in the end. I was a connoisseur. I had a whole collection." Ellery cleared their throat. "It's apparently much safer than hockey games or, you know, swinging a pipe around an alley and beating up inhabitants of the Other World."

Knox snorted. Then winced. "Ow," he said softly, then carried on. "That makes sense."

Ellery lightly placed their hand in Knox's, sliding their fingers into his. "Are you okay?"

"It hurts," he said. "Things are . . . blurry. Swimmy?" he said. "Is that a word?"

"You're probably a little dazed."

"Once the world stops spinning, I'll use my magic and I'll be fine."

"That sounds like a good plan."

There was a moment of silence between them. And Ellery wasn't quite sure what to do besides sit and hold Knox's hand and think about how weird the whole night had been.

"I'm sorry," Knox said into the silence.

"You didn't do anything wrong. That woman shouldn't have punched the security guard."

Knox grimaced. "Not about that."

"About what, then?"

"A secret," he answered, subdued. His free hand rested on his abdomen, and he stretched out his fingers, then curled them into the bloody fabric of his shirt. "I have a secret."

Oh. Ellery's whole body stilled, except for the suddenly cold thrum of their blood in their veins. Knox was obviously in pain, and hurt, and not quite with it. It wouldn't be fair to push, despite Ellery's internal panic. "That's okay. You can keep your secret."

"You won't like me when you know. And I want you to like me."

"Because you need me for the bargain? It's been signed in blood. I think it's a solid contract."

Knox's brow furrowed. "No. Not about the bargain. I want you to like me. You're cute. Special. Brave. I like you."

Ellery's eyebrows shot up. Their breath left them in an audible whoosh. "You like me? I thought you liked Aubri?"

"Aubri?" Knox scrunched his nose, then pouted. "Who is Aubri?"

"The pixie."

Knox slid down on the pillow and sighed. "Oh. No." He ran his thumb over the back of Ellery's hand. "Can we do your version of fun?"

"We don't have to."

Knox stuck out his bottom lip. "But I want to. Please?"

"Oh." Ellery's heart fluttered. "Yeah. That would be . . . fun."

"Good." Knox opened his eyes, steadied the ice pack, and squirmed until he sat up. "That's the point."

"What? Now?"

Knox blinked several times, long eyelashes fluttering, bruises stark against his pale skin. He swung his legs, and Ellery had to jump out of the way so as not to be kicked. He settled his feet on the floor, then slouched down in the middle of the couch until his neck was supported by the back of the cushion and the ice pack was still balanced on his nose.

"Okay," he said with a gasp. "There. Ready."

"To do what?"

"Watch a horror movie."

"You're ridiculous. You've been clocked in the face. Your nose is probably broken, you definitely have a concussion, and you want to watch a horror movie?"

"Yes."

Incredulous laughter bubbled out of Ellery's mouth. They ducked their head. "Okay. Who am I to argue? But first, snacks. Any preferences?"

"Nothing that takes effort to eat."

That made a strange kind of sense. Ellery searched the cabinets and refrigerator and found some wrapped cupcakes and package of soft-baked cookies.

On their way back to the couch, Zada's timer went off with a series of beeps.

Knox removed the ice from his face. His cheeks were a mixture of bright red from the cold and blue from the bruises. His nose was swollen, and despite Ellery's efforts, there were still smears of blood around his mouth and cheeks. He looked awful, but then he smiled, bright and lopsided, with his hair sticking up from the couch, and he was the best thing Ellery had ever seen.

Ellery sat next to Knox on the couch, and they flicked through the channels until they found a horror movie that had just started.

"I hope this isn't too frightening," Knox said with a grin. "I don't know if I can handle it."

"We've seen worse. I think we'll be fine."

"Maybe," he said, catching Ellery's hand in his. "As long as you're here, I'm sure I'll be okay."

Ellery's mouth went dry. They were certain that Knox could hear the now thundering of their pulse as he snuggled close. Ellery took a breath and tipped to the side, laying their head on Knox's shoulder. It wasn't quite comfortable, but Ellery reveled in the closeness, the feeling of warmth and companionship.

Knox had said he had a secret, one that might change Ellery's perception of him. But that could wait. It was late. They were safe on the couch watching a bad film, cuddled together. Ellery decided to just enjoy it.

15

ELLERY

ELLERY WOKE UP WITH A STIFF NECK. THEY DIDN'T REMEMBER falling asleep, only the end of the first movie and the beginning of the second and Knox's warm, dry hand clutched in their own. They groaned as they turned their head, eyes fluttering open, to find the spot beside them empty. A smile ghosted across their face as the words *he likes me* ran on loop in an intrusive drumbeat inside their brain.

Stretching their arms upward, they spied Knox on the other side of the couch. His bare back, and the muscles flexing beneath, was on display as he changed out of his bloodied shirt. Ellery's heart quickened at the expanse of pale skin.

Knox shoved the ruined shirt into his bag, then slipped on a clean one. And Ellery could breathe again.

Knox turned and grabbed the journal teetering on the edge of the couch, then jolted when he caught Ellery's gaze.

"Oh," he said. "You're awake."

Ellery yawned, trying to act nonchalant and not at all like they'd just been caught creeping on him. Knox was back to his inhuman self; his nose was no longer purple, and the bruises and the blood from the day before had all disappeared. Ellery couldn't help feeling like their fragile conversation from the previous night was in danger of fading away as quickly as Knox's injuries.

"Yeah, I'm awake. Unfortunately. What time is it?"

The corner of Knox's mouth quirked. "Later than you think. Charley and Zada have already left for the day."

Ellery sat bolt upright. "What?"

"Charley said she'd tell Diego that you were ill after the game last night."

"I hate missing work," Ellery groaned.

Knox frowned. "Because you need the money?"

Ellery stood and scrubbed a hand over their face, wiping the sleep from their eyes. "Yeah. But I also don't want the diner to realize that I am basically superfluous and that they could probably handle what I do with the current staff. Diego did Charley a favor hiring me, and I doubt I could find another job in this economy."

Knox looked away, his hair falling over his eyes, his profile god-like. Ellery tucked their arms around themself.

"I'm sorry," he said sincerely.

"Why? It's not your fault. You didn't cause this winter, and you certainly didn't have to persuade me to stay up late last night watching bad movies."

Knox paled; his lips went bloodless. His long fingers wrapped around the leather-bound spine of the book, and he gripped it tight. "Yeah. Of course."

Ellery bit back a sigh at Knox's abrupt turn of mood. "What's that?" they asked, indicating the book.

"Arabelle's journal," Knox said softly. "I took it the night she . . . died."

"Oh."

"It's mostly her work, but it also has her thoughts and some weird poetry."

And that was something that Ellery hadn't really asked yet: what Arabelle had sold her soul for. "What . . . what was her bargain?"

Knox ran his hand over the cover. "The knowledge of life."

"The what?"

"Arabelle wanted to make a potion that would defeat death. But since that is the realm of the goddess, the shades wouldn't allow her that. So she asked for the knowledge to create a potion that would extend her life until she chose to pass on."

"Wow. That's amazing."

Knox's mouth pinched into a bitter twist. "It is. But the shades came for her as soon as she figured it out."

"So she never had the chance to use it?"

Knox shook his head. "No." He sighed, then returned the book to his bag. "Anyway, enough about that." He rubbed his hands together. "I want to have more fun. Another human experience."

Ellery closed their eyes. "And what is on the agenda for today?"

"A sleepover."

Ellery glanced at the window. "It's, like, ten in the morning."

Knox shrugged. "Yes. Yes, I know. But it's freezing out, and I have noticed that you are not a fan of being outside in the cold. Or anywhere really that's not the apartment."

"You're not wrong."

"Besides, it sounds fun. Staying in for the day. With you." A blush swept across his cheekbones.

Ellery's stomach fluttered. Their whole body went hot. "Okay. That's fine. How do you envision your sleepover?"

Knox grinned. "Movies. Pizza. Ice cream. Doing each other's makeup? Gossiping? A pillow fight?"

Ellery raised a finger. "Movies, pizza, and ice cream are fair game. I'm horrible at makeup; we'd need Zada for that. I have no gossip, as you and Zada and Charley are the only people I know. And you literally had a concussion last night, so a pillow fight is also out. But we can still make it fun."

"Sounds great," Knox said, making jazz hands.

Ellery shook their head and heaved a playful put-upon sigh. They crossed to the kitchen for a glass of water. "I can't believe I get stuck with the familiar who wants to live out every teen drama fantasy," they said as they filled their glass from the tap.

Knox laughed, his eyes crinkling at the corners. "What? I'm technically a teenager."

"You're immortal."

"So? I'm totally a teenager. I even have the weird adolescent impulses."

Ellery choked on their drink, wheezing as the water went down the wrong pipe. They plunked their glass on the counter, coughing, eyes watering. "What?" they managed after a few seconds.

Knox's brow furrowed. "I literally ran away from home. Are you okay? What did you think I meant?"

"Nothing!" Ellery said quickly, mopping up the spilled water. "How about you pick a movie or TV show and we get this party started?"

Ellery disappeared into the hallway and pressed a hand to their thundering heart, mouth open and cheeks flushed. They weren't going to survive this day if Knox kept saying things like that and acting innocent on top of it.

Zada wasn't kidding about this crush business. Ellery's emotions were out of control, but in the wildest, most exhilarating way. A small voice that sounded a lot like Charley reminded Ellery to be careful, that it was called a "crush" for a reason. And, to be fair to the voice, Knox had said something about having a secret last night. But he'd also told Ellery he liked them. And, for once, Ellery wanted to follow Charley's advice to not make other people's problems their own. Whatever the secret Knox had, it wasn't their issue. And instead of worrying about the money they were losing by not working today, Ellery decided they'd enjoy the fact that they had a cute boy who liked them and a rare day off to spend with him. Ellery wanted to bask in the crush. They wanted it so badly.

After Ellery freshened up and changed out of their outfit from the night before into a pair of pajamas—because what else did you wear at a sleepover?—they placed a grocery order that included popcorn and ice cream and all sorts of toppings to go with it. Ellery knew they would be judged for ordering ice cream in the middle of a snow flurry, but well, it'd been snowing for years; there was no way that everyone gave up ice cream just because it was winter.

They went back into the living room and settled by Knox on the couch, feet up on the coffee table. Knox draped a blanket over both of their legs.

"What did you choose?" Ellery asked, hoping their voice came out even and not at all affected by Knox's proximity.

"This scary television show about teen witches, werewolves, and wyverns," Knox said, gesturing toward the screen. "Have you seen it?"

"No, I haven't. But I heard it's good."

Knox grinned as he tapped the play button. "Let's see if they get any of the lore correct."

The groceries arrived during the second episode, and they paused the show to each make massive ice cream sundaes. After the fourth, Ellery ordered their pizza and made a face when Knox advocated for pineapple, but added it to half anyway.

During the fifth episode, with Knox leaning into their side, Ellery had seen enough. They threw up their hands.

"Oh my goddess, don't trust that guy!" they yelled at the screen. "He's trying to lure you into the trap. Why are you believing him?"

Knox huffed in amusement. "You really think he's the bad guy?"

"Of course! All signs point to that dude. He's totally shady."

"But he's been nothing but nice. He's given her no reason not to trust him."

Ellery crossed their arms. "No, but she's naïve to think he doesn't have an ulterior motive. Blind belief only causes problems. And she's just setting herself up to be hurt."

Knox raised his eyebrows. Ellery dropped their hands and scrunched down in the blanket, blushing under Knox's intense attention.

"I mean, maybe."

A character screamed onscreen, but Knox didn't look away from Ellery. "You said your family prays to the goddess, but you didn't believe me when we first met."

Ellery debated pulling the blanket completely over their head. "Belief is difficult for me," they said.

"Why?"

"Because my parents believed, and look where it got them. They prayed and prayed, and their prayers went unanswered. Instead of taking matters into their own hands, they waited for some mystical solution. One that never came. I grew up believing that they knew best because they were the adults, and it hurt when I realized that they *didn't*. That I had to be the pragmatic one."

Knox's jaw clenched. "I'm sorry."

"It's not your fault. You said you ran away. I basically did too. I came here to earn money for my family, but that wasn't the only reason I left. I couldn't handle it all anymore."

"Do you think you'll go back?"

"I don't know. Maybe? Maybe not. It's hard to trust them. It's something that's bled into my other relationships as well."

"With Charley and Zada."

Ellery nodded. "I love them both. And I want to trust them when they tell me that they love me too, and that they want me here, or that it doesn't bother them that I invaded their space. But like I said, it's difficult."

"I understand," Knox said, though he sounded pained. "I know you don't trust me."

Oh. "I believe that you are what you say. And I trust that you'll hold to our bargain."

Knox frowned. "It's signed in blood. I have to follow it."

"I'm sorry," Ellery hastened to add. "It's a me thing. It's not you. I promise. And for the record, I really—"

A knock at the door cut Ellery off, which was fortuitous because Ellery didn't know how to navigate whatever situation would arise from blurting out their feelings. Especially if what Knox had said in his concussed haze the night prior was true—that he liked Ellery in return.

Ellery scrambled off the couch and opened the door to accept the pizza. They brought it over to the table and handed Knox one of the paper plates stacked on top.

"It's fine," Knox said, helping himself to a slice of pineapple pizza. "I understand."

"Do you?"

"You've been hurt by people you loved. It's made you wary. That's nothing to apologize for." He gestured toward the TV. "Just like August refuses to let Manny into the circle yet, because of her cheating ex-boyfriend."

Ellery huffed in amusement. "Yeah. Something like that."

Knox smiled. "Hopefully, though, once you get to know someone, you'll be able to trust them."

Ellery ducked their head. "I'm trying."

"Now," Knox said, settling back onto the couch, "let's see if this other character is really the bad guy as you say."

Within the next few episodes, Ellery was proven wrong: the

character was not the bad guy, but he did wind up dead, and then undead. Sometime during the last few episodes of season one, Zada waltzed into the apartment and stopped short.

"Well, this is a mess," she said, eyeing the pizza box, drink glasses, and empty bowls containing remnants of ice cream, pretzels, and popcorn. "Oh," she said, pointing to the television, "is this that werewolves, witches, and wyverns show? I only made it to episode nine. Which one is this?"

"Eleven, but episode ten was filler," Ellery said.

"Budge over," she said, dropping onto the couch, effectively squishing Ellery closer into Knox's side. Knox was forced to drape his arm over the back of the couch, so Ellery was snug against him. "I can't believe that one guy wasn't the evil one," Zada said, eyes glued to the screen. "Too bad the writers killed him off."

"He's an undead now," Knox offered helpfully. "Episode ten wasn't completely filler."

"Oh, awesome." She jutted her chin at the pizza box. "Do I smell pineapple?"

"Yes."

"Excellent," she said, stealing a slice.

The episode opened with the characters at a loud house party dancing and drinking from red plastic cups, flashing lights bathing them in different colors, fast music overwhelming the speakers.

"That looks fun," Knox said. Ellery didn't miss his wistful tone, and apparently neither did Zada.

"A party?"

"Yes. I don't think I've ever participated in something like that. With humans," he clarified.

Zada hummed in acknowledgment.

That's how Charley found them hours later, the three of them huddled together on the couch, Ellery half asleep on Knox's chest,

Zada curled into Ellery's other side, and Knox with wide eyes watching the final episode of the season.

"What's this?" she asked.

Zada waved her hand and shushed her. "Almost over, babe."

"Is this that dragons show?" she asked, squeezing into the tiny space left on the couch. Ellery grunted as Zada knocked in their side, which forced them to squeeze closer into Knox, which was not such a hardship.

"Wyverns," Knox corrected.

"Oh, I wanted to watch this," she said, settling in.

"Spoilers, babe. This is the last episode."

Charley shrugged. "No worries. I'll watch from the beginning later."

Ellery lifted their head. "You are literally chaos in human form, aren't you?"

Charley beamed. "You're just now realizing?"

Knox and Zada shushed them both as the episode reached its climax. Five minutes later, they all stared at the screen. Knox's mouth hung open.

"That's *it*?"

"They didn't reveal the killer," Zada said in disbelief. She gestured at the screen. "And they left Grant stuck in the cave with Manny, and it's about to be a full moon!"

"And Pala doesn't know their magic won't work against the wyverns and is walking straight into a nest," Knox said. "Ugh." He jabbed the off button on the remote. "Cliffhangers are so disappointing."

"Well," Charley said gently. "I heard it was renewed for a season two. That's good news, right?"

"Unless it's filming right now, it won't air anytime soon," Zada said, bottom lip in a pout, arms crossed over her chest. "And Knox . . ." She trailed off.

Knox's body went taut under Ellery. Ellery peeled themself from where they'd been draped over him.

"Oh," Zada said, hand over her mouth. "I didn't—"

"It's okay," he said with a forced smile. "Anyway, at least the show has given me an idea," he added, rubbing his hands together, "for my next human experience."

Ellery's heart sank, because they already knew. "A party?" they hazarded.

Knox grinned. "A party."

16

ELLERY

THE NEXT MORNING, CHARLEY SWISHED THE REMAINS OF THE almond milk in the carton and frowned as she poured the scant amount in the blender with her pile of fruit. "What kind of party are you thinking, Knox?"

Knox sat up quickly from his sprawl on the couch. "Like the one from the TV show yesterday."

"So, like a frat party," Charley clarified.

Ellery did not like the sound of that, but Knox had indulged their preference for a low-key day at home yesterday. It was only fair to continue checking off items on Knox's list. "Didn't you have enough rowdy adventures at the ice hockey game? There was blood."

Knox blinked. "Is there blood at frat parties?"

"Only the good ones," Charley said, wistfully.

"You need help." Ellery said, deadpan.

"They can get kind of wild," Zada said as she painted her nails at the kitchen table. "But I actually know of a party tonight at one of the frats on campus. They won't mind a few more people squeezing in."

Charley bounced in place. "I haven't been to a party in so long. I would love a night of dancing."

Ellery huffed. "You mean grinding against people on a dance floor to bad music in a public setting."

Charley beamed. "Like I said, dancing."

"Anyway," Ellery said, "Knox said that parties attract supernatural beings for a lot of reasons. We could find some answers tonight, if we play our cards right and don't drink anything out of a sketchy punch bowl."

Knox bit his bottom lip. "The energy of a party would draw attention, and we need someone who has information about my queen. Satyrs are known party lovers, and if there were any in this area, they would definitely show up to one. And satyrs are children of the forest, so they would be a good start."

"Then it's settled," Charley said, hands clasped. "We're going to a party!"

Several hours later, Zada confidently pushed into the frat house. Ellery envied how effortlessly Zada, Charley, and even Knox melded into the crowd.

Even with Zada's help choosing their outfit and applying their makeup, Ellery felt like a child playing dress-up. They wondered if the college kids could tell that Ellery hadn't even finished high school. When no one stopped them at the door, they let out a grateful exhale.

"Anything?" Charley leaned over and asked Knox while they took off their jackets in the entryway, adding them to the pile on a table by the door.

He shook his head. "Not yet. But the night is still young."

"If you're a vampire," Ellery muttered.

Charley snorted. "It's not even that late. And I thought you said there was no such thing as vampires."

"Yeah, well, things have changed since I said that."

"Anyway," Zada said, fixing her braids. "Our mission is twofold. Look for supernatural beings and have fun. Knox, keep an eye out for your . . . friends. And for all of us, don't drink from anything that you didn't pour or open yourself. And don't accept any candy that looks strange."

"And in case we get separated, we'll plan to meet back here in an hour to check in." Charley pointed a finger in Knox's face, then Ellery's. "Don't forget and don't be late."

Knox nodded seriously. Ellery checked their phone and set a timer to vibrate in their pocket.

"Okay," Zada said, slipping her phone into the back pocket of her tight jeans. "Into the fray."

The beat of the music pulsed through Ellery's sternum. They could feel the thump of it in the soles of their feet, reverberating through their bones. It was everything Ellery hated, but Knox stared eagerly at the dance floor, smile wide and bright. Ellery sighed and resolved to try and enjoy, well, whatever this turned out to be.

The room was packed to the brim with people. The air was humid with body heat and smelled of perfume and cologne and bad decisions. As they followed Zada and Charley through the chaos to the living room, Ellery squeezed themself inward as far as they humanly could to avoid bumping their shoulders and elbows into anyone. They didn't need a repeat of the hockey game.

All the furniture had been pushed against the walls to create a makeshift dance floor. A disco ball hung from the lighting fixture above them. And a crowd of people danced and jumped to the music, yelling along to some grating pop song, their drinks sloshing everywhere.

Charley squealed and immediately jumped into the madness of the dance floor. Zada followed, laughing, and soon they were swallowed by the crowd.

Ellery sighed.

"You okay?" Knox asked over the music.

Ellery forced a smile. "I'm great."

"You're lying."

"Yes. I am. But don't mind me. Go dance. I'll find a corner to stand in and watch."

Knox glanced toward the whirl of people dancing with undisguised excitement. Ellery gently pushed his shoulder. "Go. Have fun. I'll be fine. Seriously. Just come find me when you're done."

"Are you sure?"

The sparkling lights of the disco ball swept over Knox's features, highlighting the glitter Zada had swept over his cheeks and the gloss of his lips. Ellery's whole body flushed, and they half contemplated joining him for at least one dance, but they squashed that idea when the music changed and the crowd noise rocketed to an earsplitting level.

"I'm certain."

Knox looked back to the heaving mass. Ellery spotted a flash of Charley's hair in the middle of the mess.

"Go," Ellery said. "Seriously. Have fun, Knox."

Knox grabbed Ellery's hand and squeezed their fingers, giving Ellery his trademark dazzling smile. "Okay. Thank you."

"Just try not to charm everyone. And hey, if you feel any of your friends, let us know!"

Knox exhaled loudly and ran a hand through his hair. "Right. Yes. I will." He pointed at Ellery. "See you in an hour."

And with an excited grin, Knox stepped into the crowd and was immediately swept into the mayhem of jumping bodies. Ellery couldn't even feel mad about it, seeing him join Charley and Zada in whatever the hell they were doing with their limbs.

Feeling lost, Ellery made their way to the kitchen and filled a red plastic cup with soda from a bottle and squeezed their way back into the living room. They found an empty window ledge that, after a quick test, seemed sturdy enough to support their weight. They perched on it and took in the party. A couple made out in a nearby dark corner while a few people gamely tried to carry on a conversation on the couch pushed against the wall. Ellery inadvertently caught a few stray words and winced when they realized it was more of an argument than a conversation and that two friends were likely breaking up over a third.

Ellery turned their attention to the dance floor and couldn't help but giggle when they saw Knox flailing along with the song, laughing with Charley and Zada. A burst of absolute fondness swelled within Ellery at the sight, and they couldn't stop the smile that broke forth even if they tried. But they didn't want to stop it. They enjoyed it, the fluttering in their middle, the affection that warmed them from their core. It was ridiculous to feel this much for three awkward people, but Ellery did, and they almost abandoned their drink and joined them. But a group of other partygoers, who had undoubtedly been pulled into Knox's orbit by the gravity of his charm, attached themselves to the trio, and Ellery stayed where they were. Their fingers curled around the red cup, the plastic dimpling and crinkling under their fingertips. Ellery couldn't begrudge the people who had become star-struck by Knox's presence one bit. They knew the feeling.

They took a sip of their drink, content to sit there and enjoy the party in their own way.

"Having fun?" someone asked, sidling up next to Ellery, their arm brushing along Ellery's forearm.

"Huh?" Ellery replied. They tore their gaze from Knox learning a popular social media dance from two guys and looked to their right.

"I asked if you were having fun?"

It was a guy. And he smiled at Ellery, a little shy, with a duck of his head and a tentative hunch of his shoulders. He had bright blue eyes and blond hair that hung in his face, and he held an identical cup to Ellery's. He was cute, in a non-Knox way. Ellery could tell by the way he fumbled with his drink that he was nervous. They looked over their shoulder to check if someone else was the target of his question, but the only people around were the couple making out in the corner.

"Are you asking me?" Ellery asked, pointing at themself.

"Yeah," he said, scratching the back of his neck. "I saw you across the room and thought I'd come over and say hi because . . ." He trailed off.

"Oh," Ellery said. "Oh." This had not happened before. No one had approached them because, well, Ellery hadn't ever really put themself in a situation to be approached. And it was kind of flattering. But not quite wanted. "Okay. Um. Hi."

"Hi," he echoed. "So are you having fun?"

"Sure, if you count watching my friends make fools of themselves on the dance floor as fun."

He laughed too loudly for the joke. "Does that mean you're here with someone?" He propped his shoulder against the wall and angled his body toward Ellery, partly blocking the room from Ellery's view.

"I'm with them," Ellery said, peering past the guy's ear and gesturing to where Knox jumped in a circle with Zada and Charley to the beat of something fast. "I mean, I'm here with *him*. And my cousin and her girlfriend."

The guy's gaze flickered to Knox.

"You're with him? Or you're *with* him?"

Ellery narrowed their eyes, because ouch. "Um . . . at least one of those. Why?" It came out sharp and offended, a little bitter.

The guy held up his hands. "Hey, no offense intended. I saw you four come in together. I just . . . know what he is and didn't realize they mingled with humans."

Ellery tensed. "You know . . . ?"

"That he's not from around here," the guy said, tilting his head. He made a vague gesture with his hand.

"Not from the college?"

The guy laughed. "No. Not from the college, the city, or the *realm*, for that matter." He leaned in, his breath hot on the shell of Ellery's ear. "Because neither am I." He drew back, his blue eyes glittering.

Oh. *Oh.* This guy, with the perfectly parted blond hair and crystal-blue eyes and flawless skin and a sharp jaw and a knowing, sly smile was supernatural. His gaze was intense, and he reached out and touched Ellery's hand, his long fingers slipping around Ellery's wrist. His fingertips were cool along Ellery's skin, and goosebumps bloomed in the wake of his touch. The pulsing music fuzzed into the background, and the edges of Ellery's vision blurred as Ellery's senses zeroed in on the guy's smile, the white of his teeth and the ruby of his lips. He really was good-looking, and Ellery should be flattered that he had deigned to talk to them, to approach them at all.

Ellery blinked, shook their head, and the commotion of the party roared back into focus. They gently pulled their hand from his grip and took a stumbling step to put distance between them. They felt a little dizzy and they looked down into their cup, but all they could see were the bubbly remnants of their soda.

"Need a refill?" the guy asked.

"Huh?" Ellery lifted their head, met his gaze again, and felt heat surge into their cheeks. "Oh. No. I'm good."

"So, even if you are here with him, can you at least give me your name? Since I basically humiliated myself coming over here to talk to you?" he asked.

"And why did you do that? Come over, I mean."

"Because you're cute," he said with a shrug, as if it was a simple truth. "And I wanted to see if I had a shot. I don't, obviously, but still."

"Oh. Um. I'm Ellery."

He held out his hand. "Nice to meet you, Ellery. I'm Hale."

Ellery shook his hand. His grip was strong, and his skin was cold, like he'd just walked in from outside. Which was probably why Knox hadn't sensed him when they'd first entered the party.

"Nice to meet you. We were hoping to run into someone like you to ask a few questions."

Hale raised his eyebrows. "Really? How fortuitous. What kind of questions?"

"We're trying to find information about the queen of the Other World."

Hale's gaze flickered toward the dance floor. "Huh. Interesting. Well, I have answers if you want them."

Ellery's heart thumped. "You do?"

"Of course." He swirled the contents of his cup, then set it down on a nearby table without taking a drink. "I've met her. I talked to her recently, actually."

Ellery's eyes widened. Knox had been unable to reach her. But if this guy had been successful, maybe he had a way to talk to her. Maybe Knox could send a message. "Seriously?" Ellery licked their lips. "You've talked to her?"

Hale's gaze dropped to Ellery's mouth. "Oh, yeah. And I'll tell you all about it. But the music is so loud in here. It's difficult to converse. Come on. I know a place we can go."

Ellery glanced to the dance floor. They couldn't see Knox now, swallowed up about the bodies. But they caught a glimpse of Charley and Zada. Knox had to be with them.

"Okay. Cool. Let me just get my friends."

"Wait. Friends?" he asked, frowning. He took a step backward. "I didn't sign up for an interrogation."

"Oh. Okay. I'll just grab Knox. He knows the best questions to ask anyway, and—"

"Ellery," he said, his voice deep, almost a command. Ellery felt compelled to look at him, to peer into the depths of his eyes. "This is a one-time offer." He touched their arm. "It's now or not at all."

Ellery's throat went tight. "But—"

"It'll be fine." He smiled, all teeth, oozing with charisma. "I promise."

Yeah. Yeah, okay. It would be fine. And if Ellery could get this information, then Knox could send a message with his magic, and they could break the winter. They couldn't pass up this opportunity. They had a weird feeling it would all work, everything would be fine. Just like Hale promised.

"Okay."

Hale's palm was dry and cool against Ellery's sweaty one, and his grip was tight as he dragged Ellery from their space by the wall through the crowd. They bypassed the kitchen, walking through a large dining room that led to a darkened hallway with a laundry alcove. The corner was small and close and smelled strongly of cleaning supplies, but it was quiet, the music muffled by the walls separating them from the dance floor.

There was another couple who had found the spot as well, and they stood near the wall, giggling as one of them placed a large hand on the indent of the other's waist.

Hale paused and narrowed his eyes. "Leave," he said without pre-amble, his voice authoritative and firm.

Their conversation ceased immediately. They straightened from their casual slumps and left through the nearby back porch door. They didn't protest, they didn't speak; they didn't even look at Ellery as they passed, their expressions blank, a far cry from the two people who had been having a good time. Ellery's pulse ticked, and they felt suddenly uneasy.

That was weird. In fact, now that they were alone with Hale in the darkened area, Ellery realized that this was a bad idea. A really bad idea, and they wondered how their judgment had led them there. Why had they followed? They knew better. Hale's body was far too close to theirs, with barely any space between them. With a shaking hand, they reached into their pocket for the acorn, only to find it empty. Because it had broken. The night of the hockey game. And Ellery didn't have a protection charm.

"You know what? I think I've made a mistake," Ellery said, detangling their hand from Hale's. "I'm going to find Knox."

"You're not," Hale said.

Ellery froze. They couldn't move. They swallowed in fear.

"Let me go."

"I don't think so," Hale said, pushing Ellery's shoulder so they were forced into the alcove, hidden by the accordion door. Hale's grip on Ellery's shoulder tightened as he pushed them against the wall, stuck between a shelf of cleaners and the washing machine. Hale loomed over them; one palm pressed flat next to Ellery's head, and his other hand rested on Ellery's neck. Hale squinted at Ellery's face. "You're too good to pass up. A human who's somehow involved with the liminal? There has to be something special about you."

"There's nothing."

"I don't believe that." He grabbed Ellery's chin and tilted their face up. "And yet you were so easy to lure away. Has he taught you nothing?"

Ellery jerked their head, only to smack the back of it against the drywall. "What are you?" they demanded.

"Isn't it obvious?"

"No." If he'd met the queen of the Other World at some point . . . that meant he had crossed the barrier . . . and the only people who could do that were either citizens of the Other World or the dead.

Hale rolled his eyes. "I wasn't lying when I said I'd met the queen of the Other World."

"But you haven't talked to her recently."

"Depends on your definition of recent."

Ellery's blood went cold. "What do you want?" Ellery's voice came out far shakier than they wanted, and Hale merely smiled.

"Nothing you can't afford to give," he said, running his thumb over Ellery's bottom lip. "I could feel it the moment you walked in, and it only thickened as you stood there and watched them." He made a disgusted face. "The deep affection you have for them. It's been a while since I've felt a pulse of emotion that intense. I couldn't pass up the chance." He cupped Ellery's jaw, the skin of his palm so cold and so smooth. "Now, close your eyes, Ellery."

Ellery's eyes slid shut without their permission. They trembled. Their phone in their pocket vibrated against their hip, but they were unable to reach for it. "What are you doing?" they breathed. "The chance for what?"

His voice was a shiver against Ellery's mouth. "A meal."

17

KNOX

KNOX HAD NOT HAD SO MUCH FUN IN HIS LIFE. WELL, AT least in this life. He twirled in the middle of the dance floor and bumped into Charley, who let out a loud peal of laughter. She caught his hands and tried to coax him into a couples dance that they both utterly failed at. They ended up doubling over laughing until Zada tapped him on the arm.

Knox straightened as Zada pointed at her watch.

Oh, it had already been an hour. Time really did fly by when he was having fun.

He looked over his shoulder to check on Ellery, who had found a quiet perch by a window. Huh. They weren't there. They must've gone to the foyer where they had agreed to meet. Maybe Knox could convince them to join them on the dance floor. Just for one dance. Maybe more, if they decided it was as fun as Knox thought it was.

Knox jerked his thumb toward the entrance of the house to signal to Zada that he was going to go check for Ellery. Zada nodded in affirmation.

It wasn't difficult to push his way through the crowd, though there were a few people who tried to tug him back. He smiled in return and gently disentangled himself until he was able to stumble toward the foyer.

He skipped his way to the entrance, expecting to find Ellery, intent on wrapping them in a hug and transferring some of his happiness to them. But the foyer was empty, save for the large pile of jackets on the table.

That was weird.

Maybe they'd gone to get a drink.

Knox maneuvered through the heaving throng in the living room and into the kitchen. There was a small crowd in there as well, but no Ellery.

A worried knot began to tighten in Knox's chest. He knew Ellery had set an alarm to meet after an hour. What could be keeping them? Maybe they'd stepped out for fresh air? Despite the cold?

"Looking for your friend?" a girl at the table in the kitchen asked.

"Yeah," he said. "Have you seen them?"

She arched an eyebrow. "I saw them with the only other good-looking guy here."

That did not sound like Ellery at all. Knox's stomach sank. "Where?"

She shrugged. "They went toward the back of the house."

Knox left the kitchen and made his way deeper into the house with a growing sense of urgency, squeezing past groups in small rooms and corridors, calling Ellery's name over the noise to no response. His worry grew as each new person he ran into was not Ellery. Toward the back of the large house, he turned a corner and found a dark hallway that led to a door. Could Ellery have gone out that way to cool off and forgotten the time? He hoped that was the case. He strode to the door and grabbed the knob, intent on checking the outside, when he heard a whisper.

Off to the side was a small room. A shuffling sound came from the laundry alcove, behind the half-folded door. A cold chill crept down Knox's spine as he moved closer, and that was when he noticed the sense of wrongness that filled the space, one that he recognized.

His breath caught.

Undead.

He quickly crossed the small area and wrenched the accordion door open.

The undead hunched over Ellery, lips hovering above Ellery's own. Without hesitation, Knox yanked him away by the collar of his shirt, the fabric ripping in his grip. The undead staggered backward out of the alcove, breaking the connection. Ellery's eyes fluttered open, and they slid down, landing in a heap on the floor.

Furious, Knox shoved the assailant to the end of the hallway, hard enough for his shoulders to smack soundly against the wall. Calling forth a burst of magic, Knox pinned him, golden tendrils of his power wrapping around the undead's wrists and throat.

"Familiar," the undead hissed, struggling against Knox's magic. "Release me." His voice was deep, authoritative, but the compulsion didn't work on Knox.

"No," Knox answered through clenched teeth. His whole body was tense, anger and worry threaded through every particle of his being.

The undead licked his lips, then pouted. "This is unfair," he whined. "I didn't even get a taste."

Knox's magic constricted in response. The undead let out a gasp of pain as his head slammed back against the wood.

"Knox," Ellery whispered.

Knox spun and dropped to his knees. "Ellery," he said, reaching out to grasp their hand. "Are you okay?"

Ellery raised the heel of their hand to their forehead and winced. "I think so. I have a headache. What happened?"

"You were charmed."

"Charmed?"

"By this creature. It will wear off shortly. Can you stand?"

Ellery grimaced but nodded. Knox slid closer, guided Ellery's arm over his shoulders, and wrapped his arm around their waist. Together they stood. Ellery was wobbly but kept their feet, leaning heavily into Knox's side.

The undead cried out. "Oh, come on," he said, straining against the magic bonds. "This is so unfair. I just wanted a snack. Nothing that would have done them harm. I'm hungry. Please?"

Ellery made a face.

"You're gross," Knox said, the magic tightening again. "What are you doing here, anyway? Your kind is not allowed in a city."

"Who says?"

"The rules. My queen has strict laws regarding—"

He scoffed. "Your queen hasn't enforced the laws in years, so why should I follow them?"

"What?" Ellery asked, still dazed. "What is he? What did you do to me?"

"I wasn't lying. My name really is Hale. Why don't you come over and look into my eyes, and we'll talk more about—?" The words abruptly ended in a choking sound as Knox's magic squeezed over Hale's throat.

"Knock it off," Knox bit out. He turned back to Ellery. "He's an undead. He was a human, but he died, traveled to the Other World, and has been banished back to the human realm to wander aimlessly until the queen decides he is ready to return. It's meant as a punishment. But some of them enjoy it."

"It *is* a punishment," he gasped. "Being among humans but being unable to feel emotions or connections to anyone. Not even able to enjoy any physical aspects of humanity either. That is, until one of my brethren taught me how to feed off the emotions of the living." He licked his lips. "The taste of human emotion is like nothing you'd ever imagine. Joy. Sadness. Anger. Lust. All delicious, though they leave me feeling a little empty. But love? It's like a drug. And I almost managed to siphon some off your little friend here, until you interrupted."

Ellery's body stiffened under Knox's arm.

"If emotion is all you were after," Knox asked, "why did you lead them to a dark corner?"

Hale clucked his tongue. "I don't like having an audience when I feed. That's all. It's nothing nefarious. Not all undead are the same. I don't kill humans. I don't drain their life force, if that's what you're thinking. Because one, that's wasteful, and two, that draws attention. Also, I prefer small meals. A little bit at a time is filling enough."

Knox narrowed his eyes. "And yet you needed to use your charm."

"As if I would be able to get dear Ellery to agree by normal means. Not with you in the picture."

Ellery rubbed their sleeve over their eyes and shook their head as if ridding themself of the undead's charm. "You lied about having information about the queen."

"Of course I lied." Hale rolled his eyes. "You were just so delectable, standing there with the biggest heart eyes I'd seen in ages and the affection just dripping off you."

Ellery ducked their head, the strands of their hair hanging in their face.

Knox frowned and drew them closer to his side.

"But if Ellery is off the menu, I wouldn't mind some of that righteous anger rolling off you, familiar." Hale smacked his lips.

Knox made a face. "You are going to leave this party and go back to whatever forsaken little hole you're supposed to be living in."

"Right. That's not happening," Hale said with a sneer. "You can't enforce your queen's rules. From what your friend has said, you can't even talk with her. So here's what's going to happen. You are going to release me, and I'm going to find a different bite."

Knox gritted his teeth. His magic wavered, and Hale's grin widened.

"You can't hold me forever," Hale said.

"You're right," Ellery said. "He can't. But before he releases you, we're going to make a deal."

Hale's gaze snapped to Ellery. "What?"

"Yeah, what?" Knox echoed.

Ellery turned their back to Hale, dipped their head, and dropped their voice. "He's been to the Other World, correct?"

"Yes."

"Which means he could go again."

Knox nodded slowly. "Yes."

"If we can't figure this out, we could at least try to use him to send a message to your queen. He could help us break this winter. Right?"

Guilt burned in Knox's gullet. "Ellery," he said, sighing.

Ellery stared at him with wide, hopeful eyes, their jaw set in determination. "Right?" they said again. And Knox wilted.

"Yes."

Ellery gave him a sharp nod, then turned on their heel back to Hale. "Knox will release you, and you're going to leave and have a long meditation on consensual *snacking*." They shivered as they said it. "And you're going to owe us a favor."

"These are terrible terms. What do I even get out of it? Who taught you how to strike a bargain?"

"Oh, I've learned from the best." Ellery stepped close to Hale and yanked up the sleeve of their shirt, exposing their wrist. They held it up to Hale's face. "A taste, right?"

Hale laughed. "I'm not a bloodsucker. I don't want your veins."

"Then what—"

"A kiss."

Ellery visibly gulped.

Jealousy welled up fast and hot, and Knox crowded along Ellery's back. "Is that really necessary?"

Hale smiled. "With all the emotion sparking from you, I'd almost think you were human. But we all know you're not." He winked.

"You don't have to do this," Knox said to Ellery, a little more pleading than he would've liked. "We can just let him walk away."

Ellery shook their head. "It's fine," they said. "I have plenty of emotions to share. And it means he won't prey on anyone else at this party. Right?"

"Fine. I won't. And I don't actually take anything from you," Hale said, eyes glittering. "I only sample it."

"You leave after," Ellery said, holding up a single finger. "And you owe us."

"Deal," Hale said eagerly, his gaze focused again on Ellery's lips.

Knox didn't like this at all. But it was Ellery's choice. And they had chosen to follow through on the off chance it would lead to breaking the winter. Though it wouldn't help, because Knox was the reason for the winter to begin with. Which meant they were entering this bargain under false pretenses and—

"Wait," Knox said.

"What now?" Hale asked.

"Ellery, there's something I have to tell you, and—"

"Ellery! Knox!" Charley's voice rang out from down the hallway.

Ellery's eyes went wide. "Sorry, Knox. It'll have to wait."

Then Ellery tilted their face up, leaned in, and smashed their mouth to Hale's. Hale's eyes slid shut on impact, a glow emanating from where his lips touched theirs. He inhaled deeply, like a drowning man gasping for air, as magic shimmered between them. He pushed into the kiss and made a low, hungry noise.

And okay. That was enough. Knox could not take any more.

Ellery must've thought so as well. They yanked away, then hurriedly swiped their sleeve over their mouth, expression pinched with disgust.

Hale exhaled. "Wow," he said. "You were not lying. You are full of emotion."

"Knox! El!"

Knox released Hale from his magic, and Hale stumbled forward on his feet, a little stunned.

"Leave," Knox said.

Hale bowed unsteadily to the pair of them, then slipped out the back door.

"There you two are," Charley said, dragging Zada behind her. "We've been looking all over for you."

Zada smiled and shook her head. "We haven't, really. We literally found you in, like, five minutes."

"Still." Charley flailed her hands. "We didn't know if they were together. Or if they were separated. If they had left. Or were in trouble."

"You sound like a hysterical mom," Ellery said, arms crossed. "We were fine."

Charley made a face. "Well, excuse me for worrying about you, cousin. I'll just go back to dancing and having fun."

"You could do that."

"Okay," Zada said, holding out her hands. "Since we're all here anyway. How's everyone? Knox, you doing okay? You look a little tense."

He *was* tense. His shoulders were near his ears, his hands were balled into fists, and he could feel his teeth grinding together. He took a breath and tried to relax and plastered on a smile. "I'm fine."

"Wow. That was not at all convincing," Charley said. "We can leave and go home, if you want."

"Actually," Ellery said, chiming in, "Knox and I were talking about going back home together, but you two can stay. Have fun. Party for a bit."

Zada raised an eyebrow. "That in no way sounds suspicious. Knox, are you sure you're okay?"

"Yes," Knox said. "I'm fine. I am an immortal being with magic. We're fine. Fine. Nothing happened."

"The more you talk, the less convinced I am," Charley said, tapping her chin.

"I agree," Zada said. "But we trust you both. If you say you're okay and want to go back to the apartment, then we're okay with that."

"We are?" Charley spun around and eyed Zada. "Seriously?"

"Yes. We are. I'm certain that if something were to happen, they would alert us."

Charley narrowed her eyes. "Okay. We are."

"They're *responsible* young adults. Who have had discussions regarding certain activities. And know how to be *responsible.*"

"Why are you saying 'responsible' like that?" Charley asked, mimicking Zada. *"Responsible."* Then an expression of understanding crossed her features. "Oh. Now I get it."

Ellery dropped their face in their hands and groaned. "Oh my gods and goddesses," they whispered. "That's *not* what happened."

"All the same," Zada said, looping her arm through Charley's, "be careful heading back, and text us once you're home."

"We will," Ellery muttered through their fingers.

"Oh, and Ellery. Your lip gloss is smeared." Zada said, touching the corner of her mouth. "May want to take care of that."

Knox's eyes widened and his stomach swooped when he caught on to what Zada was insinuating. "Oh! They think we—"

"Let's just get out of here," Ellery said, tugging on Knox's sleeve.

Knox followed blindly, bumping into people as Ellery pulled them through the house and toward the front door. Because all he could now think about were Ellery's lips. And kissing Ellery. And how nice that might feel. And how much he wanted to—not just to complete his checklist of human experiences, but because it was Ellery.

On autopilot, he slipped on his coat and stumbled outside into the cold, following Ellery down the front steps before pausing on the concrete path that connected the sidewalk to the front door.

Ellery's heel slipped on a patch of ice, and Knox grabbed the bend of their elbow, steadying them.

"Are you feeling okay?" he asked.

Ellery shrugged. "I'm fine, really. We could go back in if you wanted to finish dancing. I don't mind. I just wanted to get out of that hallway."

Knox shook his head and started walking away from the house, toward the campus. Ellery fell in step beside him.

"No. I don't think I could have fun anymore," he admitted. "I was so worried when I couldn't find you and then so angry when that undead dared to . . ."

"You did go a little intense with the magic on Hale. It was surprising." Ellery nudged Knox with their shoulder and raised an eyebrow. "Are *you* okay?"

"Yes. As long as you are."

Ellery scrubbed their sleeve over their mouth. "It was a little weird, the whole feeding-off-my-emotions piece. But the feeling of being charmed was worse. And there were those few moments that I thought I had been ensnared by an evil being and that my death was imminent."

Knox shuddered. "I'm sorry." He cast a glance at Ellery. They were scrunched down in the fabric of their coat, and their steps were quick to keep up with Knox's long strides. But they didn't appear shaken or upset, only contemplative, their lips pink and pursed, their eyebrows drawn together in thought.

"Is there anything I can do?" Knox offered.

Ellery suddenly paused under a streetlight. "Actually," they said, hands in their pockets, face tipped up, their features bathed in soft yellow light, "you could kiss me."

Knox froze. "What?"

Ellery shrugged, though they couldn't really sell the forced nonchalance. "You could kiss me if you wanted."

And yes. Yes, Knox did want that. It was all he had been thinking about since Ellery had kissed Hale a few minutes ago. He took a small step forward. "Are you sure?"

"Yes. You don't have to, though," they said. Their smile trembled at the corners. "It was just an idea."

Knox curled his hand into the fabric of Ellery's jacket. "Do you want me to?"

"Yes. He was my first kiss. I want you to be my second." Ellery stilled, the wisp of their breath curling around them. "You really don't have to if you don't want to. His lips were cold. And kind of gross. And the whole taking-of-emotions thing was super weird, and—"

"I want to," Knox said.

Ellery lifted their chin, the light from the lamp highlighting the blush that seeped across the bridge of their nose into their cheeks, either from the cold or from Knox's attention. "You do?"

"Yes." Knox tucked the strands of hair that escaped from beneath their hat behind their ear. "If that's okay."

"Yes."

"Okay."

Knox bowed his head, closed his eyes, and brushed his lips across Ellery's. He had seen people kissing in movies and TV shows for years, but it did not prepare him for the shock of it. His heart thundered, and his hands shook where they fisted into Ellery's coat, and every nerve went alight with a shivery longing.

Knox pulled away slightly, and his eyes fluttered open to find Ellery staring back at him in disbelief and awe, glossy lips parted. Ellery curled their hand around the back of Knox's neck, fingers digging in, and pulled Knox back in.

They collided, Ellery's bottom lip catching in the seam of Knox's mouth, and it was perfect. And they kissed again. And again. Impatient and a little desperate and awkward. But it was amazing, the slide of their lips, the little gasps from Ellery's mouth against his, the pressure of Ellery's hands sliding along Knox's shoulders, then down the curve of his back to rest in the dip of his spine. Kissing Ellery was intoxicating, and Knox wanted to indelibly stamp the details into his memory—the race of his pulse, the warmth of Ellery's mouth, the heat of their body close to his. In that moment, all his worries and fears and guilt ceased to exist.

A whistle and a catcall from a passing car broke through the haze. Ellery jerked backward, eyes wide and startled. They peered over Knox's shoulder at the slow-rolling vehicle full of heckling college kids and started giggling uncontrollably, burying their face in Knox's chest.

"Oh my gods and goddesses," they said, pressing their words into Knox's body. "That was embarrassing."

Their laughter was contagious, and Knox chuckled as he wrapped his arms around Ellery. He pulled them close, resting his chin on the top of their head. "At least it wasn't Charley."

Ellery snorted endearingly with laughter. "She can never know. She'd never let me live it down."

"Live what down?" Knox asked.

"That she was right."

"About?"

"Seeing many kisses in my future."

Knox grinned wide. He fiddled with the clasp on Ellery's coat. "Did you like it?"

"Wasn't it obvious?" Ellery said. "Yes. Yes, I liked it."

Knox ducked his head. "Good. I'm happy." Which was an understatement, but Knox didn't want to put words to the feelings sloshing around in his middle.

"Me too," Ellery said with a soft smile. "I wouldn't mind a few more."

Knox slid his hand along Ellery's cheek then leaned in again. They kissed under the lamplight. Knox reveled in every press of their lips, every clench of Ellery's hands against his waist or in the fabric of his jacket, every soft sigh, every shiver. Until Knox realized the shivering had more to do with the cold than the kisses.

He pulled away. "It's cold."

Ellery blinked, mouth parted, each deep breath a puff of fog. "Yes."

"We should go."

They nodded. "We should." Adjusting their jacket and scarf, they swooped in and stole one last swift kiss. "Come on," they said. "It's late. Let's go home." Ellery held out their hand, and Knox took it and laced their fingers together.

It hit Knox then, the amount of affection he held for this human he'd known for barely a few weeks. Maybe it was all a product of the situation, and maybe it wasn't supposed to happen this way, but he couldn't deny that the feelings he had for Ellery were intense and real.

The trip back to the apartment took longer than Knox would have liked. Tension stretched between them as they glanced at each other, mouths red and faces pink. Knox wanted to ask what it meant for them now that they had kissed. Had it changed anything at all? Had Ellery only wanted to kiss him to erase the feeling of Hale? Or had they had wanted to kiss because of the fondness Hale had alluded to that Ellery held for him? But he was afraid asking might dissolve the closeness between them. Ellery leaned against Knox on the bus, their body wilting against his own as the fatigue from the late hour and the drain from Hale caught up with them.

Luckily, the buses in the college part of town ran more frequently than in others, and within an hour, they tumbled into the apartment.

After kicking off their shoes and removing their coats, they both readied for the night. Ellery disappeared for a few minutes, and Knox quickly changed his clothes, peeling off the tight jeans and the shirt Zada had suggested for their night out. He slipped into pajamas just as Ellery emerged in their sleeping clothes, face scrubbed and free of makeup.

Ellery drank a glass of water as Knox disappeared to brush his teeth.

Once they were both done, they stood awkwardly in the living room, facing each other.

Ellery's hands twitched. "Do you want—"

"Yes," Knox said immediately.

Ellery smiled. "You don't even know what I was going to ask."

Knox shrugged. "No. But that doesn't mean I don't know what I want."

Ellery swallowed. They gestured to the mattress. "Do you want to sleep with me tonight? Just sleep."

"Yes." It came out breathy and a little choked with the realization that he wanted more than one night. He wanted to stay with Ellery in the human realm for as long as he could. But he couldn't, not with the knowledge that he was responsible for the winter, for the last few difficult years of Ellery's life. The guilt that had dissipated in the light of Ellery's enthusiastic kisses surged back into his throat.

Ellery arranged the blankets, grabbed Knox's pillow from the corner of the couch, and placed it next to theirs. They slid into the bed and beckoned Knox to follow.

He did, hesitating slightly on the edge of the mattress before taking a breath and curling under the blankets, his head resting on Ellery's pillow. Ellery faced them, arms folded close to their body.

"Thank you," they said.

"For what?" Knox asked, panicking slightly because he didn't know where to put his hands. He settled on tucking one under his cheek beneath the pillow and keeping the other resting between them, until Ellery snuggled closer, took Knox's arm, and draped it over their waist.

"For saving me from Hale. I shouldn't have gone with him." Their blinks were slow and heavy, the late hour catching up with them once they were horizontal.

"He charmed you. That's not your fault. It's what he does." Knox squirmed closer. "I'm just glad I found you."

"Me too." Ellery shifted, their foot brushing Knox's under the covers, until their legs were tangled together. "Is this okay?"

"Yes."

"Was the kissing okay?"

"Also yes."

"Can we do it again?"

"Yes," Knox said, bending close. He pressed his lips to Ellery's, quick and sweet.

Ellery grinned. Then they yawned, and their eyes slid shut. "Oh, was there something you wanted to tell me? You mentioned it, but Charley cut us off."

Knox blanched. He swallowed. "Tomorrow. I'll tell you tomorrow."

"Okay." Ellery's breathing evened, easing toward sleep. "I trust you. And I know it's impossible, but I wish you could stay."

Shame was a knife in Knox's ribs. "I want to stay," Knox said softly. "I want to stay with you."

The corners of Ellery's lips quirked upward. "Then stay."

"If only it were that easy."

Knox wished he could. Knox wished he could stay a century with Ellery and with Zada and Charley, wished he could live as a human until Ellery didn't want him any longer, or until Ellery made their own trip to the Other World. Knox wanted so much to kiss and cuddle and *love*. But even if he could stay a decade or two with Ellery, that meant the winter would persist. And that also meant more creatures like Hale would invade human spaces, would encroach in places they weren't supposed to be, hurt innocent people. No, five years of disruption was enough, had ruined the lives of all the beings in the area, and it was time for Knox to make things right, to take the vial and go home.

Once Ellery was asleep, Knox eased out of the bed and quietly snuck over to his duffel bag. He removed the journal from the top and flipped it open to where his list was tucked inside. He checked off the item at the bottom, added another, and checked it off as well since he was certain he'd fulfilled it, then added one last task.

One that might be the most difficult of them all.

18

ELLERY

"I HATE TO BREAK THIS UP," CHARLEY SAID, STANDING OVER THE mattress. "Because really it is too cute. Like, tooth-rottingly sweet. If I continue to stare, I'm going to get a cavity. Look at you two, curled up together like puppies. But we have things to accomplish today."

Ellery peeled one eye open at Charley's obnoxious voice. They were tangled up with Knox and a blanket and it was the best, most comfortable sleep they'd had since they'd moved to the city, and they were loath to be woken from it.

"Go away," they said, voice gruff.

"Nope," Charley said, popping the P. "I'm afraid that the day awaits, and you must rouse or be forgotten."

"Then forget me," Ellery muttered.

Knox's arms tightened around them. And Ellery felt like a jerk when they thought about the possible reason why—the soft conversation they'd had as Ellery had drifted asleep, the ghost of Knox's wish to stay, and the knowledge that when he no longer could, he'd pass the barrier and lose the memories of this human life.

Ellery hadn't forgotten the secret Knox had mentioned when he was concussed, and they hoped it was that fact that he didn't want to leave, that he wanted the conditions of their bargain to continue, even if it meant never being able to contact the goddess and find the reason for the ceaseless winter. Some small selfish part of Ellery agreed, especially if it meant more kisses and more nights together.

Ellery shifted closer, buried their face into Knox's chest, the soft fabric of his shirt a safe haven from their inevitable future and the hurt that would accompany it.

"Come on, Ellery. We need to hit a few stores today. And think of it as another fun thing for Knox."

"Fun?" Knox's voice was a rumble against Ellery's cheek. "How?"

Zada's voice echoed from the kitchen. "Mall scenes are a classic teen-movie trope. Granted, our mall is not as busy, and lots of shops have closed, but at least there's a food court and a bookstore and a few clothing stores, one of which sells punny T-shirts."

"Like the ones Grant wore in the werewolves, witches, and wyverns show?" Knox asked, his voice sweet in Ellery's ear.

"Exactly," Zada said.

"No," Ellery groaned. "Don't let them persuade you with their capitalistic ways."

Charley laughed. "We might even be able to catch a movie this afternoon in an actual movie theater."

Knox perked up. "Really?"

"With popcorn."

"I'm sorry, Ellery." Knox patted their back. "But there's a movie theater and a food court."

Ellery sighed. "Yeah. I get it."

They untangled, and Ellery did their best to smooth down the fluffy bird's nest of their hair while Knox jumped from the mattress and rummaged through his duffel bag.

Charley clapped her hands. "Great! We're leaving in thirty. I want an iced coffee and a pastry from the coffee shop on the mall's first floor, and I don't want to have to fight people for the last one. It can get pretty nasty. So we need to get moving."

She flounced back toward her room, which left Ellery and Knox alone. Ellery stood.

"Hey," they said, cheeks hot.

"Hi," Knox returned with a smile.

Ellery coughed shyly into their fist. "Are you okay this morning?"

Knox tilted his head. "Yes. Are you?"

"Yep."

"Good."

Ellery fidgeted, rocked back on their heels. "So. We're both good."

Knox shook his head fondly. "Yes. We are."

"Great. This is not at all awkward."

Knox laughed. He rested a hand on Ellery's waist, his long fingers warm and steady even through the thick fabric of Ellery's shirt. "It doesn't need to be." He swooped in and kissed them firmly before pulling away. "See?"

"I'm convinced," Ellery said with a smile.

Knox grinned in return. "And when we go to the mall, I'm going to hold your hand. And once we both brush our teeth, I'm going to kiss you again. Probably not in front of Zada and Charley, but it's definitely going to happen. If that's okay with you."

"I find these terms agreeable," Ellery said with a sharp nod.

Knox's smile dimmed as Ellery inadvertently drew attention to the cloud of their inevitable parting that hung over their heads. And Ellery wished they could snatch their poor choice of words out of the air and shove them back down their throat. Instead, they took his hand and squeezed his fingers.

"Hey. Let's just enjoy it. For as long as we have it."

Knox swallowed. He ruffled Ellery's already messy hair, his expression one of such open fondness, Ellery's heart threatened to break. "Okay."

"Hey, El!" Charley called, then appeared in the doorway, phone in hand.

They jumped apart, but not before Charley entered. She gave them a knowing smile, then winked. "Oh, am I interrupting?"

Ellery glared. "What do you want?"

She held out the phone. "It's your mom."

Oh. Ellery had managed to avoid the last few phone calls, too caught up in the supernatural to be readily available, which was ironic on levels Ellery didn't want to examine. So they guessed they should take this one.

"Hey, Mom," they said, balancing the phone between their ear and shoulder. They squeezed by Knox, briefly touching his arm as they did so in an affectionate gesture before settling in one of the kitchen chairs.

"Ellery," their mom greeted them. "How are you?"

"I'm okay. How are things?"

She sighed, her weariness unmistakable over the line. "I was wondering, and I hate to ask this, but do you have funds available?"

Alarm bells immediately went off in Ellery's head. Their mother had never outright asked for money. "I get paid in a few days. Why? Is something wrong?"

Knox paused from where he was tidying Ellery's bed. He cocked his head to the side, obviously listening.

"The electricity has been cut off. We couldn't pay the last bill. We're burning wood in the fireplaces for the house, but the greenhouses . . ."

Ellery's whole being went cold, goosebumps rising along their arms. "I thought I was sending enough."

There was a beat of silence before their mom continued. "I know you've been giving a little to Charley each month for rent, but if she can spare it this time . . ."

Ellery bowed their head. "Yeah. I'll . . . I'll send the whole amount as soon as I get it. I have a little in my account I can send now."

"Please."

"I'll do it right now." They took out their own phone, tapped into their bank account app, then sent everything they had, save a few dollars. "Okay. Sent," they said. "It's not much."

"Thank you," their mom said. "I didn't want to put this burden on you."

"It's fine," Ellery said quickly, uncomfortable. "I have to go."

"Okay. Talk to you again soon. Goodbye."

"Bye," Ellery said, and hung up. They passed the phone off to Charley, who stared at them with a sad expression.

"Is everything okay?" she asked tentatively.

"Um," Ellery said, casting a quick glance to Knox, who was doing a bad job of pretending to not eavesdrop. They forced a smile. "Not really, but uh . . . I'll figure it out. Anyway, mall, right? Let's . . . um . . . go to the mall."

"We don't have to."

"It's fine!"

Charley held up her hands. "Okay. You two get ready. I'll get Zada."

Once Charley left the room, Knox sat on the back of the couch. "Are you okay?" he asked.

Ellery deflated. They stretched out their arm on the table, then lay their head on their bicep, peering at Knox through the untamed dark strands of their hair. "I'm fine. It's just . . . my mom sounded defeated and scared. I don't think my family can survive much longer, even with me leaving. And I feel like I've failed."

Knox stepped forward. He took Ellery's hand in his. "You haven't failed. You're doing your best."

Ellery took a deep breath. "I know. But my best doesn't seem to be enough."

Knox swallowed. "I'm sorry." He looked away, his jaw clenched. "Look, I need to tell—"

"Hey! Lovebirds!" Charley said, clapping her hands as she came back into the kitchen. "Get ready! There are scones at stake! Let's go!"

Ellery groaned but sat up. "Is sugar all you think about?"

"Um, no. Coffee is also high on my list. Chop-chop! I'm serious." She pulled out her phone and set a timer. "I'm leaving in thirty minutes. With or without you." Ellery grumbled but got up from the table to start getting ready for the day.

It only took twenty minutes for Knox and Ellery to be presentable. Zada spun her car keys on her finger as they locked the door behind them, and they walked up the stairs toward the parking garage. A fresh layer of snow crunched under Zada's tires as she carefully drove on the back streets toward the mall. Despite the chill in the car, Ellery didn't put on their gloves and instead slid their hand into Knox's, their entwined fingers resting on the seat between them.

Knox glanced down, and the smile that blossomed across his face was worth enduring any temperature.

Despite the time being late morning, and on a weekend at that, the parking area was mostly deserted. Only a smattering of cars sat in the spaces, and the lot had barely been plowed. Part of the mall was under construction; large tarps hung over the beige concrete face with scaffolding in place. The section that was open to the public was peppered with abandoned storefronts, marked by rain-stained outlines of the letters that had once spelled out popular store names. It was depressing, but it was their best option for hitting all of Charley's errands in one place.

Charley exited the car and inhaled. "Nothing like the fresh air of the country."

"We're still in the city," Ellery said, tugging up the zipper of their light jacket. They'd chosen something less bulky than their regular coat because at least the mall was heated. "We're, like, fifteen minutes from the apartment. You can see the college campus's clock tower right over there."

"Yep. It's just a different atmosphere out here," Charley said, hands on her hips.

"You are the literal weirdest."

Zada linked arms with Charley. "You're bizarre. I love you."

Charley threw her head back and cackled. "I love you too," she said, smacking a kiss on Zada's cheek while giggling. "Let's go get a donut or a scone or a turnover. Any of the above. And a flavored coffee. Something sweet." Charley pulled Zada toward the entrance, the pair of them dancing around the large drifts of snow from the latest flurry.

Ellery held out their hand, and Knox pushed away from where he leaned on the car and took it. "Come on," Ellery said with a slight tug. "Let's get to the bakery before Charley eats all the good stuff."

"This doesn't look like in the movies," Knox said, his brow furrowing as they entered the mall.

The interior was bleaker than the exterior, if that was even possible. The second story was roped off, all the stores having been relegated to the first floor. The entrances to the powered-down escalators were wrapped in caution tape. Large tarps were draped around the skylights, the floor below water-stained from the snowmelt. Bright lights flickered overhead, buzzing on and off like a drunk bee. There was no one else in sight, Charley and Zada having already skipped around the corner toward the coffee shop. It was eerie being the only people in what should have been a bustling beacon of economic strength.

"Well, it kind of does, if the movie is a zombie apocalypse."

Knox frowned.

"Hey," Ellery said with a squeeze of his hand. "We can still have fun."

"That's not—" Knox cut himself off with a start. He abruptly rubbed his chest. "There's something here."

Ellery's eyes widened. "You mean something like you?"

Knox nodded. "Yes."

"Is it friendly?"

"I don't know." He sighed. "I'm not sure seeking out other creatures is such a good idea. It's all well and good when they're friendly, like Lorelei or Aubri, but Hale was a different story. That undead shouldn't have been within the city limits. It's part of the deal when being sent back to this world from the Other World. He should've never been able to enter that party."

"But like he said, your queen isn't enforcing rules. She isn't here anymore."

Knox pinched the bridge of his nose. "I'm aware."

"Maybe we can ask whatever *is* here. They might have answers."

"I don't know. It could be dangerous. Possibly even something worse than Hale."

Ellery tapped their fingertips across their lips. "I've been thinking about that too. Maybe the favor that we ask of him is to go back to her. He can cross the barrier, right? Maybe it won't affect his memory like it does yours. Maybe he can meet with her and find out what's going on."

"Ellery," Knox said on another sigh. "That won't work."

Frustration sparked inside Ellery. "Knox, I know we talked about you staying here. And if we do find information about your queen, then it might break our deal. But we'll just make another one. Okay? One that will let you stay here for much longer and maybe even be here in the spring and summer. We could have so much fun together. We could be together." They pressed their mouth shut when Knox's expression became even more pained. "Unless you don't want to?"

"I want to!" Knox said, gripping Ellery's hand tighter. "I want to be in this realm, Ellery. At first, I was just afraid of what I'd find when returning home. And I wanted to rebel a little, play at being human. But then I met you and Charley and Zada. And you became my friends, and I realized just how much I'd been missing. I want relationships. I want to hang out with Zada and watch TV shows and go dancing with her. I want to make breakfast with Charley and listen to her tell stories about her day and help her make tips at the diner. And I want to be with you. I want to kiss you. I want to watch horror movies with you and run around the city with you. I want to be able to love you. The way you deserve. But I can't. And I'm so sorry." His voice choked on the end. "I'm so sorry."

He closed his eyes and tears spilled from the corners, rolled down his cheeks. He ducked his head and covered his face with his hand.

Ellery was stunned. Their budding annoyance melted away. They pulled Knox close, stood on their toes, and wrapped their arms around his shoulders. "I'm sorry," Ellery said. "We'll figure it out. I promise. There has to be a way. And we'll find that way. Even if I have to ask every supernatural creature in a hundred-mile radius. Even if we have to leave here and go to where she is paying attention and beg."

"I can't leave. I'm tied to my crossroads."

Ellery grimaced. "Maybe I'll go, then. And find a crossroads and make a deal and—"

Knox tore out of Ellery's grasp, scrambled backward until there was a foot of space between them. "No!" He dashed the tears away as his chest heaved. "No. None of the shades can be trusted. They'll do something to you, because they know you're special to me. Our bargain is the only thing holding them back right now, and even that is tenuous."

Ellery raised their hands. "Okay. Okay," they said, placating, though their heart raced. They didn't quite understand what was happening, what had changed in the time from when they'd woken up cuddling to this moment.

Ellery blew out a breath, tucked their hands into their coat pockets. "Do you still want to look around the mall? If not, we can go somewhere else."

Knox bowed his head and stared at the patterned carpeted floor. "Look. I have to tell you something. I've been putting it off, but it's time."

Ellery's heart dropped. "Time for what?"

"To keep my end of our agreement." Knox gently took Ellery's elbow and guided them farther into the mall, toward a bench by a dry fountain. He plopped onto it, and Ellery eased themself down too.

"Arabelle. She . . . um . . . When she called me . . . she bargained her soul for—"

"The elixir."

Knox nodded. "But what I didn't tell you was that the shades—"

Ellery caught a flicker of movement in a shadow by a nondescript corner. It was in the hallway that led to the bathrooms, and the shadows weren't even that thick, but they moved, slid across the floor in a smoky writhe. Ellery's breath caught. They grabbed Knox's hand where it was twisted in his shirt.

"The shades."

Knox jumped to his feet and spun around. Ellery followed, a cold sweat breaking out over their skin.

"Run," Ellery urged, grabbing Knox's sleeve. "We should run."

But Knox stood frozen. Indecision and guilt warred across his handsome features.

The shades coalesced from the shadows and rose vertically, rolling fog turned corporeal. The trio stared at them with their blazing red eyes, and Ellery shivered, remembering the twisted root and bone beneath their cloaks.

They hovered, unblinking, and slunk across the floor toward them. "Knox," they called in an eerie singsong. "Ellery." Ellery's name was a discordant rasp that caused a line of fear to trickle down their spine.

"Please," Ellery said as the trio approached. "Please, let's run."

"Yes," Knox said, glancing to the side, catching Ellery's frightened gaze. "Okay."

Ellery moved first, dragging Knox behind them as they ran. Realizing they couldn't risk the shades following them through the more populated areas of the mall, Ellery made for the back side, toward the department store they'd seen with scaffolding and the missing lettering. Their sneakers squeaked on the patches of floor where the carpet had been removed and the linoleum peeked through. A curtain of plastic hung over the entrance of the large anchor store, and Ellery pushed through, pulling Knox behind them.

"Ellery," Knox protested. "They can follow me anywhere there is shadow."

"I know. But this is a construction area. There has to be some kind of iron here." Ellery looked upward, spying an abandoned workplace near the skylights. Not only did it appear as if there were a smattering of tools, but there was also a large patch of sunlight on the second floor. "Up there," they said, jerking their chin.

"Ellery."

Ellery didn't listen, their heart pounding, focused solely on protecting Knox and themself.

Ellery ripped through the caution tape across the escalator entrance and bounded up the stairs, Knox hot on their heels. In the blinding sunlight, Ellery found a pile of tools on a workhorse. They grabbed a hammer.

"I know it's not pure iron, but maybe it will—"

"Ellery," Knox said.

"The handle is plastic. Maybe you can hold this? And I'll go with the wrench."

"Ellery."

"And we'll fight them off. You have magic. You can blast them with light, right? I wish I had a way to contact Lorelei, because her help would not go amiss at this moment, but—"

"Ellery! I'm the reason for the winter!"

Knox's voice broke through Ellery's panicked rambling like a hot knife slicing through butter. They stilled as the words tumbled through their mind, then took root. Snapping their head up, Ellery's heart lurched at Knox's expression. The tears at the corner of his eyes and the absolute naked sorrow written across his face told them he wasn't lying.

"What?" Ellery asked softly. "What?"

"I'm the reason," Knox said, pressing two fingers into his chest. "The shades sealed off my crossroads from the queen's sight when Arabelle made her deal."

Ellery blinked back tears. "Why?"

"Because they wanted the potion she was making. They wanted to be human. To come alive. They thought that Arabelle's elixir would allow them to do that." He reached into his coat, pulled out an object, and held it up. It was a vial of sparkling liquid. "This elixir."

The blue and purple clashed together in a tumult, a storm trapped in a bottle. It was beautiful and terrifying. "The elixir of life?"

"Yes."

"I don't . . . I don't understand."

"I stole it when I ran. It's too dangerous to fall into mortal hands. I knew they were interested in it, but I didn't know that they had some convoluted plan to rule the earth. I didn't know until that night at the diner, when I took the trash to the alley."

Ellery remembered that night. Knox had disappeared while Ellery and Charley closed the diner. Ellery had been afraid that Knox had run off with Aubri the pixie. Instead, he had been meeting with the shades. "You've known that long?"

Knox looked away, the sharp cut of his jaw jumping as he clenched his teeth. "Yes." He swallowed. "I was selfish. I wanted more time with you and Zada and Charley. So I didn't tell you. I should have. I know that. But . . ." He trailed off.

Ellery took a step back, their thoughts a whirlwind. "So if you had just gone back to the Other World after your contract with Arabelle ended, like you were supposed to . . . ?"

"Then this winter would have ended three weeks ago." Ellery didn't know what face they made, but Knox hastened to add, "I promise you; I didn't know. I didn't know until they told me."

"The winter has lasted five years. And you've been here the same amount of time?"

"When I came, it was the beginning of winter five years ago." Knox's shoulders slumped. "I should've put two and two together—my appearance and the long winter—but my purpose was to help Arabelle, not to question, not to disobey."

"I don't . . ." Ellery took another step. "I don't know what to say. I don't know what to do."

"Nothing!" Knox raised his hands. "You don't have to do anything. I can't let the shades have the potion. I'll have to go back to the crossroads on my own. And I'll show the queen what they did, and the winter will end."

"How? You'll forget when you cross the barrier."

Knox clasped the vial in his fist. "The elixir will have to be proof enough to the queen that it was the shades." He looked away. "She's going to be furious. But I have to trust that she'll be fair."

Ellery's fierce anger quickly shifted to alarm. "Furious?" they asked. "Why? You haven't done anything wrong!"

Knox huffed. "I literally ran away."

"You had good reason. You didn't know what had happened. You thought she'd forgotten you. You deserve to have a chance to live in the human realm like you want. To make your own choices. You don't deserve her anger."

"El—"

"We'll write a note!" Ellery gasped desperately, cutting him off. "We'll escape the shades, and then we'll go back to the apartment, and you can write a long note to yourself. About the potion. About what's happened. We just need a few more days. We'll fulfill the bargain, and I'll take you to the crossroads myself and—"

A cloud rolled in front of the sun, casting the landing in shadow. "Ellery," Knox said with a soft smile. "I'm out of time. I need to go back now."

"But . . . but you'll forget everything," Ellery said, frantic. They closed the distance they had put between them and Knox and grabbed Knox's hand. "You'll forget us. You'll forget *me*."

Knox bit his trembling lower lip. "I'm liminal. That's what I'm supposed to do."

"No!" Ellery shook their head. "No. We'll find paper and a pen right now. But I just . . . I don't . . ." They licked their lips and held up their hand. "I need . . . I need a minute." Ellery's chest tightened. Their eyes burned. They had to get away, to get a breath, to have a moment alone. They turned on their heel, still clutching the hammer with a white-knuckled grip, and ran. They pushed through a set of EMPLOYEES ONLY doors and into the spacious back room of the department store. It was dark and stuffy, with no windows or natural light. Filled with boxes of merchandise, mannequins, empty shelves, and displays, it was obviously abandoned, more than likely written off by the owners of the chain.

A wave of fear broke over them. Ellery stumbled toward the nearest light switch and flicked the toggle. The overhead lights didn't come on. Sighing, Ellery pressed their forehead against the wall. They shouldn't have left Knox. He was alone against the shades, but he had magic, and all Ellery had was a hammer. And a broken heart.

Ellery pinched their eyes shut as tears welled and sobs clogged their throat. This was the hurt that Charley had warned them about.

The inevitable end. Unfortunately, it was happening the day after they had finally come to an understanding, with their expressions of mutual affection and their wishes to stay together.

Ellery had known that Knox had a secret. He'd confessed as much. But they didn't know it would be this, that his existence prolonged the winter that had ruined Ellery's and thousands of other people's lives, the one that Ellery desperately wanted to end. And they didn't know how to reconcile that. They should be angry that Knox had lied, but they weren't. They were heartbroken.

Taking a steadying breath, Ellery pushed away from the wall.

Okay. That was enough wallowing. They needed to find supplies to write a note so they could ensure their boyfriend wasn't punished in another realm. They needed to figure out the steps after that, and the shades were still out there and—a hair-raising cackle echoed through the room, followed by the sounds of something scurrying across the floor. Ellery spun, eyes wide in the gloom, heart pounding. The eerie laugh came again, followed by the scratch of nails on linoleum.

The door behind them burst open, and Ellery let out a strangled yelp as Knox appeared, the raspy voices of the shades right behind him. He slammed it shut, throwing his body against it and sealing it with a burst of bright light from his palm. The magic crawled over the door, down to the floor, toward the ceiling, and thinned out along the entire room, crackling with golden light.

"Knox!"

Knox grabbed their elbow, facing Ellery, gaze intense, gold eyes blazing. "Once our bargain breaks, I'll have enough magic to fend them off one more time. That should give me enough of a head start back to the crossroads."

Ellery clutched at Knox's arm. "But you haven't finished your list."

Knox smiled. "There's only one thing left on it." He tucked a strand of hair behind Ellery's ear. "To tell you the whole truth."

Ellery shook their head. "No. I don't want to hear it. There has to be another way."

"Our bargain has to break, Ellery."

"But I don't want you to go."

He cupped Ellery's cheek. "Ellery—"

Another laugh echoed in the small space, chilling and terrifying, and Knox paled. His hand dropped from Ellery's face as he peered into the darkness.

Ellery spun to face the sound. They gripped the hammer tightly. "There's something else in here with us."

"We can't stay here," Knox said, voice shaky. "We have to run."

The doors shuddered, vibrating inward, and they both skittered away. Thin hairline cracks appeared in Knox's magical barricade.

Ellery clutched Knox's hand, their palm clammy, their fingers trembling. "What do we do?"

The knocks against the door continued, and the fissures spider-webbed outward as the stress on Knox's magic intensified.

Knox grabbed Ellery's hand and slapped the vial into it, curling their fingers around the elixir.

"You take this. When the shades come in, they'll chase me farther into the room, and then you should be able to run out the door. Understand?"

"But—"

"The bargain is still intact. I still have magic. I'll be fine. But I need you safe. I'll find you after."

"I don't want to leave you!"

Knox smiled, though his expression was grim. He nodded to a vacant spot by the door. "Hide there. Once they're in, run out."

Reluctantly, Ellery took a few steps to the side behind a row of boxes to hopefully go unnoticed. Knox focused on the door.

The laugh rang out again, nearer this time, and the hairs raised on the back of Ellery's neck as a hot breath skirted across their skin. They tore their gaze away from Knox and whipped around to come face-to-face with a gruesome visage.

The wraith smiled, wide and menacing, baring a row of broken, bloody teeth.

Ellery's surprised cry was choked off by a veiny hand closing around their throat. Then all they knew was pain.

19

KNOX

KNOX NARROWED HIS FOCUS DOWN TO THE DOOR AND THE warmth of his magic pulsating in his chest, the roar in his ears blocking out the cracking sounds from his protective shield as the shades tried to force their way through.

The sound of Ellery's panicked, aborted yell, followed by a wet, gurgling gasp and an ominous laugh, cut through Knox's concentration. He wrenched his gaze away from where the magic barricade trembled, and his heart stopped.

A phantom.

Fear gripped him. The remnant had Ellery in its grasp, its bony fingers wrapped around their throat, holding them aloft so only their toes scraped the floor. It held a knife in its other hand, the blade gleaming red. Blood dripped on the floor in splatters, a crimson stain rapidly growing on the front of Ellery's clothes.

No.

It laughed and thrust the knife forward. The blade plunged into the folds of Ellery's jacket with a sickening slick crunch. It grinned, knuckles wrapped tight around the hilt, as Ellery twitched helplessly in its grasp.

"No," Knox breathed in horror and disbelief.

The phantom turned its face slowly. Dark, greasy hair hung in chunky strands over its wrinkled, colorless skin. Its eyes were slashes of yellow set in sunken sockets. It was a specter in rags, a wraith fueled by pure malice.

What was it doing here? Phantoms dwelled in dark, abandoned places like swamps and ghost towns. One didn't belong in the back room of a mall. It didn't belong here, holding the person most dear to Knox in its hands as their lifeblood drained out of them.

It slowly cocked its head to the side in horrible, creaking stop-motion. Its bruise-blue mouth pulled taut in a parody of a smile, then it nodded in recognition.

"Familiar," it said, voice a rusty scrape as if it had never spoken before.

"Release them, phantom. I'm warning you."

It shook its head, skeletal fingers flexing along the hilt of the knife. Then, with a flourish, it ripped the blade out, and Ellery cried, tears streaking down their pale cheeks.

"Knox," Ellery said, their voice a pained whisper. "I'm sorry."

His initial horror was quickly consumed by an incandescent fury, a thousand times more potent than what he'd felt the night with Hale.

He had no remorse when he turned the full brunt of his magic on the phantom.

The blast ripped from Knox's body in a torrent, a white-hot flash of lightning, a combination of all his frustration and fear and despair burning through him from his core to his fingertips, aimed at the sinister wraith.

It screamed.

Ellery fell from its grasp like a puppet with its strings cut, hitting the floor with a sickening wet thump.

Another blast and the phantom writhed, its decayed, translu-cent body catching alight, cracking and breaking apart from the fury of Knox's magic. It convulsed under the onslaught as it burned into nothing but a harmless puff of smoke.

Knox's chest heaved. The smell of ozone and sulfur permeated the space, turning his stomach. The air shimmered with heat and power, but otherwise the phantom was gone.

Knox wasted no time dropping to Ellery's side, blood instantly wicking into the fabric of his pants. He pushed Ellery's limp body over to their back and ripped open their jacket. Twin wounds, one high on Ellery's side, the other above their navel, gushed blood, the warm wetness spreading out around their body in a puddle. Knox covered the deeper one with his hands, adding pressure in an attempt to stop the bleeding. He reached for his magic, but he didn't know what to do. What was he supposed to do? This wasn't a bruised nose on his own face. He couldn't fix this. He pushed harder down on the gash, but there was no response from Ellery at all, no twitch in pain from under his palms, no groan or low curse. Nothing.

Panicked, Knox tapped their cheek. "Ellery. Wake up."

Their eyes were barely open. Their skin had turned a sickly gray. Blood dribbled from the corner of their mouth. Knox pushed his hand through Ellery's hair, knocking off their knit hat, hoping to elicit something, anything.

"Ellery," Knox said again, grabbing their shoulder and shaking. Their head lolled to the side. "Ellery!"

Knox gripped their chin and leaned close, gold eyes staring into Ellery's vacant brown. "Ellery," he said again, voice choked.

Ellery blinked, rousing. Their fingers twitched next to Knox's knee, and Knox grabbed their hand.

They mouthed something that looked like *goodbye*, but Knox shook his head. "No. Don't. Ellery, please."

Ellery mustered a smile, a weak, a bloody stretch of their lips, and squeezed Knox's fingers.

Knox cupped their cheek. "Ellery. No. Don't go. You belong here. Not there."

Ellery didn't respond. Their smile slipped. Their fingers went lax in his grip, and their eyes slid shut.

"No," Knox said again, resting his forehead on Ellery's unmoving chest, squeezing his eyes shut as tears streaked down his cheeks. "No. Don't go. I want to stay with you. I want to love you." His breath hitched. "I love you."

The magic in his chest, once a brilliant flame, dimmed to an ember, and he felt it with excruciating clarity: the moment his tether to the human realm snapped, their bargain breaking as Ellery's breaths stilled.

Knox bowed his head, his grief as real and acute as the moment he'd realized he'd been abandoned, but worse, so much worse, and tears spilled from his eyes, mingled with the blood on Ellery's cooling skin. He'd never hurt like this before. He felt sliced open, a horrible deep pain, and he curled against it, a whimper escaping from between his clenched teeth.

The protective shield around them burst in a shower of sparkles; Knox's magic was no longer strong enough to sustain it. He lifted his head as the shades oozed into the room. He instinctively turned to face them, releasing Ellery's limp hand, and his fingers brushed over an object.

The vial.

Knox grabbed it and lifted it in his palm. It was intact. The colors inside continued to clash and swirl.

He cast a glance at the approaching shades and hesitated. Without the potion, he'd have no evidence and no way to explain. He'd surely be punished.

But that was a small price to pay.

He uncorked the vial with his thumb, grabbed Ellery's chin, tipped their head back, and poured the contents down their esophagus. He pinched Ellery's lips shut and hoped it would work, hoped that he had been fast enough, hoped the elixir of life would be effective for the dead.

The shadows around him flickered and grew as the shades rose from the ground to encircle him and Ellery. He kept his gaze locked on Ellery's body, searching for a sign that the magic of the potion was working. It had to work. *Please let it work.* He directed his thoughts to his queen, to any other god who might listen, and hoped, *hoped,* that Arabelle's death hadn't been for naught.

"What have you done?" the shades hissed.

"Where is the potion?"

A smoky hand reached for Ellery's mouth, and Knox snarled. He pushed it away with a feeble blast of magic.

"You've wasted it." The shades trembled in anger. "The human is almost dead. They will be in the queen's realm shortly."

Knox shot to standing. "Almost dead?" He pressed a bloody hand to his chest. "Almost? But our connection snapped."

The shades' eyes blazed. "Because you met the terms," the leader scoffed. "You've experienced all the human moments from your list. They know the reason the winter continues."

"Your bargain is at an end," another added.

Knox's eyes widened. His broken heart lurched, and he dropped back to Ellery's side. Ellery wasn't dead. There was still a chance.

"Ellery," he said. He took their hand, threaded their fingers together. Their palm was warm. "Ellery," he said again, voice deep, commanding. "Come back." He took a breath. *"Please."*

A subtle glow began beneath the skin of Ellery's throat, soft and timid.

"That's it," Knox encouraged.

It blossomed slowly, unfurling down toward their wounds, careful and searching. Knox watched, muscles tense, as the magic stitched the slashes closed with golden tendrils. It seeped through their limbs and surged into their cheeks, turning their skin flushed and warm.

Ellery's body jerked and they gasped. Their eyes stayed closed. They were unconscious, but they were alive.

Alive.

Knox sobbed. He hid his face in Ellery's shoulder, reveled in their raspy breaths, and cried.

The shades scoffed in disdain as they watched. He'd almost forgotten they were there. But now that the terms of his bargain with Ellery had been met, the call of the Other World could no longer be ignored. It beckoned him. His time grew short.

He kissed Ellery's cheek, then their forehead.

In Ellery's pocket, he found their cell phone and pressed Charley's name. The screen wavered, but the call went through, and Charley picked up after one ring.

"El! Where are you? We found this hilariously weird T-shirt that we want to buy for Knox, and—"

"Second floor. Department store, back room." He was proud his voice only slightly wavered. "You need to hurry."

"Knox? What's going on? Why are you up there? It's closed off. Are you okay?"

He winced, closing his eyes. "No. Hurry."

"Where's Ellery?"

"Ellery is here. But I have to go."

"What?" Charley demanded.

"Thank you for everything."

He dropped the phone next to Ellery, knowing that Charley and Zada were no doubt running up the stairs toward them.

He stood and faced the shades.

"Okay. I'm ready. Let's go."

"The queen will not be pleased."

Knox shrugged. "No. Not once she finds out what you've done."

"You have no proof."

The tallest shade huffed. They gripped Knox's shoulder with a smoky hand. "And you will not remember." Knox granted himself one last glance at Ellery, alive, glowing, covered in blood, but as beautiful as they had been when they'd first met. "No," Knox said with a trembling smile. "I won't. But it was worth it."

Smoke and magic engulfed his human body, the tug of the Other World insistent as the passage welcomed him back, and in an instant, he disappeared.

20

KNOX

WHEN HE OPENED HIS EYES, HE WAS IN FRONT OF THE queen's throne, standing on the ribbon of green moss that led from the dais to the door at the back of her grand hall. He blinked, his memories already fading, the knowledge of his last human life ebbing away with every moment. He scrunched his eyes shut, placed his hand on his chest, and knew, *knew,* there was something he hadn't wanted to forget. Something he *needed* to remember, but it slipped through his fingers until it was out of his grasp entirely. And that unnerved him, because even though his emotions had been dulled, they were still present, an overwhelming blunt pressure that made his chest tight and his stomach ache.

What had happened?

"Knox."

He snapped his eyes open. He had never materialized right into the goddess's presence before. Usually he returned by the docks and had the whole walk to the palace to gather his composure, to reacclimate to his home. To shed the skin of his previous life before he spoke to the queen and reported for his regular duties upon his return. But he did not have that ability this time, and her voice trembled through his frame, setting his teeth on edge.

His queen sat in front of him on her massive throne. She was a goddess, beautiful and terrifying, and she loomed over the court, domineering in both size and presence, physically bigger and taller than any of her creations, and more substantial than any human soul. She glared down her nose, seemingly irritated, and Knox quivered under her intense gaze. Her hair, the green-blond color and texture of corn silk, hung down her back in intricate braids, and her crown of gilded leaves perched brilliantly even in the gloom of their world, glinting in the low light. Underneath her olive skin, her power glowed in golden waves, emanating outward, a sign of her anger.

Knox bowed quickly at the waist. "My queen." His skin broke out in a sheen of sweat, and he hoped that he was not the source of her ire. But even if he was, he couldn't give an accounting of his actions.

"Rise and tell me where you have been."

Knox furrowed his brow. "In the human realm."

"And what have you been doing there?"

He bit his lip, a bad habit of his. "I'm not certain." He kept as still and silent as possible as she weighed his answer, his shoes leaving indentations on the moss carpet.

At her side fluttered a stack of messages, the kind he would send during an excursion through the crossroads. But there didn't appear to be many, and they were weathered and wrinkled, not his usual pristine magic notes. What was going on?

Her fingers flexed around the arms of her throne as she hummed. "And you three?"

She pinned her chilling gaze to Knox's right side, and he startled when he realized the three shades who managed his crossroads were there as well. They shivered, their cloaks rasping across the stone next to him, and Knox stared, confused. They were different somehow. Not quite as they should be.

"With the humans."

"Trying to capture the familiar."

"He fled after his duties were completed."

Her grip on her throne tightened. A snake slithered through one of the gaps in the twisted branches and stone that made up her seat.

Her attention swung to Knox. "Is this true?"

Knox squirmed. A memory pricked at his consciousness, one he had tried to hold on to. But it hovered beyond his reach. "I don't . . . I don't know."

A murmur rose among the beings of her court at his answer. Her mouth flattened into an annoyed line, as if forgetting his time in the human realm was his fault instead of a feature of his liminality, how she had made him.

"He ran," the leader of the shades hissed, pointing a gnarled finger at Knox. "As soon as he was released, he ran away from his duties."

"He begged a nymph to use her voice against us."

"He signed a bargain with a human in his own blood."

The goddess raised an eyebrow. "These are serious accusations." She gently picked up one of his letters from the pile. "You sent very few messages, Knox. And they have only just arrived," she said evenly. "Each one exudes an inappropriate fascination with the human realm."

"He *loves* them," a shade accused.

"He wants to live among them."

"With one in particular."

A stab of grief, as sharp and painful as a blade, sank into his middle. He bit down a gasp and squeezed his hands into fists, frustrated that he couldn't remember any details. He could only feel the tumult of emotions whirling in his chest. Something, or someone, that had left an imprint on his being.

The queen flipped through the pile of tattered pages, her eyes narrowing on the last one. Her gaze flicked to the shades. She set down the notes and laced her fingers.

"There are many matters at hand," she said. "And I am unsure whom to believe. The familiar with no memory but with a preoccupation with humans and their realm, or the shades who have returned to me not like themselves."

The shades shuddered, their cloaks rustling in the otherwise stillness of the room.

"You must trust us, my queen." The leader bowed.

"We are faithful, unlike the familiar."

"He did this to us. With help from the human."

Knox bristled but didn't respond.

"Based on their accounts, it appears punishment is in order."

Knox's stomach dropped. His knees trembled. They had to be lying. Right? He wouldn't have done those things . . . would he?

"Thankfully, we have another witness." The queen smiled, though it was sharp. "Where is the soul the shades ensnared?" she demanded of the others gathered in the room, a mixture of palace servants, spirits, and familiars like Knox. "Bring her to me."

The soul of a woman floated forward. She hovered, her visage clear and strong, like she had not been in the Other World long and had not yet forgotten her human self. The longer souls remained in the Other World with the queen, the more amorphous they became, until they were nothing but a rounded cluster of lights, with little memory of anything beyond their existence there. Most moved on to the next step, but for those who stayed, the existence could be a reprieve or a punishment. The oldest souls dotted the sky, lit the paths and grounds outside of the palace, and floated above them now, casting a soft greenish glow on the proceedings.

However, this one still retained her human appearance. She approached warily, but when she glanced at Knox, recognition passed across her features.

"Knox?" she asked.

He startled. "Yes?"

"It's me," she said, pointing at her chest. "Arabelle."

Knox shook his head. "Sorry. I don't remember."

"You were my familiar."

Oh. This was new. He'd not met the souls of those he'd worked for before. Or if he had, they had not introduced themselves to him.

"Was I a good one?"

"Yes." She gave him a hesitant smile. "You were friendly."

Oh. He smiled, and a small pinch of human emotion sparked in him. A memory flashed across his mind's eye—of two women, one with brown skin and a calm air and a fond smile, the other with wild red hair and a loud laugh—but the vision faded quickly.

The queen cleared her throat, and Arabelle turned her attention to the throne and bowed.

"Spirit," the queen said. "Did you make a bargain with these creatures?"

She nodded her head. "Yes."

"And what was that bargain?"

"No!" The third shade cried. "She cannot be trusted. She will lie."

"Silence!" The queen's voice boomed. She gestured to Arabelle. "Speak, spirit."

"I bartered my soul for the ability to make an elixir of life."

Loud gasps and harsh whispers emanated from the onlookers. The queen's expression turned thunderous.

"Where is the contract?" she asked, her voice low and strained. She glanced toward her servants. "Search these miserable creatures."

The shades shared a glance, then bent their heads. The middle one reached into their robe and removed a glowing scroll.

The queen called it to her hand. She unrolled it, eyes searching, her eyebrows pinched. "You have kept secrets," she said to the shades. "You entered into a bargain that is against the very rules I have set as monarch of this realm."

The trio dropped to the ground, prostrating themselves in a show of abject humility. Knox skittered to the side, afraid and confused, his eyes wide.

"It was for you, our queen."

"To harvest another soul for your reign."

"It was not a danger. Not until Knox stole the vial!"

She frowned. "And who sealed your crossroads from my sight?"

One of the shades snapped their head up. "It was the familiar."

"Knox's correspondence proves it was not him." She grabbed the note and held it up. "I have not yet received a response to any of my messages," she read. "Please send one when you are able. I am worried but hope you are well." She slammed it down.

"You sealed your crossroads and region from my sight and have caused unimaginable suffering to the humans there. You have blocked prayers from the faithful. You have affected the human realm in ways that violate the pact between myself, my brother, and my sister. And you have allowed a human to create an elixir that places our very realm in danger. What do you have to say for yourselves?"

The trio writhed on the moss carpet, shivering in fear. "Have mercy, queen of the Other World, goddess of the dead and of magic. Have mercy on your humble creations."

"Mercy?" she scoffed. "Like that you have shown the humans and creatures of that region? Those who have lost their lives, their homes, their families, because of an unending winter that you orchestrated. And for what gain? To become these pathetic creatures? Half alive, half dead."

One had the audacity to raise its head, his hood falling away to reveal his visage of bone, tree, stone, and soil, his red eyes gleaming. "We merely wanted the life of a familiar, my queen. To move about freely in both worlds. To live among the humans and return to our home."

"That is not your role!" she snapped. "That is not why you were made."

It bowed again, knees tucked under, torso flat, forehead pressed to the stone. "Forgive us, your majesty."

She lifted her chin and glared. "Where is the elixir now?"

"Knox used it!"

"To save a human!"

"Look at his garments!"

Knox trembled and looked down at himself. His clothes were indeed covered in dark crimson stains. He patted his torso and found no wounds of his own. Had he done what they said? That didn't sound like him. He would never do something against his queen's wishes. Would he? His heart pounded. Unless . . . unless what they had said was partially true—that he had been close with a human.

The queen clenched her jaw. "You have been unchecked for too long," she said, addressing the shades. "You've made a mockery of my name, have been the reason for the disbelief that now permeates the region of the world that you were supposed to maintain. You've become a liability, and as such I have decided to reassign you."

They shook. "Thank you, majesty," they said in unison.

A slow smirk stole across her face. "Do not thank me yet. You are to report to the wayfarer doors."

Knox winced. The wayfarer doors were located deep in the realm, farthest away from the boundaries to the human world, and were where souls continuing their journey would pass through to their next location.

The shades wailed. "But dear queen, our beings are now half alive; the distance from the barrier will be agony."

She tented her fingers. "That is why it is a punishment. You should be grateful that you have not been destroyed and I am giving you a chance to redeem yourselves." She motioned to the guards. "Take them."

Several of the guards descended on the shaking shades, grabbing them by their cloaks and dragging them out of the room. The shades cried and twitched, but there was little they could do. The main door shut behind them, muffling their anguish.

The queen sighed and turned back to Arabelle. "These fiends took advantage of your wants for their own ends. I apologize on their behalf for their treachery." She held her palm beneath where the scroll hovered. "I release you from these terms." Fire immediately engulfed the paper, and in an instant, all that remained was a small pile of ash.

"Thank you. But I don't understand what that means."

"You are no longer bound here. You may proceed forth to the next stage of souls. And if you have a request, I will grant it if it is within my power."

"I want to go home. I want to go back."

"That I cannot grant."

"But that was the point of the bargain. I wanted to live, to stay on earth and continue my work."

Knox involuntarily flinched at her words, and a soft sorrow settled over his shoulders, though he didn't know why.

"Your servants took me before my time and in your name."

The queen frowned. "They took advantage of the situation, yes. But it was your greed and thirst for power that led you to bargain with them in the first place. You are not blameless."

"No, but I don't want to be here. I want to go home."

"You are dead. Your body is dead. You cannot return to the human realm."

"She can," Knox said softly, daring to contradict his queen. "As an undead." As he said it, a strong twinge of anger and revulsion scorched through him. He pressed a hand to his chest, unsure why he'd had such a strong reaction to the thought of an undead. That hadn't happened before either.

The queen shot him an annoyed look. "That is considered a punishment."

"Not if it's what she wants."

"What is that?" Arabelle demanded. "What is an undead?"

"Your soul is sent into a body in the human realm. You are not alive. You are not dead. You are not human. But you are able to roam the earth. There are rules that you must follow. No contact with friends or family. Limited contact with humans in general. You return to me when your time is completed, and I deem whether you are able to proceed to the next stage."

"May I think about it?"

"Not for long," the queen said sharply. "You have already been in my realm beyond the time I normally would grant for those who are sent to be undead. It will take more power than I would like to find a body and release your soul, so do not waver."

Arabelle bowed. "Yes, goddess."

"You are dismissed, spirit."

Arabelle bowed again and floated away. Once she had exited through the palace wall, the queen motioned to Knox.

"Step forward."

He stood in the center of the carpet and faced his queen.

"As for you," she said, tone sharp. "You are not without fault. At the very least, you have been truant. If what the shades have reported is true, you have also been reckless, entering into a bargain with a human. You stole a soul from me by giving the human the elixir. And you have shown faithlessness in your creator. What do you say for yourself?"

"I . . . I must have had a good reason."

Her eyebrows shot up. "A good reason?" She stood, her form towering and massive. "A good reason to defy your queen?"

Knox craned his neck. "Yes."

"There is no good reason to defy me," she snapped. "For your truancy, you will be sent to the cells until the time I deem fit to release you."

Knox ducked his head. The cells were dark and lonely, but at least it wasn't the wayfarer door. Hopefully, she would only make him stay there to make up for the length of time he was gone. He could handle a few weeks. "I understand."

"Meanwhile, if it is proven that you are as traitorous as the three shades, I will strip you of your liminality and close your crossroads."

Knox's legs gave out, and he fell to his knees. That meant he would *never* be able to return to the human realm. He pressed a hand to his chest, where an unrelenting ache pulsed beneath his skin. He didn't know what it meant, why his feelings remained intense and persistent even after crossing the barrier, but if she closed his crossroads, he'd never have a chance to find out.

"No! Please." He clasped his hands. "I don't remember what happened, but whatever it was, I am certain it was to serve you." Except he *wasn't*. He wasn't sure at all, not with the pinpricks of memory and the splashes of emotion clinging to his consciousness.

She slowly sank back onto the throne. She considered him. "I will gather my own information. Until then, take him to the cells," she said with a wave of her hand.

Knox wilted.

His hopes for a quick stay in the cells was dashed. It could be a day or a decade of waiting to see if she uncovered any additional information, if the consequences of his actions in the human realm were more far-reaching or severe than he knew. And then she would come and take away his liminality, alter his very makeup. The anticipation of her decision would be a torture of its own, and he might have a long time to wait for the result.

He didn't fight the servants who grabbed his arms, and he ignored the snickers of the other familiars who watched from the sidelines. They guided him from the throne room, out of the palace, and down a dark path toward the docks. There was a small outbuilding, one that even souls typically avoided, which housed the rarely used cells. When he was let inside, there was no one else there.

He stepped into the cell nearest the entrance, and the door clanged shut behind him. The servants left, closing the outer door, and Knox was left alone.

There was a narrow bed, and he sat heavily on the edge. He didn't need to rest, but it would be nice to stretch out. He kicked off his shoes and lay down.

He closed his eyes and parsed through the fleeting bits of memory that remained. A plate of food, a warm hand in his own, a kiss. He wanted to remember.

But he was not created to do so.

Looking for a temporary escape from his situation and his scattered thoughts, he slipped into an uneasy sleep.

21

ELLERY

ELLERY LURCHED AWAKE WITH A PANICKED GASP, KNOX'S name on their lips. They rocketed to a sitting position, arms flailing, pain shooting through their torso like lightning. The last thing they remembered was falling to the floor after the *thing* had released them. Knox had called it a phantom. But they didn't remember anything after. It was all dark, and where was Knox? It was still dark. Why was it dark?

"Knox!"

"Whoa," Charley said, grabbing Ellery's arms. "Calm down. You'll hurt yourself."

"Knox," they gasped. "Where's Knox?"

Charley's arms tightened around them, and Ellery twisted in their grasp, then cried out in pain.

"Stop, El. You'll hurt yourself."

"You're safe," Zada said, her voice coming from Ellery's other side. Zada's calm tone permeated Ellery's panic. She cupped the back of Ellery's neck firmly. "You're safe."

"Open your eyes," Charley said gently.

Oh. Ellery's eyelids were leaden, but with effort they pulled them open.

They were met with Charley's concerned face, but beyond her shoulder, slightly out of focus, was the living room couch. They were in the apartment. Somehow they'd made it home. Charley sat on the bed next to their hip. Zada knelt on the other side.

Ellery's chest heaved. They met Charley's gaze. Her eyes were red. Her lips chapped, like she'd bitten them raw. Her cheeks were damp with tears. Ellery's stomach churned, and they turned to Zada.

Zada appeared slightly more together, but she too was not her usual impeccable self.

"What happened?" Ellery breathed.

Charley threw her arms around Ellery, wrapping them in a tight hug, and cried. Zada joined, and the two of them crushed Ellery between them.

"Don't ever do that again," Charley said, squeezing. "Please. I can't live through it. I can't."

"What?" Ellery asked, straining to look around the living room. Knox's duffel bag was by the couch. But Knox was not there, and Ellery furrowed their brow in confusion. "I don't remember."

"Knox called us," Charley said. She hadn't released Ellery, and Ellery didn't think she would anytime soon. They sagged into the embrace, exhaustion lingering behind their eyes even after waking, and pain real and sharp between their ribs. "And we found you."

"Found me?"

"In the mall," Zada said, voice choked. "On the second floor, covered in blood, a knife nearby and an empty vial, but no sign of Knox. It smelled horrible too."

"Burned popcorn, but like a whole different level of disgusting."

"We have no idea what happened. We thought you were dead...."

Charley sniffled. "That was the worst moment of my life. Seeing you like that. I thought . . ." She pressed closer. "Don't do that again. My poor old heart can't handle it."

"You're twenty," Ellery deadpanned. "How long have I been asleep?"

"Three days," Zada said gently. She smoothed down Ellery's hair. "We've been taking care of you, but we weren't sure you'd wake." Zada sighed deeply. "We're so happy you're okay."

But how? How were they okay? Ellery accepted their tangled hug for a moment longer, then disengaged carefully from the pair of them, weakly pushing Charley away when she wouldn't let go. They patted down their torso, grimacing when they touched the sore spots. Lifting their shirt, they discovered a nasty scar above their navel and another on their side, right under the edge of their rib cage.

"Ellery?" Zada's voice was tentative. Her fingers twisted in the sheets. "Do you remember how you got those?"

Ellery swallowed. "The shades were at the mall. They chased us, and we went to the second floor. And Knox and I had a disagreement— or well, he told me something that he'd been hiding—and I ran into another room. There was a . . ." Ellery swallowed. "A phantom in there." A tear slipped down Ellery's cheek. "It stabbed me."

Zada grabbed Ellery's trembling hand. "We found the knife."

Charley gasped. "But then how . . . ?"

Ellery shook their head. "Knox used his magic. I think he destroyed the phantom, but by that point I was barely awake and . . ." They gestured to the closed wounds.

"We haven't seen Knox since he called us. He sounded upset on the phone, but when we arrived, he was gone." She bit her lip. "He thanked us for everything. We haven't heard from him since."

A lump formed in Ellery's throat. "Did you see anything else?"

"No," Charley said softly. "Just the knife and a small bottle."

Ellery stiffened. "A vial?"

"Yes!" She jumped from her place on the mattress, padded quickly across the room, and snatched something off the counter. She held it up. "This."

Ellery's eyes widened. It was empty. *Oh.*

"Ellery?" Zada prodded. "Do you know what was in it?"

"The elixir of life," Ellery said.

"The what of what?" Charley asked, peering into the vial, twisting it around. "Does this have anything to do with your bargain signed in blood?"

Knox had saved them. Knox had used his proof to save Ellery, to keep them in the human realm. Ellery licked their dry lips, their heart seizing in their chest.

"Charley, could you bring me my coat?"

For once in her life, Charley didn't comment or question, merely retrieved the coat from the main hall, stepping around a bucket catching a drip from the ceiling. Wait. That hadn't been there before.

"What's the bucket for?" Ellery asked as Charley handed the coat over.

"Oh!" She clapped her hands. "The most wonderful thing happened. Two days ago, spring came."

Ellery's breath caught. Tears sprang into their eyes. "Spring?"

"Everything is flooded, though, and we have leaks everywhere. It's a mess. And it's not quite summer, like it should be. But the city and the surrounding areas are gradually warming up."

And Ellery knew. They reached into their jacket pocket and removed the small scroll. It no longer glowed. And when Ellery unrolled it, a tear dripped right onto Knox's signature with all the flourishes and curlicues, smearing the ink. Ellery pinched the paper between their fingers and as they pulled, it slowly ripped.

The terms of the bargain had been met. And with spring arriving, it only meant one thing.

Knox was gone.

Ellery doubled over, clutched their chest, and heaved a sob.

"Ellery?" Zada asked, rubbing their back. "What does it mean?"

"He's gone," Ellery gasped. "He's gone."

"I'm so sorry." Zada tugged Ellery close. "I'm so sorry."

"I didn't even get to say thank you. Or goodbye."

"Oh, El," Charley said, joining them back on the bed. She grabbed their hand. "I'm sorry, too."

Ellery allowed themself to be comforted, pressed their face to Zada's shoulder. They cried for what felt like hours, tears dampening the fabric of Zada's shirt, their heart breaking despite the promise of spring.

The story poured out of them in between sobs—how Arabelle had been tricked by the shades, how Knox had had to return to the Other World for the winter to end, how he'd wanted to *stay* with them but knew he couldn't. How they had only just made a promise between them to enjoy what they had for as long as they could and only having the one day together. How he must have used Arabelle's elixir to save Ellery's life. Ellery's heart broke—not only for themself, how they would miss Knox and any chance they'd had at loving him, but also for how he'd had to leave the place he wanted to be. It pierced Ellery to their core, deeper than the phantom's knife, and all they could do was curl into Zada and Charley's embrace and cry.

Eventually Ellery's tears dried up, and they slumped into Zada's arms. With Charley pressed against their back, Ellery fell into slumber.

"Ellery," Charley whispered, nudging Ellery awake some hours later. "Your mom is on the phone. She's called a few times since yesterday, so I can't keep putting her off. Are you up for it?"

Groggily Ellery pushed up on their elbow, eyes still shut but palm up and open.

"Hey, Aunt Nance," Charley said, all bright and chipper. "Ellery is just up from their nap. Yeah, they've been under the weather the past few days, but they're feeling better. Here they are!"

Charley slapped the phone into Ellery's palm. Ellery opened their eyes and put their mom on speaker, then fell back to the pillow.

"Ellery?" Her voice was loud in the otherwise stillness. "Are you there?"

"Yes," they answered.

"Oh, good! I've been so anxious to talk to you ever since the seasons changed. Isn't it wonderful?"

Right. The seasons had changed. Because Ellery's kind-of boyfriend had sacrificed himself to save Ellery's life and had been taken against his will to the Other World, and the goddess was now able to perceive their part of the world again.

Ellery squeezed their eyes shut, tears trickling out the corners.

"Yes. It's great."

"I knew praying to the goddess would work."

Ellery grunted, then turned their face into the pillow.

"But enough about that. You never did send your paycheck."

Ellery winced. "I'm sorry. Like Charley said, I've been sick. I can send it."

"Well, there might not be a need. Now that it appears the seasons are changing."

"Right. That's good."

"It is! And I think it's time for you to come home."

Ellery jolted fully awake. "What?"

"You need to finish school. And we need you here to help run the farm. And I'm sure Charley and Zada would love their own space again."

Ellery recoiled. They loved living with Charley and Zada, and they had come to love the city. And they couldn't . . . they didn't see themself returning to the place that had hurt them so much, even if it had been a supernatural misunderstanding. Even if their parents needed them.

"I . . . I don't know."

"You don't know? What don't you know?"

"I would rather stay here."

"What about school?"

"Online courses. Or I'll enroll in a high school here for my last year."

Their mother made a disapproving noise. "Ellery, you've worn out your welcome with Charley. She's young and in a relationship and is too kind to say it, but she is ready for you to come home as well."

Ellery cringed. They looked to Charley in the kitchen, who had clearly overheard despite her clanging of pots and pans, her face a thundercloud. She stomped over.

"Hey, Aunt Nance. Sorry for interrupting, but I couldn't help but overhear, and that's just not true. Zada and I love having Ellery. We were actually just discussing finding a bigger apartment so Ellery could stay longer."

Ellery startled. "Really?" they mouthed to Charley.

Charley crossed her arms and gave a curt nod. And despite the heartbreak of the past few days, Ellery allowed themself a soft smile.

But silence reigned on the other end of the line. Then came a sigh. "Ellery—"

"I'm not ready to come home," Ellery said. "Not yet. I can finish school here. And I have a job, and if I want to, I can continue with classes at the local college, like Zada does."

"We need you here."

Charley's hand rested on the crown of Ellery's head, and Ellery took a breath. "I'm sorry. But I think it's best for me to stay where I am."

Another silence. Then a huff. "Well, maybe you'll change your mind before school starts again."

Ellery's first instinct was to bite out an "I won't," but instead they swallowed it down. They were too exhausted to fight about it. But knowing they had Charley's and Zada's support only bolstered their resolve to stay.

"I have to go," Ellery said, voice soft. "I'm tired."

"I hope you feel better soon. We'll talk more later."

"Bye, Aunt Nance!" Charley yelled, overly cheerful. Then she swiped the phone from the pillow and ended the call. She made a face.

"Now I know why you never want to answer her calls."

Ellery gave Charley a half-hearted smile. She eased down to Ellery's side and brushed their unruly hair from their face.

"I'm proud of you."

"For abandoning my family?"

"For putting yourself first. For not returning to a situation that only hurt you. For trusting what I said about Zada and me wanting you here."

Ellery mustered a smile. "Maybe some of what you said sank in."

"Good," she said with a short nod. "Anyway, how are you feeling?"

"Like I was stabbed."

Charley frowned. "I'll get you some pain medicine." She wrung her hands. "I hate to be that person, but what are you going to do now? And what," she said, pointing over her shoulder, "are we supposed to do with that?"

Knox's duffel bag sat propped against the side of the couch.

"I don't know."

Charley smiled. "May I make a suggestion for the immediate future?"

"Sure."

"Take a shower?"

Ellery surreptitiously sniffed, and yeah, Charley had a point. With her help, Ellery stood. They bit back a groan, because even though they were alive and the potion had brought them back from the brink of death and healed their wounds, they still hurt. Charley propped Ellery against the couch, and Ellery held on to the back of it with a tight grip.

Charley patted their arm. "I'll get everything ready. Just wait here."

She bounced toward the hallway. Once she was gone, Ellery stared at the duffel bag. Knox had never revealed what he'd had in it, other than some clothes and Arabelle's journal. Ellery missed him fiercely, and maybe being near his things would ease the ache.

Ellery plucked the strings holding the bag closed and opened the top, revealing Arabelle's leather-bound journal. They hefted it in one hand, wondering if Knox had added any of his own thoughts to the pages. Ellery hoped so. They balanced it on the arm of the couch and unwound the leather string holding it closed. They flipped it open, and a small piece of paper slid out.

With a grunt, they reached down. It was a slip from Charley's order book, covered in flowery handwriting that Ellery would recognize anywhere. It was a list. The header stated *Things to Do*.

"What's that?" Charley asked, towel draped over her arm.

"It's a list that Knox wrote."

"A list of what?"

At the top was simply *Find my friend*, which had a checkmark beside it. After that, *See the city*, followed by *Make other friends*, and those were also checked off.

"It's a list of everything Knox wanted to do in the human realm."

Ellery scanned the different activities and their breath caught. In the middle, it said, *Kiss someone*. But "someone" had been scratched out and replaced with Ellery's name.

"What's it say?"

Ellery's hand trembled as they read the remainder. They closed their eyes, tears spilling down their cheeks.

Charley gently took the paper. "Oh," she said softly. "He checked off 'Fall in love.'"

Ellery swallowed.

"'Stay' has been crossed out. And 'Tell the truth' doesn't have a check. Do you know if he had a chance—?"

"He did," Ellery said. "He told me the truth."

"I'm sorry. I know he wanted to stay."

Ellery opened their eyes, took a breath, and blinked back the tears. "He did. He really did. He told me about how much it meant to him that he was friends with you and Zada. He wanted to be with us. To be with me."

Charley squeezed Ellery's hand. "It's so unfair. The entire time he was here, he was either under Arabelle's command or running from scary shadowy things." Charley wrapped her arm around Ellery's shoulders. "I'm glad he did have some fun times with us, though. And I'm really glad he had that vial. I don't know what I would do without you," she said, giving Ellery a squeeze.

Ellery frowned, Charley's words striking a chord. Knox had used the vial to save Ellery's life. He'd given up the only proof he had of the shades' misdeeds. And they had run out of time to write a letter. Which meant he'd have no way to prove what the shades had done. And without his memories, he would have no way to explain his own actions.

"Charley, I have to make sure he's okay," Ellery said. Their gaze dropped to the list. "And I need him to know how much he meant to me."

Charley scrunched her nose. "How?" She wagged her finger. "You are *not* bargaining with those creatures. I won't allow it."

Ellery shook their head. Even if they could find the correct cross-roads, Knox had bluntly stated that he didn't want Ellery making a deal with the shades either. "I don't know how, but I have to."

Charley sighed. "Let's get you in the shower first, then we'll talk."

She looped her arm around Ellery's waist and guided them from the living room to the kitchen. A shock of pain ripped through Ellery's torso, and they stumbled, grabbing the edge of the counter for support. Their hand knocked into Charley's keys and sent them skittering to the floor.

"Whoa," Charley said. "Are you okay?"

Ellery stared at where the dyed rabbit's foot and the googly-eyed corn had landed on the linoleum. They sucked in a harsh breath. "I have an idea."

"And what's that?"

"We entreat a minor god."

22

ELLERY

THE CORN SHRINE TEEMED WITH VISITORS.

The last time Ellery had been there with Knox, there had only been a handful of people walking around, and their view of the whole area had been unobstructed. Now, since the weather had warmed, the weird corn statues and the visitor center and the walkway were swarmed.

Ellery craned their neck but couldn't see past the crowd, and they were knocked from behind when they didn't move fast enough in the queue.

"Ugh," Zada said, her shoulder banging into someone as she followed Ellery weaving through the mass. "It's a row of corn statues, not a priceless painting. I don't understand the appeal."

Charley squealed when she saw the cart of tourist memorabilia. "It's so tacky. I love it. I need that corn shirt like I need air."

Ellery rolled their eyes. "Can we focus, please?"

"Do you see him?" Zada asked.

"No." Ellery squirmed. "I need to—" They forced their way between a group of people clustered around one of the fences. "Sorry. Sorry. I just need to get over there."

Once through and finally free, Ellery made it to the corner where Bram had loitered previously. He wasn't there, though a black feather rested on the very boundary of the attraction. Ellery slowly picked it up, then twirled it in their fingers.

"Is that his?" Charley asked.

"Yeah. And so is that." Ellery jerked their chin to the broken windmill.

Charley made a face. "Yikes. That shrine has seen better days."

An answering caw came from a tree overhead. Ellery whipped their head around and looked up. A large black bird hopped on a branch, feathers ruffled, eyeing them in disdain.

"Bram?" Ellery held up the feather. "We need to talk."

The bird made another noise and turned its head away, feigning indifference.

"Please? I'm entreating you."

Charley leaned and whispered into Ellery's ear. "Maybe we should've brought him an offering."

"Maybe."

Ellery tamped down their frustration. The last time they'd interacted with Bram, they had been rude. Well, kind of rude. It had been in defense of Knox, and Bram really had been the rude one, and there'd definitely been some snobbery involved, but Ellery could do this.

"I'm sorry for last time," they muttered.

The bird angled its neck and cawed.

"I said, I'm sorry for last time." Ellery's shout drew attention from a few guests, but they quickly went back to their own business after a moment. "I shouldn't have been rude," they continued in a softer voice. "Knox explained there was some kind of hierarchy I don't understand as a mere mortal being. So I apologize. I just need a moment of your time, and then I'll leave you alone. Promise."

The bird flew away, and Ellery's heart sank.

"That wasn't me."

The trio spun around. Despite the warmer temperatures, Bram still appeared in a long black coat with his large boots. He wore thick dark sunglasses, and he kept his hands tucked into his sleeves as he crossed his arms. His hair was perfectly styled, and if Ellery didn't know the arrogance—and the power—that lurked beneath, they'd think he was almost handsome.

"But nice to know that you recognize you were rude at our last visit."

"Sorry." Ellery gestured vaguely toward the tree. "I didn't know what you looked like in your messenger form."

"Much more magnificent than that," he said with a twist to his lips, "I assure you." He glanced at Charley and Zada, and his eyebrow rose. "Where's the familiar?"

Ellery swallowed. "That's why we're here, actually. I was wondering if I could ask you a favor."

He scoffed. "No."

"I need a message sent."

"I said no, human." Then he paused and leaned in. "Oh. Not quite human. *Interesting.*"

Ellery shivered. They decided not to deal with the implication of that comment just yet and plowed onward. "Knox may be in trouble. I just need you to check on him. And take him this." Ellery fished an envelope out of their pocket.

Bram remained expressionless. "No."

"Please."

"No."

"I'll bring you an offering. What are your favorite things?"

Bram smirked. "No."

"But—"

"I told you before. I am a messenger for my king only. Not for almost-humans, and not for familiars from the Other World. And I'm certainly not a babysitter." A feather slid from the bottom hem of his coat. "Now, if you'll excuse me, I do have things to do."

Zada scoffed and crossed her arms. "Like what? Stare longingly at your broken shrine? Rustle a few leaves? Oh, I know—maybe there's a pie in a windowsill that needs cooling."

He slowly turned his head, a frown marring his features, his movements almost menacing. "And who are you?"

"Just a human."

"And you feel knowledgeable enough to comment on the duties of a god?"

She crossed her arms and mustered her best unimpressed expression. "Come on, Ellery. This is a waste of time. I bet he can't even enter the Other World."

Bram bristled. "I'm a messenger for the gods." He removed his hand from the folds of his coat and pointed a clawed finger to his chest. "I can easily traverse between all three godly realms and as I want along the earth."

Zada shook her head, her braids swinging. "Ellery has found you twice in this same location. That kind of makes it seem like you're just as stuck as we are."

"Ah. I understand. Your feeble human mind cannot grasp how the barriers between the realms work, much less how a god travels."

"I mean, your beak is moving, and all I hear is *blah blah blah.*"

Bram tensed, his shoulders straight, his chest puffed. More feathers slipped from his sleeves. He held out his talon. "Fine. Give me the letter."

"Uh . . . ," Ellery said. "I'm not so sure."

"Do you want the letter delivered to that familiar in the Other World or not?"

"I do."

He made a grasping motion. "I'll do it, then. Come along, not-human."

Carefully Ellery slid the envelope into Bram's claw. "Okay. Um . . . please be careful. And um . . . thanks?"

"You owe me."

Ellery did not answer in the affirmative. They didn't know every-thing about the gods' magic, but after all that had happened, they'd at least learned to be careful about making deals. They weren't about to confirm a transaction, even if it was just verbal. Especially not to a capricious god.

"Anyway, just please make sure he's safe and he's . . . happy."

Bram slid the letter into his pocket. He looked Ellery up and down. "I don't know what you've done, not-human. But I will deliver your message."

"How will I find you again?"

He pursed his lips. "I'll find you." And with that, Bram puffed out of existence, leaving a thin trail of smoke and a few stray feathers swirling in the wind.

"Are they all that dramatic?" Charley asked.

Ellery nodded. "Yeah. So far."

"Also, kitten, goading him into doing what we wanted was amaz-ing. So smart." Charley jabbed Zada in her side. "You just poked that fragile ego until he gave in. Genius."

Zada shrugged. "I've encountered his type before." She squinted at Ellery. "Come on, El. You look peaked. Let's get some dinner and get you back to bed."

Ellery acquiesced, though they didn't think they would be able to rest until they knew Knox was okay. They missed him. And they wouldn't be able to let their worry go until Bram returned.

23

KNOX

OVER THE NEXT FEW DAYS, MOST OF THE MEMORIES FADED, save a stubborn few.

The most vivid of these was a kiss.

While Knox couldn't picture the person's face or remember their name, every time the memory stirred, the phantom pressure of the kiss tingled against his lips, and strong feelings of affection swelled within him.

He pressed his fingertips against his mouth, reveling in the emotion. He stretched out along the cot, the wails and cries of new souls from the docks wafting past his door. The cell's proximity to the incoming boats meant he rarely had a reprieve from the sounds. He'd gotten so lonely, he'd even begun to wish the souls would visit him. But not even old souls dared to wander into the small outbuilding.

Knox was used to some level of loneliness in the Other World, even when he'd been staying at the palace. But at least there he'd had his instruments and his freedom to roam. Here he just had the darkness and his own thoughts.

A squawk from the entrance drew his attention. He sat up straight when he saw the raven perched in the outer door's small window. The bird hopped through the bars, then floated lazily to the floor in the still air.

In the next moment, a god stood in front of him, dressed in black, with black hair and black sunglasses and black boots. Knox scrambled to his feet.

"Familiar," the god greeted him with a nod. "I have a message for you."

"For me?" Knox pointed to his chest. "Or for my queen?"

"I didn't misspeak. It's for you," he said, annoyed, and reached into his pocket. He removed an envelope and held it in his talons. "This is from your human."

Knox carefully took the missive. "What? My human?"

"Yes. Short. Brusque. Eternally frustrating. That human. And that is a message they wanted me to give you."

"I don't understand."

The god sighed. He rubbed his brow. "The human wanted to ensure your safety in this realm. And they wanted you to remember . . ." He cleared his throat as if uncomfortable. "The affection they have for you. No, they didn't tell me to say that, but I read their letter. However, based on your puzzled expression, it seems you have already forgotten them."

"I have." Except—was this human responsible for the kiss? "I think."

"And myself, I assume."

"We've met?"

"Yes." He shook his head. "Such a waste. All that magic, and you can't even remember falling in love with that human."

A sudden burst of fresh weeping echoed outside, but Knox tuned it out as background static. He sucked in a breath. "What?"

The messenger shuddered, disregarding his question. "Though I understand," he said as he looked around, making a face at Knox's quarters. "I've only been here a few minutes and desperately want to leave. If I knew how much better the other realms were, I'd want to forget them too, just to be able to survive this place." He wandered around the small space, making a face as he poked the wall with his talon. "What is this building? Is this where you live? I don't know how you'll even read the message in this gloom."

Knox swallowed, unsure how much to reveal to this god, but he seemed to know Knox, and he might know what happened. "I'm in trouble."

"Really?" the god asked. "I hadn't noticed."

"Can you . . . can you tell me what happened? What I did?"

The god crossed his arms. He cocked his head to the side and regarded Knox. "Well, what I've heard from my sources is that you made a bargain with a human, and then you gave them an elixir, and now they're not quite human."

Knox's breath caught. "So it's true."

The god gestured to the bars between them. "I had assumed this was the punishment. Is it not?"

"This is for being truant."

The messenger god sneered. "Truant? What a ridiculous charge. If this is the cost for missing a few days of duties, what will she do when she realizes what else you've done? Because she will find out, familiar. Your human is not subtle, and they have already entreated me on your behalf. Who knows what else they'll do."

Knox gripped the message, the paper crinkling between his fingers. "The queen said she would close my crossroads and remove my liminality."

The god frowned. "Oh, the human will not like this." He tipped his head back and spoke to the cracked ceiling. "What have I been dragged into?"

"What do you mean?"

"Your human is reckless and protective and in love." He pushed his glasses back up his nose from where they had slid. A particularly loud soul drifted close, sobbing about the beloved family they'd left behind. The god shook his head. "Poetic, isn't it?"

"What is?"

"How love remembers." He didn't elaborate further. "Anyway." He rubbed his hands together. "It's time for me to depart. Unfortunately, I'm certain I'll see you again."

With a puff of smoke and wisp of feathers, the god turned into his messenger form. He fluttered up to the window and gave one last caw, then flew away.

Knox sat back on the bed and, with a flourish of magic, allowed a single flame to flicker into existence to illuminate the darkness.

The queen would know that another god had crossed the barrier. She'd come looking. He had to hurry.

With shaking hands, he opened the letter.

A piece of paper fell out of the envelope. It was a list in Knox's handwriting with a header of *Things to Do*, and he stared at the different items that were checked off. Ones he must have accomplished. Among the checkmarks were two that stood out immediately.

Kiss someone Ellery.

Fall in love.

Oh. He pressed his fingers to his mouth. He had really done those things.

Below his list was a note in a different handwriting.

I believe in you.—Ellery

And though Knox didn't remember the person who had written the note, he knew the weight of those words, the significance of belief. There was probably a deeper meaning he was missing, one that pertained specifically to him and this human, and the dulled feeling of frustration and grief tugged at his core. He closed his eyes and hoped, *hoped*, that one day he would find out what that was.

24

ELLERY

"ELLERY, YOU'RE NOT GOING TO GO TO WORK, MUCH LESS BIKE there," Zada said, grabbing the handlebars of Ellery's bicycle. "You are still recovering from basically dying, so I think it's okay if you miss a few more days."

Ellery scowled as they stood on the sidewalk outside the apartment building. Zada blocked their path as Charley frowned from her side. The sun was high, and the air was warm, and the streets were damp from a summer shower.

"But I want to go."

"El, I thought we'd talked about this."

Ellery looked away. "You talked. I maybe listened."

Charley sighed loudly. Zada released the bike and rubbed her brow.

"Can you at least give us a reason?" Zada said, dropping her arms. "So we can understand."

Ellery clenched their jaw. "I need the distraction." They took a shaky breath. "Everything reminds me of him."

"Oh, El," Charley said sadly. "We get that. We do, but—"

A caw from overhead interrupted her, and Ellery's attention snapped to where a large bird with midnight plumage stared down at them from atop a streetlight.

"Bram?"

The raven floated lazily to the sidewalk. In a short puff of smoke and a snap of magic, Bram appeared in human form. He brushed off a few feathers from the shoulders of his long black coat. His hair was pulled back in a ponytail; his sunglasses were dark where they rested on the bridge of his nose. But when he smiled, it wasn't sharp and calculating like it had been the last time they'd met. It was softer, genuine, almost friendly.

"Human," he said pleasantly. "I've delivered your message."

"You saw him?" Ellery asked, voice a timid breath. "How is he? Is he okay? What does he remember?"

Bram held up his hand. "He's physically fine for now. But he didn't remember me."

Ellery knew he wouldn't, but to have it confirmed, to hear it from a god, was disheartening in its own way.

"What do you mean, 'for now'?" Zada asked.

Bram arched an eyebrow. "It was bad enough dealing with one of you," he said, tone dripping with irritation, "but now there are three of you. And I still have not seen any kind of offering."

Charley waved her hand. "Offering. Yes. Got it. Now squawk. What did you find out?"

He huffed in annoyance, and a stiff wind blew down the sidewalk. Feathers swirled at his feet. "He's been punished. Imprisoned in a cell for truancy. But when the goddess learns of your existence," he said with a nod to Ellery, "she'll close his crossroads and strip him of his ability to ever again cross into this realm."

Ellery dropped their bike. It clanged to the concrete. Zada grabbed their arm as Ellery swayed where they stood.

"Ellery's existence?" Charley asked. "What do you mean?"

"A human who was given an elixir of life. A soul that will never need to cross into the Other World. A threat to her reign."

Zada's grip tightened. "Is Ellery in danger?"

Charley grasped Ellery's other arm. "From the shades?"

Bram shook his head. "That trio of shades has been dealt with by the queen, banished to the depths of the realm. Ellery is in no more danger than any human, but the familiar will be once the queen realizes."

Ellery clutched Zada's hand to steady themself. "Without the ability to cross the barrier, he wouldn't be a familiar at all."

"He'd essentially become a shade," Bram confirmed. "And it's not *if* she discovers you, Ellery. It's *when*." He gestured at Ellery's body. "You're no longer an inconspicuous human. You will be easy to find."

Ellery broke into a cold sweat. Knox would lose a part of himself. He would never have the opportunity to return. He'd be stuck in the Other World for eternity, never able to watch bad TV shows or eat pineapple pizza or make friends or do whatever other ridiculous thing he wanted. "We have to clear his name."

Charley's eyes widened. "Wait, what?"

"We have to save him." It sounded unbelievable, and impossible even, but Ellery grasped on to the thought. "I can't believe I've wasted all this time waiting while he's been imprisoned."

"Okay, hold up. First, you were sleeping for several of those days, so don't beat yourself up over that. Second, I don't think that's what Bram meant. We should think this through."

Ellery wrapped their arm around their aching middle and grimaced. "I'm not asking for permission, Charley. And even if this means you ship me back to the farm after all is said and done, okay. But I'm going to try and get him back."

"I would never send you to the farm! It's just . . . I don't want to see you get hurt again, and this is dangerous and—"

"I agree with Charley," Zada said. "It's dangerous. And I don't want to find you bleeding out again in an abandoned department store." She raised her hand, effectively cutting off the fierce rebuttal on the tip of Ellery's tongue. "But as we said when we first met him, Knox obviously needs our help, and we should offer it if we can, within reason." She shrugged as Charley gaped at her. "What? We should at least see if there is a chance."

"We?" Ellery asked.

"Of course. He's our friend." Zada smirked. "There are several different types of love, kid. Even if your love for Knox differs from my love for him, it doesn't make mine any less valid."

Charley beamed. "Gumdrop, I love the way you word things. Okay. I'm in. Just . . . where would we even start?"

That was a good question.

Bram cleared his throat. "You may be different now, human, but you can't just wander into the Other World. Even I had trouble entering her realm, and I'm a god." He shook his head, fending off Charley's inevitable follow-up question. "I'm not returning to that place anytime soon."

Ellery's thoughts spun. "I think I know someone else who can."

Bram's eyebrow twitched. "If it's that undead who wanders around the city, be careful. He cannot and should not be trusted."

"Yeah. That's him. How did you know?"

"He comes to my shrine sometimes. To stare."

"You all are very weird," Charley said.

"I wouldn't expect you to understand." Bram folded his arms back inside his coat. "When he's not here, he's often on the college campus, feeding."

Ellery shuddered at the memory of his cold lips on their own: the sensation of their fondness being drawn from them in a slow, steady stream, the split-second hollowness after. How Knox's kisses had chased all that away. "He owes me a favor. He has to help."

Bram wrinkled his nose. "Gods don't deal in favors. Friendly word of advice, not-human. Next time you entreat a god or a goddess, have an offering ready." He tilted his face toward the sunlight. "We're vain creatures. We want to feel worshipped and revered. Like we're above it all, even if we're as shallow as your kind."

"At least he admits it," Charley said under her breath. Zada elbowed her in the side.

He leveled his sights back on the trio. "If you do intend to travel to her realm, you'll need more than a trinket, especially if you plan on returning." He adjusted his glasses. "Not all of us are as magnanimous as myself."

Ellery licked their dry lips. "Would a protection charm—?"

Bram let out a derisive huff, cutting Ellery off. "Not against a goddess in her own realm." A shiver of fear skimmed down Ellery's spine. "Right. So any suggestions for an offering?"

He slid his sunglasses down his nose and peered at Ellery with his dark, dark eyes. "The thing that made you what you are now."

And with that, Bram puffed out of existence, leaving a thin trail of smoke and a few stray feathers.

"Dramatic much?" Charley said with a roll of her eyes.

Zada squinted at Ellery. "What did Bram mean? Did that make sense to you, El?"

Ellery's thoughts tumbled. The elixir had made them not quite human. And while Ellery didn't know all the effects, it had kept them alive and prevented their soul from traveling to the Other World. The goddess of the dead probably wouldn't want that knowledge circulating among humans. And on the last page of Arabelle's journal had been a recipe. . . . If that was the last thing she had worked on before the shades had claimed her soul, they could remake the potion. That had to be it.

"Arabelle's journal," they blurted out. "It's in the apartment." They turned and ran back inside.

"Hey!" Zada called after them. "Your bike!"

Ellery ignored them. They slammed into the apartment and crossed the room where Knox's duffel bag still leaned against the wall. They opened it. Arabelle's journal sat at the top where Ellery had placed it.

Hope fluttered in Ellery's chest. It was a dangerous thing.

"You could have at least locked up your bike," Charley grumbled as she entered the apartment a moment later. "And I guess this means you're not going to work either?"

Ellery held up the journal. "Arabelle found Knox's crossroads and made a bargain with the shades. She probably wrote some of that down. We'll start there."

Charley made a skeptical face but sighed. "Fine. Coffee first, though. Then we'll brainstorm how to save your boyfriend from his punishment in the land of souls."

25

ELLERY

After a perusal of Arabelle's journal and a loud discussion around the kitchen table, the three of them conceded that they needed assistance. Even if what they found in the journal made sense, which most of it didn't, and even if they could find the correct crossroads, to which Arabelle had only left vague directions, they would still need help creating the potion. They found the recipe in the last entry Arabelle had made, but the ingredients were weird, and some of the instructions were complicated.

At least they had a place to start.

Ellery pounded on the stage door with their fist. Charley and Zada stood shoulder to shoulder with them, and despite their incessant hovering, Ellery was grateful to have them there. After the past few days, their heart felt just as beat-up as their body, and they were happy to have all the support they could get.

Ellery pounded again. "Lorelei," they shouted. "Open up!" Their voice cracked with frustration on the third syllable.

No response.

At least the weather was warm, unlike the last time Ellery had been there. And they weren't being chased by living shadows. But those small details did nothing to improve Ellery's feeling that the chances of their success were decreasing with every minute spent waiting. Ellery jiggled the doorknob, kicked the frame, then knocked continuously until the side of their fist was red from the impact.

"Open up, Lorelei! Or I'll tell everyone that—"

The door swung open while Ellery was midswing, and they stumbled over the threshold, only just catching themself from barreling right into the minor goddess herself.

"You'll tell everyone what?" Lorelei asked, vibrant blue eyes narrowed. Her silver hair was pulled back in a high ponytail, and she wore a pair of designer jeans and a flowy green blouse. She crossed her arms and tapped the toe of her expensive heels.

Ellery stared. Then hastily gathered themself. "Um . . . nothing. That was just—"

"An empty threat. I'm aware." She studied her nails. "What do you want, human?" Then she paused, her brow furrowing, her gaze darting to Ellery's face, then sweeping over their frame. Her eyes narrowed further. "What happened? Where's Knox?" She opened the door wider, beckoning Charley and Zada inside.

"That's a conversation for a safe space," Zada said.

Lorelei led them to her dressing room. Once inside, she closed the door firmly.

Ellery sank onto the couch, trying to hide their wince. Charley and Zada followed, and the three of them squished together.

Lorelei eyed Ellery from her perch across from them. "You . . . you've changed."

"So I've been told."

She arched an eyebrow. "You're aware?"

"Yes." Ellery ran a hand through their hair. "It doesn't matter. Knox has been taken to the Other World. And we need to save him."

Lorelei scoffed. "To what end?" she asked, sitting demurely in the chair across from them. She crossed her legs.

"He's in trouble. His queen punished him, and she is going to take away his ability to cross the barrier," Ellery said.

Lorelei's mouth flattened into a thin line. "I see."

Ellery leaned forward in their seat. "So you understand why we have to fix this. We have to save him."

Lorelei sighed. "Humans," she muttered. "Well, mostly-humans. You fail to realize that once Knox crossed the barrier back to his home, he lost his memories." She leveled Ellery with a sympathetic look. "He won't remember you."

Ellery's stomach twisted into knots. "I know."

"But you hope he will," Lorelei said with a pitying smile. "You hope he'll see you and remember the affection you had for each other. I see it all over you."

Ellery ducked their head. They didn't acknowledge Lorelei's statement, but they didn't refute it either. "You've known him the longest out of everyone. Wouldn't he be miserable being stuck in the Other World with no ability to return to the human realm ever?"

She rubbed her temples, expression pinched. "I don't know. Yes. Probably. Possibly."

"Then we have to clear his name. We have to show the queen he wasn't at fault."

"The risk of meddling in another god's affairs, even for a minor goddess like me, much less a human, is not worth it."

"We know the risks," Ellery said.

"Do you?" Lorelei held up a manicured finger. "One, you're messing with the supernatural; there is always a risk for you humans. Two," she said, adding another finger, "you'd have to strike a bargain with the shades, and we all know that option by its very nature is unsafe."

"We're not going to do that," Charley chimed in, elbows on her knees. "Knox warned us, so we have to find another option."

"Well, the only other option would be to travel to the Other World and plead his case. But that is absolutely ridiculous and impossible for a human to do so without dying. Only human souls can cross the barrier. Not human bodies." She dropped her hand. "And before you ask, no. Even gods and goddesses don't travel there unless they absolutely must."

Ellery gritted their teeth. "We know, but I'm not completely human anymore, am I?"

A slow, understanding smile spread its way over Lorelei's face. "You were when I first met you. You're not now. What did you do?"

"I drank a potion a witch made."

Her eyebrows quirked. "Oh. Well, it worked." She hummed, the tune beautiful and soothing as she regarded Ellery. "You're not immortal," she said. "Not like me. Not like Knox. But I think your physical self could cross the barrier and return unharmed."

Ellery folded their shaking hands. "How do I get there?"

"Wait!" Charley burst out. "I thought the plan was to first ask Lorelei or Hale to go on your behalf. And you would go if there were no other options."

Lorelei snorted. "I'm not venturing to the Other World. I'm returning to my river and then visiting my father and grandmother in the Oceans. A realm in which I'm welcome. Besides, I imagine my beautiful river is flooded from the snowmelt and will need to be tamed. I'm waiting a few more days so it's not completely frigid, but I'm not staying in this city any longer than I have to."

"What would . . . ?" Zada trailed off. The couch jostled. "What would Ellery need?"

"What?" Charley asked. "Ellery is not traveling to the land of the *dead*. Their mother would *kill* me."

Ellery lifted their head. Zada's hand rested gently over Charley's. "It's not our decision, babe. And I'd rather Ellery had all the tools and information they need than rush in. Which they will do," she said, shooting Ellery a glance, "if we don't help."

"But, muffin, it's the *Other World*. Knox doesn't even remember Ellery. The queen is a goddess. A goddess of *souls*."

"She is," Lorelei chimed in. "But she is fair."

Charley grunted and tugged on a lock of her hair. "And you're dead set"—she paused, scrunching her face at her own poor choice of words—"I mean, you're certain?"

Ellery nodded and took a breath. "I am."

Charley closed her eyes, waved her hand as if centering herself, and took a breath, then opened her eyes again. "What does Ellery need? And how do we get there?"

Lorelei smirked. "An offering."

"Bram made that clear," Zada said.

"Oh, you've already talked to the bird-god? You're really invested, then."

"Yes," Ellery said.

"Well, the offering can't be the regular burnt, scented votive crap. Like, a real offering. One she can't refuse."

"About that," Zada said, leaning forward and handing Lorelei a piece of paper. "Can you help us find these ingredients?"

Lorelei perused the paper, her lips pursed. "I think I can help. But even with this," she said, waving the paper, "you'll need a way in. I can get you to the correct crossroads, but I can't open the door, much less cross the barrier without an invite. You'll either need to call the shades or find someone who can cross on their own."

Ellery gulped. "I know someone who can help. We'll have to find him quickly, though. With the goddess's attention restored, he's not quite allowed in the city."

Lorelei tented her fingers. "Interesting. I believe I've met him before. He loves a good gathering."

"Yeah, that's him."

"He should be able to get you in. This plan doesn't sound as futile as I originally thought." Lorelei spun in her chair and grabbed a pen from her desk. She scribbled something on the paper and handed it back to Zada. "Start there for ingredients. And that's my number underneath. Text me when you have the offering ready, and I'll keep an eye out for the undead."

Ellery slumped in relief. "Thank you for all your help."

"Knox is my friend. My immortal existence would be boring without the chance of him popping back into it at any given time." Lorelei gave them a tight smile. "I know you are determined to travel to her realm, but be prepared for what you may find. By all accounts, the Other World is not like any other realm. It may be frightening for a mere somewhat-mortal."

That sounded ominous, but Ellery was prepared. They had a lifetime of watching horror movies under their belt. They had fought shades. They'd insulted a messenger god. They'd almost died at the hands of a phantom. They were ready for what might come next.

26

ELLERY

"NOT THAT I'M COMPLAINING," CHARLEY SAID, TWIRLING A pencil through the red strands of the ponytail she'd gathered to keep it out of her flushed and freckled face. "Because it's great that the spring or summer or whatever we're in has returned. But it's so hot in this kitchen, I could die."

She fanned herself with her hand.

"You're literally complaining."

"Don't start with me." She wagged her finger in Ellery's direction. "Do you have those chopped root thingies ready so we can add them to this disgusting mess?"

Ellery returned to the cutting board, knife in hand, and diligently and awkwardly cut the sturdy root. It was almost carrot-like in texture and thickness, but it definitely did not look like a carrot and did not smell like one either.

Arabelle's journal was propped in front of them, held up by the toaster, pages pinned open with Zada's hair clips. Ellery squinted at the handwriting.

"I don't think we're supposed to combine these until after we shake in the soil from the graveyard."

Charley gagged. "I can't believe you drank this."

"I'm pretty sure I was almost dead at that point, so . . ." Ellery trailed off and scooped the tiny bits of root into a bowl. Charley shivered despite the heat.

She grabbed the wooden spoon and slowly stirred the concoction, which was a mixture of honey, red wine, garlic, and corn oil. Which didn't sound completely horrible, until they added the stagnant pond water. They didn't have a cauldron, so they had settled for using a slow cooker, since many of their other pots were currently collecting water from the leaks in the ceiling.

Between Zada running around to every alternative grocery store and herb shop in the city and Lorelei assisting, they'd managed to gather just about all the ingredients. It had taken two days to track everything down, and Ellery bristled against the loss of time. But they were grateful for the help from the others. Even if they had been more annoyed and moody in those two days than actually thankful. At least Charley and Zada had understood.

A thin trail of smoke wafted between them as the smell of something burning reached Ellery's nose.

"Oh no," Charley said, hurrying over to the stove. "I hope I didn't char the horsefly wings."

She yanked open the oven and waved her oven mitt to disperse the tendrils of smoke. Sliding the cookie sheet out, she set it by the stove burners. "A little crispy, but they should work. I guess. But what do I know? I'm not a witch."

Ellery's brow puckered in concern as they regarded the charred remains of the bugs.

Making the potion had turned out more arduous than they had anticipated. Granted, it had taken Arabelle five years to perfect it, and it was literally the key to life, so Ellery should've been more realistic about their expectations and abilities.

They sighed and leaned forward to consult the book. "Okay, so those can be stirred in with the chilled pomegranate juice and then set aside."

"On it," Charley said, using a spatula to scrape the wings into the juice mixture. "So I have to be honest—when Knox walked into the diner the first time a few months ago, I didn't think it would lead to, well, *this*. But that's life, I guess."

Ellery drummed their fingers on the countertop. The viscous mixture in the slow cooker bubbled. "Thanks for all your help, especially with . . ." They gestured helplessly to the mess they'd made of the kitchen. "You didn't have to."

"Of course I did." Charley grunted as she stirred. "It's for you. I'd do anything to help make you happy. Even if I had to peel wings off dead flies and bake them."

"No, but you and Zada welcomed me, and I never really thanked you for that. And you told my mom I could stay." Ellery bowed their head and knotted their fingers. "I'm grateful for everything you've done for me these past months. Thank you."

Charley ruffled Ellery's hair. "You're welcome. You are my favorite cousin. And I love you. And I can't wait for us to find an apartment that's bigger and not dripping," she said, gesturing to the buckets and pots placed around the apartment. "And I only ask one thing in return."

Ellery made a face. "What?"

"That we get to do more fun stuff together. Like this." She wrinkled her nose when a thick bubble in the mixture popped. "Okay, not exactly like this. But fun stuff. Together, as a family. That's all I want."

"Okay," Ellery said with a nod. "I can do that."

Charley grinned wide. "Great. I have so many plans."

The front door opened. "Plans for what?" Zada asked, tromping in. She held up a sandwich bag. "For this cemetery dirt, I hope."

Charley squealed and clapped. "Yes! Excellent. Thanks so much, bunny. This was the last thing we needed."

Oh. It was. Once they sprinkled in the soil, they would add the chopped root and top it off with the pomegranate juice and baked flies. They were almost done.

"Great," Zada said, shrugging out of her jacket. "Because this is gross, and I want it out of my kitchen."

"So much same," Charley said. "Okay. Let's do this."

Ellery removed the lid from the pot and gently shook the contents of the bag over the top of the liquid. Then they added the root, and Charley poured in the fly juice.

"Turn the heat up," Ellery said, nodding to the instructions. "And stir."

Charley turned the knob on the pot. Zada grabbed the spoon and mixed vigorously.

"Is . . . is this really what it's supposed to look like?" Charley asked, peering in. "It's sludge."

"And smells like a farm," Zada added. "How did Knox carry around a vial of this without us noticing?" She pressed a kitchen towel to her nose. "I'm going to throw up."

Ellery ran their finger down the directions and the ingredients, brow furrowed, anxiety rising, because the potion failed to look anything like what had been in the vial. "We used the wax from a candle that had been burned for a ritual, right?"

Charley nodded. "Stole it off the shrine myself."

"And there are three dog hairs?"

"From Ms. Smith's Pomeranian down the hall."

Charley wrinkled her nose as the mixture began to boil in earnest. "Okay. We've ruined the slow cooker. There is no using this again."

"Maybe it's because we're not magic." Zada switched arms as she stirred. "Arabelle was a witch, right? She must have had some magical ability or ingredient that we're obviously missing."

Ellery abruptly stiffened. Magical ingredient. Oh. *Oh.*

"Gods and goddesses, I know what it is."

"What?"

Ellery darted out of the kitchen to where Knox's duffel still leaned against the couch. They opened the top and rifled through the clothes inside.

"Remember when Knox and I made the pact? He didn't have magic at the time, but we used his blood to seal the deal. He mentioned that Arabelle had used his blood as an ingredient in a potion."

"Blood?" Charley shouted. "Where are we going to get Knox's blood?"

And there it was. Ellery yanked out the bloodstained shirt Knox had worn the night of the hockey game. The attempts to wash and salvage the shirt had been in vain, but thankfully Knox hadn't thrown it away. Instead, he'd merely shoved it to the bottom of his bag. Ellery lifted it up. "Right here."

Charley jerked open the junk drawer. "Aha!" She brandished a pair of scissors. Together they cut off a small scrap of bloodied shirt.

"I hope this works," Ellery muttered.

"Have a little faith." Zada winked.

Ellery took a breath and dropped the tiny bit of bloodied cloth into the potion. Nothing happened as the fabric floated along the top. But once the liquid seeped in and the fabric sank and the dried blood oozed into the concoction, the whole pot shook as the sludge thinned; its color changed from mud brown to a midnight blue swirled with purple sparkles.

The whole slow cooker began to shake as the potion bubbled and thrashed in a threatening tempest. A wave spilled over the side, hissing and steaming against the hot exterior of the pot.

"Oh no."

"Grab the lid."

"Turn off the knob."

Zada reeled backward, spoon in hand, while more of the swirling chaos broke over the side, splattering all over the counter. Charley lunged forward and slammed the lid in place. Ellery switched off the power and unplugged the device from the wall, but the pot continued to shake, the liquid slamming against the sides.

"What do we do?" Charley shouted as she leaned all her weight on the lid. "Did this happen with the vial?"

"I don't know!" Ellery yelled, fingers scrambling around the junk drawer. "But at least this is the right color!"

Ellery grabbed a roll of duct tape, and between the three of them, they managed to secure the lid with a crisscrossing design of tape. A lot of tape.

Charley wiped the sweat from her brow. "Wow. So that's done."

Zada peered through the glass top into the pot. "I can't believe that's the secret to life. It's . . . pretty."

"Do you . . . do you want to drink some?" Ellery didn't really know what it had done to them, other than bring them back from the brink of death, and that the local gods and goddesses seemed to think they had changed enough to be able to wander into the realm of souls.

Zada jerked backward. A glob plopped on the floor. "No. Thank you." She nudged Charley with her elbow. "Do you?"

Charley hummed. "No, I don't think so. I know what's floating in there, for one. But for two, I think I'll be happy with whatever time I'm allowed." She reached out and took Zada's hand, laced their fingers, and nuzzled into Zada's neck. "As long as I'm with you, sweetcakes."

A pang lanced through Ellery's middle, and it was not the stab wound. They looked away and stared out the high window, where the blazing sun peeked through the curtains. They missed Knox; they missed him so fiercely, they ached with it. They wished he was there so they could stand in the sun and feel the warmth of its rays and hold hands as they went on some kind of adventure together.

"El, did you hear me?"

Ellery snapped from their daydream. "Huh?"

Charley had her hands on her hips. "I said, what's next?"

The slow cooker danced on the countertop. Ellery's palms grew clammy. They were so close to the finish line, so close to the end. They gulped. "We call Lorelei."

"Found him!" Lorelei called brightly as she rounded the corner of the corridor from the club to her dressing room. "He was right where I thought he'd be."

Ellery shot up from the couch as Lorelei pushed the body forward, the person smacking into the swinging door before stumbling into the room.

"Ow," he said with a grunt. Hale glared at her over his shoulder as he righted himself using the back of the couch, then rubbed a red spot on his forehead. "Manhandling? I expected better from a goddess." He tugged the hem of his expensive shirt and smoothed out the imaginary wrinkles. He was as handsome as he had been the night of the party, with his perfectly styled blond hair and bright blue eyes, but Ellery could sense the unnaturalness about him now, the danger. "And what is the meaning of this? I was minding my own business—"

Lorelei scoffed. "You were loitering around the campus, waiting for news about the next social gathering you could crash."

He huffed. "And you grabbed me. In broad daylight, no less."

"People clapped."

"Heathens," he said with a sneer. "Besides, I don't know what I've done to anger you, goddess of the river, but whatever it was, it didn't warrant being dragged across town."

He glanced around the room, then stilled, his mouth dropping open.

Ellery wiggled their fingers. "Hi, Hale."

He narrowed his eyes. "Oh, it's you." He peered at Zada and Charley, who stood just behind Ellery. "Where's your familiar friend? Is he going to strangle me with his magic again?"

"No."

"Good. It took an entire day to be able to talk without squeaking." He licked his lips as he focused on Ellery. They squirmed. "But that was a small price to pay for the absolute deliciousness of—"

"I'm calling in my favor."

Hale's eyebrows shot up. "Already?"

"Yes."

He shrugged. "Well, all right. I'd thought you might sit on it for a decade or so, but what do you want, human?"

"You're coming with us to the crossroads. And you're going to open the door to the Other World."

Hale burst into loud, obnoxious laughter. He wrapped his arms around his middle and guffawed right into Ellery's face. He even slapped his knee in insufferable delight.

Ellery set their jaw.

His laughter petered out. "Oh, you're serious."

"Yes."

"I hate to break it to you, but that's not quite a fair exchange. I mean, it was *one* kiss, and not a great one at that. I only managed to draw a tiny bit of affection from you before your boyfriend broke us up. It wasn't even a full meal. More like a snack."

"You kissed him?" Charley said with a gasp, thrusting her finger in Hale's direction. "Really?"

Hale grinned. "I'd give it a three out of ten. Nice warmth, a little too much force, and far too short for the favor you are requesting. But I wouldn't be averse to a little kiss from—"

"Don't," Lorelei warned.

Hale pouted. "You all are no fun. And thus my answer is no."

Ellery crossed their arms. "You agreed that you owe me, and this is what I need. So I hope you are ready for a little road trip."

"Oh, and who is going to make me?"

Lorelei hummed a tune as she cracked her knuckles, the threat of her voice obvious.

Hale gulped. "Fine. I call front seat."

"Not on your life," Zada muttered. She spun her keys on her finger. "You're lucky you're not being tossed in the trunk."

"You wouldn't be so disrespectful if you knew the extent of my powers. One look into my eyes, and I could change your mind. You might even hand over those keys and let me drive us to a secluded location."

"Ew," Charley said. "You're gross."

"Hey!" Hale pressed a hand to his chest in mock affront. "That's an unwarranted maligning of my character. I'll have you know that ever since my rendezvous with that little human and our subsequent heart-to-heart, I've committed to consensual snacking only. I was merely making a point."

Lorelei grabbed his upper arm. "That's enough. Let's go, undead."

"Ow. Ow!"

Lorelei dragged him behind the procession, out of the building, and to Zada's car parked on the street. The pot of potion had been left on the front seat, which, in hindsight, had not been the smartest idea.

A caw and a flutter of wings caught Ellery's attention, and they paused before sliding into Zada's car. Bram stared down at them from the SIREN'S CLUB sign.

"Um . . . hi?"

Bram hopped down to the sidewalk, and after a flash and a crackle of magic, he appeared in front of Ellery in his human form.

"Human," he said pleasantly.

He peeked into the back window of Zada's car. Lorelei was squished in the middle, a barrier between Hale and Charley. "Aw, you found the undead. And the river nymph is also along for the ride, I see."

"She's guiding us to the crossroads."

He tapped his foot. "Is there room for one more?"

"You want to come with us? Why?" Ellery asked, brows drawn together. The metal of the car door was hot under their palms in the midday sun. A blast of cold air skirted across Ellery's back as Zada turned on the air-conditioning, a feature they hadn't used in the last five years.

Bram shrugged. "I'm interested now." He tilted his face toward the sun. "And I'm in a good mood. I've missed the warmth."

"Um . . . okay? I just . . . There's not a lot of room."

"Don't worry. I won't take up much space."

A plume of smoke later and Bram flew into the car, balancing on the armrest between the driver's seat and the passenger's, his feathers ruffling in the air from the vents.

Ellery slid in, the container of potion held tight in their arms.

Zada's eyes were wide as she threw the car into drive, pulling out of the parking spot onto the main road. "I'm driving a god, a goddess, an undead creature, my girlfriend, and my girlfriend's cousin who is no longer completely human to a crossroads in the middle of a corn field, to rescue a familiar from the powerful goddess of souls." She smiled tightly. "This is fine."

"Isn't it great, blueberry?" Charley piped from the back. "Road trip!"

Ellery sank into their seat, balancing the tumultuous potion on their lap. They wished they could match Charley's enthusiasm, but Charley wasn't the one who would be walking into what basically constituted the afterlife to plead to a powerful goddess, one Ellery had turned their back on years ago. Fear beat a continuous drum in their chest, and the pressure built behind their eyes. But they fought it all down, put on a brave face, and held on to the fact that it would be worth it. Because if all went right, then they would see Knox soon.

27

ELLERY

"IT'S THE NEXT ONE, ZADA. I'M SURE OF IT," LORELEI SAID AS Zada drove down the brown pea-gravel road.

Lorelei held Arabelle's journal open on her knees; she had been guiding Zada based on Arabelle's cryptic notes and her own memory since she'd turned off the interstate an hour ago. The route cut through several single-stoplight towns that were too small to warrant an exit off the highway. Though they were hours away from Ellery's home, it was all eerily familiar to them: the long stretches of flat land, the skinny roads that sliced through swaths of farmland, the gas station a few miles back with the tiny convenience store and only two working pumps. The whole area was an echo of where Ellery had grown up.

Zada slowed when they came upon an intersection featuring a weathered wooden post off to one side. Nailed to the pole was a piece of plywood.

BEWARE OF BARGAINS MADE HERE.

Ellery gulped as Zada eased the car over. The intersection was nondescript. It was literally in the middle of nowhere. To most, it would appear to be a weird location for a place of power. But a crossroads was a liminal space, a threshold. It made sense that it would be where the veil between their realm and the Other World was thinnest.

"This must be it," Charley said, leaning over both Lorelei and Hale to look out of the window.

"Did the warning sign give it away?" Hale snapped. "Or was it the literal magic radiating from that spot?"

"Magic?" Charley flopped back in her seat. "I can't feel anything."

Ellery gripped the slow cooker. Hale was right. They'd felt magic before—when they'd signed the bargain in blood with Knox, when the shades had approached, when the phantom had held them in their grasp—and this place was soaked in it.

They all pushed out of the vehicle. Ellery's knuckles turned white from the grip they had on the pot of potion.

"This is Knox's crossroads," Lorelei said with a nod, snapping the journal shut. She breathed in deep. "I can hear my river," she said dreamily. She closed her eyes.

"It's close?" Charley asked, looking around.

"Miles away. But it's calling to me."

"Then release me and go, goddess."

She snapped her eyes open, her grip still tight on Hale's arm. "Not until you open the doorway and fulfill your promise, you sniveling creature."

With a spark of magic, Bram turned into his human form. He crossed the road and wandered around the marked post, bending close to inspect a fresh and brilliant bouquet of colorful flowers, a few votive candles, and a stack of pomegranates. He pushed his glasses to the crown of his head and squinted in the sunlight. "The doorway is not here."

Ellery froze. "What? Where is it?"

Hale sighed, long-suffering, and rolled his eyes. He jerked his arm away from Lorelei. "It's right there."

Off to the side was a large tree with a twisted trunk. The branches spread out above them, casting shade along the roadside. It was tall and old and beautiful, and Hale approached it with narrowed eyes and a wary step. He pressed his ear to the wood and hummed beneath his breath. "Prepare to be amazed, humans. And god. And goddess. And whatever you are now," he said to Ellery. Then he rapped his knuckles twice with a flourish and stepped back.

A ripple of magic crackled outward, and the outline of a doorway glowed gold in the bark. With the tip of his finger, he pushed. The door swung inward.

A gust of stale wind blew out, and deep in the oval of darkness, the sound of faint, plaintive wailing reverberated .

"There. Off you go, Ellery." Hale smiled wide and bright. "Have fun. Don't eat or drink. Don't touch anything. And don't anger her or, well, you'll be there a long time."

Ellery's hands shook on the container of potion. They approached the oval and stared into the pitch black, mouth dry, heart racing.

Bram appeared at Ellery's shoulder. He held up a coin in his talons. It gleamed silver in the afternoon light. "For the boat ride." He tucked the coin in Ellery's jacket pocket.

"Boat ride?"

He huffed. "Did you even do any research? You have to cross the river to get to the palace. And you're not a newly arrived soul, so you will need to buy passage."

Ellery's gaze flickered to Hale.

"He's right," Hale said, patting his pocket. "I have my own coin to pay my way when it's time for my return." He waved his hand. "Just take the one coin, though. It would be presumptuous to have one for the return trip, when it's ultimately her decision if you are allowed to leave."

"I . . . I . . ."

"Stick to the road," Bram continued. "Don't touch the water. Go right to the palace. Don't get sidetracked by the souls who want to talk to you. Some of them are just lonely, but others have ill intent. They can't physically impede you, but they will trap you in a conversation, and you won't know how much time has passed."

Sweat broke out on Ellery's brow. Their whole body trembled.

"Do you want to come with me, Bram?" they asked hopefully.

Bram crossed his arms. "No. One recent trip was enough. And I don't want to garner anyone's wrath by wandering into realms not my own."

"Oh," Ellery said. "Makes sense."

"Don't touch the water. Stay on the path. Have a coin. Don't talk to the souls," Charley said, ticking the rules on her fingertips. "What if Ellery follows all the rules, but the queen is still pissed? What's to keep her from smiting them where they stand?"

"Tradition," Lorelei and Bram said in unison. They looked at each other, and Bram rolled his eyes, gesturing for Lorelei to elaborate.

"It's bad form for a god or goddess to hurt a human who is beseeching their assistance in good faith. And Ellery is still mostly human." She raised her finger. "I said it's bad form; I never said it hasn't happened. It has. But it's generally frowned upon. If she were to violate this etiquette, then her brother and sister would not be pleased."

"Oh, great. El will be protected by etiquette and sibling rivalry."

"It's fine, Charley," Ellery said, nudging Charley with their elbow. "I'll be okay."

"She might not kill you, but anything else in that realm can," Bram said. He glanced at the elixir. "And you might be the only human I know with the ability to anger her enough to break that tradition. Tread carefully."

Ellery gulped, then nodded.

"Ellery," Zada said softly. "You don't have to. No one will think any less of you if you decide this is beyond the boundaries of what you can handle."

Ellery closed their eyes and steeled themself. "It's not just for him. I want to see him one more time." Ellery glanced to Charley. "This is for me, too."

Charley gave them a watery smile. "Okay."

"I'm going. I just need a minute. It's so dark."

The oval doorway almost looked opaque, and if Ellery hadn't heard the noises coming from within and felt the light breeze, they'd think the entrance was painted on the bark with absolute black paint instead of there being an actual hole.

"The souls will light the way," Bram said.

"Wait," Charley yelled. She sprinted back to the car and threw open the trunk. Grabbing Zada's school bag, she upended it despite Zada's protest, then opened the emergency pack Zada kept in the back and shoved a large flashlight and a pair of headphones inside.

"Here," she said, crossing the road, looping the strap over Ellery's head to rest on their opposite shoulder. The bag hung at their hip. "Flashlight for the dark. Headphones to help block out the souls if they try to talk to you. They muffle sound—not completely, but it's better than nothing."

"Thank you."

"You have your coin?" she pressed.

"I just gave it to them." Bram scowled.

"I'm just checking!" Charley patted the pocket and nodded when they felt the hard circle. "This is my beloved cousin. I want them to return in one piece. Okay?" she said to Ellery.

"I'll be fine."

Charley wrapped her arms around Ellery's shoulders in a crushing hug. "I know. We'll be waiting."

Ellery clutched the pot, blinking back their tears. They turned and faced the group. "Thank you all for your help." They lifted their chin. "I'll be back soon."

Then they turned and faced the opening. And stepped through the black.

28

ELLERY

ELLERY SHOULD'VE KNOWN THAT CROSSING INTO ANOTHER realm would be more difficult than merely stepping through a hole in a tree. But it still caught them off guard when the darkness physically squeezed them on all sides, as time and space bent around them in the moments of that first step.

When their foot touched the ground, they stumbled but righted quickly, watery eyes snapping open. In the space of a breath, they were on the other side. They turned and looked behind them, and the entrance was an oval of pure white light, like staring directly into the sun. They spun around, blinking away the brightness, then took stock of their surroundings.

The air was thick with the smell of damp soil and the taste of rain. The atmosphere was one of perpetual gloom, the floating, glowing balls of light above them casting everything in a greenish-yellow swirling glow. A low hanging fog rolled over the land-scape, thin in some areas while thick as clouds in others. The most disconcerting aspect was the lack of noise. Off in the distance came the gentle lap of water on a shore, but otherwise Ellery was sur-rounded by an oppressive silence. There were no birds chirping, not even the rustle of leaves on the wind. The wails they'd heard when on the other side were now absent, as if the beings they'd emanated from had drifted along on their journey.

The path in front of Ellery was narrow and winding, made of packed earth lined by overgrowth that encroached along the edges. It dipped downward, then curved away in the darkness, disappearing into the fog.

Ellery shook. They couldn't help it, no matter how tightly they locked their joints and muscles. Their teeth chattered as adrenaline coursed through them on the backs of fear and uncertainty. They could turn around. The oval of white light was a beacon in the murk. No one would judge them. Zada had said so. But Ellery couldn't. They wouldn't be able to live with themself for the rest of their now undoubtedly long life if they didn't follow through.

Ellery glanced at the pot clutched in their hands, peering through the glass top at the swirling blue and purple. It continued to roil inside, giving off its own soft light. This potion had started the whole mess, and Ellery had gone and brewed a second batch in a slow cooker in their cousin's kitchen.

With one last glance over their shoulder at the exit, Ellery took a breath, then their first step of their journey. The road wound through rolling hills covered in low spindly grasses, devoid of any movement or life, not even a breeze to rustle the blades. Bram had warned them not to stray from the path, but as they walked, the farther they ventured, the harder the trail became to follow. The fog was gray and dense and obscured everything in front of them. Ellery looked over their shoulder and found the way to the oval surprisingly clear, as if informing them it would be easier to just go home.

"Okay," they said softly. "I get it."

They gripped the pot more tightly. They wouldn't give up. Not so easily.

Their pace slowed to a crawl as they carefully felt out each inch of the path with their feet before moving. The prickly growth that lined their route snagged on the skin of their ankles, raked across the fabric of their jeans.

Ellery squinted into the gloom, but wispy smoke streamed in front of their face and wreathed around them, blocking their sight. They took another tentative step, too close to the edge of the trail. A vine shot out. The thick greenery slithered around their ankle, ensnaring their foot. They cried out in fear and yanked their foot free. They stumbled, then fell.

The pot smacked the ground first, but Ellery managed to keep their grip. Their knees hit next. The impact jarred their body so hard, their teeth clacked, but at least they hadn't spilled the potion.

"Fuck," they whispered as they breathed hard. Their pulse raced. Their body shook with panic.

But from the vantage point of their knees, they were beneath the fog and could see clearly. Rummaging in the slouchy bag at their hip, they pulled out the industrial flashlight. With a flick, a beam cut through the gloom, and in the distance, Ellery made out a marker with a sign on it. A crossroads. The road made several twists and curves between where Ellery knelt and the signpost, but at least Ellery had a destination in mind.

"Okay," they said. "One step at a time. Just keep going. Stay in the middle of the path."

They stood, brushing off their hands, hoisting the container under their arm, holding the flashlight with the other.

And that was how Ellery spent the next few hours. Putting one foot in front of the other, terrified of becoming hopelessly lost in the fog, of being wrapped in sentient foliage, of losing their chance to see Knox, of never making it back to the human realm.

Their arms and back ached, their skin stung with scratches from the overgrowth, and their ankle had swelled from the tumble, but finally, *finally,* they made it to the sign.

Several other paths joined into a wider road, in a convergence that Ellery realized must be roads that came from other crossroads. They paused at the mouth of their path and scuffed their heel, digging a divot so that later, when they left, *if* they left, they'd be able to find the correct way.

From that spot the road continued in a straight, broad line, and thankfully the fog cleared. Ellery stashed the flashlight back in the bag, not wanting to drain the batteries unless it was absolutely necessary, instead using the bobbing balls of light high above them to navigate. The silence was crushing; the only sound other than their own footsteps and nervous breaths was the sound of water, which grew louder the longer Ellery walked. It was difficult to discern anything beyond a few feet in the darkness, so it startled them when they turned a gentle curve and found themself on the bank of a river.

The river was wide, the color of pitch, save for the froth sliding along the shore. A wooden boat floated next to a dock that jutted out from the shoreline. The boat was nothing special, free of adornment and featuring only slats for seats.

This was the river Bram had spoken about. The next obstacle in Ellery's journey to the palace. Ellery walked along the dock, then gingerly stepped into the boat. It bobbed beneath them, rocking unsteadily when they stepped in, but they managed to sink to sitting, setting the potion on the bottom of the boat between their feet.

There were no oars or any other means to propel the boat across, and Ellery was unsure of what to do next. They reached into their pocket and removed the coin Bram had given them. There was no one to hand it to and no coin slot like an arcade game anywhere they could see. Ellery leaned forward and placed the coin on the seat in front of them and waited. Nothing happened.

"I wish to cross," they said, their voice loud in the quiet. "I have a coin."

No movement. No sound. No response at all.

Think, Ellery. Think. Bram had said not to touch the water, so they couldn't paddle their way across using their hands. There was nothing in the boat—no rope, no sails, and Ellery couldn't pry a slat loose to use as an oar. They propped their elbow on their thigh, chin in hand, and absently tapped the edge of the coin against the wood as they thought.

Beneath the boat, something tapped back.

Frightened, Ellery jerked back as the sounds reverberated from beneath their feet. The boat rocked dangerously.

Oh.

Their heart pounded even harder than when they'd walked through the barrier. A ripple of water circled the boat, like a large fish was just beneath, running a loop around the perimeter. Ellery pinched the coin between their thumb and forefinger and held it over the side, and once the ripple appeared nearby, they dropped it. It fell into the river with a plunk. And just below the surface, Ellery spied a blue-veined hand with wicked black fingernails catching the coin in the flat of its palm. Bony fingers curled around the shiny circle, and the hand disappeared beneath the water.

The boat lurched forward. Ellery fell backward to the bottom.

Scrabbling upright with a pounding heart, Ellery hunched into a ball and shoved their feet under the seat in front of them as whatever was beneath propelled them forward across the turbulent river. Ellery gritted their teeth against the trembles that still wracked them. A wave jilted the boat to the right, almost pitching Ellery into the river. They grabbed the sides, holding on for dear life as the vessel rocked.

The boat dipped deeply to the left after another high wave, and the fingers and knuckles of Ellery's hand touched the frigid water. They yanked away, but it was too late.

The blue hand breached the surface, wrapped terrifying fingers around Ellery's wrist, and pulled.

29

ELLERY

Plunging into the cold water was a slap to Ellery's senses.

Their breath punched out of their lungs. Their mind whited out in absolute fear as the creature pulled them deeper into the darkness. Their chest squeezed with the need to *breathe*, but Ellery had at least enough awareness to keep their mouth closed.

The fingernails scraped along their skin, and the pain sliced through both the ice and the panic. Their brain finally kicked over from "freeze" to "fight."

Ellery wrenched their arm, viciously twisting it in the creature's grip until they broke away. Once released, they kicked toward what they hoped was the surface. It was so dark, and the river undulated, tossing them around like a cork until they were totally disoriented. They only knew to swim opposite from where the creature dragged them, so they did.

It grabbed for them again, its hands pulling Ellery under by the strap of their bag. Ellery twisted, kicked out as hard as they could, but with every movement forward, their assailant would pull them just as far back.

Ellery's lungs burned. Water rushed in their ears. They were going to drown, or worse—become trapped in this river at the mercy of whatever was in the water with them forever, unless they *did* something other than flail. They reached into the bag at their hip, fumbling for the flashlight, hoping it was waterproof. They switched it on and instantly wished they hadn't.

The beam cut through the stifling dark and shone right in the face of Ellery's attacker.

If Ellery thought the phantom was terrifying, this being was a thousand times worse. Large, filmy eyes bulged from its face, its flesh so thin that the light illuminated the skeleton beneath. Fins sharp as knives, fangs and gills and hair that floated like pale, clumped seaweed all around them. Ellery clamped their mouth shut lest they scream.

The creature hissed at the light, threw up one hand, and cowered. Ellery swung the heavy end of the flashlight down on where it had hooked its claws in the pocket of their hoodie, smashing the barrel against its knuckles. It released them and shrieked, an inhuman sound that rattled through the water, then disappeared into the depths.

Ellery picked a direction and swam. They broke the surface a few moments later and gulped mouthfuls of air, tears leaking from their eyes, mixing with the froth of the river.

Ellery spun, swinging the flashlight in every direction, hoping for land. They nearly cried when they spotted the boat in the near distance. With the last of their flagging strength, they swam toward it, knowing if the creature returned and pulled them under again, they would not have the energy to fight it.

Thankfully, nothing hindered their swim, and they breathed a sigh of relief when they touched the side of the boat, wrapping both hands around the edge. They hauled themself over the side.

They fell into the boat, next to the still-intact pot of potion, and breathed. They clutched the flashlight to their chest as they broke down. They didn't know how long they lay there, sobbing, shaking, doubting every decision that had led them to that point, cursing their own stubbornness, but when they finally gathered themself, they noticed the river had calmed. And they were moving.

Ellery cautiously sat up. They pushed the wet strands of their hair out of their eyes, and sure enough, the boat cut through the still water. They breathed deep, centered themself, and thanked Charley for her foresight in giving them the flashlight. If they made it back, they owed her a fruit basket.

The rest of the ride somehow felt like both an eternity and mere seconds. The boat slowed as another rickety wooden dock appeared through the gloom. A strange glow surrounded the area, and it wasn't until the boat eased alongside the arrival point that Ellery knew why. Souls. Spirits. Hundreds and hundreds of the newly dead had arrived from other boats at the same time, and the image of them, faded human likenesses emitting an inner light, illuminated the area.

They disembarked from their boats, floating along the ground. Some wore expressions of shock, others grief. They muttered to themselves but didn't interact with one another, their attention turned inward or toward the path in front of them. A few let out unearthly wails.

Ellery carefully disembarked and stepped onto the dock, slow cooker under their arm. They reached into their damp bag and pulled out the headphones. They were the vintage kind that went over their ears, because Zada was a lover of everything retro. They slipped them on, held the potion close to their body, and walked along the wooden dock until it reached the shoreline. A sandy path led from the shore, which gave way to a road of cracked stone. Ellery maneuvered through the crowd, desperately hoping not to bump into, or rather pass through, anyone. Head down, they trained their eyes on the few feet in front of them as they walked.

"You don't belong here," came a voice from too close to their side.

The soft tone permeated the headphones. And despite the gentleness, Ellery recoiled. They risked a glance to their right to see a young woman hovering. She was beautiful, with a round face and long flowing hair, and when she smiled, a burst of warmth shot through Ellery's middle, one that contrasted with the frigid atmosphere around them. Ellery met her sad gaze, her large blinking eyes, and Bram's warning swam in their head. Ellery flinched away.

"It's okay," she said, the headphones not completely blocking the sound of her voice. "You can tell me your secrets. I'll keep them for you."

Ellery hurried their steps, but she kept pace, floating effortlessly alongside them.

"Won't you talk to me?" she asked, plaintive. "Please."

Ellery hunched their shoulders.

She sighed. "Please talk to me. Stop and stay awhile. I'm so lonely. We can be friends. I'd love to be your friend."

Ellery shivered. They went as fast as they safely could while carrying the pot of potion and navigating around the large fissures in the stone.

"You're no fun," she said with a pout. "I wouldn't keep you long. Only a few years."

"Don't listen to her. She wants to trap you." A stale breeze washed over Ellery's skin, and a sweet voice rumbled against their cheek. "I need you to take a message to my family. Please."

"No. Choose me. I have a family too."

"Ignore them. Talk to me. I miss home. *Please.*"

Ellery pressed their lips together. The headphones muffled the sound of the clamoring voices but did not block them completely. However, without them, Ellery knew the whispers would've become intrusive, turned into thoughts and compulsions instead of merely annoyances. Yet tears pooled in the corner of their eyes. Sweat gathered in the angles of their body. Their breaths came in short staccato pants. What would these specters do if Ellery spoke? What would they do if they didn't? Were they going to follow Ellery the whole way?

Another joined. And another. All of them whispered, begging Ellery for favors, enticing Ellery to stay, offering companionship and love, but they were not who Ellery wanted.

"You're pretty. Come talk with me."

"I'll listen to your secrets."

"I'll stay, unlike him."

"I'll love you like your parents don't."

Ellery shrank as the comments became more personal, more barbs than enticements. They soldiered forward, arms wrapped tightly around the potion, shoulders drawn, making themself as small as possible while they hurried.

Focused only on their steps, they didn't realize they'd made it to the palace until they came to the base of a set of stairs shaped from stone and packed earth. Ellery paused, and for the first time in what felt like hours, they looked up. The palace towered over them—a magnificent structure made from carved rock and the roots of ancient trees, interwoven tightly into walls and towers. Glowing orbs floated around the spires, illuminating the creatures that scurried between the gaps. Ellery shuddered.

In front of them was the entrance, a steep set of stairs lined with ornate statues. At the top, a stony set of dogs stood sentry on either side of an arched wooden door that was open a sliver.

As soon as Ellery took their first step onto the staircase, the ghosts dispersed with a collective sound of displeasure. Ellery eased off the headphones, leaving them looped around their neck just in case.

They heaved a breath and began their climb. The stairs stretched out in front of them. They climbed, higher and higher, the muscles in their arms straining against the weight of the pot.

Ellery crested the final step and paused. They were infinitely fatigued. They were certain they'd been in the Other World for *hours*, but time was difficult to discern and moved in dizzying slips and slides. As they caught their breath, a strange breeze pulled in and out of the crack in the door, almost as if the palace itself were alive. The effect was so unsettling after being around the dead that Ellery froze. On the other side of the door was a literal goddess who was so powerful, she hadn't even noticed an entire city under her purview falling to ruin for half a decade. What if she refused to even see Ellery? What if she did and decided to punish them for all of eternity for their insolence? It wasn't until this very moment that the fear fully hit them. The river creature and the lonely souls were nothing compared to the terror that Ellery could have made it all this way only to fail. Not only could they fail to clear Knox's name, but they could lose their own future, too. What would Charley do if they never came back? What would their family do? They bowed their head. A drop of sweat rolled down their nose, then dripped onto the stone beneath them.

What would happen if they merely . . . stopped? Would they have to walk back to the crossroads? Could they even cross the river? How would they leave without seeing the goddess? Was it possible?

Ellery shook their head. No.

Knox.

This was for Knox. Knox, who had saved them from the phantom. Knox, who had kissed them so sweetly. Knox, who had a bright smile and a brighter laugh, and who had given up his freedom, possibly forever, just so Ellery could live. If there was a chance they could return the favor, they had to try.

Ellery took another step, reached out to the door, and pushed.

30

ELLERY

THE STONE DOG SCULPTURES ON EITHER SIDE GROWLED at them, low and menacing, and a shiver shot down Ellery's whole body at the sound, but thankfully they didn't move as Ellery wriggled through the narrow opening.

The hall was huge. Massive pale fluted columns held up the vaulted ceiling, which was a tangle of stone and wood and vines. Beautiful, twisted trees, much like the one at the crossroads, lined a ribbon of moss that led to a raised dais. Atop the dais was a massive throne, and sitting on that throne was the goddess herself.

She towered over the room in stature and presence. She wore a crown of gilded leaves atop her corn-silk hair, and gold glittered at her throat like ripened wheat. Her dress was long, cinched at her waist, and knotted over one shoulder. Twin torches crackled at her sides, the flickering flames caressing her olive skin, while snakes slithered through the branches that made up part of her throne.

She was too beautiful to stare at directly, and as Ellery stood on the other end of the mossy carpet, they averted their gaze.

"We don't often receive living human visitors to our realm," she said, her voice even and measured but powerful, a rattle in Ellery's bones. "Approach."

Ellery walked quickly to the front of the room despite their shaking knees. Whispers followed their steps. Ellery kept their eyes on their feet, too scared to look for the origin of those voices.

Once in front of the goddess, Ellery set down the pot, then bowed.

"What is *that*?" she asked, tone filled with disgust.

"An offering for the queen of the Other World."

"I have no use for human gadgets."

Ellery swallowed. "It's not the gadget that I offer, goddess, but the contents."

"And what are the contents?"

She sounded bored, almost insulted that Ellery would deign to interrupt her time with something so trivial.

"It's an elixir of life."

The atmosphere turned suddenly dense. Ellery heard a scuttle to their right as a figure appeared. It grabbed the pot and scampered up the dais to the throne.

Ellery straightened, watching intently as the goddess peeled back the duct tape and lifted the lid. She sniffed the brew, which had quieted in her presence. Her plump pink lips turned down into a frown, and her dark marble eyes fixed on Ellery.

She leaned forward and flicked her wrist.

A prickle of power caressed Ellery's exposed skin; the goddess's brow furrowed, and her frown deepened. "So the shades' account was true. This is how you crossed the barrier," she said, gripping the arms of her throne. "Yes," she said at Ellery's wide eyes. "I was aware of your progress. Admirable. For an imbued human."

Ellery shuffled nervously under the goddess's scrutiny. They didn't know what to say, what to do. Did they blurt out what they wanted? Did they wait until she asked?

"An elaborate offering." She raised her chin and stared at Ellery down the slope of her nose. "And you traveled all the way here instead of leaving it at a shrine. You must want something. Or, should I say, someone."

Ellery's throat tightened. "Knox."

"He is unavailable." She relaxed into the curve of her throne, and a large snake emerged from behind her and slid along her shoulders. "Though you may already be aware. The messenger god was sent by you, yes?"

Ellery nodded sharply and gritted their teeth. "I would like to see Knox."

A knowing smile spread across her features. "Oh," she said. She clucked her tongue in pity. "He won't remember you. Memories and emotions are fleeting. Maybe not for you humans, as your lives are tragically short, but for gods and goddesses and immortal creatures, they last but a moment."

Ellery balled their fists. "I'm not in love with him, if that's what you're implying," they said. "I could be. I could love him. If he were allowed back to the human realm. But that's not why I'm here."

"Then why are you here?"

"I know you've punished him for running away. And I know you plan to punish him even further for the other things he did. So I'm here to keep that from happening. I'm here to clear his name."

She cocked her head to the side. "How do you know I haven't already stripped him of his powers?"

"Because you weren't certain," Ellery said confidently, despite literally shaking in their shoes. "You were blinded to his crossroads and the region around it. You couldn't trust what the shades told you, and Knox couldn't remember. And if everything he told me about you was true, then you would have waited for more information. He said you were fair."

"Your appearance proves his guilt. You've doomed him, human. I will carry out my punishment."

Ellery trembled. Their heart raced, and their mouth went dry. "Before you do, please let me see him."

The goddess lazily drummed her fingers on the arm of her throne. "Fetch Knox," she said to the audience. "I want him present for this conversation." She scanned Ellery from head to toe. "So he may see the consequences of his actions."

A figure skittered from a pile of leaves and took off running to do her bidding.

Ellery crossed their arms. The Other World was cold. They attempted to not appear nervous in front of the goddess and whatever other creatures lurked about, but they couldn't stop the tremors that wracked their frame.

As they waited, she narrowed her eyes. "You don't even believe in me."

Ellery grimaced.

"Oh yes. I know. I can see through to the heart of you right now. Your soul is naked here, and I see no belief there for me, even as you stand in my presence."

"You abandoned us. You abandoned *him*." Ellery clenched their jaw. Anger and frustration bubbled in their chest. "Why should I believe in a goddess who left us to our fate when we begged for her to return?"

"I am a goddess," she said, in a sibilant hiss. "My actions are above the reproach of humans."

"Then why do we try? You want to be worshipped but not held accountable. You want our offerings and our love and devotion but don't offer anything in return except a flimsy shield of faith. So no, I don't believe in you. I don't have faith in you."

"Then what do you believe in?" she asked, fingers tented.

A side door opened, and Knox stepped through, flanked by two servants. Even in the muted light, he was as handsome as ever. He was still dressed in his clothes from the day at the mall, and Ellery flinched at the amount of blood splattered across his shirt. His bare feet padded lightly across the stone, and he bowed when he faced the goddess.

Ellery's gaze locked on Knox, and their words tumbled out to answer the goddess's question.

"I believe in him," they said.

Knox startled and spun, golden eyes wide. Ellery couldn't become distracted, even though it was so good to see him again, so they plowed on.

"I believe he told me the truth when he talked about how kind and just you really are. I believed him when he talked about his love of certain foods and TV shows, and how he loved talking to people, and how he wished to make friends. I believed him when he said that he liked kissing me."

Knox's hand raised to his mouth, and he pressed his fingertips to his lips.

"And I believe in justice. He saved me, and it's my turn to save him."

"Who are you?" Knox breathed. His mouth had dropped open, and twin spots of pink painted his cheekbones. He looked confused and stunned and achingly hopeful.

Ellery couldn't pretend that the question didn't hurt. They clutched the spot above their heart. "Someone who knew you in another life. Someone who could love you."

Knox smiled politely, vacantly. "Oh." His gaze flickered to the queen, then back to Ellery. "I'm sorry. I don't remember you."

"I know." A lump caught in Ellery's throat. A tear slid down their cheek. "It's okay."

He frowned. "But you're upset."

Ellery shook their head. "No. I'm happy to see you. Really happy to see you."

"You are?"

"I've missed you. So much."

"It's only been a few days," he said softly.

"A few long days."

Knox bit his lower lip, and the familiarity of the gesture struck Ellery like a punch in the gut. Knox ducked his head, inched closer. "Did you . . . send a message?"

"Yes. I did."

"And you traveled here? For me?"

"Yes."

He inched closer, his fingertips grazing the sleeve of Ellery's hoodie, still wet from the river. "Can I . . . can I kiss you?"

"Yes," Ellery breathed.

Carefully, gently, Knox leaned in and pressed a hesitant kiss to Ellery's mouth. His lips were cold, and tentative, but Ellery sighed into it anyway, hoped Knox could feel their affection and their faith and their longing in the quick touch. He pulled away, eyes wide, mouth open, staring at Ellery in awe.

"Can I . . . ?" Knox asked, lifting his hand.

Ellery nodded.

And Knox cupped Ellery's cheek in his palm, fingers brushing the shell of their ear, threading through the still-drying strands of Ellery's hair. He ducked in again, kissed Ellery once more, confident, sure, and Ellery basked in it, knew it was more than likely their last. They wanted to remember every moment Knox's lips were against theirs, the feeling of his thumb swiping along their cheek.

A sound from the court made Knox step away once more. But he didn't go far, staring at Ellery's face. He pressed his fingers back to his lips, brow furrowed. "I think—"

"That's enough." The goddess's voice boomed through the hall.

Ellery startled and wrenched their attention back to the goddess.

"You've made your journey. You've presented your offering. You've spoken to Knox. You're finished."

Ellery took a breath, steeling themself, taking strength from Knox's presence. "No."

"What?"

The air froze. Her tone was angry, but Ellery stood their ground, despite every alarm bell of their limbic system ringing in their head at the danger in her voice. But they'd overcome everything thus far, and they would not back down.

"Not until you pardon Knox and grant him freedom. He may have broken your rules, but he doesn't deserve your punishment. It was the shades who allowed the potion to be created. They closed the cross-roads and created the winter. They allowed Knox to believe he'd been *forsaken* by his creator. He did what he thought was best in the circumstances. You can't fault him for that."

"He should have retained faith in his queen, in his *goddess*. Instead, he placed his faith in a human."

Ellery lifted their chin. "A human who has traveled through the Other World to save him from the goddess who would punish him. How was he wrong?"

Knox's gaze swiveled between the two of them. He wrung his hands in distress, and Ellery ached to take one in their own and lace their fingers together.

"You forget yourself. You are not wise to question me."

"Speaking of questions, have you ever asked him what he wants? He might not tell you, but he told me. He wants to have a chance to live in the human realm. Not as a familiar tied to a bargain, but as a being who is not bound to the whims of others."

"I grow tired of you," the goddess sneered. "Your offering allowed you to speak to him. Nothing more."

"That offering, yes." Ellery reached under their hoodie and T-shirt and removed a hidden waterproof pouch. They removed several pieces of folded paper and held them up. "But I still have these.

The instructions and recipe for that potion." They jutted their chin to the pot that lay at the goddess's sandaled feet. "And I have enough ingredients, including Knox's blood, to make it several times over. I can distribute it far and wide, make endless souls who never have to pass through the Other World, as long as the earth continues to exist." Ellery straightened to their full height. "I have all the time in the world, so I've been told. I won't stop."

Her experssion was murderous, but Ellery couldn't turn back now, especially as Knox watched them in undisguised awe.

"You did all that?" he asked in disbelief. "For me?"

"Yes. Of course. You're . . . you're worth it."

Knox's brow furrowed. His gaze dropped to his clothes, and he brushed his fingers over the bloodstain on his shirt. He squeezed his eyes shut as if trying to remember, and after a moment, his hand bunched in the fabric. He inhaled sharply as his eyes snapped open, and he met Ellery's gaze. Recognition briefly flitted across his features, as if a piece of memory had broken free.

"You're okay," he breathed.

Hope fluttered recklessly in Ellery's chest. "I am."

He smiled in relief, then frowned and shook his head, as if the memory had slipped away.

Ellery knew right then that merely saving Knox from the queen's punishment wouldn't be enough. It would never be enough. They needed Knox to have a chance to return. To have a choice in what he wanted. And deep down, Ellery knew they just needed Knox in their life.

They cleared their throat, drawing the attention of all in the audience chamber. "Now, beloved goddess, you can pardon Knox right now and . . ." Ellery licked their lips. "And allow him a choice to return to the human realm."

Knox gasped. Murmurs broke out among the crowd around them.

Ellery quickly talked over them. "Or you can expect to see a lot fewer souls traveling through here."

The goddess abruptly stood. The palace floor trembled. The torches on either side of her flared. Her servants all dropped to their knees, except Knox, who stared at Ellery like they were the sun.

"You dare—?"

"Yes." Ellery cut her off. "I do."

She held out her palm. "The papers, then."

Ellery released the journal pages, and they caught on a sudden breeze and fluttered into her hand. The goddess perused the words, scowl firmly affixed. "Knox."

Knox whipped around and faced her. "Yes, my queen?"

"The human has successfully bargained on your behalf. You are hereby pardoned. Despite your many transgressions, you will remain a familiar, and you will not return to the cells."

Knox bowed to the queen, then turned to Ellery. "Thank you," he said softly.

Ellery smiled. "No need to thank me; you saved me, after all."

"I . . . I did?"

"More than you realize."

Knox reached out to touch Ellery's hand, but his gaze flicked to his queen, and he withdrew.

"But," she continued, holding up Arabelle's notes in her fist, "this does not grant Knox the ability to leave this realm. He will remain here until he regains my trust." She smiled tightly. "Which will take time to repair."

Despair cut through Ellery's middle. Their heart plummeted. They were so close. They'd come so far. "What about giving him a choice?"

"These are the terms of this bargain. Unless you have something else to give?"

Ellery looked around hopelessly. They dropped to their knees, rifling through their bag, hoping there might be something of interest to the goddess. The flashlight, the headphones, an old pen . . . none of it was useful. Ellery tore at their clothes, turning out their pockets to find nothing but lint.

They stood back up slowly and turned toward Knox. "I don't have anything," they choked. "I'm sorry. I don't." Their voice broke.

Knox took their hand in his without hesitation. "It's okay."

"It's not okay!" Tears blurred Ellery's vision. The stubborn hope that Ellery had clung to, that everything would work out, that it would all be okay, disappeared in a flash. How had they ever thought they'd be okay leaving Knox again? Was this what Knox had felt when he'd watched Ellery dying on the department store floor? Was this anguish the last thing he'd experienced in the human realm before being taken away? "I've failed."

Knox shook his head. "No. I'll remember this," he said. "I'll remember the human who saved me." He tucked a piece of Ellery's hair behind their ear, and Ellery melted beneath the familiar touch. "We'll see each other again."

Ellery shook their head. "No, we won't. Because I . . ." They trailed off. They faced the queen, craned their neck upward to her figure, which towered over them. Her expression was blank, but her knowing gaze was fixed on Ellery. "I do have something."

"And what is that?"

"My soul."

Knox's grip on their hand tightened.

The edge of the queen's mouth quirked upward. She scoffed. "One human soul is not equivalent to the life of a familiar."

"It might not be. But I drank the elixir. My soul doesn't ever have to pass through your realm. I'm lost to you. But that's not the real problem." Ellery boldly took a step forward, untangling their fingers from where Knox clutched them. "I'm evidence of your inability to control your own creations." They pointed at their chest. "Don't think I haven't noticed that you haven't granted me permission to leave. But you can't hold me forever, because I *am* human, and etiquette dictates you can't hurt me since I am beseeching you in good faith. Your brother and sister wouldn't be pleased."

Her mouth pinched. "And how do you plan to alert my siblings?"

"I have a god of the wind and a goddess of a river standing right outside that crossroads, awaiting my return." Ellery wasn't certain that Bram and Lorelei were still there, but they did know that the queen couldn't take that chance. "You can't afford to trap me, but you can't afford for me to leave as I am. Because it will show your world how weak you really are."

She lifted her chin. "You are foolish to speak so brazenly in my own court."

"I'm right. And you know it. So here's *my* deal. Take whatever power the elixir has granted me, and my soul will have to pass through your realm. It will be like the whole thing never happened, other than the winter, but I have faith you'll be able to spin that in your favor some way."

She slowly lowered back to the throne. "In exchange for Knox returning with you to the human realm."

"No," Ellery said. "In exchange for him having the *choice*."

She narrowed her eyes. Ellery had the disconcerting feeling that if she could've killed them, she would have.

"Fine. I will allow it."

Ellery slumped in relief.

"With the following conditions. Knox, you may follow this strange human back to their realm. But you will have no magic there, and I will not answer your messages. You will toil as humans do until the average span of human life has ended. And then you must return, only to reenter my service as a familiar."

Knox furrowed his brow. "Or?"

"Or you may remain here and carry on as you have for centuries, existing between the two realms."

Knox's throat bobbed, but he didn't respond.

"As for you," she said, addressing Ellery. "As you leave, do not look back, or you will risk breaking this bargain. If your belief in him is as solid as you claim, you will have no need to peek over your shoulder."

She gestured, and another figure appeared from behind a tree and flicked a coin to Ellery. They caught it and shoved it into their pocket.

"When you pass through the barrier into the human realm, you will leave any effects of the potion behind. Now go."

Ellery closed their eyes as they turned, not risking a glance at Knox lest that break the tenuous bargain. They hurried away, out of the throne room, through the crack in the door where the sculpted guard dogs perched. The trip down the stairs was far easier than the climb up, and at the bottom, the ghosts didn't bother with their temptations.

Without their threat, Ellery's thoughts were able to spiral about Knox's decision. It undoubtedly had to be difficult. He clearly only remembered Ellery in fragments. He'd have to give up his magic. He'd have a chance at one life, and one life only. Ellery believed that Knox would make the decision that was right for him, even if that choice wasn't Ellery.

At the docks, Ellery settled into the boat and waited a few moments, straining to hear any footsteps over the wails of the dead, hoping to hear Knox's familiar voice. When neither sound reached their ears, they tossed the coin into the water, knowing better than to tarry in case the goddess changed her mind.

The coin hit the water with a plunk, and the boat lurched forward. The ride was quick and less turbulent, as if the river knew the goddess's demand for Ellery to leave. Once on the other side, they began the long, slow trek to the crossroads. With each step, and with the silence hanging over them like a shroud, Ellery's hope dwindled.

They found their notch in the packed dirt and, with a sigh, selected the correct winding path. There was no fog to hinder them. Their whole body tensed against the want and the need to look backward, but they set their shoulders and continued on. As they rounded a hill, the oval portal appeared in the distance. It was no longer blazing white but dark with a purple sheen.

Trudging toward it, Ellery's body sagged with exhaustion and sorrow. Knox had not caught up to them. They heard no footsteps or shouts behind them, no acknowledgement that he was there. He'd chosen to stay.

Ellery closed their eyes and paused, swaying where they stood. Tears dripped down their cheeks, born of fatigue and sadness. They took one moment to wallow, to silently lament that Knox had not chosen them and a human life. Then they wiped the tears away, opened their eyes, and took peace in the knowledge that at the very least Knox had been pardoned. He was free, and Ellery's debt had been repaid.

The trek to the portal didn't take long at all, and with one last breath, Ellery stepped through to the other side.

31

KNOX

KNOX FROZE IN PLACE.

The figure of the human grew smaller as they walked out of the throne room.

He closed his eyes and willed his memories to surface. All he could see were flashes of an undead and the messenger god and a river goddess. But nothing of this human, except the phantom feeling of a sweet touch of lips against his, and a sense of comfort and safety. That didn't seem like enough to entice him to give up everything he'd known. To surrender his magic. To abandon his queen.

And yet . . . the familiar tug beneath his navel—the one that tethered him to whatever human had made a deal for his assistance, the one that guided him back to his crossroads when his time in the human realm was over, the one that called him back to the Other World—that comforting, gentle pull *lurched* after the human. Knox rubbed the spot, brow furrowed. He'd associated that feeling with home for his entire existence, but it had shifted. What was it that the messenger god had said? That love remembered?

"Knox."

The human had traveled all that way. For him. Through the fog and across the river and through the spirits and to the palace. Fought their way to him, if their bedraggled appearance was any indication of the struggle. Bargained, not *for* him, but for his freedom, for him to have a *choice*. And he had a choice.

No one had ever done that before.

"Knox," the queen said again, interrupting his musings.

"Yes?"

"You do not have long to decide."

He licked his lips. "What of my memories?" he asked, breathless.

"What of them?"

"If I choose to leave, will I get them back?"

Her tone barely veiled her annoyance when she responded. "You haven't been here long. If the emotions tied to them are strong enough, they may return to you when you cross the barrier. But the longer you linger here, the harder they'll be to reclaim."

"So, if I didn't love them . . ."

"Then you won't remember." She said it flippantly, as if it was a foregone conclusion that Knox could not have a connection to this human stronger than the one he had to her.

He faced his queen on her throne. "But I could." He knotted his fingers. "I *could*."

She scoffed. "You've seen firsthand how fickle humans are, how their attention flits from one thing to the next, the regret they bring with them about the poor choices they'd made over their lifetimes. You would want to bind yourself to that?"

Knox ran his hand through his hair. "I don't know."

"Furthermore, you could follow and find out they don't love you. They could be using you for their own ends. You'd risk a happy life here, with occasional excursions there, for what? A few decades with a human who you don't even know."

And that was the crux of it. "Who said my life was happy here?"

She paused, then her lips curled in disdain.

"Did you even notice I was gone?" he pressed.

"Just because I allowed the human to question me does not mean you have the same privilege."

Knox stepped forward. "I want to make an informed decision."

She pursed her lips. Her fingers flexed on the arms of her throne. "It was only five human years. You were not gone long."

"Of course." And yet it had only been days and this human missed him, missed him enough to venture across entire realms. And in the recesses of his heart, he missed them too. That was the uncomfortable ache that had resided in him since his return, the hollowness he couldn't shake.

Knox bowed. "Thank you for this choice, my queen." Then he turned and walked down the mossy carpet to the exit.

"Where are you going?" she demanded.

"To think."

She huffed. "Make a wise choice, Knox," she warned. "You may not like all the consequences."

He paused, then turned. "No, I might love them instead."

32

ELLERY

"ELI" CHARLEY CRIED AS ELLERY STUMBLED THROUGH THE portal to the other side. "You're finally back!"

Ellery fell into her open arms, resting their forehead on her bony collarbone. The sky was dark, but stars sparkled overhead, and Ellery was so relieved they had left the foggy gloom of the Other World behind. With a groan, they allowed the bag to slide from their shoulder and thunk to the soft ground beneath the tree.

The door in the tree swung shut with a bang of finality, the edges of the entrance melting back into the wood, the magic glow dimming until it faded out and the tree was just a tree again.

"How long have I—?"

"Three months."

Ellery snapped upright, gasping. "Three months?"

Zada slammed the door of her idling car shut, which was pulled to the side of the road, and joined them. "Charley," she admonished. "Why would you do that?"

"Because when I say 'two and a half days,' it sounds great in comparison to three months."

Ellery blinked. "What?"

"You've been gone two days, Ellery. Almost three, but that's all." Zada shot an admonishing look at Charley, who shrugged.

"Oh, that's . . . not bad."

"See!"

Zada elbowed Charley. She reached out and rubbed Ellery's upper arms. "You're freezing. And damp. Are you okay? What do you need?"

Ellery trembled. They were indeed cold to their bones, now just realizing it in the contrasting warmth of the summer night. "You stayed?" Ellery asked.

"Of course." Charley pushed her fingers through Ellery's hair, brushing back the wayward strands. "We had faith that you'd come back as soon as you could."

"And we wanted to be here for that," Zada added with a soft smile.

"We made really good friends with the gas station attendant down the way. And Lorelei and Bram brought us things we needed. Otherwise we haven't left." She sniffed her armpit. "So don't judge us, okay?"

Faith. Ellery squeezed their eyes shut and hugged them both fiercely. "Thank you."

"Of course."

They held on for far longer than was socially appropriate, but Charley merely patted their back and smoothed down their hair. And Ellery took comfort in it, held on a little longer, knowing that once they let go, there would be questions with difficult answers.

But Ellery could only hide in their cousin's embrace for so long, and they reluctantly stepped out of Charley's arms.

"Where are the others?"

Charley rolled her eyes. "Around. They've been checking in periodically. Bram comes and goes as he pleases. Lorelei went to inspect her river. And Hale . . . He weirded me out, so we sent him on his own way after he asked to feed from me for like the fifth time."

Ellery snorted. "He is creepy."

"Yeah. You'll have to tell us all about why you kissed him. But later. First, what happened? What about Knox? Did you see him?"

Unbidden, tears welled in Ellery's eyes. "Yeah. I did," they answered, voice thick.

"And? Did he remember you?"

Ellery shook their head.

"Oh, El." Charley wrapped her arms around Ellery's shoulders and pulled them in again. "It's okay."

"At least she pardoned him," Ellery said, tears burning the backs of their eyes. "That's all I wanted. And in the end, she gave him a choice to stay or leave. He just didn't choose us. He didn't choose me."

Charley squeezed them tighter. "I'm so sorry."

Ellery sniffed. "I knew he wouldn't remember. I knew this was the most likely outcome."

"Yeah. But it still sucks."

That surprised a teary laugh from Ellery. "Yeah. It sucks."

"Come on, El," Zada said gently, guiding them to the car. "Let's go home."

"And you can tell us all about how you traversed a supernatural realm and met a goddess!" Charley said, making excited jazz hands.

Zada tipped her head back in fond exasperation. "Or not. We could order pizza and watch movies. I heard a trailer dropped for the new season of the werewolves, witches, and wyverns show."

Ellery brushed away their tears with the back of their sleeve. "Yeah, that sounds good."

With one last look at the crossroads, Ellery quietly said goodbye to the person who had taught them to believe.

They sighed deeply and turned away. They opened the back door of Zada's car and had one foot inside when a rustling sound made them pause. Their heart pounded. It was probably a bird. It could even be Bram, but hope was a stubborn thing, and Ellery turned, leaving Zada and Charley bickering behind them.

The branches of the tree shook. The outline of the door in the bark glowed. A ripping noise broke the otherwise silent country road. A flash of light followed, and a figure tumbled out of the oval, his back foot catching on the edge. He tripped and caught himself with his hands on the asphalt, then slowly stood.

It was dark, with only the light from Zada's headlights, which were focused the other way, but Ellery would recognize that tall frame anywhere.

"Knox?" Ellery's voice was choked.

Knox whipped around, raising a hand to shield his eyes and squint through the darkness. Brow furrowed, lips pulled down in a frown, he appeared confused as he tilted his head up to the stars shining above them, then to the crossroads and Zada's car idling, the headlights cutting a swath through the darkness. He startled when the door in the tree banged shut. He stared at it, then his golden gaze settled on Ellery.

"Sorry for the delay," he said, rubbing the back of his neck. "The path was longer than I thought." Then he smiled brightly. "Hi, Ellery."

Ellery gasped. "You remember?"

"As if I could forget you." He knotted his fingers. "Some things are hazy, but the longer I stand here, the more comes back."

"Knox!" Charley said with a yell.

He waved. "Hi, Charley. Hi, Zada."

"How?" Ellery licked their lips. "Not that I'm complaining, but you . . . I don't . . . What?"

Knox crossed the space between them. Carefully, he took Ellery's hands in his own, wrapped their fingers in his large palms, and held them close to his chest. He bent his head, rested his forehead on the crown of Ellery's hair, and breathed.

"A very smart bird-god told me that love remembers, and even though I couldn't remember your name or your face, I remembered you. I *missed* you. And anyone who would venture into the Other

World for me, and take on all the obstacles that led to the palace, had to be someone special. So I trusted what you said and, well, here I am."

Ellery tucked themself closer. "I'm glad you did. I missed you so much."

"Thank you," he whispered. "For believing in me."

Ellery grinned. "Anytime."

Knox folded Ellery into his embrace, and Ellery wrapped their arms around him and pressed their face into his chest, never to let go again unless they absolutely had to.

"So," Zada said, drawing out the vowel, "this is sweet and everything, but I'd like to go home now."

With red cheeks, Ellery disentangled from Knox. He smiled brightly, gold eyes shining. "Sounds good to me, but can we make a stop first?"

"Sure!" Charley said. "Come on, though. This country living is wreaking havoc on my skin."

"We've literally been here two days."

"And I have a blemish. Right here," Charley said, dramatically pointing at her chin.

"You're so adorably weird."

Ellery slid into the back seat, Knox following. They sat next to each other, thighs pressed together, Ellery's head on Knox's shoulder, Knox's arm draped around Ellery, pulling them close. Their free hands tangled as Zada and Charley bickered fondly in the front.

"Hey, Knox, please tell me we're going toward the city," Charley said over her shoulder.

"Yep. I know the way. Trust me."

And Ellery did, wholeheartedly. They trusted this little family they'd formed. They'd make mistakes—everyone did—but Ellery knew they'd never hurt them intentionally, and that they'd be there for Ellery with no expectations. And Ellery would be there for them, would love them, and in the end, that was all that mattered.

Some people chose to believe in the supernatural. That was what Ellery's parents had chosen. But for Ellery, they'd put their faith in the people who loved them. Even if one of them actually was supernatural, and one of them had questionable judgment in life partners, and the other was certifiably bizarre. But Ellery wouldn't have it any other way.

Content, they leaned into Knox's side and enjoyed the ride home.

33

ELLERY

IN THE MIDDLE OF A BUSTLING NEIGHBORHOOD, IN THE MIDDLE of an awakening city, at the end of the summer, Ellery Evans laughed at the antics of their coworkers as they hauled another plastic tub of dirty dishes across the metal counter toward the deep kitchen sink.

"Pickup order for Arabelle," Charley said, poking her head through the swinging doors. "Called in about twenty minutes ago. Hot weird guy should be here soon."

Ellery dropped a dish into the industrial sink full of suds with a plop. They quickly untied their apron and hung it on the peg by the wall before ducking into the employee bathroom. They ran their hands through their hair, trying to tame the longer strands. Their shirt was a lost cause, splashed with suds, but they blotted it anyway with dry paper towels to try and mop up the worst of the splotches.

The last day of the summer was hot, and even hotter in the diner's kitchen, and sweat dampened the hair at the nape of their neck and at their temples. They ran a wet paper towel over their face, trying to cool the heat of their cheeks, but the flush didn't fade. Between the diner and the fact that Knox was dropping by soon, they couldn't scrub the pink away if they tried.

It was the last weekend before Ellery started their senior year at the city high school. Which meant after the next two days, the opportunities to hang out with their boyfriend would greatly diminish. So despite the two of them already having plans for a date when Ellery got off work, Ellery wouldn't waste any time or opportunity for interaction. Especially since Knox had chosen to live with Arabelle in her apartment for now, to help her readjust, and until Ellery had developed a new routine with school.

Beyond starting their senior year, Ellery didn't have a plan other than to graduate. Then maybe they would take a few classes at the college. Or maybe they would work a year to figure things out. It was up in the air.

Satisfied that they were as presentable as possible, Ellery slid out of the bathroom.

"Hey!" Diego called before they could disappear to the seating area. "Not too long. We have the lunch rush soon." He wagged his spatula at Ellery. "I'm running a restaurant, not a dating service."

The restaurant had seen a steady increase in customers, so much that Diego had hired a few new waitresses and another dishwasher, since Ellery was planning to head back to school.

Ellery's blush deepened. "I'll be right back."

He huffed, then waved Ellery away.

Two months since the region had righted itself, the populace was gradually returning. The abandoned places were no longer abandoned, which had led to a few conflicts between the supernatural beings who had moved in during the winter. Knox helped when he could, though it wasn't easy without his magic. He had to be more careful when he interacted with other supernatural creatures now. So most of the time he chose to be with Ellery or with Arabelle.

Charley and Zada had been lucky enough to find a new place before prices skyrocketed. It was a two-bedroom near the college and the high school, so Ellery would be able to walk with Zada every morning. Charley still worked at the diner, but she'd surprisingly made a new friend and spent many of her days at the corn statues rebuilding the windmill shrine.

"Without Bram's help, we wouldn't have Knox *or* Ellery," she said, a touch defensive, when she'd showed up at the apartment with a new hammer, a car full of two-by-fours, and several cans of paint. "It's only polite."

Zada and Ellery had merely shrugged. Leave it to Charley to befriend a grumpy wind god and offer to rebuild his shrine.

The bell above the door rang, and Ellery scampered to the front. Knox waltzed in, dark sunglasses over his golden eyes, hair so dark, it glinted blue in the morning sun. He smiled brightly, and without so much as a hello, he tugged Ellery close and planted a kiss right on their lips.

"Hi!" he said, voice mischievous and cheerful.

Ellery's heart fluttered. "Hi," they said softly. They stepped away, very aware of several of the new staff's eyes on them. "Pickup order for Arabelle?"

"Correct. How'd you know?"

"Oh, I have a sixth sense about these things."

"That's venturing dangerously close to belief in the supernatural. I thought you were a skeptic."

Ellery shrugged. "My horizons have been broadened."

He laughed. "Good."

Charley bustled past, pushing a paper bag into Knox's arms. "For you," she said, pausing on her way to take drink orders. "Tell Lorelei I say hi and hope she's doing well."

"I will," Knox said with a nod.

Lorelei had returned to her river, but Knox visited her often. He liked talking with her and learning more about his past lives, and how they'd known each other before. He'd regained almost all his memories of his last lifetime, which meant he'd also regained his love of television shows and movies. They were all deeply invested in the new season of the werewolves, witches, and wyverns show, though Ellery would vehemently deny it if asked. Also, once Knox had remembered how they'd originally parted, with Ellery dying on the department store floor, he'd been extra clingy, loath to leave Ellery's side.

"Also, game night tomorrow. Zada says you'd better be there."

Knox nodded. "I will definitely be there."

"Good." She poked the end of her pencil into Knox's cheek. "You do not want to disappoint my girlfriend."

Ellery sighed as Charley sauntered away to flirt with a table of customers.

"How's Arabelle today?"

The paper bag crinkled under Knox's grip. The order technically wasn't for Arabelle, since she could no longer enjoy human food. But Knox loved the sentimentality attached to calling it in under her name, since it was the way he'd initially met Ellery and Charley.

"Arabelle . . . ," he answered, trailing off. "Is adjusting. She's an undead in a body that's not hers, since hers was . . . well . . . Anyway. Hale has helped a little."

Ellery raised an eyebrow. "Hale?"

"He's horrible, and I still don't like him at all, but he's been useful," Knox grumbled, then cringed, as if it pained him to admit that Hale had any redeeming qualities.

The sound of a spatula rapping against the counter meant Ellery's time was up. "I have to get back to work."

Knox frowned. "Already?"

"I'll see you after. Pick me up?"

"Of course. I'll be here."

Ellery stood on their tiptoes and kissed the corner of Knox's mouth. "See you soon."

A pink blush swept over Knox's cheeks. "Not soon enough."

Ellery shook their head and tamped down the swell of affection that threatened to overwhelm them. Knox was too sweet.

"Go before Diego throws you out."

With a wink and one last lingering look, Knox left the diner, paper bag tucked in the crook of his arm. Overcome with fondness and contentment, Ellery watched him walk past the window and down the sidewalk until he was out of sight.

"Ellery," one of the new staff asked, sidling over. "Was that your boyfriend?"

"Yeah."

"I wish my boyfriend looked at me like he looks at you," she said, leaning against the hostess stand. "How did you convince him that you hung the moon?"

Ellery pushed a wayward lock of hair behind their ear, then grinned. "Honestly, you wouldn't believe me if I told you."

Some days Ellery could scarcely believe it themself. But they had Knox's promise in their ear, his kiss on their lips, a trusting relationship, a home with their two best friends, a newfound understanding of the world, and an unburdened blissful future that stretched far out in front of them. And they were able to share it with the people they loved and who loved them in return. And that was better than any bargain.

ACKNOWLEDGMENTS

HELLO READERS. THE LAST ACKNOWLEDGMENTS I WROTE were for *Spell Bound*, and I talked about how the themes of that book were so deeply personal to me at both the time of writing the book and then later at the time of writing the acknowledgments. As I parse out what I want to say for *Otherworldly*, I find myself echoing that same feeling—that the themes presented were personal when I was writing the book and are still personal as I write the last words that will be included. *Otherworldly* is a book about embracing and about letting go—two simple acts that can be so difficult at times, both of which I've had to face recently. Thankfully, I've had several folks in my corner as I've worked through the challenges of this past year.

First, I want to thank my family. Especially my spouse, Keith, and my brother, Rob. My brother and I lost our dad in 2019, and in the beginning of 2023, we said goodbye to our mom. It's been difficult to say the least, and I'm thankful for the almost daily phone calls between us—often with Rob, myself, my sister-in-law Chris, and Keith all on the line. Not so much the phone calls about who gets the antique coffee table, but the ones where we just joke and laugh about the ridiculousness of life in general. And thank you, Keith, for being my person, my constant as we navigate it all together.

Next, I want to thank my agent, Eva Scalzo. Thanks, Eva, for being there, for being understanding, for continuing to champion my work, and for guiding me along this journey.

Thank you to the team at McElderry Books, especially my editor, Kate Prosswimmer, who I have been lucky enough to work with on four different books. Thank you for all your hard work and expertise, which has made this book so much better than the hot mess of ideas I had in the beginning. Thank you to the cover illustrator, the amazingly talented Sam Schechter, who once again created an absolute stunning rendition of the characters. I honestly cannot thank Sam enough for lending their talent to this book and the three previous ones. Also, thank you to the cover designer, Becca Syracuse, for this beautiful, beautiful cover. And thank you to Nicole Fiorica, Alex Kelleher, and Thad Whittier for also being amazing members of the team. It really has been a dream to work with you all.

Special thank you to DL Wainright, who provided feedback and ideas when it came to the folklore of this novel. Having DL to bounce ideas off and to guide me in finding the resources I needed on particular subjects was endlessly helpful. And thank you, October Santerelli, for being a sounding board and offering encouragement and support during the creative process. Also, many thanks to my BFF Kristinn and my bestie Amy Y for their continued friendship and for being there for me this past year.

Thank you to my internet family and pocket friends who have been there for me as I work through both creative challenges and life ones as well. My internet family always comes through, and I can't thank them enough for sticking with me this past decade.

Many thanks to all the authors who supported my last release in a ton of different ways, such as joining me for events, sharing social media posts, and even providing blurbs. They are amazing colleagues and I'm so excited to continue to support them and their works—Julian Winters, Carrie Pack, Steven Salvatore, Ryan La Sala, Jason June, Robbie Couch, Beth Revis, S. Isabelle, and Rachel Menard.

I'd like to thank my local amazing indie bookstore, Malaprop's in Asheville, which has been so kind to me the past few years. The booksellers are awesome and if you are ever in the Asheville area, please drop by and say hi to the staff, specifically Katie and Stephanie.

Lastly, I'd like to thank everyone who reads this book, who either purchased it or borrowed it from a library. Thank you for allowing me to entertain you for a few hours. I'm very appreciative of your time. I hope you enjoyed reading this story as much as I enjoyed writing it. Until next time, I hope you stay safe and happy.

Thank you,

F.T.